Plots with Guns

PLOTS

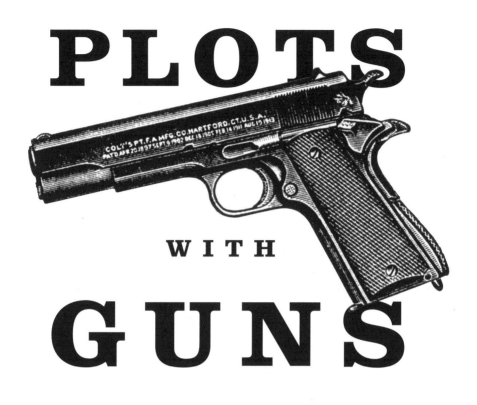

WITH
GUNS

A Noir Anthology

Edited by
Anthony Neil Smith

Dennis McMillan Publications
2005

FIRST EDITION
Published September 2005

This first edition of Plots with Guns consists of 1,000 cloth-bound copies and
156 copies bound in quarter-morocco pigskin with
hand-made paper-covered boards. The morocco
copies are signed by all the contributors.

Dustjacket and all other artwork by Michael Kellner

ISBN 0-939767-51-1

Dennis McMillan Publications
4460 N. Hacienda del Sol   Tucson, Arizona 85718
Telephone: (520)-529-6636   Email: dennismcmillan@aol.com
Website: http://www.dennismcmillan.com

CONTENTS Plots with Guns

This book is dedicated to those who know
that the best purpose of life is to create
something that will make
others feel better

Plots with Guns

Introduction:
"What It's All About"
Anthony Neil Smith

In 1999, Hunter Hayes and I started the online magazine *Plots with Guns* because we wanted to publish stories with balls that no one else was willing to take a chance on. We were grad students in creative writing, and it seemed our love of crime fiction drew either sneers or "Isn't that cute" sentiments from our colleagues, although our professors loved it, encouraged it. So I was writing literary stories about Pentecostals and bad relationships for class, sneaking in the occasional crime lark if I felt the characters were fully realized enough. Hunter's work was more the "dirty realism" of his fave Brit writers like Martin Amis, although with a reserved Carveresque tone that really drove the awfulness home. Eventually, we found a sympathetic ear in poetry student Victor Gischler. Not your typical poet—he memorized *Simpsons'* episodes and drank the cheapest possible beer. When he let slip that he'd had a story accepted by *Cozy Detective Mystery Magazine* (you've never heard of it, trust me), the friendship and mutual griping society concerning the lack of venues to publish hard-boiled crime fiction had begun.

Sure, we were aware of Gary Lovisi's fantastic *Hardboiled* digest, sort of our dream market, but it wasn't published very often. We had yet to discover the ground-breaking *Blue Murder* online, although we eventually did and even got ourselves published in it. What we wanted, what was missing, were the pulps. The flim-flam paper and crappy writing that hid jewels among the cow shit. The first stomping grounds of our heroes Hammett and Chandler. The in-your-face art and the non-apologetic plots. The point was to *move* you without you having to think about it too much. Yeah, we talked about how cool it would be to create the next *Black Mask.*

Being grad students, though, we also wanted the thing to have some respect in the literary community. Who said pulp and literature had to be mutually exclusive? Why not try to raise the bar? We were already aware of Otto Penzler's new *Best American Mystery Stories* anthology series, an offshoot of the literary *Best American Short Stories.* If those guys were saying the crime field deserved an annual round-up that concentrated on high quality writing and storytelling, then it was something to shoot for—a literary journal of hard-boiled and *noir* writing. Pulp for the Twenty First Century.

That idea didn't last long. We were broke and had no idea where to start when it came to getting a journal together. Fun to talk about in bars, though.

Soon, I was working as an editor for *Mississippi Review Web,* the online edition of the respected literary magazine, and also working with an experimental online version of our in-house student lit mag, *Product.* I tapped Gischler to help out, and Hunter was already on board. My boss taught me the ins and outs of web design so I could format the stories and poems coming in. He had this web-stuff down cold, and I learned pretty quickly.

It occurred to me soon after that, and I brought it up to Victor and Hunter, that we should go ahead and publish our crime magazine on the cheapest possible paper we had—the world-wide web. See, I had a personal website attached to my email account, and I hadn't yet figured out what exactly

2

to do with it. So why not use it as a launching pad for our magazine? My one mistake here: I tried to change the name.

"Criminal Arts Quarterly" or some such bullshit.

Gischler says it was "Con Job" or some other such bullshit.

Whatever it was, it wasn't good.

"So what about that *Plots with Guns* name? Every story has a gun in it."

I was skeptical. "A little blatant, isn't it? Who would take it seriously?"

"You *have* to call it *Plots with Guns*. That's the coolest thing ever."

(Okay, he didn't say it was the coolest thing ever.)

I gave in. Besides, Hunter and Victor were right—we *should* be blatant, and we should have a ridiculously hard-boiled attitude, and we should concentrate on contemporary stories, not period pastiche. And, yes, every story had to have a gun it in, somehow, someway.

I told *Thrilling Detective* website editor Kevin Burton Smith about our plan, and he said, "But what if the perp kills someone with a knife?"

I said, "Then we don't take it. Take that shit to *Plots with Knives*."

We found some clip art of guns, dirtied them up all rusty, and formatted three stories—our own. We weren't doing it to give ourselves a place to publish so much as we wanted to show writers kinda-sorta what we were looking for. One of those three was Gischler's "Headless Rollo," which famously became the first chapter of his Edgar-nominated debut novel *Gun Monkeys*. We started telling lit mags and crime websites and discussion groups about the new zine, and then we waited.

We had a crappy counter to check how many people visited the home page. Most of the first several hundred hits were the editors themselves. Our baby needed wings.

3

But the stories started arriving. We tapped a couple of other grad students at Southern Mississippi for pieces, received work from decent writers who stumbled across our path, received quite a few pure stinkers, cobbled together an issue, and decided to make this a quarterly concern.

After a couple of issues, people started to notice. We jazzed up the art, gloried in many more raw submissions, and carved out our attitudes with each passing month, finally deciding to turn this into a bimonthly and grab even more attention. We wanted to be a pulp, after all, but we certainly couldn't keep up a weekly or monthly pace.

So…that's the beginning. From there, we just kept doing what we needed to do, and eventually the audience grew until we were being read by many more people than we could've imagined. Who'd a thunk it?

• • •

The gun gimmick came from a story Hunter Hayes told us one day about a workshop experience involving a writer who decided to take out revenge on the page with a pulpy tale of a guy who machine guns everyone who's ever done him wrong. Not a good piece of writing, but amusing. How can you critique that? The stunned students kept their mouths shut. Eventually, the instructor told them, "Well, sometimes a story just needs a gun."

We decided early on that the gun didn't need to be the point of the story. We didn't even need gunplay. I accepted a story in which a character *threatened* to have a gun (and until it was revealed he didn't, I argued that the fear of the gun made it real enough for me). What's the old adage? "If a gun appears on the mantel in the first act of a play, it must go off by the third act?" We said, "If a gun shows up on the mantel, someone should take an ax to a head and then talk about his favorite meats before sticking his head in an oven, or have the mantel should fall on his head." As long as the thing is in there and you've written a great contemporary crime story that got us hot and bothered, we welcomed you aboard.

In the introduction for a special issue of *PwG*, novelist and critic Robert Skinner wrote: ". . .the American story is often one about a gun. . . . The gun reflects the dark side of the American nature. As much as we may admire the warrior or avenger who gains justice or vengeance with his gun, we fear him a little, too." He goes on to say that the gun is "necessary to bring closure to a story seething with violent emotion."

Or at least to make everything more vivid. The moment a gun is pulled, all the colors are brighter and all the noises are louder, and the flow of life is incoherent for those moments. Instead of allowing time for the characters to reflect endlessly or the writer to describe in deathless prose all those darlings Faulkner pleaded with him to kill, the gun forces action, truth, and emotion. Love it or hate it, it's hard to sit on the fence when the bullet has your name on it.

• • •

We grew. We landed a story in *Best American Mystery Stories* (Scott Wolven's "The Copper Kings"), and we were all over the runners-up list for several years before sneaking in again with Timothy Williams, and then again with Wolven's story from our final issue at the end of 2004. We also garnered respect from writers we admired, morphing from star-struck fans at our first Bouchercon in Washington, D.C., to a recognizable brand in the following years. We said we ran *Plots with Guns,* and many times caught a glimmer in some-one's eye, a comment like, "Yeah, I read you guys. Strong stuff."

I eventually bullied Gischler into an official editorship, even though he'd been a "shadow editor" for the entire time anyway. He brought a column called "Hard-Boiled Dixie" along with him, and if you read all of them from beginning to end, you watched the process of a writer in ascent, from a small press novel that couldn't get arrested until it got an Edgar nod, to a big book deal with a major publisher, to a guy who needed more time to write his books, so he stepped down as columnist and editor and bought himself a mandolin.

Hunter Hayes stepped down as well to start his family and move more into his Ph.D. studies in British Literature. While here, he gave us an edgy psychological sensibility and helped define the direction we believed *noir* fiction was heading and where it *should* go next.

We so admired the attitude of one of our writers, Trevor Maviano, that after he made a splash with his in-your-face short story "Blood Money," we brought him on-staff as an editor. He also wrote a column called "An Earful from Maviano" in which he gave us his unfiltered thoughts on writing, the publishing biz, and living a hard-boiled life instead of pretending.

Many readers tell me that they always read the columns of both these guys before looking at the rest of the issue. Well deserved.

Through it all, I was happiest when one of these guys or any of our writers received praise, award nominations, fan mail, attention from agents and publishers, or just got themselves a publishing credit they were proud of. When we began this trip, the noir magazine seemed to be either dying or on watered-down life support. We'd like to think we gave it an adrenaline shot. We published writers who couldn't get looked at by the "safer" mystery mags, and they gained cult followings. That was the good stuff. Our "Crimedogs" were top-notch writers who loved *noir* fiction and crafted it as well as their twisted minds could conceive. They've made this all worth it.

• • •

One more little-known fact: "Crimedogs" was originally the name Gischler thought up for us when we played the quarter trivia machines during grad school at our favorite bar, Bubba's, a wooden shack on the edge of some piney woods. Maybe because we were all carrying on as puppies of the Demon Dog himself, James Ellroy, or maybe because we were dirty and liked to bark loud, the name stuck. And we got plenty of high scores.

• • •

Why'd we shut down the magazine? We were tired. After five years, the only way to keep it going at the level we wanted would've been to turn it into a business. We weren't ready for that. Add families, jobs, and our own writing careers, and it became an overflowing plate.

We're not completely finished with *Plots with Guns,* though. The anthology in your hands is proof of that. In addition to stories from the magazine that we feel define our attitude and vision pretty well, we've invited some new stories from some heavyweights–a peek into the future, perhaps. We're going to find ways to invoke *Plots with Guns* whenever the spirit moves us, maybe in the direction of a print edition, or more anthologies with original stories, or . . . who knows? If we know there are enough people who want more, who are we to keep it in the grave forever? Let it claw its way out and stink up the world while searching for fresh meat.

Until then, enjoy this baby that Dennis McMillan has helped us birth. He's a man after our own hearts, the type of publisher we want to be when we grow up. Ain't it a beauty?

Big thanks to everyone who has ever appeared in *Plots with Guns.* You know we love you. You folks, well, you're the real deal.

Here's a Crimedog who caught onto PwG early on and supplied us with juicy pulp tales one after the other. This was the first, dark and funny—maybe even crippling. We ran a couple of other Speedy stories as time went on, and eventually Hansen took one and developed it into his first novel, Street Raised. *He's a wild man and he demands your attention.*

Speedy's Big Moving Day
Pearce Hansen

That's him now," Joel said softly. Skip followed his brother-in-law's gaze to see a tall man just closing and locking the door to the downstairs apartment. As Skip watched, the man turned and trundled down the front walk toward them. His face reminded Skip of a mournful Doberman.

Joel took a hesitant step toward the man, then paused, just outside kicking range. "'Scuse me, Speedy. You got a minute?"

Speedy stopped and rotated on the balls of his feet until he was facing them dead on. His hands dangled empty at his sides as he looked at them expectantly.

"Something?" Speedy didn't move.

"My brother-in-law here has a problem. I told him you can fix problems, sometimes."

"Sometimes. Depends."

"Yeah, well, I can't help him with this one, but maybe you two can make some arrangement. I'd owe you one. Skip, this is Speedy; Speedy, this is Skip." Joel turned to walk quickly up the sagging wooden porch steps and into his apartment. He didn't look back.

8

Skip was very aware of his relative youth and scrawniness as he looked up at the older man in front of him. Speedy stood as straight as a Marine drill instructor, and his wolfish face was utterly still as he watched Skip rub his hands on his pants legs.

Skip spoke first. "I have this problem, like Joel said. I been sharin' a house with some people over in Alameda, a couple of pot dealers. I mean, sure I partied with them, what's a few bong hits? Everybody does it, right?"

Speedy nodded. "Sure."

"Anyway, this gangbanger chick Darla moved in, and since then things been gettin' wilder and wilder. Like she just took over, you know? And she comes to me tonight, and she says they're tired of my raggedy ass, that some crack slingers from over here in Oakland will give them twice what I'm payin' for a place to deal from. So she kicks me out—and she kept all my stuff, too!"

Speedy had studied Skip's face owlishly as he listened. "What about your roommates? Did they back her up?"

"Yeah!" The anger he'd repressed up until now welled forth onto Skip's face. "And I thought they were my friends!"

"Why didn't you tell her to take a hike? Why'd you let her run you off like that?"

"She's packed, man. All her friends are packed, too. Me, I'm not into guns. I called the cops; all they did was give me a form to fill out. I came to Joel for help, but he ain't willin' either. He just pointed me at you, said you had a rep for gettin' things done."

Speedy shrugged, his gaze flicking over his shoulder reflexively as if to see if anyone was creeping up behind him. Nobody was that Skip could see. "Maybe I do. You got wheels?"

"Yeah. That's my truck over there." Skip looked down the block.

9

Speedy followed his gaze and looked at Skip's battered green pickup parked a little way off under the sulfurous glare of a streetlight. He nodded once more.

"How much money you got?" he asked then.

Skip licked his lips. "Uh, about five Cs."

"Okay. You keep three hun starting over money. Sleep on somebody's couch, I don't care. I get the other two hundred, half in advance for expenses. For that, you get your stuff back, and some payback."

Skip pursed his lips for a moment, then bobbed his head up and down. "It's worth it to me. Whaddayou got in mind?"

"Wait here," Speedy said, and went inside his place. He came out a few moments later, carrying a burlap-wrapped bundle. "Now we go for a ride." They got into the pickup and took off.

Speedy was living on San Pablo Avenue. They drove down it now, past the sullen glow of the trash fires, and the hookers who hooted and beckoned at them. In the near distance, the sewing machine chatter of an Uzi was answered by the business-like cough of a shotgun blast. Skip concentrated grimly on his driving–this was one neighborhood he didn't want to have a fender bender in.

At Speedy's direction, they turned down a side street with most of its streetlights shot out. As they drove past a rundown apartment building, he said, "This is the place." Skip parked the truck and killed the engine. Speedy made no immediate move to get out. His eyes scanned the street ceaselessly, and when he spoke, his voice was quiet. "We're going to meet some people. Keep your mouth shut, and do exactly what I say. Got it?" Skip nodded.

They got out of the pickup, Speedy carrying the burlap bundle down by his leg. From a darkened doorway down the block came the harsh tinkle of a breaking bottle followed by several angry voices. Speedy glanced over but didn't slow his pace. He continued toward the entrance to the apartment building, with Skip following close behind. The front door swung open freely, the latching mechanism smashed beyond repair. They continued through the lobby and up three flights of garbage-strewn stairs without incident. They stepped out into the third floor hallway and walked down the corridor, stopping in front of a gouged and scarred door, originally painted blue. There was fast, vicious music pumping loudly through it. Speedy rapped several times on the door—someone inside turned the music off abruptly. The door whipped open hard, and several skinheads with baseball bats filled the doorway like pitbulls crowding a dog run. "Speedy-man!" the largest one said with a feral grin. "And a new playmate!"

Speedy advanced on the skinz and they swung out of his way like gates. He stopped just inside the entrance and waved his client in after him. Skip stood right next to Speedy as the large skin closed the door behind them. The apartment was a den of skinheads and bootwomen, with at least a dozen standing and lounging around, smoking and drinking beer. There were holes punched in the walls, which were covered with graffiti, mainly three-legged swastikas and declarations such as "Bay Area Skinz Rule!" as well as various racist comments, most of them misspelled. Cigarette butts and broken glass littered the floor. A couple of skinz lay passed out on a stained mattress in the corner, almost buried in empty beer cans; from the look and the smell, one or more of their friends had urinated on them. On another mattress a naked couple was fucking. The guy was on top, and Skip watched his pale buttocks rising and falling as he hunched himself savagely into the girl below; Skip suddenly realized the girl was staring blankly up at him past her lover's burly shoulder, and he looked quickly away, reddening in embarrassment. Two shorthaired bootwomen sat at the only table whispering to each other and eyeing Skip and Speedy. Their eyes

11

glittered, and their laughter was like broken glass. Skip felt every eye in the room was on him.

Seated on a ripped, broken-down easy chair in the center of the room was a skinhead with a tattoo on his shaven skull, depicting a corpse-worm burrowing in and out of his head. He was naked to the waist, wearing red suspenders and covered with scars. A battered Louisville slugger leaned against his leg as he held court among his werewolves. "Speedy," he rasped, extending a beer to his visitor. "What can we do for you?"

Speedy threaded his way to the beer and cracked it open, swilling half of it down in a single guzzle.

"I need some backup, Buzz," he replied at last. "Two guys with bats should do it. Quick job, in and out, three-way split." He turned toward Skip. "Lay a hundred on the table for beer money." Skip complied, and the room relaxed almost visibly.

Buzz nodded. "I think for this that me and Fuck-up should suffice." He stood, stretched, picked up his bat, and called "Fuck-up!" over his shoulder.

A skin squatting on his hams in the back corner rocketed to his feet. He was an upright slab of beef, his neck and shoulders dwarfing his bald head. His eyes had all the expression of the buttons on a rag doll's face. "Fetch a bat," Buzz commanded. "We have business." Both men donned bomber jackets with hooded sweatshirts underneath.

Fuck-up picked a bat from the pile by the door, and the four men filed into the hall, trooping down the stairs and out the front door. Skip slid into the driver's seat. Speedy rode shotgun; Buzz and Fuck-up rode in the bed. Skip saw that they had their hoods up, covering their shaved skulls. As he pulled away from the curb, it occurred to him to wonder why a coven of racist skinz would choose to live in one of the blackest neighborhoods in Oakland. He shrugged the question away.

He drove his truck past the loitering armies of homeless in downtown Oakland, down the neon drenched length of Broadway into the Alameda Tube and underneath the Estuary, the engine sounds of the truck moaning back from the filthy tile tunnel walls as they passed beneath the countless tons of water above. Traffic was light. They emerged onto Webster and abruptly hit the main drag. Sailors from the nearby naval base mobbed the sidewalks, wandering between their watering holes: the bars and massage parlors, the pool halls and cheap hotels. Among them prowled the scavengers and predators that fed off them. As they waited at the stoplight at Lincoln, a young sailor on his hands and knees projectile vomited into the gutter as passersby jeered. His girlfriend for the evening looked on blankly, snapping her gum in indifference.

Skip turned left on Lincoln. After a few blocks, he turned left again and drove down a side street into a residential neighborhood. The streetlights were fewer in this area, and there were large pools of darkness between them. He pulled over to the curb, engine running. "That's the place three houses down," he whispered unnecessarily, and pointed. Speedy looked and saw Skip's erstwhile home: a house about the size of a postage stamp with a lowered red mini-truck parked in front.

"Park as close as you can," he ordered. Skip didn't respond for several seconds.

Fuck-up leaned around from the truck bed and glared into the open passenger's window. "Let's get a move on!" he griped hoarsely. "I want more beer!"

Skip took a shuddering breath and said, "All right." He pulled out from the curb and rolled slowly up to the house, parking directly in front of the mini-truck. The crew climbed quietly out of the pickup. Speedy was again carrying the bundle along his leg–Buzz and Fuck-up carried their bats

13

behind their backs. The group moved up the front walk, stopping at the base of the porch steps. The porch light was off. Rap music was leaking out the door, the bass notes hitting with the impact of a muffled rubber hammer. It was loud, but not quite loud enough to warrant the neighbors calling the cops.

"All right," Speedy said. "Buzz, Fuck-up, you know the drill. I'll go in first, you two follow: fan out and back my play. We'll make the split after." Speedy turned to his client. "Skip, you'll shut the door behind us. Stay on the porch and wait for my call." Speedy looked at his client. Skip was staring fixedly at the house like a mouse hypnotized by a snake. "Skip," he hissed, and touched the man's arm. Skip jerked as if he'd been awakened from a dream he didn't want to remember.

"What?" he asked dully.

"Give me the key to the front door," Speedy demanded, and held out his hand palm up. Skip fumbled in his pocket, produced the key ring, and thrust the door key into Speedy's hand.

"Is the lock a knob, a deadbolt, or both?" Speedy asked him.

"Deadbolt."

"Good." He looked at Skip appraisingly. "Relax. You'll do fine." Speedy made a last quick scan of the neighborhood. All the surrounding households were plugged into their nightly television fix–there was no traffic, no pedestrians. Just the night wind sighing through the trees in the front yards. He turned and led the way as the group crept silently up the steps onto the porch. Speedy stuck the door key between his front teeth and pulled the burlap sack off what was now revealed as a double-barreled sawed-off shotgun, clean as a whistle and glistening with gun oil. He handed the sack to

Buzz. Speedy pulled back the hammers, cocking both barrels, and depressed the safety button. Holding the sawed-off in his right hand, he used his left to insert the key in the lock. He gently turned it until the bolt unlocked with a metallic thud that Skip was sure could be heard by everyone in the house, even over the music. Speedy removed the key, handing the ring to Skip. He grasped the knob, again with his left hand. Even gentler now, he turned it until it wouldn't turn anymore. "Show time," he said softly. Then he briskly pushed the door open, and took a long stride into the room.

"How do," he drawled. Through the open door, Skip saw all five heads in the pot smoke-filled room whirl to face Speedy. They all had looks of what Skip interpreted as stupid surprise on their faces. From Speedy's right, Darla, green-eyed hellcat of a girl, came charging at him, and a hulk in a trench coat ahead of Speedy was fumbling for something under his arm. Speedy lunged forward and stuck his shotgun against the bridge of Trenchcoat's nose, hard enough to break the skin. The hand under the trench coat froze. Glancing to the side, Speedy kicked Darla's legs out from under her. She toppled over hard against the wall and slid down to crash on her side on the floor. Speedy's initial lunge had cleared the doorway enough for Buzz and Fuck-up to follow him in, bats brandished over their heads and skinheads gleaming. The marks froze as the two skinz spread out and threatened the group from both flanks. Neither man blocked Speedy's field of fire. Skip shut the front door from outside and leaned against it for a moment before turning to scan the rest of the sleepy block in frantic paranoia. His heart was pounding as he looked for any sign that the neighbors had noticed anything, but he didn't think anyone had. He didn't think anyone inside had seen him yet either, or even knew he was involved with this. He'd wanted to make them pay before, but now part of him wanted to just hop in his truck and split

15

before any of his roommates saw his face. But he wanted his stuff, and he suddenly realized he'd do anything to get it back.

Through the door Skip heard muffled conversation he couldn't make out, then the sounds of a short, sharp commotion. The door opened to reveal Speedy standing in the opening. "C'mon in," he commanded, and Skip obeyed. The stereo continued thumping mindlessly as he reentered the house he'd been evicted from earlier in the evening.

Everyone was there, and their eyes bored holes in him as he entered the room. Chris and Anthony, his pothead roommates, were gaping and goggling at him as they sat dazed on the sofa. Chris, a fat young man with a face like Herman Munster, yelped, "I can't believe you did this!" His friend Anthony, a pale dark-haired ghost, only stared with his mouth hanging open.

Trenchcoat's eyes were watering, the tears overflowing onto his broad cheeks. Blood from his cut nose was now dripping steadily off the end of his chin as he sat holding his injured knee without saying a word.

Gangbanger Darla knelt on the floor, her red hair hanging over her face. Her shirt was ripped down the front, and she had her arms crossed, hands holding her top to keep her breasts from spilling out like frightened puppies. She was shivering, whether with rage or terror Skip couldn't tell. Still, he figured if her looks could kill, they all would have been greasy smears on the floor

There was a man sitting in the easy chair Skip didn't recognize: he was a weasel-faced shrimp in an Oakland Raiders starter jacket, and he radiated cool.

Buzz was going from person to person, frisking them quickly but thoroughly, sticking the loot in Speedy's burlap sack. Fuck-up hovered to one side, slapping his bat against his palm; he looked disappointed that nobody was making trouble.

Speedy handed Skip his keys. Skip said nothing to anyone, carefully avoiding any eye contact as he hurried down the hall leading to the back of the house. He turned on the light and stared down in dismay at the scattered heap of his previously boxed belongings. The cockroaches had already rifled through it, but he figured he didn't have time to see what was gone. He just wanted this over with. He quickly tossed the stuff on the floor into one container or another, picked up a precarious stack of boxes, and carried it to the front room.

Speedy held the sawed-off at his waist, left palm pressing down on the barrels. He wasn't aiming at anyone in particular, but he didn't have to: if he cut loose in these close quarters, he'd splash the marks all over the wall like broken balloons full of red paint.

Under Fuck-up's watchful eye and eagerly hovering bat, Buzz was still looting the room's occupants. Guns and rolls of bills and IDs (for future modification or sale) were going into the sack even as Skip walked across the room.

A low coffee table dominated the space between the sofas, with several half-empty forty-ouncers on it. The reeking water from a knocked-over bong dripped off the table onto the red shag carpet, and a large plastic bag bulging with what looked like high-grade sensemilla lay open in front of the Retros. A smaller bag filled with rock cocaine sat in front of Weasel-face. As Skip set down the stack of boxes by the front door, he saw Buzz scoop up both bags and eye them reverently before casually sticking them into his coat pocket.

"In the sack," Speedy said firmly. Buzz swiveled his head up to favor Speedy with a flat stare. Speedy stared right back, brows raised questioningly. "Everything goes in the sack," Speedy said, almost apologetically. Buzz abruptly turned away and dropped the plastic bags into the burlap sack with the rest of their plunder. Skip went back to his old bedroom to get the rest of his stuff.

Skip had finished moving his reclaimed belongings to the door, where it stood in a disordered tower of odds and ends. He stood next to his stuff, grinning nervously at his former persecutors.

Speedy's eyes were locked onto the roomful of marks, in targeting mode. "Time to split. Skip, take your stuff and wait in the truck. Make it one load," he said. Skip opened the door, picked up his things, and awkwardly staggered out with the stack teetering precariously over his head. Fuck-up threw up his hood, held his bat behind his back and followed him. Just as he went out the door, Skip saw Buzz looking at Speedy strangely for a moment. Then, the bag clutched tightly in his hand, the skin strode out the door to follow the others.

Skip tried to be careful as he deposited his stuff in the back of his truck, but the tower of boxes toppled over to spill across the bed. As he looked down in consternation, twin presences loomed up on either side of him, boxing him in: Buzz and Fuck-up.

"We'll take the keys," Buzz said, his hand outstretched. His other hand still clutched the sack of loot in a seemingly unbreakable grip. Neither of the skinz made any overtly threatening move, but they didn't have to ask twice. Skip's hands were shaking as he dug his keys out of his pants pocket. They were still shaking as he watched the two beefy skinheads climb into his truck and drive away, the ancient engine whining with effort. His shoulders slumped as he watched all his possessions disappearing into the night. Loose comic books and scraps of his personal paperwork swirled up from the truck bed in the back draft to drift into the gutter like trash.

He looked up at the house to see Speedy standing in the open door watching the receding taillights of the pickup. Speedy looked even more mournful than usual.

Speedy whirled and disappeared inside. Skip heard him bark some orders, then Speedy ran down the steps to join him at the curb. Trenchcoat's harsh chuckles leaked out the open doorway to follow him.

Speedy had somebody's keys dangling in his hand. "In the mini-truck!" he ordered, as he switched off the alarm and unlocked the driver's door. He slid in and opened the passenger door. Skip got in and started to speak, but Speedy brusquely gestured him to silence. His eyes snapped back and forth like they were on rubber bands.

"Where's the nearest place that sells beer?" he asked abruptly after a moment.

"Uh, the School Store, three blocks down," Skip muttered. He jerked his chin in the same direction the pickup had disappeared in. His face was red with embarrassment, and he wouldn't look at Speedy at all.

"We'll swing by there first," Speedy said, his voice seeming to attempt a display of confidence. Skip wondered whose benefit the attempt was for. Speedy started the mini-truck and headed out, doing not one mile over the speed limit. As they departed Darla cautiously stuck her head out the front door and goggled after them, like a mollusk peeping from her burrow. Behind Darla in the house someone finally turned the music off.

Skip could see the neon sign of the market ahead of them, flickering fitfully. It was a mom-and-pop, the storefront flush with the sidewalk. Sure enough, his pickup was parked in front, bold as you please. There was no sign of Buzz and Fuck-up. Speedy pulled the mini-truck around the corner from the entrance and stopped.

"You wait here. When I honk the horn, leave the keys in the ignition and come running." Speedy got out under the too-revealing streetlights. He stuck the sawed-off down his waistband, flipped his Pendleton shirt over it, and walked

19

around the corner, trying to look casual but walking as stiff-legged as he were a grenade about to go off.

It seemed like forever went by then, but it couldn't have been more than a minute or two before Skip heard a short blast on what was recognizably the horn of his old pickup, and he ran around the corner as if propelled by a slingshot. He saw Speedy standing next to the open driver door of the truck holding the reclaimed burlap sack of booty. Then he saw Buzz and Fuck-up standing over by the store entrance, and stumbled a little. Neither one of them had their Louisville sluggers, but Skip could see the bat handles sticking out of his heap of possessions in the truck bed. Amazingly, Speedy seemed to have everything under control. The two skinz stood passively looking at nothing in particular as Skip hurriedly walked around the driver's side of the truck, staying well out of reach of Buzz & Fuckup as he did so—he wasn't about to tempt fate. As he eagerly climbed into the truck, Speedy ambled back over to the skinz, who still hadn't moved.

"The marks' mini-truck is around the corner with the keys in it," Skip heard him say. "That's your cut from this job—that, the beer, and the beer money Skip already gave you. Okay?" Both skinz visibly relaxed.

"Okay." Buzz said. Speedy backed away toward Skip's pickup, then opened the door and stuck his leg inside, preparing to enter. "Speedy!" Buzz called after him. Speedy froze and looked at him, tensing a little; he still held the sawed off ready.

Buzz stood carefully still, both his hands showing. "It was a big haul, and it was right there. You know how it is?"

Speedy nodded. "Sure. I know how it is." He finished climbing into the pickup and handed the keys across to Skip. "You can drop me off at my place." As they pulled out, Skip looked over his shoulder and watched the two skinheads putting the beer in the bed of their new mini-truck. Both of them were smiling.

Skip drove them back down squid-infested Webster Street, then under the waters of the Estuary, up Broadway through downtown Oakland, and along San Pablo Avenue to Speedy's front door. The two men sat silently at the curb in the truck for a few moments; each was engrossed in his own thoughts. Speedy finally turned to Skip.

"Was that enough payback for you?" he asked. Skip's mouth opened for a moment in surprise, and then he furrowed his brow. Finally, he nodded, his eyes shining. Speedy smiled, as briefly as a flashbulb in a darkened room. "Good," he said. "Then I'll have the rest of my fee now." He accepted the hundred dollars from his client, and put it in his pocket with the loot from the rip-off. Speedy reached into the sack and pulled out a four-barreled derringer, hefting it a few times in his hand. "You know, Darla and her friends may come looking for you." Speedy held the little pistol out to Skip, offering it to him.

Skip looked at the derringer for a long moment, then shook his head vigorously. "Naw, man. I told you I'm not into guns." Still, he felt a growing fascination with the power this little piece of metal represented. People will do what you say, a voice whispered as his hands began to creep toward it as if against his will.

But he'd waited too long. Speedy shrugged and put the derringer back in the sack. "Suit yourself." Skip watched as Speedy climbed out of the pickup with his sack of booty and stuck the sawed-off down his waistband. Speedy unlocked all the dead bolts on his front door and disappeared inside, shutting the door behind him. Then Skip started the truck and drove off to find somewhere else to live, somewhere not in Alameda.

21

The Czar of Noir, Eddie Muller, is also one of our drinking buddies at conventions. We love his writing, the way he reexamines post war America through his noir *lens, as seen in* The Distance *and* Shadow Boxer. *He knows so much about* noir *that you should just sit back down if you're thinking of challenging him.*

He let us run with this story for our "Big Shot" issue, where we asked several hot mystery writers to contribute a piece in exchange for, I swear, a free drink. Almost everyone we asked said yes. But we owe Eddie more drinks than just the one. "Wanda Wilcox" was nominated for an Anthony Award at the 2004 Bouchercon convention. For that, I need to buy the guy a bottle.

Wanda Wilcox is *"Trapped!"*
Eddie Muller

I found her in the forgiving twilight of the Coach and Horses, alone in a corner booth. She was sifting through a jumble of stuff dumped from a ratty clutch, the black velvet worn to a high shine. Several dead drinks awaited removal. A fresh one sat at hand, awaiting execution. Lipsticked butts overflowed an ashtray. She'd galloped through Happy Hour, but still looked strong for a stretch run.

I hung by the bar, watching the cigarette smoke mingle with her swirled-up bleach job. The hair was like a beacon, throwing a signal from her glory days. Those platinum waves, loosely set, seemed to keep her head above bourbon.

"Look, pal," she suddenly said, still poking through her junk. "If you're gonna keep staring, least you can do is buy a girl a drink. How 'bout getting us both a Manhattan? 'Fore you blow a fuse trying to figure out where you seen me before."

"I know where I've seen you," I said, stepping to the booth. "*Corner of Fear and Desire. Vicious Blonde. Wish Me Hell.*"

Her head cocked defiantly. The tar-bar jutted. She inhaled a little vestigial dignity. A sliver of Hollywood's old glamour cut through the hazy torpor of the Coach and Horses.

"You're Wanda Wilcox."

It wasn't that long ago that Wanda's bright tousle, its piled

23

curls hinting of an energetic afternoon in some Bel-Air bungalow, had caught every eye at Ciro's and the Derby. She outshone the showgirls at the Florentine Gardens. Wanda knew how to work it, unabashed. Always leave a hot flash for the tabloid boys.

"Remember this?" I pulled a photo from my portfolio and carefully set it next to her detritus: a group shot of budding starlets, circa 1950, preening for a flak's camera: Piper Laurie, Mona Freeman, Barbara Bates, Peggie Castle, and–front and center, blonde and bountiful–Wanda Wilcox.

"Oh, yeah. Eagle-Lion was about to sign me up. Then Jack Warner stepped in. Jesus, look at Piper. . . . They pimped us as the Hollywood Press Association's six 'Baby Stars Most Likely to Succeed.'"

She stared silently at the picture, examining each face. Still comparing, still competing. Onto the table I clumsily wedged a compact reel-to-reel tape recorder and jacked in a microphone.

"Oh, shit," she moaned.

"Took me a long time to find you. I want to make the most of it."

While I fumbled with a tape, she slid a photocopy of a clipping from the portfolio. It was from an old *Hollywood Reporter*:

New Queen of the Clubs
By Harrison Carroll

The glittering clubs along the Sunset Strip have crowned a new Queen—Warner Bros.'s blazing blonde bombshell, Wanda Wilcox, who is turning heads nightly as she winds her superb curves through all the hottest spots. Wanda is hoping to take a step up to A-list pictures, having moved to Warners' after several years in Universal-International's stock player training program. The impression Wanda made on audiences in Eagle-Lion's *Corner of Fear and Desire* is almost as impressive as the one she's making on the local club scene.

She didn't wait for me to roll tape:

"If I made one decent picture, it was Wish Me Hell. *That's what I say to Cagney just before I shoot him. I got to kill the star and say the name of the picture—not bad. I got that part because the producer wanted to bang me so bad he couldn't see straight. But I did okay in it. I just talked the way I talk and stumbled around and didn't get all formal. It was fun—my specialty. The reviews called me 'natural.'"*

Girls like Wanda Wilcox came to Hollywood from places like Colquet, Minnesota or Odessa, Texas, or Bent Elbow, Iowa, in search of The Montage. You know, the scene in the movie where the story upshifts into the highlife—free-flowing champagne, popping flashbulbs, gleamings roadsters, lavish bouquets, besotted admirers, and a worshipful Sugar Daddy in the middle of it all, pulling the right strings.

Wanda lived in The Montage. As Sugar Daddy she cast actor Raymond Clement, whose onscreen specialty was suave European urbanity. It contrasted spicily with Wanda's blatant allure: milk-fed farm girl tipsy in Metropolis.

"Lots of guys fell for me, but Ray fell hardest. Worldly as he claimed to be, he'd never known anybody like me. He courted me from Hollywood to New York and everywhere in between, sending flowers and champagne every day we were apart. He announced our engagement at 21 and the papers ate it up. We were The Aristocrat and the Party Girl."

"You had the world by the tail," I said, grinning.

"I had men by the balls," she corrected. "Same thing."

The key to The Montage, of course, was to keep it moving. Never let the eye linger. Don't let them see that the golden filigree is gilt paint on plywood, that the nightclub walls are suspended on cables, that Hollywood's most continental actor

25

is a wife-beating alcoholic who'd never been closer to the Continent than Coney Island.

Not that there wasn't sufficient reality to go around. Like the night Raymond Clement kicked open the door of an apartment in the Garden of Allah to find his fiancée on her knees, with up-and-coming Guy Madison in her mouth. Clement had hired detectives to follow his betrothed.

"He figured that a girl who was as good at it as me must get lots of practice."

"Was he right?"

"Isn't that why you're here?"

One of Clement's hired dicks copped some extra coin selling the dirt to *Confidential.* "Up in Wanda Wilcox's Bedroom" was tawdry and true. But even a scandal rag like *Confidential* drew the curtains before stating the precise, fleshy facts. Sin mags understood the value of the readers' imagination in the sordid communion between seller and buyer.

"The shitty publicity hurt. See, here's how it is— Hollywood's run by a club of tailors and junkmen who sell your tits and ass while praising Mom and apple pie. They don't know what to do with a girl who likes to fuck and doesn't care who knows it. Those Mama's boys hated me for that."

Here's a scene for you, hotter than any Wanda made for the masses. Picture this: a cloudless day, high noon at a Beverly Hills pool party. Wanda's lounging on a chaise at poolside, scoping the action, waiting on another Chi Chi. A swarthy, broad-shouldered guy pulls himself up out of the pool, the water glistening over his muscular body. Wanda stares impudently, eyes sparking behind her dark glasses. Her gaze hones in on his soaking swimming trunks, and the swollen contents.

"After the thing with Guy Madison, Raymond didn't break off the engagement—that's how hopelessly he was in love with me. But

everything changed when he went to New York for a few weeks. That's when I met Jack Stanton."

As he walks past Wanda, Stanton gives her an appraising once-over: she's filling a snug two-piece white suit, suntan oil sizzling on her skin. She feels like pastry, hot from the oven. A houseboy sets a fresh cocktail on the table beside her. She lifts her sunglasses and squints into blinding whiteness. Her eyes need to confirm the intuition creeping up her thighs. Her lips draw into a wicked grin when Jack Stanton's silhouetted figure looms closer, his shadow sliding over her body.

"Never being the religious type, I didn't go in for all that God and the devil mumbo-jumbo. I knew, even when I was a little girl, that the devil didn't live in some fiery cave at the center of the earth, and that he didn't have a pitchfork and horns and all that silly crap—"

Wind riffles the canvas of the cabaña. Wanda, on all fours, clutches a beach towel in her fists. Dropping her head, she bites into her damp, discarded bathing suit, the tang of chlorine stinging her lips and tongue. She throws back her hips to catch the full measure of every thrust.

". . . I learned first-hand that the devil lived in a two-bedroom bungalow out in the Canyon and made grubby little B pictures. Yes, he did have a horn, and he knew exactly what to do with it."

Like Wanda, it was Jack Stanton's body that busted him into the movies. A swishy Goldwyn talent scout ogled his muscles while he was lifeguarding in Ft. Lauderdale in the late thirties. Stanton was from Evanston, Illinois; like Wanda, a Midwesterner. And just like her, he paid his dues as a stock company frame-filler before becoming a bigger fish in an endless swamp of "B" programmers. Always the virile ladies' man. The part fit him like a Trojan.

In '44, he married sexy, black-haired Vicky Lord. They did a photo shoot for a second-rate men's magazine in which they look like slumming gods descended to earth to soak up

27

the sun and stain all the clean sheets. It skirted the limits of "good taste," and the spread was eighty-sixed. Stanton didn't give a damn. Once he was wise to the set-up, it never bothered him that he couldn't crack the A-List. For the big boys–Power, Gable, Taylor–fame was like a choke-chain. Half of them were nances anyway. Down on Stanton's rung, anything went.

"Jack laughed at the fantasy machine. He had no fear. He couldn't be embarrassed, couldn't be intimidated. He never did anything he didn't want to do, and when he wanted to do something, he did it– anytime, anywhere. Didn't care what anybody thought."

A motorcycle cop pulls over a convertible way up on Mulholland. One A.M. in the City of Angels and this guy is doing about seventy, blowing off stop signs. The cop sidles up, holster unsnapped. Shines a flash on a guy he makes for an actor, though he can't place him. But that's definitely Wanda Wilcox next to him, legs up on the leather, touching up her blond waves. The cop shifts the beam around, catching the driver's lap–fly spread wide, cock out, smudged with lipstick. "It's called Crimson Nymph," Wanda explains. Jack Stanton howls, a coyote in the Hollywood hills.

Back at Wanda's place, night and day smear into each other, over and over. She spends what seem to be endless hours in the tangled sheets, cum-drunk and aching.

"Here's the thing, the gist of it, so listen good. Most people, Jack said, live their whole life in fear. . . ."

Stanton pours himself a double bourbon and sips it through a tight smile. The bedside lamp casts harsh shadows across his face. Wanda raises her leg, pressing her foot to the side of his head. He clutches her ankle.

". . .Fear of losing money, of being humiliated, of dying. . . ."

On the floor are her nylons, torn, tossed aside. Her lacy brassiere in a twisted knot. His shoe. A belt, yanked from his jumbled trousers. Heavy drapes, almost drawn.

"*. . .I'm not like any of them,' he said. 'Because I know how it's all gonna turn out. . . .*"

Through a gap in the drapes, the face of Raymond Clement. Ashen, stricken.

"*. . .I know exactly how my life is going to end.*'"

Raymond Clement bays like a whipped dog at the window of 1815 Courtney Terrace. Stanton yanks open the front door and is on him like a wolf on a rabbit. Passing headlights throw the yard into stark relief, a split-second honed razor sharp: Clement stumbling backwards, mackinaw flapping, trying to fend off his naked attacker. Wanda rushing through the door, wrapped in a sheet that trails on the ground.

"*Poor Raymond. Jack had been a Golden Gloves boxer. He went berserk. I'd never seen anything like it.*"

Bones in the older man's face split apart as Stanton's fists pound through his flailing defenses. Wanda screams—louder, more believably than she ever mustered for a camera. Clement hits the grassy slope and slides toward the sidewalk. Stanton drops a knee into his gut and hunkers in to keep punching. Drool slops from his mouth as he pummels lefts and rights. Wanda tries to clamp herself on Jack's back, to stop the slaughter. She catches his elbow flush in the eye as he winds up for another punch. Wanda crumples on the damp lawn, the sheet unraveling around her. She watches the beating through her fingers, crying, until the approaching sirens finally end it.

"*It was amazing that Raymond lived. He had to have surgery to put his face back together. And the press—oh Christ, did they have a field day! After that, I was more famous than I'd ever imagined!*"

Hollywood itself will take a beating when the juicy news of this sordid romance goes out over the wires for the world to read. What has always puzzled me about this romantic trio is how Clement, possessor of a well-trained mind, could play around in this league of daffy dillies and muscle developers.

I watched her read the clipping, thought about pausing the tape. The Coach and Horses was eerily quiet; Happy Hour had segued into suppertime. We were the only ones left in the joint. She lit another smoke and gave the barkeep the high sign.

"That was the peak of my fame, I guess. All I had to do was follow my agent's advice: act ashamed and beg Raymond to take me back. The producers and press flaks would have patted my head and said 'good girl' and laughed the whole thing off. But it was too late for that . . . I couldn't let go of Jack. He'd put this thing in my head about knowing 'how it all turns out.' He told me I could know, too, if I just let myself go. That's all I had to do, if I wanted to be as fearless as him. And I wanted it. In the worst way."

Wanda went back to the Courtney Terrace bungalow. Back to the sheets. That's where one night she understood, for the first time really, how movies are made.

Jack's black valise was open on the bed. Looking at it, she thinks: *Close-Up.*

She closes her eyes. *Black.*

Cut, she thinks. Her head swivels to the right.

Eyes open—new shot: Her wrist, lashed to the bedpost by a floral necktie.

Eyes close. *Black. Move camera.*

Open: Jack Stanton's face, smiling, darkly. Watching her. *Black.*

Open: His belt, snaking from its loops, snapping free. *Black.*

She imagines a camera near the ceiling, looking down, observing them. She sees herself below, as if suspended, gleaming white, open to some ancient secret.

"We got pretty high one night, and when we got high, we got

dangerous. He could make me do anything, that man. Not that I wasn't game. We went at it like it was a title fight. Lost all track of time. And when I thought I might actually die, the bastard leans down and whispers hard in my ear:
   "'See it. Right now—see how it all turns out.'"
Wanda's eyes go wide with horror. She's staring right at it, shooting up from some unknowable place, a place further down than her deepest unconscious.
   Stanton, inside her, feels her whole being change. She's different then, they both know it.
"Good girl," he breathes in her ear. "Now you know."
She panicked. Most of us would. Ran right back to Raymond Clement. They got hitched in Wanda's hometown, on September 28, 1951. In the wedding pictures you can see the scars of the groom's facial reconstruction.
   On the honeymoon, Clement noticed that his bride would suddenly go blank, drifting away in the middle of a meal, or a party, or during their sadly indifferent sex. Once, while he was shaving in a hotel bathroom, he caught her reflection; she was in the doorway, staring down at nothing for what seemed like forever. He was to afraid to speak.
"Everybody thought I'd be 'normal' once I got married. But it was impossible. Nothing can be normal once you know how you're going to die. Knowing how it was all going to turn out made Jack wild and brave. He didn't think any of that reckless shit could kill him, you see? But me, I could only stare at the image in my head, looking for clues as to when it was coming. It scared the living shit out of me."
"You really believed that?" I asked. "Jack Stanton had you convinced he could see the future?"
"What, I'm the first woman to believe some guy has all the answers? Men convince women of all kinds of shit, all the time. I'll love you forever. Have my baby. I'll make you a star. What's the fucking

difference? Jack just took it to the end—his way of having complete power over me, I suppose."

Seven weeks after Wanda Wilcox married Raymond Clement, she opted for the express route: force-fed herself a handful of red devils. Clement found her splayed on the marble floor of their ornate His & Hers bathroom. He kept vigil by Wanda's hospital bed, never letting go of her hand. Two interminable days, during which Raymond Clement actually recalled long forgotten prayers from his catechism. When she finally came to, Clement got his reward.

"Jack," I murmured. "Thanks for being with me, Jack."

Maybe Clement craved the punishment. Maybe it was penance for being such a bastard in his younger days, for all the times he socked his wives in boozed-up rages. Now, all he wanted was for this young angel to love him—to forgive him the way he forgave her.

Wanda stared out the big picture window of their living room, into the lights of Hollywood. Clement's head rested in her lap, like a dog's. He was old enough to be her father, and he looked it.

"Raymond said 'I'll try to be young again for you.' That's when I knew it was time to go. He didn't deserve that kind of humiliation."

Wanda Wilcox and Raymond Clement were divorced fifty-three days after they'd tied the knot. Jack Stanton was named a correspondent in the suit. That was back when it took a year for a divorce to become final in California. Wanda went back to work like a prisoner on death row. She was a pariah at Warners; they wouldn't put her in a picture. Instead, they loaned her on a leash to make crap like *Monster and the Maiden*. Raymond Burr turns into a monkey and falls in love with her. Wanda knew not to expect a life-line to be thrown to her. She was strictly freelance now, drifting in show business purgatory.

32

Next thing she knew, Robert Beauregarde, a Poverty Row producer who specialized in bottom-feeding on fallen stars, hit on the bright idea of teaming Wanda Wilcox and Jack Stanton in a picture. Some creaky western claptrap shot in the hills of Burbank. It was a hell of a reunion: the stars' trailers were lousy with dead soldiers. Professional drinking, to the last drop: no laughs, no shiver of dangerous excitement. Just hammering in the coffin nails, one after another. Booze ravaged them. Stanton got gaunt and haggard. Wanda went soft and puffy.

"Even though I tried to run away, I couldn't. Pretty soon, I did end up just like Jack—without any fear. Because I didn't give a good goddamn about anything."

Jesse James' Treasure blew through theaters nationwide in less than a week. The picture that had more staying power, albeit for a limited audience, was the one Jack and Wanda, and a couple of other upright citizens, shot one night in the Olympic Auditorium in downtown L.A. It became wildly popular after-dinner entertainment within private screening rooms in tonier parts of town. Any studio executive who was "with it" sent their boys around to scrape up a copy. It was a show-stopper, the smutty climax to many A-List dinner parties.

"Jack fucks me in the boxing ring. I'm sure the critics found me 'natural.' Anyway, it killed whatever was left of my career. I didn't care. I hated the whole game, all those miserable hypocrites."

Jack Stanton eventually dumped Wanda for a fresh starlet, Janis Hyde. Dead in the water, Wanda clutched for her own lifeline: a furniture importer from Nogales, who had a little ranch right on the Mexico border. George Something.

The desert didn't suit her. Only made her more thirsty. Early in '55 she ditched the husband and found her way back to L.A. Got a room in a flop not far from her old stamping grounds and tried to work herself back into the show biz orbit.

33

"Nobody wanted my tits and ass anymore. So who needs the movies, anyway? Cut out the middleman, I say. I took my wares straight to John Q. Public."

Wanda started hooking to pay the rent. Trolled the clubs for soul brothers. Figured she was doing them a big favor, being a famous movie star and what not. When things got slow, she'd stroll Sunset and nail guys in their cars, right at the stoplights.

Popped for passing bad checks in a local market, she made a big scene in her threadbare housecoat and slippers, all the bottles crashing to the floor when the cop tried to yank the bag away from her.

"I'd spent thousands in that lousy place over the years, and they humiliate me over a hundred bucks worth of booze. Miserable shits."

This time, the tabloids barely noticed.

Go deep in the files of the LAPD and you'll find Wanda Wilcox's mug shots and rap sheet. Solicitation, mostly. A sympathetic judge, remembering her a studio confection, tried to pull her from the drain. She agreed to regular sessions with court-appointed psychologists.

"I told 'em what I'm telling you—about the vision, about how Jack put the picture in my head of how I was gonna die. All the headshrinkers told me the same thing: I was trying to destroy myself. The vision was just a 'projection' of my own fears. They tried to convince me that I secretly craved death, because I felt guilty and inferior. What bullshit! I'd had ten times the life they had! Did they know what it felt like to be picked up by Howard Hughes in a limo at the Waldorf on their twentieth birthday? Or how it felt getting screwed by Gary Cooper or Gregory Peck, men I'd dreamed about when I was a little girl? I made that happen! What did these stupid doctors have in common with me?"

"That's true?" I asked, "The stuff about Cooper and Peck?"

"Don't be naive," she said. "Those shrinks should have been paying

34

me *for all the stories I told 'em. All the cocktail party chatter I supplied."*

Whatever she thought about it, the counseling helped. Wanda pulled herself together and started earning legitimate money. She worked as a shampoo girl in a Beverly Hills salon, biting her tongue while the customers wagged theirs with non-stop industry gossip. Nights, she worked as a cocktail waitress, struggling to smile politely whenever some jerk made a crack about how she overflowed her snug little uniform.

When she'd saved enough, she left L.A. once more, fleeing to a place called Searchlight, Nevada. Just her and a two-room cabin, at the foot of the mountains.

"My hope was that God and the world might forget all about me, and that I might live in peace with myself, all alone. Too bad I kept reading the paper. . . ."

JACK STANTON WIFE SLAIN
Actor Held in Shooting

The victim was an attractive young woman named Lisa Rogers, who was a dark-haired dead ringer for Wanda Wilcox. She was shot in the head in the Palm Springs home she shared with her husband of three years. Stanton was arrested and charged with murder. When the trial opened, Wanda was among the hundreds of spectators who thronged the Indio courthouse.

"I had to go—maybe this was the proof that Jack's vision thing was a crock of shit all along. Maybe he'd end up in the gas chamber instead. Then I could shake off his damn curse."

On the stand, the defendant looked wasted. He reenacted the incident with a replica gun—the actual weapon, one he'd used in all his movies, was never found.

"He claimed that the gun went off accidentally during an argument."

35

Wanda sat in the back of the courtroom throughout the trial, wearing that most disingenuous of disguises, the dramatic sunglasses and scarf ensemble. The camouflage was unnecessary. She was swollen past recognition. But Jack Stanton, being ushered from the courtroom by his attorney, turned and looked right at her. Wanda saw all kinds of emotion cross his face. Except confidence.

"I knew Jack. I knew the truth. He'd aimed that gun right between his wife's eyes."

The jury ruled voluntary manslaughter. Stanton drew a five-to-fifteen stint in Soledad.

"He might never live through it," Wanda Wilcox said cheerily.

She lifted what was left of her latest Manhattan and waved it at all corners of the Coach and Horses, a gracious gesture to the departed. "So I'm celebrating, you see. That's why I agreed to talk to you. I'm free! The curse is lifted."

"Congratulations."

I stared at the tape, which spun inexorably toward the end of the reel. I belatedly toasted her with the remnants of my only drink.

"Jack always said that he was gonna die alone on the floor of some skid-row dive," she went on. "His ticker was just gonna give out on him. What do you think the odds of that are now? Don't you think he'd have seen a prison sentence? Jesus H. Christ, can you believe what I've done to myself, the time I've wasted believing in that goddamn vision? I'm gonna make a fresh start of it and just forget that whole other life, the movies and the parties and the booze and all that. My parents just retired to San Diego, and I'm headed down there to stay for awhile. They'll have me back. I know they will. We haven't talked in a long time, but I know in my heart they'll forgive me. Then I can get back on track again. It's never too late to turn things around. Do you know that in

36

Mexico they tie oranges around the necks of stray dogs to keep them from getting rabies? That's *faith,* you see. Oranges? How the hell do they stop rabies? But maybe it doesn't matter, so long as you believe. I think I'm ready to. I think I'm ready to have a future."

She kept on rambling, watching the tape go around, until it finally spooled right off the reel.

Then: "Twenty bucks and I'll give you a blow job you'll never forget. Real movie star stuff."

A hot prickling spread across the nape of my neck. I pulled out a twenty and pushed it across the table. She lowered her eyes, sadly, then scooped it up along with all her stuff and shoved it into the clutch.

"That's okay," I said. "Take the money. We'll leave it at that." We both stared at the tape recorder. I wondered how much of her story was bullshit, just more show biz, even at the bottom of the barrel.

"What I really want," I said, "is to know what you saw in that vision–how'd you think it was gonna turn out?"

She showed me a stone-cold gaze and leaned toward me, angry and defiant.

"That's what you want for your money? My death scene? The Big Kiss-Off? And you think *I'm* sick? Here I'm offering you something real for a few minutes, and you want the morbid shit instead. That what gets you off?"

I didn't say anything. I pulled the tape off the machine and slid it into its little square box.

"Okay," she finally said with a sigh. "Dead on the floor. I look like hell, like some fat Minnesota housewife in a cheap terrycloth robe from the five-and-dime. I'm all blue. My eyes are wide open and my tongue is bloated out and–"

"Okay, okay. I'm sorry."

"There she lies . . . the Baby Star Most Likely to Succeed."

She stood without teetering and surveyed several hours

worth of spent booze and tobacco. She lifted her head and smiled at me.

"But today's a good day," she declared. "'Cause now I'm betting against the house. Jack's only been in the joint a few months, but he'll probably slug some guy before too long and get his throat cut—and I'll realize once and for all that 'knowing how it all turns out' was just more of his shit."

As she walked past, she trailed a finger over my shoulder and jaw. One last affectation: The Grand Exit.

"Frankly," she said, pushing open the heavy door, "you got way more than twenty bucks worth. Even without you-know-what."

She stepped across the threshold into the Strip's neon smear, into her future.

• • •

SIX MONTHS LATER I added another clipping to my Wanda Wilcox file.

On May 8, 1967, Wanda Wilcox's father found her on the bathroom floor of his San Diego home, dead from both a heart attack and liver failure.

She was forty years old.

On August 7, 1972, eight months after his early parole from Soledad State Penitentiary, Jack Stanton died in a North Hollywood transient's hotel. No cause of death was listed in his brief obituary. And nobody cared to ask.

This is the first story we published from Tim Wohlforth, a prolific writer who has collected an impressive list of publications over the past several years. "Crip and Henrietta" is a hoot—a pierced-punk babe with an attitude and a paraplegic private eye make a winning team. So much so that we published a few more in the series too, including one called "Jesus Christ is Dead!" How could anyone turn that down?

Crip And Henrietta
Tim Wohlforth

I thought I'd fired you," I said as I looked up into Henrietta's green eyes. She hovered over my table in the back patio behind Raleigh's Ale House on Telegraph Avenue in Berkeley, California. I must say she looked worse than the last time I saw her. Spiked green hair. An emaciated pale face suggested she had spent years in a Bosnian concentration camp. Enough damned metal piercing her nose, eyelids, lips, ears, and tongue that I was afraid she'd clink if she smiled. No problem because Henrietta never smiled.

"You're not getting rid of me that easy, Crip," she said, sneering at me.

"Come to poke a stick into the spokes of the wheels of my chair?" I asked.

Henrietta was about as politically correct as Rush Limbaugh. Seemed to delight in pressing my buttons. Thought the whole idea of a paraplegic private eye was a contradiction in terms. Sometimes I thought she had a point. That's why I made the mistake of hiring her as my legs. But most of the time I'm more than happy to hide my wheelchair behind a web site, called "Tom Bateman, Investigations," and make a meager living doing skip traces and selling supposedly confidential information.

"I came to hire you."

"You've got to be kidding," I said. "You kept telling me I'm some no account freak."

"Well, you are. Without me around you're useless."

"So why do you want to hire me?"

"Okay, I admit it. I need you."

I'll be damned if it didn't look like she was going to cry. I knew she must be in some really deep shit to make such a confession. It was as close as she had ever gotten to saying something nice to me. I wasn't sure I could handle a warm and fuzzy Henrietta. I gestured for her to sit down on the bench opposite me, waved at a barmaid, and ordered her a pint of Full Sail. She reached into her jeans pocket with a thin, bare, goose-pimpled arm covered with bluish cult tattoos and withdrew a crumpled pack of Camels. She lit up.

"Puff the other way. That's one reason why I fired you. Stunk up my house. Ashes all over the place. Cigarette butts."

"You're a fuckin' tight ass."

She blew smoke in my face. So much for warm and fuzzy. In some weird way I missed the lady. At least I knew where I stood with her. No phony patronizing.

The place was filling up with students, some attempting to study as they sipped their ale, others loudly arguing about philosophy and literary criticism. Someone behind me, who smoked Gauloises, launched into an oration on the differences between the "Jamesonians" and the "Bloomians." Ah, Berkeley.

"So what's the problem?" I asked.

"You got to find somebody for me."

"Easy. Just hit a few keys on my computer and the job's done."

"This one's not that simple. The guy's been kidnapped."

40

Kidnapped? Heavy duty. Henrietta was definitely in over her depth. Me, too, for that matter. I could handle myself and carried a gun. But I preferred small cases for small change. And little risk.

"Tell me about him."

"Reads books. Thinks big thoughts."

"Definitely not your type."

"Name's Daniel Freidman. He lives in my apartment building off Telegraph. A weirdo. He's an ex-Commie."

"Never thought you would be interested in politics."

"Chills me out. But Daniel's different. He just talks and talks about anything, everything. Kinda like spending time with an encyclopedia that smiles."

"You really care for the guy."

I never could figure out Henrietta's tastes. Like why she chases after me and then spends her time insulting me. But the lady is loyal. I give her that.

"He got burned, Crip, real bad by this weird political cult, the Workers Socialist Party. They had him working twenty hours a day. The main guy was sleeping with all the young chicks. Runnin' around in a fancy car. So he quit."

"What's the problem now?"

"He took off yesterday. Left a note. Said he was returning to the old movement. I just don't believe it."

"People do, you know. It's like religion. Deep down they never really lose the faith."

"Not Daniel," Henrietta insisted. "He hates them."

"I think I'd like to buy a book."

"What?"

"Come if you like."

I put on my calfskin driving gloves, wheeled the chair out from behind our table, spun its specially forged titanium wheels, took off towards the door, and then out onto Telegraph Avenue. My eyes burned from the car exhaust coming from

41

the busy street. A whiff of French roast hit my nostrils as we passed patrons sprawled on the sidewalk, backs against the front of Philosophical Grounds coffee house. All along the street, vendors were setting up their stands for the day. Silver jewelry, incense, tie-dyed tee shirts, anarchist bumper stickers.

Henrietta ran after me, panting. "Slow down, Crip. Don't want a heart attack."

"Then quit smoking."

. . .

I entered a long walkway just off Telegraph Avenue with Henrietta at my side. She knew better than to try to push me. I was not about to be dependent on her or anyone for locomotion. I came to a halt in front of Red Books. I sat in my chair, taking in the window display.

An immense photo of a man dressed in camouflage khaki, black ski mask over his face, charred pipe sticking out his mouth, dominated the window. He was surrounded by a truckload of similarly attired peasants waving Kalashnikov rifles and red flags. A sign proclaimed, "Viva La Zapatistas!"

"Holy shit," Henrietta said. "This where you hang out and get your jollies?"

"Run by a friend of mine. If anyone knows about this group that kidnapped your friend, it's Maggie."

I saw Maggie emerging from a backroom, holding a container of coffee. A Mao cap, boasting a bright red star, perched jauntily on top of her head. A quite pleasant sight with straight prematurely gray hair, bobbed and stylishly cut neck length. She wore a black turtleneck jersey that accented her well-shaped body and matching skin-tight ski pants. She swung open the bookstore door and waited for me to get through with my chair.

42

"Introduce me to your young friend." Maggie placed her emphasis on the word "young."

"Meet my sometime associate, Henrietta."

She turned to Henrietta and began her pitch. "We've got the complete works of Stalin, also Lenin. Have you ever read *Red Flag?* Want a sample copy?"

"All I read is the *Enquirer,*" Henrietta said, "and then only when they feature two-headed babies from outer space."

A pile of *Red Flag*s sat by the door stacked under a table covered with brightly colored leaflets. I could barely get my chair into the place.

"Who's that fuckhead in the ski mask in your window?" Henrietta asked. I would have kicked her in the shins if I had kickable feet. The last thing I wanted was a lengthy lecture from Maggie about the Revolution in Chiapas.

"I need your help," I said before Maggie could launch her pitch. "Henrietta appears to have lost a friend. Claims he was kidnapped by the Workers Socialist Party. What do you know about them?"

"Revisionists."

This was no revelation since, in Maggie's book, "revisionist" means someone who disagrees with her.

"No doubt, but do they go around kidnapping people?" I asked.

"Possible." Maggie rested her coffee on a copy of Stalin's *Foundations of Leninism.* She turned to Henrietta and asked, "Who's the guy?"

"Daniel Freidman."

"Ah," Maggie said thoughtfully. "Very, very interesting."

"So you know him," I said.

"Of course. Comes in here all the time. Once a top figure in the WSP. Then he quit. Sure he was kidnapped? He's speaking at a WSP rally Friday."

"No way," Henrietta said. "Daniel hates those creeps."

43

Maggie walked over to the leaflet table and handed me a hot red one. Damned if she wasn't correct. I passed on the leaflet to Henrietta.

"How can they make him front for a group he hates?" Henrietta asked.

"Easy enough," Maggie said. "They get to someone close to you and threaten to harm her. Then you do what they say."

"Think, Henrietta," I said, turning to her. "Is there someone close to Daniel outside of you?"

Henrietta held up her hand to silence us. She was thinking. Not something she does very often, so it didn't come easy for her.

"There was someone. He was crazy about her. Back in New York. That's why he can't relate to other women. Told me she was a dumpy little woman with two children. Sara's her name."

"Great. I just punch 'Sara' in my old computer. Then narrow it a bit by adding 'New York City' and end up with only a 100,000 hits. Got to have a last name."

"Used to be married to a top party leader. Party brass forced him to divorce her. First name begins with 'J.' John? No, Jack. That's it."

"Jack Geller," Maggie said.

"You sure?" I asked.

"Got to be," Maggie said. "Only Jack in the top leadership of the WSP. And I do remember some story about him being forced to dump his family."

"We're off to see a computer," I said as I whirled my chair around. Maggie leaned over me and gave me an affectionate kiss on the lips. If it wasn't for her damned politics. Henrietta glowered.

• • •

"That's all I need," I told Henrietta as we whizzed down Telegraph towards my cottage. I cruised through the bustling crowd of students and professors. A young man wobbled by on a unicycle, dressed as a clown. I almost collided with a large, middle-aged woman in a full-length dress. She was unfolding a table to display her jewelry.

"I have a name and a city," I continued. "Also a former husband's name. In ten minutes I'll have her phone number, her bank balance, terms of the divorce settlement, current address."

"They should lock up people like you," Henrietta muttered between puffs on her Camel.

I was not nearly so cocky inside as I pretended to be in front of Henrietta. The problem was I was caught up in her quest. It hit me personally. I took some shrapnel in the spine over in 'Nam. Stuck in a chair for the rest of my life because of a war I didn't understand. A war we lost. Maybe a war nobody won. Came back and joined the Vietnam Veterans for Peace. Lasted one demo. Yet it did give me respect for people like Daniel. If they had been more successful earlier on, maybe I wouldn't be in a chair. So I felt I owed those rads something. Finding Daniel would be my way of paying back.

The key was Sara. I had to get her out of their clutches. But how? A scheme shaped in my head. Crazy enough to work. Cost bucks. I needed to call a PI I knew in New York City to dig up some information. Then a quick trip to the Big Apple.

I turned to Henrietta. "Pack your bags. We're going on a trip."

"I haven't got a bag."

"How about a toothbrush?"

"Piss off."

• • •

45

Sara Geller stood in front of the window of her apartment on West 95th Street in New York City. A misty rain descended upon the rooftops of the apartment houses that stretched out in front of her. She fixated upon a flock of pigeons swirling over one tenement roof. A lone figure, little more than an inch high in her distant view, slowly swung a long pole to keep the birds in flight. He stood near a little shack that was the pigeon loft. She felt a connection with the figure, all alone on that wet roof. He had his birds. All he needed to do was drop his pole and they would flock back to him.

She had her own pole swinging. She had sent her two children off to school. She feared for them. The children and herself, like the pigeon keeper and his flock, were being watched. She knew who was doing the watching. The WSP people. The ones who had broken up her marriage. But why? Why torment her again after all these years?

The phone rang. No one ever called her. Who could it be? The WSP people?

"What do you want of me?" She shouted into the phone without waiting for the person on the other end of the line to speak. "You've already done enough to destroy my life."

"I'm not who you think I am," an unknown voice said. "I mean you no harm. Need your cooperation to help Daniel. Daniel Friedman."

"What about Daniel?"

"My name's Tom Bateman. I'm a private investigator from Berkeley, California. I've just arrived in town. I'm working for a friend of Daniel's. She's convinced the WSP has gotten to him. Using threats to harm you to control him."

"But why?"

"I don't know the answer to that one. All I know is he has suddenly become important to them. They're forcing him to speak at a rally the end of the week. Is someone watching you and your children?"

"Yes. I recognized them from the old days. Goons from the WSP."

"Then I want you to do just as I tell you. You and the children are going on a little trip. Don't pack a thing. Just take the kids to Hebrew school. This time you go inside. I'll contact you."

"How will I recognize you?"

"Ever meet a paraplegic rabbi?"

"No."

"You will."

Sara hung up the phone. Anything to get those bastards. Anything for Daniel. But fear returned. Her flock. Their safety.

• • •

A feeling of peace came over Sara as she walked with her two children into the temple on Broadway. Sara wore her brown suit, with a plain white blouse, and sturdy, comfortable brown shoes. The skirt on the suit felt snug. She must be gaining weight. Daniel had liked her on the heavy side. A musty aroma hit her nostrils, almost causing her to sneeze. She smelled centuries of Jewish culture. The room reflected a tradition brought over from Europe. The ark, with the *torah* inside, floated at the end of the room, the floor its sea.

She was brought up in a secular Jewish household. Then came Marxism, faith in socialism and the party. The break. Nothing but emptiness left inside her. She had returned to the faith of her ancestors. It was good for her. For her children.

She led the children from the prayer hall into a side room, teeming with children. The boys, all with yarmulkes on, played roughly with each other, while the girls formed little knots, talking and giggling. Rachel, her daughter, dashed off for a group of girls her own age, while her son, David, stood by her. Rabbi Finkel, a round man about forty with little hair on his head, came up to her. He wore a black suit and a wrinkled white shirt with an open collar.

"Wonderful you could help us out today and take the children on a little trip," Finkel said. He winked at her. "Afraid I can't make the trip myself. A good friend, Rabbi Breitman, has volunteered to take charge."

"Breitman?" Sara asked.

"Not to worry."

Rabbi Finkel took Sara's hand in his plump one and, oblivious to the youthful chaos around him, ploughed across the room. He steered her towards a tall, thin man sitting in a wheel chair. He wore a yarmulke with a black hat sitting precariously on top of it.

"It's me, Tom Bateman. All you've got to do is herd your kids and the others out of here and into a waiting school bus I've parked outside."

• • •

Sara, with her two children next to her, sat directly behind Tom Bateman. Even though she had just met him, she felt a connection, a trust. She would do as he said. For David. To get back at the WSP swine. Bateman occupied the driver's seat of an orange school bus that had Hebrew writing, painted in black, on the side panels. He had a broad grin on his face. A dozen or so noisy, restless kids filled the rest of the bus.

"Where did you get a school bus with wheel chair access?"

"Easy. Used for special ed."

He started down the street. Sara looked through the rear view mirror and spotted a maroon Chevrolet. It pulled out into the traffic from a parking spot near the end of the block. She recognized the two men in the front seat. WSP.

"They're following us!" she said.

"Figures."

"So what are you going to do?"

"Count on a little help from New York City traffic. Then make my move."

The yellow school bus putted down Broadway, with the maroon car right on its tail. How was Bateman going to lose their tail? Had she been right to trust him?

At that moment the light turned yellow in front of them. He jammed on the accelerator and forced the bus into the intersection. Brakes screeched. The shrill sound of a police whistle pierced the air. A taxi almost slammed into them. Shouts. Curses. Sara gripped Rachel tightly. Children cried. Bateman paid no heed. He drove like a madman. She didn't mind risking her own life. But she was risking the lives of her children. He forged ahead. Sara glanced back. The Chevy was caught up in a snarl of traffic.

The bus reached the next corner. Red light. Without slowing down, or giving his left more than a quick glance, Bateman swung a right. More screeching brakes. He barreled down a side street. He drove that damned old school bus like it was a sports car. What had she gotten herself into? She started to speak but was smashed against the side of the bus. Bateman turned right again. The children regained their composure and started shouting encouragement. Young David's voice boomed, "Go, Rabbi, go." Those in the back cheered.

Bateman jammed on the brakes and stopped in the middle of the narrow, one-way street. What was he up to now?

"Okay," he said. "See that gray van?"

"The one with a that weird woman standing next to it?" Sara asked.

"That's Henrietta, my assistant. She's going to drive you to the Catskills while I take the rest of this mob to the Jewish Museum. Now."

He pushed a lever and opened the door. She grabbed her two children and ran towards the scowling green-haired woman, who had a cigarette dangling out of the corner of her mouth.

• • •

I made my way down the middle aisle of the Slovenian Hall on Telegraph. I had buried Sara's letter under my blanket. Right next to my .45.

Henrietta bounded ahead of me, eyeing everyone she passed as if she was checking out an exotic animal zoo. The hall was filling up. Around three hundred people packed the place. It seemed that every radical who hung out on Telegraph Avenue had made it to the meeting.

A huge banner over the speakers' podium declared "Forward to Socialism–The Workers Socialist Party." Red flags and portraits of Marx, Lenin, Ché Guevara, Malcolm X, and Fidel Castro draped the side walls.

A hush came over the audience as the speakers filed in to occupy their places in a row of chairs behind the podium.

"Far fuckin' out," Henrietta said. "That's Bridget Stanhope, the movie actress."

She pointed to a thin, middle-aged woman with dazzling blue eyes, the kind that made you feel she was looking just at you. She had exquisite cheekbones, while a touch of wrinkle enhanced her beauty. Mature, majestic, almost imperial. Shoulder-length, strawberry-blond hair.

A soft smile of recognition crept over her face as a man about her age, wearing an ill-fitting suit, took the seat next to her. Big head, small body, like a prematurely aged child.

"There's Daniel," Henrietta exclaimed. "Looks like she knows him."

"Fits."

"What do ya mean?"

"That's why they needed him. He's the key to her. She's money, fame, property."

50

Next came a middle-aged man in a rumpled open collar white shirt. He had a dome-like high forehead, bald on top, long gray hair flowing from the sides to shoulder length. Pot belly. The ruddy complexion of a drinker. Looked like an aged gnome who had imbibed a little too much nectar. He nodded to Bridget and walked unsteadily to the podium.

A broad-shouldered muscular blond man with a mustache sauntered in, paused for a moment behind Daniel, and then found a place to stand in the corner. His cold eyes scanned the audience and came to rest on Henrietta and me. Or so it felt. I noticed a bulge under his suit jacket near his armpit. This was the fellow to watch.

There was something definitely wrong with the scene. Retro 60s. But it was not the 60s. Someone was perpetuating the past for contemporary evil ends. My money was on cold eyes as the someone.

The gnome tapped the microphone. He introduced himself as Barry Emerson, the National Secretary. He chronicled the ills of capitalist society, occasionally stumbling over a word or blurring his speech.

The audience rose from their chairs, clapping, and chanted "Two, four, six, eight. Who do we really hate? The capitalist state! The capitalist state!" They didn't stop. They just kept chanting and chanting. It seemed to go on for hours, but maybe it lasted ten minutes.

I heard screeching next to me. I'll be damned if Henrietta wasn't on her feet as well, screaming at the top of her lungs with the best of them, face getting red. Most color I'd ever seen in it.

The audience quieted down and Henrietta found her seat.

"Never knew you were such a radical," I whispered.

"Oh, fuck off," she muttered. "Just trying to blend in."

"You succeeded."

Bridget Stanhope rose from her seat and floated to the

podium. She held out long, gracile fingers to cut off the applause that erupted in the hall. Then she smiled graciously and began to speak. She told a story about her days in Mississippi in the summer of 1964. Lost one night in redneck country, her car followed by Klansmen, she narrowly escaped death.

"The driver of our car is here on the platform with me. It was none other than Daniel Freidman. I owe him my life."

The place burst into tumultuous applause. Daniel rose from his seat. Bridget rushed over to him and enveloped him in kisses.

"Fuck all," Henrietta said. "Daniel never said a word. I didn't know he was a hero, for Christ's sake."

"Now," I whispered.

I spun the wheels of my chair to turn it and then propelled myself into the aisle. Henrietta followed me. The crowd was standing, clapping and pounding their feet. No one noticed me. If they had, who would stop a paraplegic? Daniel was slowly walking towards the podium with what looked like a prepared speech in his hand. I reached the front of the podium just as Daniel appeared at the back of it. I handed Sara's letter to Henrietta. She leapt on the stage and pressed the paper into Daniel's hand, whispering into his ear. Cold eyes came running towards her. She jumped back to the floor of the hall.

Daniel quickly read the letter. A smile came over his face. He looked like a different person, rejuvenated. He raised his hand for silence. The roar continued. Bridget, who stood next to him, flicked her wrist in the direction of the crowd, as if she held an invisible magic wand. Immediate stony silence.

"I want to thank Bridget Stanhope for bringing back a flood of warm memories of our common struggle that summer of '64," Daniel began. "When I returned to New York that fall, I joined the WSP." Cheers went up from the audience. "It was a beautiful party then. Dedicated to world socialism. I gave myself wholly to it. But it changed." He turned towards cold eyes. "It changed when Philip Gaynor joined the leadership."

Gaynor grabbed Daniel. Emerson rose from his seat and headed Daniel's way. Bridget touched Gaynor's arm with a fingertip. He dropped Daniel reluctantly, a vicious scowl on his face. Emerson froze in place.

Gasps came from the audience. Shouts of "Traitor. Fink."

"Let him speak," Bridget said, "and then Comrade Gaynor can answer him. He saved my life. I owe him that much and far, far more."

"Gaynor turned Comrade Emerson," Daniel said. "He encouraged his drinking, womanizing. In time he was running the WSP. Emerson became nothing more than a figurehead."

I saw the muscles tighten in Gaynor's face. He loosened his jacket and reached underneath it.

"I found out later," Daniel continued, "and I have the evidence, that Gaynor was sent in by the FBI under their Cointelpro program to disrupt us. When the FBI abandoned that effort, Gaynor stayed to run the WSP for his own gain."

It was too much for cold eyes. Ignoring Bridget, he flung open his jacket, pulled out a pistol and pointed it at Daniel.

"Lower your gun, Mr. Gaynor," I said, yanking out the .45 from under the blanket covering my legs.

I released the safety, pointed the barrel of the gun at Gaynor, and began to squeeze the trigger. He turned towards me and hesitated for less than a second. I shot, hitting him in the arm. His pistol fell to the floor. Emerson bolted out into the audience, heading for the back door.

"Get the CIA assholes," Henrietta screamed.

She leapt into the air and threw her whole body at Emerson bashing into him feet first. He sprawled on the floor. Henrietta jumped up and came down on his belly, knocking the air out of him. She straddled him and gouged his eyes with her long green nails.

Daniel approached Bridget and whispered into her ear. Then he walked her towards the door behind the platform. I wheeled over to Henrietta, who was still sitting on top of Emerson, banging on his head with her fists. I held Gaynor in my gun sights. He fell to the ground and gripped his bloody arm. His eyes were on his gun. It was a good three feet away.

"That's not a good idea," I said.

"Holy f…".

"Just grab the goddamned cell phone in my pocket," I said, "and dial 911."

Laura is well known for the Tess Monaghan series of novels set in her native Baltimore, and she's been a trooper with us in all our hard-boiled dirtiness. As she once told me, "Don't underestimate my taste for truly nasty stories. I wanted to be a hardboiled writer when I grew up, just took a wrong turn somewhere." But she's got hard-boiled all over her writing—the way she unflinchingly opens the door to some disturbing issues in her book Every Secret Thing *and this story, "The Babysitter's Code," which provided a jump-start for her most recent novel,* To the Power of Three.*

Her drink of choice as payment for this story? A "Sea Breeze."*

The Babysitter's Code
Laura Lippman

The rules, the real ones, have seldom been written down, yet every girl knows them. (The boys who baby-sit don't, by the way. They eat too much, they leave messes, they break vases while rough-housing with the kids, but the children adore the boys who baby-sit, so they still get invited back.) The rules are intuitive, as are most things governing the behavior of teenage girls. Your boyfriend may visit unless it's explicitly forbidden, but the master bedroom is always off-limits, just as it would be in your own house. Eat what you like, but never break the seal on any bag or box. Whatever you do, try to erase any evidence of your presence in the house by evening's end. The only visible proof of your existence should be a small dent on a sofa cushion, preferably at the far end, as if you were too polite to stretch across its entire length. Finally, be careful about how much food you consume. No parent should come home and peer into the Pringles' can—or the Snackwells' box or the glass jar of the children's rationed Halloween candy—and marvel at your capacity. There is nothing ruder than a few crumbs of chips at the bottom of a bag, rolled and fastened with one of those plastic clips, or a single Mint Milano resting in the last paper cup.

Terri Snyder, perhaps the most in-demand babysitter in all of River Run, knew and followed all these rules. Once when she was at the Morrows' house, she discovered a four-pound can of pistachio nuts and got a little carried away. And while the canister was so large that it provided cover for her gluttony, the shells in the trashcan left no doubt as to how much she had eaten. To conceal the grossness of her appetite, she packed those shells in her knapsack and the pockets of her ski jacket. Riding home in the front seat of Ed Morrow's Jeep Cherokee, she realized she was rattling softly, but Mr. Morrow seemed to think it was the car's heater. The next time she babysat for the Morrows, she found another canister of pistachios, a sure sign of trust.

But then, the Morrows were among the most generous clients in Terri's circle. Most families, even the rich ones, hid what they considered precious—not just liquor, which interested Terri not at all, but also expensive chocolates and Macadamia nuts and the asiago cheese dip from Cross Street Wine & Cheese in Baltimore. The last was especially dear, a souvenir from the parents' hip, carefree lives, when they lived where they wanted, with no worries about school districts, much less backyards and soccer leagues. The asiago dip was like the tiny little treasures that pioneer families kept in their sod houses—a single silver spoon, a pair of diamond earrings, a china-head doll. Almost laughable, yet touching somehow, a symbol of a foreign land from which they had chosen to exile themselves for some vague dream of betterment.

Terri always found these forbidden snacks, but left them undisturbed, obeying another unwritten rule: You may snoop all you like, but you must not move or in any way tamper with the secrets of the houses left in your care. Read the dirty books and magazines by all means, catalog the couple's birth control (or lack thereof), poke through medicine cabinets and those mother lodes known as nightstands, but make sure everything and everyone is tucked in its respective bed before the parents return home.

The fathers' cluelessness is understandable, but why would mothers, most of them former babysitters, leave so many embarrassments to be discovered? Yet Terri never stopped to wonder about this. Like most teenagers, she assumed her generation had invented depravity—and she was not entirely off the mark. Her clients remembered their pasts as one might remember a dream—hazy, incoherent, yet vaguely satisfying. Indulged in their youth, they had little need for rebellion in adulthood, and even less energy for it. Those who know the gin-soaked suburbs described in Cheever and Updike would be disappointed in River Run, where there was so much money, and so little imagination. Sure, there was a sex toy here, a prescription for Viagra there, but Terri's systematic sleuthing did not uncover anything truly shocking—not until the day she found the beautiful little handgun, no bigger than a toy, nestled in Mrs. Delafield's lingerie drawer.

Now the Delafields had been considered odd from their arrival in the community two years ago. Mrs. Delafield ("Call me Jakkie, it's short for Jakarta, can you believe it? My mom was nuts.") was very young, so young that even an incurious teenager such as Terri could see she did not belong in this overdone, over-large, grown-up house in River Run's Phase V development. Local gossip put her at no more than 25, which was worth gossiping about because Mr. Delafield was 52. He was divorced, of course, with children in college, and now he had Mrs. Delafield and the baby, a shockingly large child of 16 months, a child so big that he was having trouble walking. Hugo's short, chubby legs simply could not propel his mass forward, and he continued to crawl, when he deigned to move at all. It was hard, looking at Mrs. Delafield, to figure out how such a huge child had come out of this lanky size 2, with hips narrower than most of the boys in the River Run freshman class. No one knew what Mrs. Delafield had been before she was Mrs. Delafield. The one time Terri had dared to ask, Mrs. Delafield must not have understood the question because she said: "Oh, I was at my height when I met Mr. Delafield. You have no idea. I can't bear to look at the photographs because I'm such a mess now." Her hands shook, she chewed her nails when she thought no one was looking, and her hair was an odd shade of yellow. And she was the most beautiful woman Terri had ever seen outside a magazine.

No one knew why the Delafields had chosen River Run, not at first. For while River Run was an extremely desirable place to live–great school district, beautiful countryside, and convenient to I-83, that was the locals' litany–not even its biggest boosters expected billionaires in their midst. The grandest house in Phase V could not compete with the waterfront estates outside Annapolis, or even the rambling mansions on Baltimore's north side. Plus, Hugo was so young, and the Delafields so very rich, they didn't have to worry about public schools.

The mystery was explained when Mr. Delafield's corporate helicopter landed with a great, ear-shattering roar in a clearing behind his property, acreage dedicated as permanent open space according to the master plan for River Run. The community and the River Run board fought the helicopter, of course. Mr. Delafield insisted he had been promised use of the land, that he would not have purchased the house otherwise. Yet the Delafields decided to stay in the house even after a zoning judge decided Mr. Delafield could not use the land. The corporate headquarters for his pharmaceutical company were in Harrisburg, Pa., no more than an hour's drive away. His chauffeur-driven Town Car pulled out of the quarter-mile driveway promptly at 7 every weekday morning and returned 13 hours later. Mrs. Delafield, who did not work, was left at home with Hugo and a live-in housekeeper, who apparently terrified her. She hired Terri to come on Tuesdays, the housekeeper's day off, and spell her for exactly four hours, from 3-7, for $5 an hour. Finding something to do with those four hours was a terrible chore for Mrs. Delafield. She tried tennis, but she wasn't coordinated. She tried shopping, but she found the nearest stores disappointing, preferring to purchase her clothes on seasonal excursions to New York. She signed up for ceramics class, but didn't like what it did to her acrylic nails. Still, she was strict with herself, throwing herself into her Porsche SUV every Tuesday as if it were a grim duty.

She always returned promptly at seven, sometimes stepping out of her clothes as she crossed the threshold–whatever she had been in her past life, it had left her without modesty. She then handed Terri $25, and fixed a drink. Terri wasn't sure if the extra five dollars was a tip or a math error, and she didn't ask Mrs. Delafield for fear of embarrassing her. Mrs. Delafield was shy about her lack of education, to which she made vague, sinister references. "When I had to leave school. . . ." or, "I wish I could have stayed for prom, but there was just no way." Sometimes, she examined Terri's armload of textbooks, as if just touching them might convey the knowledge she had failed to acquire. "Is algebra hard? When they say European history, do they mean all the countries, even the little-bitty ones? Why would they want to you to study psychics?" The last was a misreading of "physics," but Terri didn't have the heart to correct her. Instead, she told Mrs. Delafield that River Run High School had been founded at a time when there were a lot of alternative theories about education–perfectly

59

true—and that it still retained a certain touchy-feely quality. Also true, although parents such as Terri's, who had known the original River Run, were always complaining it had become a ruthless college factory.

Given that the Delafields' house, like the Delafields' baby, was so huge, it had taken Terri a while to inventory its contents. Still, the wonders of Mrs. Delafield's underwear drawer were well-known to her long before she found the gun. Drawers, really, because Mrs. Delafield had an entire bureau just for underwear and nightgowns. The bureau was built into the wall of a walk-in closet, one of two off the master bedroom, both almost as big as Terri's bedroom, but her family lived in a Phase II house. Terri had been through those drawers several times, so she was certain that the elegant little handgun she found there one March afternoon was a new addition, along with the rather nasty-looking tap pants of transparent blue gauze, with a slit where the crotch should be. Terri did not try on the tap pants, which she considered gross, but she did ease an emerald-green nightgown over her bra and panties. Small and compact, with thin legs and rather large breasts, Terri could not have looked less like Mrs. Delafield. Still, she rather liked the effect.

It never occurred to her to touch the gun, not at first. In fact, she was petrified just reaching around it to pick out various bits of lingerie. She treated it as if it were an explosive sachet. To Terri's knowledge, guns were like coiled snakes, always ready to strike. Didn't everyone know about the Shellenberg brothers, perhaps River Run's greatest tragedy? Not to mention that scene in *Pulp Fiction.*

But as time went by, and Terri kept returning to the lingerie drawers, the gun began to seem integral to the clothes she found there, an accessory, no different than the shoes and purses arrayed on the nearby shelves. It was so . . . pretty, that little silver gun, small and ladylike. Such a gun would never go off heedlessly. One Tuesday afternoon, Terri pulled on a black lace nightgown, one that was probably loose and flowing on Mrs. Delafield. On her, it bunched around the upper part of her body and tangled around her ankles. She slipped on a pair of Mrs. Delafields' high heels so she wouldn't trip on the hem, picked up the gun in her right hand, and posed for the full-length mirror at the back of the closet. The gun really made the outfit. She went into all the poses she knew from films—the straight up-and-down Clint Eastwood glare, the wrist prop, the crouch. Each was better than the last.

A trio of quick, high beeps sounded, the signal that the front door had been opened and closed. Mrs. Delafield always turned the alarm off when she went out because she didn't know how to program it. Terri, frozen in front of her reflection, wondered what she should do. Call out to the intruder that someone was home? Announce that she had a gun? But the front door had been locked, she was sure of that. Only someone with a key could have entered. Mrs. Delafield? But she never came back early. The housekeeper? It was her day off. Someone was coming up the stairs with a heavy, tired tread. Wildly, Terri glanced around the walk-in closet. The door was ajar, the soft overhead lights, so kind to her reflection, were on. She could lock herself in, but her clothes were folded on an armchair in the Delafields' bedroom. She could make a run for them, or array herself in some of Mrs. Delafield's over-sized sweats, shove the gun back in the drawer, or—

"What the fuck?" asked Mr. Delafield and, at that moment, Terri hated every adult in River Run who had fought his helicopter, even her own parents. If Mr. Delafield still had his helicopter, she would have heard him coming from a long way off.

"I'm the babysitter. Terri." She fought the impulse to cross

61

her arms against her chest, as that would only draw attention to the gun in her hand.

"Oh." A blond man with a ruddy face, it was impossible for him to be even redder, yet Terri thought he seemed embarrassed. For her or himself? "And—that? Do you bring that to all your babysitting jobs?"

She glanced down at the sweet silver gun, held at her hip as if it were a small purse. "No. No, that's not mine. It's yours."

"Not mine. You mean it's Jakkie's? Jakkie has a gun? Son of a bitch. Why would Jakkie have a gun?"

Terri shrugged, not wanting to tell Mr. Delafield that she had always assumed it was because his wife feared him, with his big, shambling body and red, red face. Now she wondered if he feared his wife, if she had overlooked some menace in Mrs. Delafield's ditziness.

"Where did you find it?" Terri's right hand, the one holding the gun, gestured loosely toward the open drawer, and he ducked his head, as if expecting it to go off. "With her pretty little panties, huh? Well, no wonder I never saw it."

The situation was so surreal, to use a word of which Terri was particularly fond at the time, she couldn't figure out how to behave. She put the gun on top of the built-in bureau and slipped on Mrs. Delafield's most prosaic robe.

"I was just looking at it," she said, as if that explained everything. "No one I know owns a gun."

"Well, I didn't know anyone I knew had a gun, either." He laughed, and Terri joined him, a little nervously.

"You looked nice," he said, as if he didn't mean it but wanted to be polite. "In the gown, I mean."

"It doesn't really fit right."

"Oh. Well, you can get stuff altered, right? Jakkie does it all the time."

Did he not know that the gown was his wife's? Or was he pretending to think otherwise, to spare Terri the humiliation of being caught in violation of almost every rule of good baby-sitting? Or was it possible that he really liked how Terri looked? Terri was terrified that he might come toward her, or touch her in some way. She was terrified he wouldn't.

"Hugo's asleep," she offered, reminding him of who she was, and why she was here.

"Hugo," he said. "You know, I have no idea where she got that name. Maybe from Baby Huey. He has too many chromosomes. Or not enough. If I had married what my daughters call an age-appropriate woman, someone 35 or 40, she would have had amnio, and we would have known before he was born. Or we wouldn't have kids at all. But Jakkie was only 23 when she got pregnant, and Hugo's a freak. He won't live past the age of five."

"He's just big."

"He is. Huge Hugo. But he's screwed up, too. I don't know what Jakkie's going to do when he dies. I wonder if that's why she bought the gun." He shook his head, disagreeing with himself. "No, she'll go into a slow, catatonic decline, refusing to eat, wandering around the house in her robe. In that robe. All these clothes, and she spends most of her time in that robe."

"Oh." Terri had grabbed it because the blue flannel looked so ordinary, the antidote to the expensive lingerie she had probably damaged, stretching it to fit her so-very different proportions. "I'm sorry, I'll –"

"It's okay." Waving his hands in front of his face, fanning himself, as if it were a summer's day instead of a late-winter one. "It's no big deal. You should keep it. She'll never miss it. Keep it."

She knew, from the River Run Self-Esteem Project, that this was how such things began. Men gave you gifts, or money, then asked for favors in return. Teachers, coaches, neighbors— the girls at River Run had been taught to assume they were

63

all potential predators, far more sex-crazed than their male peers.

"I couldn't possibly," she demurred.

"Suit yourself. Put, um, everything back where you found it."

And with that, he was gone. Terri listened to him leave the room and walk downstairs, then waited another minute before going into the bedroom to change. She then returned to the closet and made sure everything was where it belonged. She assumed Mr. Delafield would tell Mrs. Delafield what she had done, and she would lose this weekly gig, an easy $25 by anyone's standards. But losing her job did not bother her as much as the encounter itself. It was not unlike a dream she had from time to time. A man, an older one—one taller and darker than Mr. Delafield—found her alone somewhere and just . . . took over. It was at once a scary and comforting dream, one that always ended a little too soon. That was what she was feeling now—relieved, yet desirous of knowing what might have happened if Mr. Delafield had kept going. Would he have been more insistent with a different kind of girl—someone truly beautiful, like Katarina Swann, or someone weak and shy, like Bennie Munson? It was Terri's lot to fall in the middle of that continuum—pretty enough, but not a raving beauty. Nor was she like Bennie, someone who all but begged to be used and abused by the world.

Mrs. Delafield came home at seven, as always, and seemed indifferent to Terri's news that Mr. Delafield was in his den, watching television while working out on his elliptical machine. No one, not even Terri, stopped to wonder why he hadn't sent Terri home and assumed Hugo's care. For the next six days, Terri waited for Mrs. Delafield to call and say she wouldn't be needing Terri anymore, but the call never came. She went back at 3 P.M. the following week and everything was as it always was—the quiet house, the listless baby (who now seemed more precious to Terri because he was doomed), the gun in the lingerie drawer. Caught once, Terri knew she should turn over a new leaf, but she found herself in the walk-in closet within 20 minutes, modeling lingerie and holding the gun. This time, she moved on to Mrs. Delafield's evening dresses, which she had never dared touch before. She listened for the door to beep, refusing to admit to herself that her ears were straining toward that sound because she wanted to hear it. She had started a diet—for senior prom, she assured her mother, who grudgingly allowed it. Terri's mom hated diets. But it was working already, she could tell. Mrs. Delafield's things were not so tight in the waist this week.

Mr. Delafield did not come home early that day, or the next week, or the week after. He never came home early again. In April, he stopped coming home at all. His absence, like most absences, took time to register. First a neighbor realized the Town Car had stopped gliding in and out of the driveway at its usual hours. Then Terri noticed the pile of bundled-up *Wall Street Journals* in the three-car garage, placed in a basket, as if Mr. Delafield might return and want to work through two weeks, three weeks, an entire month of business news. It was only when Mrs. Delafield put out the whole collection for recycling—on the wrong day, in the wicker basket, and still bundled in their plastic wrappers, in violation of every protocol—that Terri realized Mr. Delafield was never coming back. The following Tuesday, Mrs. Delafield paid her $20 instead of the usual $25 and Terri finally understood that the extra five dollars had always been a tip, one Mrs. Delafield had decided she could no longer afford.

On the third Tuesday in May, Terri arrived to find the house full of boxes, and Mrs. Delafield flitting around with various lists, shouting into her portable phone as if the connection was bad. Yet she looked radiant, more beautiful than Terri had ever seen her, and her conversations seemed to hum with excitement. "I have so much to do," she told Terri with obvious delight. "Lawyers, realtors, moving companies–oh, it's all so complicated! But a week from now, Hugo and I will be gone, and this place will be on the market. We'll miss you!"

She headed out, full of true purpose for once, and Terri walked through the house. It was as if some careless, heedless babysitter had been here first, for all the drawers and closets were open, their contents tumbling out helter-skelter. Yet the little silver gun was still in its place of honor, lying on a bed of emerald-green silk. Terri picked it up, intending to do nothing more than hold it one more time. It fit her hand so well, looked so right. It wasn't her imagination: she was beautiful when she held this gun. Mr. Delafield had said as much. *Take it*, he had said, and she had assumed he meant the nightgown. Clearly, he meant the gun. He had been asking Terri to save him, to protect him from his crazy wife, who was capable of anything in her grief and anxiety over their damaged child. Terri had been Mr. Delafield's last hope and when she failed him, he had no choice but to leave.

Terri stuffed the gun in her knapsack; later, she would claim the act was an impulse. The emerald-green slip as an afterthought. After all, she needed something to muffle the sound of the metal. She couldn't afford the possibility that the gun might rattle when Mrs. Delafield took her home later this evening, or assume that Mrs. Delafield, like Mr. Morrow, would be polite enough to pretend that a mysterious sound was nothing more than a faulty car heater. She swathed the gun with great tenderness, placing it in the outside pocket of her beat-up bag, assuring herself all the while that when something makes you beautiful, it should be yours to keep.

Pat Lambe submitted a piece to me and another piece to Trevor Maviano pretty much simultaneously. I was happy with the story he sent, called "The Most Dangerous Animal in Louisiana," and since I consider New Orleans a "second home" in a sense, I read with interest. Strong writer. And then Maviano sends "Union Card" with a note telling me it was damned good. So, Lambe hit us with the ol' One-Two, and it paid off. He's also a frequent dinner guest at our buddy Charlie Stella's house, so we think this guy's going places.

Union Card
Patrick J. Lambe

I set the pneumatic nail gun on the ground next to the trestle I was working on, removed my ear plugs, and followed the yellow air hoses back to the two-sided plywood barrier I had constructed to mask some of the noise from the compressor. There were two men standing behind the barrier.

One of them was dressed in duct-brown colored Carhart carpenter jeans and a worn wool sweater with a lot of holes in it. The other guy was wearing Levi's and a flannel shirt, and he was sipping out of a paper cup full of coffee.

"I hope you don't mind us unplugging your compressor, kid, but it's against union rules to work through lunch break," Flannel Shirt said, pouring a little of the coffee out on the dust covered concrete.

I glanced down at my watch and tried to act surprised. "I must have lost track of the time."

The two looked at each other. "Let's see it, lad," Sweater said, his Irish accent tinged with impatience.

"See what?" I asked.

Flannel shirt looked at me with a patience that I knew was

67

feigned. "You're a little young, so I'm giving your ignorance the benefit of the doubt. You don't work on this site without a union card. Period. Now I'd like you to reach into your wallet and produce one or turn around and walk out of here."

Phil had warned me that something like this might happen, and he had instructed me what to do.

"I just started this week, and my card didn't come through yet. Why don't you come back in a few minutes when my foreman Phil comes back from lunch? He'll straighten everything out."

"Your foreman's at lunch, lad? How would you know that, being that you lost track of time and all that," Sweater said. He stepped so close to me that I could smell the Guinness on his breath that had comprised his lunch.

Flannel placed his coffee on the generator, pulled a knife from his back right pocket, unfolded it, and grabbed a length of hose in his hand, slicing through it with an ease that implied the knife had Ginsu written on the blade somewhere. "Listen up, scab, do you know anything about the history of the American labor movement?"

"Not really," I said, trying to maintain eye contact with Sweater.

"Neither do we. We don't care much about history as a matter of fact. And if you and your crew don't get off this job site, you're not going to have a history." Flannel folded his knife and put it back in his pocket.

They started to leave right as Logan turned the corner with our lunch in two paper bags he had picked up from the deli. He looked from me to them, an expression somewhere between fear and surprise on his face.

"I have two questions for you, errand boy," Flannel said. "Are you Phil? And do you have your Union Card?"

Phil must have been right behind him because he walked into the light thrown out by the halogen lamps a few seconds

68

after Logan. "I'm Phil," he said, "and if you have a problem, you can file a grievance."

Phil Groendyke had blond hair that kinked out at odd angles and blue eyes that looked like current was flowing though them. I always thought he looked like he had his finger permanently inserted into a 120-volt electrical outlet. He was sipping from a steaming cup of coffee he had purchased around the corner at Starbucks.

"We're not the type to file a grievance," Flannel said

"I guess the paperwork involved would be a little difficult for you two, with your brains being in the atrophied condition that they're in," Phil said.

Flannel and Sweater looked at each other uncertainly, no doubt wondering at the linguistic roots of the word atrophy.

Flannel shook his head before he stepped into Phil's face. "You guys don't seem to understand. This is a Union job. No card, no work." He placed his finger on Phil's chest. Big mistake. Phil threw the coffee in his face and kicked him in the stomach, only getting in a glancing blow as Flannel reeled back clutching his scalded skin.

Sweater started towards Phil, but I tripped him up before he took two steps. Phil smiled at me as he was kicking Sweater's prone form repeatedly. I kept an eye on Flannel as he sat on a spackle bucket, pouring ice water from our cooler onto his burned face.

Phil stopped kicking Sweater the moment he started to break a sweat, hauled him off his feet, and dragged him towards the entrance to the construction site. I grabbed Flannel gently by the elbow and followed them. Phil put his arm around me as we walked back to the compressor. "You did good kid, real good." He picked the empty Starbucks cup off the ground and looked at it in mourning. "That damned cup of coffee cost me five bucks."

The loading dock door opened up a few minutes later, and Mike, the owner of whatever our company was named that week, backed a twenty-four-foot rental box truck into the loading dock. I had been working for him for nearly three months, and his company had gone through two name changes in that time. I was a little surprised that Mike had rented a truck today. We used them occasionally when we had a large amount of junk to get rid of, and he had spotted an empty, unsupervised dumpster not too far from the job site we were working on; but the job we were doing—assembling trestles that would be hauled up by crane to the top of some apartment buildings—didn't produce that much wasted material. I thought he could handle it with one load in his company van.

It was just after our lunch break and I walked over to the compressor and was about to fire it up. Phil paused by me as he and Logan made their way towards Mike, who was unloading some tools out of the back of the truck. "Why don't you take an extended break, kid. It's been a tough day."

Logan looked like he was about to throw up when he passed me.

I took a seat on a spackle bucket and pretended like I was reading my newspaper as I watched Phil and Logan talk to Mike at the back of the truck. At one point they all looked over at me. I didn't even bother to act like I was reading at that point.

Logan walked towards me, picked his tool belt off the ground, and placed it around his shoulder. "Mike wants to talk to you, kid. I'd think about getting another job if I was you. I think this one just fell out of OSHA's jurisdiction." He walked out of the entrance.

"Phil tells me you did good with those Union goons," Mike said, appraising me.

"I guess so," I said.

"They're going to be back, you know."

"I know."

"Are you scared?" Mike asked.

"A little," I said.

"Good. I don't think they'll be back before tomorrow. We should be done by then."

I looked around at the pile of greenish tinged pressure treated lumber and the rolls of nails coiled and ready for the gun. "We have to build what, nearly fifty of those trestles? I don't think we're going to be done in a week."

"Those goons scared Logan off, and we need a third guy. How'd you like to work a little overtime tonight? I can guarantee you'll make more than time and half," Mike said. I had a feeling they weren't talking about the construction job.

They must have seen my eyes turn into dollar signs because they both laughed before I could accept their offer. "Greedy and just a little scared. I think you're going to do well working with us," Mike said. "Take the rest of these jackhammers off the truck and carry them over to the compressor. Me and Phil have a couple of things to discuss." I carted the jackhammers one by one, wondering at their necessity in the construction of wooden framed trestles.

We were working a rush job for a huge developer. They generally used union contractors, but there were some jobs that fell through the cracks, or were not clearly under the jurisdiction of one union, such as the punch list. After each apartment was completed, a representative from the developers would walk through and make a list of anything that had been forgotten. They would give us the list and we would go over it, fixing anything that was left undone or didn't meet the developer's standards. The Unions didn't

71

mind letting us do such small projects. In fact it saved them some work. Technically they were responsible for the finished job, and they could move onto the next big job without messing with the small stuff. The developers wanted the apartments occupied as quickly as possible, so they hired Mike to make this happen.

Occasionally a rush job came up, and the developers—instead of taking months to draw up a contract and work out details with the union contractors—would call my boss and he'd get things done quickly, and discreetly.

Van-sized air conditioning and heating units lined the roofs of the apartment buildings, generating noise and heat. An overzealous and idealistic young building inspector had refused a bribe and threatened to close the job site down if the required trestles were not installed around the units in two weeks. The Union Contractor spent the first week negotiating a price. Mike pulled us off the punch list the first day of the second week and set us up in the cavernous first floor of one of the apartment buildings.

The apartments were almost complete, but construction had been halted on the first floor of the building we were working in. It was supposed to have been a Post Office, but they had budget problems and the hammers had stopped swinging right after the eagle logo had been installed over the entrance on 66th Street on the Upper West Side of Manhattan. There was a trendy new shoe store about to open up next to the Post Office, and most of the rest of the storefronts were occupied or leased out and under construction.

The developer thought he could hide us here and planned to call the crane in to boost the trestles up on the roof after we had assembled all fifty of them.

I wouldn't have heard the union guys return if I hadn't

removed one of the ear-plugs so I could scratch an itch. I was just about to put it back in when I heard a sound like someone dropping a cement bag on the floor followed by a grunt of pain.

I walked to the other side of the job site where Phil and Mike had been going over some blueprints. Two tough looking union guys held Mike between them; a third one was punching him in the stomach. Phil sat on a spackle bucket, looking unconcerned as he waited his turn, two guys looking down at him sternly.

I returned to the compressor and waited for its natural cycle to kick back in as the pressure died down in the nail gun. As soon as it started on again, I turned it to its highest setting. I opened up the gun and replaced the half empty clip with a full one and placed two additional clips in the tool pouch attached to my waist.

I snuck back to the area where the guys had Phil and Mike and hid behind a pile of sheet rock. I removed my hammer from its loop at my belt and hurled it overhead, into the darkness across from me. The union guys looked over at the metallic sound of the hammer hitting a beam in the darkness.

I targeted the guy who had been punching Mike and squeezed off about ten rounds as fast as I could. I aimed for his body, and the impact of the nails sent him off balance. He fell into the blueprint table, scattering papers and nails onto the floor.

I swung the gun to one of the guys looking down at Phil and squeezed off a couple rounds at him. The impact threw him back several feet, and I saw blood on his hands when he examined his wounds. I ducked back behind the sheet rock and threw my crow bar over their heads in the general direction where I had thrown the hammer and heard it land on the concrete.

By the time I looked back at the scene, the union guys were

running towards the entrance, one of them supporting the first guy I had hit with the nail gun.

Phil smiled at me. "I'm glad those guys have good benefits. It looks like they're going to need them."

Mike was on his knees, throwing up on the floor. Phil and I stood over him until he had recovered. He stood up and looked at his watch. "I wanted to do this later, but we can't risk those guys coming back. Grab all of our tools and put them into the gang box, kid. Then wheel it onto the loading dock. We'll put it on last. When you're done grab a jackhammer and give me and Phil a hand."

The jackhammers kept up a steady racket as I did as instructed.

Although the insurance investigator was a young man, probably just a couple of years older than me, he had been on the job long enough to look at me incredulously after I had confirmed my boss' list of the tools we had stored in the gang box that had been stolen out of the Post Office.

"Laser levels, diamond tipped drill bits, titanium reinforced saw blades, generators; what were you guys building in there, a Space Shuttle?" he said. He looked closer at the list. "Every person in your company has their own lap tap computer, and they were all stored in the gang box?"

"We used to have them before they were stolen from us. You have to go modern to stay competitive these days," I said.

I could see Phil holding back a smile sitting in the chair next to me. We were both dressed in worn suits that we probably only wore once a year or so to weddings and funerals, and we had both been a little nervous, neither of us having spent much time in an office during the course of our work lives.

The investigator looked down at my feet. "Those are nice

shoes you got there. I priced a pair just like them a couple of weeks ago. They cost something like five hundred dollars, a little expensive on my salary, but I guess construction is paying pretty good these days."

I looked over at Phil's shoes; a different model but equally expensive. I had to agree with him, construction did pay pretty well, even without the prevailing wage provided by an active union.

After we were through cutting a hole in the shoe store wall with the jackhammers, we used handcarts to move the entire inventory into the rental truck. I followed Phil in our company van. We dropped the gang box off at one of our other job sites in the East Village; then we drove through the Holland tunnel to a dark street in Jersey City. Phil parked the truck in the street in front of an abandoned warehouse and joined me in the van, placing a pair of shoeboxes on the bench seat between us.

"I had to estimate your size, but I'm pretty good." He chuckled to himself. "If they don't fit, you can always buy a pair with your cut. You did good, real good. You earned your Union Card today, kid. I'm going to enjoy working with you on a regular basis."

I read Hamilton's vivid crime novels set in Michigan's Upper Peninsula at least a year before I ended up moving to Michigan for a job. I wrote Steve at the time, asked when he'd be around the area for a signing. Every time a new one in his series comes out, Steve takes a swing through his native state, and I was lucky enough to see him read at one of these stops. The man puts on a good show.

He's been more than helpful, offering up this twisted little noir tale for our Big Shot issue, and all it cost us was a Coke.

A Shovel With My Name On It
Steve Hamilton

One thing I know, it's the sound of a man digging a hole. I've done it enough times myself, believe me. I know the sound of the shovel hitting the ground, the thud of the dirt landing on the pile. Maybe the sudden scrape of metal against rock, then the long silence while the rock gets dug up by hand. Then the shovel again. It didn't matter what time of night it was, or how unlikely it might have been that my back neighbor would be digging a hole instead of sleeping. I knew what I was hearing.

It was after midnight. I was sitting on my deck with a cigarette, enjoying the coolness after a hot summer day, watching the clouds race across the moon. It was the kind of night where a sound carries a long way. I sat there for a long time listening to the man digging. And then I got curious. That's the kind of guy I am, like it or not.

I went to the back of my property and pushed my way through the sumac and the wild raspberry bushes. I took it slow, pulling off the prickly vines. I tried to be quiet. If this

76

midnight digger was who I thought he was, I didn't want him to hear me coming.

It was Hank, all right. I saw him there in his backyard, standing in the hole. It came up to his waist, a lot of hard digging already done. Hank took another shovel-full of dirt and threw it high in the air. Wasted effort, I thought. He doesn't know how to dig a hole. And of course as I'm hiding there in the bushes, I knew that something wasn't right. There's no good, innocent reason to dig a hole in the middle of night. Especially not a hole as deep as Hank was apparently intent on digging.

I could have gone back to my house, minded my own business. But no, I was a little too nosy for my own good. Always have been. That plus the matter of the shovel itself. I was quite sure that it was mine, the same shovel Hank had borrowed back in May, and here it was August already. Best shovel I owned, too. I wanted it back.

"Evening, Hank," I said as I stepped out of the bushes.

Hank gave out a yell, had two or three heart attacks right there in the hole, and called me every bad word he could think of. That took most of a minute because he knew every bad word there is and even made up a few new ones.

"Sorry to disturb you," I said, nice and smooth. "I'm just wondering what you're up to back here." I walked right up to the hole and looked it over like I was the County Hole Inspector. I could hear his dog barking, somewhere in his house.

"What does it look like I'm doing?" he said. Hank was a big guy. It felt good to look down on him for once.

"Nice shovel you got there," I said.

"Yeah, well, I'm busy now, so—"

"In fact," I said, "that shovel looks exactly like mine. You remember, Hank? The one you borrowed from me about four months ago?"

77

He looked at the label on the handle. "Well, what do you know. It's your shovel, all right. I'll give it back to you when I'm done. Now if you'll excuse me, I got work to do." He took a good rip with the shovel and threw the dirt at my feet.

"Kind of odd, isn't it?" I said. "Digging a hole in the middle of the night?"

"Too hot during the day," he said. He didn't stop digging. Another load of dirt landed on my shoes.

"What's the hole for, anyway?" I said, moving sideways. Now I was a moving target.

"Dog died," he said. His next load of dirt landed a good yard behind me.

"I just heard your dog barking."

"Not that dog," he said. "Another dog." He tried to lead me with his next load. It barely missed me.

"Didn't know you had two dogs," I said.

"It was an old dog, okay?" He finally stopped digging. "He never comes outside. And now he's dead, and I'm gonna bury him. Soon as I'm done, I'll give you your stupid shovel back, okay?"

"You don't have to bring it back tonight," I said. "Tomorrow's fine."

"I'll give it back tonight. I wouldn't want you to live another minute without your precious shovel."

"I'm going to bed now," I said. "I won't need it until tomorrow."

"No, as soon as I'm done, I'll leave it on your doorstep."

"No need," I said. "I'll come get it tomorrow."

He closed his eyes and held the shovel with both hands. He squeezed it so hard I could see the muscles in his arms quivering. "If you don't get out of here right now. . . ."

"I'm leaving, I'm leaving," I said. "You don't have to tell me twice. I just didn't want you to have to go out of your way. You've had my shovel for four months, after all. What's one more day?"

When I had made my way through the bushes back to my own property, I sat on my deck for a long time, listening to Hank digging. The business about the second dog, that bothered me. His German Shepherd, I saw that dog all the time. A second dog? Never.

I wanted to sneak back to watch him bury that dog. Or whatever it was. But I could hear him digging and digging for another full hour. I gave up and went to bed.

The next day, my shovel was right there on my doorstep. "Look at this," I said as I picked it up. The blade was all dinged up from the rocks he had hit. "That's the last time I ever loan that man anything."

• • •

Of course it wasn't a dog he buried that night. It didn't take me long to figure that out. I'm not a complete idiot.

Hank has a wife named Joanie. During the day when Hank is gone, Joanie likes to sit outside in the backyard sunning herself. Every once in a while I'll take a peek through those bushes. Not every day, mind you. Just the sunny days. Sometimes she'd have men over during the day to keep her company. I'd recognize some of them from around town. One day I swear I saw three separate men come visit her. She had quite a busy calendar.

On the day after I saw Hank digging that hole, the sun was high and bright and I was sure Joanie would be out there in the backyard. But when I looked, she wasn't there. The next day was perfect again. But no Joanie. It didn't make any sense.

Like I said, I'm not a total idiot. After five sunny days and no sight of Joanie, I put it all together in my mind. That was no dead dog Hank was burying. It was his wife. He found out about all the other men, he killed her, and then he buried her in the middle of the night. I actually went over there and watched him dig the hole. No wonder he wanted me to leave so bad.

I thought about it all that day and night, wondering what to do. Should I call the sheriff? Are they just going to think I'm crazy? Then something else hit me. Hank knew that I knew that he was out digging that night. He was probably thinking about that right then, wherever he was hiding. I was sure he'd come back to kill me, too. "That does it," I said to myself. "I'm calling the sheriff."

That's how I ended up standing in Hank's yard the next day, with the sheriff and six of his deputies, watching a big backhoe digging up that hole.

"What night was that again?" the sheriff asked. He was standing next to me with his arms folded across his chest.

"Saturday night," I said.

"Six days ago?" he said. "You waited six days to call us?"

"How was I supposed to know?" I said. "Every time I don't see a neighbor for a couple of days, I'm supposed to call you?"

"You saw the man digging a hole in the middle of the night," he said. "That didn't strike you as strange?"

"He said one of his dogs died."

"I thought he only had one dog."

"He said he had another dog."

The sheriff shook his head. We watched the backhoe lifting great loads of dirt out of the hole. It was getting deep fast. "Did you see anything else that night?" the sheriff said.

Before I could answer him, one of the deputies signaled for the backhoe to stop. "I think I've got something!" he called to the sheriff. We watched him disappear into the hole. When he climbed back out, he was holding a woman's shoe.

"Oh my God," I said. I felt like I was going to be sick.

"Why don't you go back in your house," the sheriff said.

80

"That's a good idea," I said. "I don't want to see this."

I went back to my own house and sat at the kitchen table with a bottle of whiskey in front of me. I wondered what was going through Hank's mind when he killed his wife. I wondered where he was at that moment, how far away he had gotten in six days. Little did I know just how ironic that thought would be. For at that very moment, the deputies were carefully removing Joanie's body from the hole. Directly underneath her, they found yet another body.

It was Hank.

• • •

"Let's go over this one more time," the sheriff said. He was sitting across from me at my kitchen table. "It was after midnight. You heard him digging."

"Yes," I said.

"You know, it's kind of funny. We looked through his house, through his garage. We didn't see a shovel anywhere."

"He was using my shovel."

"I see," he said. "You didn't mention that before."

"I didn't think that was important," I said. I didn't like where this conversation was going.

"How did it end up back here at your house?"

"Hank returned it after. . . ."

I stopped.

"After he buried his wife and himself," the sheriff said.

"No," I said. "I guess he couldn't have returned it."

"Be kinda hard to do, I'm thinking."

"I just assumed it was him," I said. "I mean, it was on my doorstep the next morning, so. . . ." I started to feel hot.

"You think I might take a look at this shovel of yours?"

"Of course," I said. "It's in the garage." I could feel the sweat starting to run down my back.

"You have to admit," the sheriff said. "This looks a little

suspicious. Hank supposedly digging his own grave, with your shovel, and you being the only witness?"

"I don't know what happened," I said. "I just. . . . Maybe I shouldn't say anything else without a lawyer."

"That might be wise," he said. "You're just digging yourself into a hole here, if you'll excuse the reference." He gave me a little smile.

"I bet he killed her," I said. "And then one of her boyfriends came over and saw what had happened." I tried to make myself breathe. Slow down. "Yeah, that's it. And then the boyfriend killed Hank and threw him in the hole, too."

"But Hank was on the bottom."

"Hank hadn't buried her yet," I said. "The boyfriend threw them both in."

"I've got to hand it to you," he said, leaning back in his chair. "You've got quite an imagination."

My head was spinning. I didn't know what to do. I should have kept my mouth shut. But before I could even think about what I was saying, it came out.

"I've seen you over there," I said.

"Excuse me?"

"During the day, when Hank is gone. I've seen you with Joanie."

The sheriff didn't say anything.

"It'll come out in court," I said. "Everyone will find out."

He got up from his chair and walked over the window above the sink. He looked out at my backyard.

"You have to believe me," I said. "I didn't do it. I didn't kill either of them."

"That's a big mistake," he finally said. He was still looking out the window. "Now I'm going to have to make up a little story."

"What are you talking about?"

"Let's see," the sheriff said. "The suspect went for a weapon.

82

A kitchen knife, let's say. I had to shoot him. How does that sound?"

"No," I said. "You can't be serious." I tried to move but I couldn't. I was frozen in my chair.

He already had his gun out when he turned to face me. "And to think I went out of my way to bring you back your shovel."

Stella writes about brutal men doing brutal things to each other, their women, and anyone else who gets in their way. But his characters feel real things like real people, and they talk about their dreams, their families, and even their insecurities in novels like Jimmy Bench-Press, Charlie Opera, *and* Cheapskates.

When I visited NYC a couple of years ago, I told Charlie we should meet up for a drink. He supplied some beer, some tequila, and then took us to his favorite Italian restaurant, all the while showing us his old haunts in the neighborhood. I owe him a few drinks, but I can't ever get my wallet out fast enough! The guy's too generous. But I'd be scared to cross him. . . .

If you ever get a chance to stop by Christina's on Second Ave. in New York, order the Penne Stella, and ask for a "Charlie" order.

Young Tommy Burns
Charlie Stella

Tommy Burns crushed one cigarette in an ashtray and reached for another. When he saw the pack was empty, he tossed it in a small plastic trash pail alongside his desk.

"Excuse me," he told the Hispanic woman tied and gagged in the chair across from him.

Burns left his small office to run up the stairs leading to the bar's kitchen. He grabbed one of the busboys and shoved a ten-dollar bill in the square-faced Mexican's apron pocket.

"Smokes," Burns told him. "Tell them Camel regulars, no filters. Don't come back here with them other things."

The kid nodded. "No filter."

"Atta'boy," Burns said. He pushed open the kitchen doors to check on the bar. It was busy but not crowded. He glanced at his watch and took the stairs back down to his office in the basement.

Burns was a short man with a thin, muscular build. He had thick, blond hair he wore greased back. His eyes were a cold, piercing blue. At twenty-nine years of age, he had already served four years for manslaughter. Three months ago, he had contract killed for the first time. The job had only paid five thousand dollars, but Burns had gained an added income collecting a percentage on wiseguy shylock money dock-workers dropped off at his bar.

Things had been running smoothly the last few weeks until

two nights ago, when he learned that his girlfriend of six months, a married woman with two kids, had cheated on him with a Puerto Rican parking lot attendant from Williamsburg. Burns had learned about it from the woman's husband, a bookmaking customer who had come to Burns to put out a contract on the Puerto Rican. The husband was not aware of the affair between his wife and Burns.

"You comfortable like that?" he asked the woman now.

He was standing in the office doorway waiting for the Mexican to return with his cigarettes. The woman couldn't respond. She didn't move.

Burns thought about the last time he'd had Maria Perez-Grecco, three days ago when he stopped at her apartment on his way home from a night of playing blackjack in Atlantic City. He'd been stuck in traffic on the Staten Island Expressway until after nine o'clock in the morning. It was a day when he figured her kids had already gone off to school.

"Anybody home?" he had asked when she cracked open her apartment door.

"No, come in," she had said, pulling the door open.

Burns found his bottle of Jameson where he'd left it, stashed in the back of the cabinet under the sink. It was half full when he pulled it out. He poured himself a drink in a Flintstones juice glass and put the bottle back. He downed the drink fast and told Maria he didn't have much time.

She had just taken a shower and was wearing a robe over black panties. She stepped out of the panties, picked the robe up around her waist, and turned to face the kitchen window. Burns pulled the curtain aside enough to see the street below. He entered her from behind and made fast work of it.

"Again?" Maria asked when he was finished. "For me now?"

Burns shook his head. "No can do." He pulled two twenties from his wallet and set them on the table. "Get yourself something."

Maria went to kiss him on the mouth. He turned his face and accepted a peck on his cheek instead. He patted her ass on his way out and said, "It's the world awaits."

It was a good thing he had with Maria, mostly because there was never anything more to it than sex. Once in a while he would have to spend an extra ten or fifteen minutes with her, when Maria insisted he get on top, and then she would cling to him afterward. Those times they would do it in her bed or on the living room rug, and it would always end the same way, with Burns tapping her on the leg and saying, "Okay, time to go."

Burns had never been comfortable hanging around any woman longer than necessary. If it wasn't for sex, he was sure he could live without them.

It wasn't that he was an unappreciative man. Burns had always left Maria a few bucks on his way out. He would tell her to buy herself something or stash it away for a rainy day. The way he saw it, leaving cash was the right thing to do.

When he first learned about Maria having a boyfriend other than himself, Burns had figured it was because she wanted someone closer to her own age who would spend time with her. Maria had just turned twenty-three when Burns first met her. She was married to a dockworker ten years her senior. Her sons were five and six years of age. It made sense that she wanted more attention than she was getting from either of the adult men in her life.

It wasn't the deceit involved with Maria having another boyfriend that bothered Burns. It was the complications, both real and imagined, that had evolved because of the guy.

For one thing, it was dirty. Burns didn't like being where another man had been. He could live with Maria's husband sharing the same space between her legs because somehow God had sanctified their sex through marriage. Burns was a believer. Although marriage wasn't for him, he could live

87

with another man banging the same woman so long as he knew it was her husband. Learning about yet another guy, somebody he didn't know, had made it dirty.

The other issue, of course, was the fact Joe Grecco wanted Julio whacked because Maria had managed to get caught in the act.

"I almost break my foot, a drywall skid drops on it," Grecco had told Burns. "I come home early and first thing I hear, I open the apartment door, my wife is screeching some guy's name. 'Oh, Julio! Oh, Julio, baby!' I mean, what the fuck, Tommy? What am I supposed to do?"

"What did you do?" Burns had asked.

"I went to work on him with a baseball bat I keep in the front closet there," Grecco had said. "I go in the bedroom and she's on top, she flies off him like a dart she sees me standing there. I nailed him across the back as he's rolling off the bed. He took another shot in the arm running out the place, but that was it. I couldn't chase the cocksucker with my foot the way it is. I figured I'd come to you instead."

"What about Maria?"

"I didn't hit her," Grecco had said. "I mean, she's a cunt, what she did, but she's my wife. I made her tell me about the guy, I scared her with the bat, but that was it. I told her I'd take care of it. I didn't say what I'd do. I just told her I'd take care of it."

"So, you're staying?" Burns had asked.

"We got two kids, Tommy. Where'm I going?"

That was two days ago. Now Burns had to deal with the situation because some spic who parked cars, a guy named Julio, like the one they made the song about 'down by the schoolyard', for Christ sake's, was feeding off the same bush he and Grecco were sharing.

He waited a full five minutes before the Mexican busboy

brought him the cigarettes. He met the kid at the foot of the stairs and pushed the change from the ten back into his hand.

"Thank you, mister," the Mexican said.

Burns nodded. The busboy ran back up the stairs. When the door closed at the top of the stairway, Burns returned to the office and opened one of the two packs of cigarettes. He sat behind his desk and put fire to his first cigarette in what seemed like hours.

"You understand the fuckin' bind I'm in now?" he asked Maria Perez-Grecco.

Again the woman didn't move. She was short and busty with thick thighs and big round eyes. She had dark hair she wore up. Her tight jeans showed the indention in her crotch. Her white pullover top, also tight, was stretched at her chest and exposed some of her stomach above her waistline.

Burns looked her over.

"Your fat fuckin' horse of a dockworking, cocksucker-motherfucker husband comes to me the night before last and wants to know can I off some guy parking cars at the BAM there, the music place over in Williamsburg. What the hell for, I ask him. What the hell happened? 'He's fucking Maria,' your husband tells me. 'He's been fucking her. He's been fucking her in my own apartment when my kids go off to school. Mondays and Wednesdays,' he says to me. 'Mondays and Wednesdays.'"

Maria Perez-Grecco sobbed under the gag.

"I almost says to him, Jesus Christ, Joe, she's going that strong, four, five days a week, you should fuckin' charge. She slips me in Tuesdays and Thursdays, your wife. I don't know when she gets around to you, pal, but she's gotta be working just as hard as you are down the docks. Maybe you should see she can join the union, get some benefits. Maybe give discounts to your brother members."

The phone rang. Burns yanked the cord out.

89

"You wanna tell me what the hell I'm supposed to do?" he asked her. "You got any fuckin' ideas?"

The woman shook her head.

"I take that gag out, you start crying, I'll put my foot in your mouth instead."

The woman rested her chin on her chest.

"Eyes fuckin' up!" Burns yelled.

The woman obeyed.

"It's not enough I'm taking care of this place upstairs, the dagos on the docks dropping envelopes off for wiseguys, I get an occasional piece of work to pay the bigger bills, now I gotta have it so's the only quiet time I have, a piece of ass on the side you'd think is safe since it's married with children, you'd think it's decent enough it doesn't make things worse than they already are, she's out fucking the town and making what's supposed to be a little peace of mind for me a fucking job I don't need or want, her husband wants me to kill one of her other boyfriends now."

Burns slammed the desk with a fist.

"Jesus Christ, this is the way of the world, isn't it?"

Maria mumbled something.

"Yeah, right," Burns said. "Shut the fuck up."

• • •

Three months earlier, Jimmy Valentine, an up and coming wiseguy with the Vigneiri crew, had approached Burns with a piece of work after a card game. Valentine and Burns had met while serving time together at Sing Sing Correctional Facility in Ossining, New York. Burns had been taken in and protected by wiseguys at the prison. He went to work for them within weeks after his release.

"I got something, you're interested," Valentine had told Burns that day as they walked across the open field in New Dorp on Staten Island. "A real mutt just come out the can."

Burns had said, "I can always use the extra scratch, Jimmy. What's it involve?"

"Not much cash up front, but it'll open doors down the road. You'll establish yourself through me. Sooner or later I'll move up and you'll be part of a strong crew."

Burns said, "No doubt you'll move up. Sure, who is it?"

It was then Valentine gave Burns the name of the man to kill. Lawrence 'Porkchop' DaVito, a twice-convicted car thief, had given up the names of two accomplices to cut his own sentence. One of the two names given up was the son of Valentine's skipper.

"You take care of this, no mistakes, it'll earn us both points," Valentine had told Burns. "But it's gotta be done so it's a clear message. You leave the cocksucker dead in the street. Wherever you hit him, he stays 'til he's found."

When Valentine passed him an envelope stuffed with small bills, Burns had pushed it back.

"I ain't done it yet. I don't wanna get paid," he had told Valentine. "No way. Not 'til it's done."

Two nights later, Burns caught Lawrence DaVito leaving a bar on Flatlands Avenue in Canarsie. It was just after three o'clock in the morning. DaVito had wobbled across the avenue and fumbled with his keys trying to unlock the front door to his car. Burns walked around the back of the car and raised his .38 to chest level. DaVito never noticed. He continued searching for the keyhole.

"Hey, asshole," Burns had said, in an attempt to get DaVito to turn.

DaVito swayed to his left instead. Burns realized the guy was too drunk to command his own feet. He raised the .38 and squeezed off two headshots. DaVito caught the first in the right temple and was instantly killed. The second bullet grazed the top of his head.

The body crumpled on the street into a fetal position. Burns leaned over and put another two shots, side-by-side, behind DaVito's left ear.

Twenty-five minutes later he was covering the gun with black electric tape. He stopped mid-span on the Marine Park Bridge, got out of his car, ran to the railing, and underhanded the taped weapon as far as he could out over the water.

Burns was back in the car and on his way before he could spot another pair of headlights. He U-turned as soon as he passed through the tollbooths and headed back towards the Belt Parkway.

He returned to Brooklyn and left word at one of Jimmy Valentine's bars in Bay Ridge that the package had been delivered. He spent the rest of the night drinking at his own bar, Tommy's Place, where he eventually fell asleep in his office.

When he woke the next day, it was from one of the kitchen helpers. He saw it was after ten o'clock. The bar would open at eleven. He had met Maria Perez-Grecco a few months earlier and had been seeing her on and off during the week, Tuesdays and Thursdays. It was then a Friday. He dialed her number prepared to hang up if Maria's husband answered.

"Hello?" Maria had said.

"Yeah, it's me," Burns had said. "You free?"

"Yes, until one. I have to take the boys to religious instructions."

"I'll be over in five minutes. Need anything?"

"Milk, Tommy, thank you. Two quarts."

He grabbed the milk from the kitchen upstairs and was at the Perez-Grecco apartment in just under fifteen minutes. He wasn't as interested in sex that day and asked for a back and shoulder massage instead. Maria perched herself on the back of the couch behind where he sat and worked her small hands deep into his muscles.

It was both painful and blissful. It was better than sex, Burns had thought. He moaned a few times when Maria's fingers caused him to flinch.

One time, he had moaned as he leaned into the pressure she was applying with her hands.

Maria had said, "You never do that when we fuck."

Burns had his eyes closed and was in heaven. He didn't want to argue. "No? What do I do?" he asked softly.

"You grunt."

"I do, huh? Why's that, you think?"

"I don't know. I wish you moaned more."

"Maybe this feels better."

She stopped massaging him. "That's not nice."

He glanced at her over his shoulder. He saw she was upset. He winked. "I'm just kidding," he lied, then patted one of her legs.

She went back to working his shoulder muscles, but remained quiet. Burns preferred it that way. He moaned every now and again just to keep her busy.

• • •

Now he crushed out another cigarette before lighting a fresh one. He looked at Maria Perez-Grecco and frowned.

"I know a guy, he got burned by a broad like you, he never went after pussy again," Burns told her. "The man is in his early forties now, I met him in the joint upstate. Good looking guy, too. He decided it just wasn't worth it anymore, chasing skirt, falling in love, getting involved more than he had to. Know what he does now?"

Maria barely shook her head.

Burns sucked hard on his cigarette. He held the smoke a few seconds before blowing it out. "Jerks himself off, he gets the urge. Or he pays some broad to do it for him, give him a hand job. That's as close as he gets to tail anymore. Says it cleared his head for business not having to think about pussy anymore."

Maria mumbled something under the gag.

Burns got up from his chair to pull the gag from her mouth. He went back around the desk to sit again.

"What?" he said.

"I can jerk you off," she said nervously. Her Hispanic accent was slight. "If that's what you want."

"I don't like doing it myself," Burns said. "I never did, tell you the truth."

"I can use Vaseline if you want. I do that for Joe sometimes. When I'm sore or not in the mood."

Burns gave it a thought. "I never tried that, the Vaseline."

"It makes him go fast when I use it."

"It does, huh?"

Maria used her head to motion at her hands.

Burns held up a finger. "Hold on a minute."

He was thinking about Joe and Maria and how the hell did that work with her having two different boyfriends, at least two, and Joe being a dockworker caveman of sorts. Burns wondered what it was like when Joe came home in the mood, or just got that way watching the television or some dirty movie on the VCR. Did Maria take care of him the way a wife was supposed to, or did she look to get him off like she was on the clock because time was money?

He asked her. Maria shrugged a few times before answering.

"Joe is Joe," she finally said. "Sometimes I get on top and make him happy that way. Sometimes I let him get on top of me. The two times I start to give him head, he stopped me. He doesn't want his wife doing that. I think he goes to hookers for that. I don't mind because it's better than he fucks them and brings what they have home to me."

"How do you know he doesn't fuck them?" Burns asked.

"I don't, except I know he likes getting head, he just thinks it's dirty if I do it."

"It is, you get it from your wife."

Maria shrugged again.

"I'm not gonna kill this guy, you know, your other boyfriend," Burns said. "Not for Joe or for you."

"He doesn't deserve to die, Tommy."

"You were my wife he does."

Maria looked away from him.

"You give him head, this Julio?"

Maria swallowed hard. "Should I start lying to you now?"

"Start? You never mentioned this spic to me before I found out from your husband."

"Julio is none of your business."

"I pick something up banging you, you got it from him, he is. You ever think of that?"

"He uses condoms."

"I fucking hope so, you already got two kids."

"Yes, to answer your question. I give him head."

Tommy felt a sudden excitement.

"Yeah, and what about you? He take care of you, too?"

Maria nodded.

Tommy was hard. He said, "I'll handle Joe with this other guy, but you gotta be more careful or maybe Joe'll do it himself, kill the guy."

Maria nodded again.

"And we're through, you and me, except for this Vaseline thing. I'd like to try that once, see how it works. Maybe we can save what we had. You take care of me and I'll watch out for you."

"I have Vaseline at the apartment."

Burns made a face. "Yeah, right. I can send somebody upstairs to the store. In case your husband double-backs from work to check on you. I know I would."

Maria motioned at her hands again.

"After I send a busboy out for the grease," Burns said. "I kind of like it this way, you tied up like that. It turns me on."

"You can put it between my tits if you want," Maria said. "I do that for Julio sometimes."

Burns was confused. "Put what between your tits? My dick?"

"With the Vaseline. It works the same way as I use my hands."

"And where do I come, on your chin, your fuckin' neck?"

Maria shrugged one more time.

Burns was disgusted. "Just stick to your hands, okay? Jesus Christ."

A full minute passed. Burns couldn't shake the image she had left him with. He crushed out another cigarette and rubbed his eyes.

"Tommy?" she said.

"What?"

"Can you untie me now?"

He didn't answer.

"I have to get the boys from school at three o'clock."

He glanced at his watch. "It's not even one yet."

"But if you want the Vaseline. I have to go home and change first. I can't wear these clothes to the school."

He had called her at the apartment when he opened up at eleven o'clock. He had told her to come to the bar wearing something sexy. They would do it in his office in the basement. When she showed, he had brought her downstairs to the office, pushed her in the chair, and tied her hands. He gagged her when she didn't stop asking what was wrong. Somewhere in the process of shutting her up, he'd lost his desire for sex.

Now it excited him having her tied. He was angry with himself for taking the gag out. He should've known better. Women couldn't help themselves. They always said the wrong things.

96

"Tommy?"

He untied her hands and helped her out of the chair.

"There, go ahead now," he told her.

"You don't want–"

"No, get out of here. Go change your clothes and pick up your kids."

"Will you call me?"

"I don't know."

"I'm sorry."

"Yeah, yeah, I know. Go 'head, take off."

Maria took the stairs quickly. Burns remembered the call he had yanked the phone cord on earlier. He put the cord back in the jack and dialed the number he suspected had called his office.

A man with an eastern European accent answered on the second ring.

"Milo?" Burns said.

"Tommy?" the man replied.

"Yeah, it's me. You called earlier?"

"At twelve-thirty, when you said."

"Yeah, I was out. You got something for me?"

"An address in Floral Park."

"That Queens?"

"It's wherever Floral Park is."

"Okay, let me have it."

The man gave Burns an address.

"And this is confirmed, correct?" Burns asked.

"It's where he's hiding," the man said. "The super is with us. He'll get you inside."

"He'll have the other thing, too, I'm assuming."

"C.O.D., yes."

"Okee dokee," Burns said. "I'm on my way soon's the girl shows upstairs."

97

"Thank you, Tommy."

"Pleasure is mine."

Burns hung up and stretched through a long yawn. The day had started off like shit having to deal with Maria Perez-Grecco ruining what little action he was getting, but once he found Floral Park on the Road Atlas he kept in his car, it would end on a profitable note.

It was working out exactly the way his wiseguy friend had said. Since killing Lawrence 'Porkchop' DaVito for Jimmy Valentine, the work and money had started to flow.

Life was good, Burns was thinking, as he uncovered the floorboard where he hid the tools of his trade. Maybe after he took care of the work in Floral Park, he'd have a few Jamesons upstairs and give Maria Perez-Grecco another call in the morning.

He might even take her down to the basement again, where next time he'd leave her hands free to work and just gag her.

Burns was still anxious to try the Vaseline. It excited him again now as he picked the Walther as his tool of choice for his work later in the afternoon.

I've seen Toth drink six pints of Guinness in the space of an hour and still function. Maybe that explains his warped view of reality that he allows us to visit in his short stories and his novels, Fizz *and* Fishnet. *This one was the first Toth piece we ran. We couldn't refuse it. It was just too insane.*

Bull Dyke
Paul A. Toth

B.D., a/k/a Bull Dyke, pulled her old junker behind the bumper of Los Angeles convertible number two million twenty-three. She twirled her single purple pigtail, the only strands of hair longer than a whisker. She watched the driver's face in the convertible's sideview mirror: Yes, B.D. knew, it was one of them, a gleamer, tossing her hair as B.D. whispered to herself, "Now, toss your hair, honey. That's it. Thatta girl." The driver reveled in her me-ness, loving herself in a sleet of self-esteem. Yes, B.D. knew, this was another self-hugger, achieving (not simply buying) a convertible. It was not a reward for hard work, no, nor result of lucky genetics, never, but rather what you get for being you, all of you, the very best of you, the you that you are and all that you can be. All those things no girl named Bull Dyke could expect in life.

B.D. stepped out of her car in the jittering shift of time between red and green. She knew instinctively this was the kind of woman who said "fuck" all the time. They wanted to be tough, like her, no holds barred, no-shit takers, heart-breakers. She knew all about why women said the word, and men, too, so she banned herself from saying it, that and frigging, fugging, fricking. She was a clean hard woman, like glass, but you couldn't scratch her with coins or jewelry. She was free of everything but the desire to intrude, to break and enter, not for profit but to upset nature's balance, horrible nature and its opposition to everything she was: clumsy, dumpy, and not at all interested in mating, mating, mating.

She walked toward the sideview mirror and studied the driver's face, the stunned expression, the visibly hysterical thought of, "I should slam on the accelerator, so why don't I?" B.D. continued coolly, just as she always hoped she would. She moved toward the apex of her sociopathic tendencies, the summit of her amoral self. For some people, these are goals, like a week without uncharitable thoughts, a kind of backwards Lent for criminals. It could be perfected, she felt, in those who did not have the natural criminal talent. She could develop it the way fat girls starve themselves skinny and mediocre girls paint themselves supreme. Still, the gun in her pocket was unloaded.

For a second, her face joined the driver's in the sideview mirror. B.D. saw both the panic of the other and her own eyes, not blue or green but a shifting combination, like marbles in the sun. Then the traffic light changed to red.

"Whum you'm wam?" the driver said.

"What? Get out."

B.D. yanked the driver's hair—or rather, stopped it from tossing any time soon. She reached inside the car, unlatched and opened the door. She hauled the girl out and calmly threw her to the ground, feeling the smooth clean action of her own biceps and the newfound grace of her wrists and forearms, thanks to the stretching regimen she had recently begun. This was why she didn't care for sex, because there was something else that she controlled and it did not require the participation of another, participation that must be anticipated and somehow magically caused. This act, this form of intimate sharing, could and must be demanded, not coerced. You could only exploit the shock of these smug debbies by popping the balloon of their trust in the universe. You smacked 'em hard and fast and before you knew it, for a moment or two, they understood what it meant not to get what they wanted. Or at least, that's what she thought any criminal like herself would know.

"I am God taking away," B.D. yelled at the driver on the ground. "I stomp you with my king foot."

The driver held her hand to her ear like a conch shell. "I campt heam youm."

B.D. bent down and snatched the keys from the driver's hand. "What?"

The driver made a cutting motion with her other hand. "CAMPT HEAR!"

"You are preening. I hate preeners. Haircut head. Quit crying."

"CAMPT HEAR, CAMPT HEAR, CAMPT HEAR–I CAMMOT HEAR YOUM!"

The words clarified, focused, solidified, until B.D. finally heard them, thought them, saw them. Her brain printed internal billboards, neon lit signs: "'I can't hear you'?" B.D. repeated.

"Uhm-hump," the driver said.

B.D. leaned against the convertible. For some reason she looked at her watch, but the time of morning did not register. Where were they? In the canyons, the canyons. She looked all around her, and, yes, there was only clear California light in the gouged canyon road, which from above must have looked like someone dragged a finger through clay. That's why there were no cars. There was only one home at the end of this particular road, where one day, after being cut off by the driver, B.D. had followed the car home.

She pushed herself off the side panel and walked over to

101

the driver, bending down beside her. "I am a bull," she mouthed, but the driver looked at B.D., straight into her eyes.

"Yourm eyes lomk limk Jumpiter."

"What?"

"Jumpiter, Jumpiter," the driver said, pointing at B.D.'s eyes.

For several seconds, B.D. watched those fingers pointing at her eyes, listening to the woman saying, "Jumpiter, Jumpiter," until she imagined twin Jupiters and began to cry, a weird, warm release of remorse. Then the two fingers jabbed straight into her eyeballs, plunging deep down into pools of black and red. They seemed to twist into her brain like drills, spiraling, shredding all perception.

B.D. felt herself roll back and tumble in the sun, spinning unevenly, like a chipped marble, light splintering as the driver kicked and kicked her. She flipped and twisted, sliding downhill how, over rocks and glass and pebbles. She felt her knees peeling grape-like on the jags and crags, and then she bounced hard twice and landed in a pool of water, in the shady ditch off the canyon road.

It took a while for the black to clear, and when it parted and allowed an image to enter it was of the driver, standing above, legs spread, one foot on each side of the ditch.

"I AM BULL," the driver shouted, tossing her hair. "ME. ME. ME. ME."

Darren Speegle is a globetrotter, but his fiction slums over on the bad side of town. This story floored me when it came in over the transom. Most times when I think of the desert, I get a dry and arid feeling all over, might even squint to keep the imaginary dust out of my eyes. But Speegle's desert is vivid like Technicolor, same as his characters in this sharp piece of work.

Johnny Holes
Darren Speegle

The diner floated on a sea of dust, an island along an endless, shifting highway, tawny from blown waves. At the road's edge a sign hung askew on a weighted metal frame, its weathered message quoting, "Best eats in the desert!" A truck tire rolled across the gritty parking lot, whoever had set it on its uneventful course—a boy, a ghost—having since evaporated. The sun, high in the vault, was a fiery red as it pounded rock to sand, bone to dust, blood to vapor.

From within the diner, they saw the man seem to materialize out of the ripples, fleshing out to fill suggested dimensions and proportions. They watched him pass by a vulture tearing at dry carrion, neither the man nor the scavenger bothering to acknowledge the other beneath the sweltering heat of the noon hour. The diner's customers, regular as the tides of the wasteland, marveled at this unexpected disturbance in the flow.

The sheriff, with his unmended nose and cockeyed way of drinking coffee, was perhaps the most notable among the set. It was no secret he had long had his eye on the aproned bulldozer of a woman behind the counter, who happened to possess the one other personality in the place.

103

As follows, the two of them were the only occupants of the Snakeskin Diner who were not agape at what they saw. Rita was more than a mite intrigued, while the sheriff was outright suspicious. Nothing and no one came marching out of the dust, north or south, unless it was bad. One eye on Rita, one eye on the front door, he checked his holster, burning his lips on his joe as he did. He hadn't tried to do so many things at the same time since last election, and then only to win back those who had gotten mad at him for jailing Dan Bottoms for selling peyote to a couple Californians.

The door opened with a chime that died as suddenly as it was born. Heat barreled into the room to be tossed about by multiple fans. A chugging air conditioner unit cowered at the intrusion but kept blowing wasted cool into the place. Rita's Saint Bernard sat below the unit, enjoying the hum, tolerating the occasional drop of condensation—or perspiration—that fell from it. As the stranger stepped by the dog, its ears did not even twitch.

Everyone at the counter stared openly, all heads nodded at the visitor. Sheriff tried to remember when last he had seen an unfamiliar face in the Snakeskin, couldn't.

Rita addressed the stranger. "How do. Where ya comin' from?"

"Last town back," he said, gesturing with a thumb.

"Oldham?"

"Oldham, yes. And before that, Wind Branch."

"My. You're making your rounds. What can I get for ya?"

"Water'll be good."

"You mean no hot coffee like the boys here? I'd swear sometimes they enjoyed the heat. Have a seat there. Gotta name?"

"Johnny."

"I'm Rita. These are the boys." She talked as she pulled a jug from a refrigerator standing plump and awry against the

104

wall. As she poured, she nodded at his pack. "Drifter are ya?"

"I suppose I am."

The sheriff said, "Hot part of the country to be driftin' in, ain't it?"

"A man's mission won't be stifled by heat," Johnny said.

"Oh?" said Rita, placing his glass in front of him. "And what sort o' missionary's a drifter?"

The sheriff cocked his head at the stranger. "You a missionary?"

"Naw, Jake," said Rita, doing a familiar akimbo. "I didn't mean it literally. I was being . . . what's the word?" She looked at the stranger, as if, by virtue of his strangedom, he should know more about it than the rest of them.

"Figurative?"

"Yup, that's it."

"Actually, in a sense I am a missionary. I'm a missionary in the way Johnny Appleseed was a missionary."

"Didn't he go around somewhere in the east plantin' apple trees?" said Rudy, who sat other side of Sheriff Jake.

"What John Chapman, aka Johnny Appleseed, brought to the rural Midwest was the gift of romance. From the seeds he planted came spring blossoms, poetry, songs, wine. I bring a gift too."

Rita leaned on the counter, maybe or maybe not conscious of her impressive bosom, the cleavage of which might have hidden any number of lost treasures. Her curiosity, however, was indisputable.

"What gift?" she said with syrup.

"The gift of holes."

Almost in unison, the counter said, "Holes?"

Rita followed up with: "You mean that figuratively, huh?"

He smiled. "Holes are outlets. Outlets free you of unwanted anger and aggression, fear and anxiety and pain."

105

"It's beautiful," Rita said.

Sheriff shot her a look of injury and reproof.

"Oh shut up, you," she said to him. "Poet you're not. You wouldn't know your emotional outlets from your button holes." She opened her eyes wide, surprised with herself for her insight.

Sheriff Jake turned to the stranger. "Okay, Johnny, how's it then? Psychology or somethin'? Some kind o' Freudish voodoo?"

"I'll need supplies," Johnny said to Rita.

"Anything," she said, meaning it.

He leaned back, counting with his finger the number of persons at the counter. "Five. We'll need that many–"

"What about me?" said Rita, teetering between feeling hurt and feeling special.

"Is that your truck out back?"

"Yup."

"Does it run?"

"Sure."

"You're the driver then. We'll have to address your–"

"Whoa, now. Look here, Johnny," Sheriff cut in, "Rita's a business to run. And as sheriff, I got duties myself. Let's say we don't go for any rides."

Johnny scrunched his brows at Sheriff Jake. After a moment, he motioned with his head towards the corner. As suspicious as ever, Jake followed him to the table, the big dog ever true to its torpor as they passed. Rita was contained by a wink from the drifter missionary. As far as the others were concerned, Sheriff saw best.

In a low voice Johnny told the sheriff, "What I'm sensing in Rita, what desperately needs an outlet, is the emotion she's concealing for you, Jake."

Jake frowned at this liberty with his Christian name, but quickly refocused on the subject.

Johnny elaborated, "The girl's head over heels for you and just won't admit it."

"Think so?" Sheriff said.

"It's certain," said the drifter. "My guess is, she's intimidated by your position. A man of your high station has got to be intimidating to a woman. Have you ever been married?"

"Back once."

"Before you were sheriff. . . ."

"That's so."

"See. It's the position. I'll bet you've had not a single real prospect since you stepped into those boots."

"Come to think of it. . . ."

"What you need to do, Jake, is step back out of those boots when you're around Rita. Get rid of that belt, that gun. Lord, Jake, you frighten *me!*"

Jake looked down at his holster. "Well, I never thought of it that way."

"Let's experiment, Jake." He turned to Rita, who looked on intently. "Five glasses," he ordered up.

"Glasses of. . . ?"

"Leave them empty. Place one in front of every man up there. Bring one back for Jake."

Puzzled, she turned to do it.

Johnny said to Jake. "Go ahead. Remove all the apparatus. Lord, you're a hard man to love."

That last word, hanging out there, sparked something in Sheriff Jake. Convinced or not, he began to doff all the leather.

Rita brought the glass but paused before setting it down, making way for Sheriff, who was placing his belt and holster on the table.

"Everyone have a glass?" Johnny asked her, looking past her at the occupied stools.

"Yup."

"Good." He raised his voice. "Now everyone take a long

look inside your glass—you too, Jake—take a long look and think about what's inside you. All the anger and fear and anxiety and pain. When we are finished, all of you will be as empty of those unpleasant emotions as the glass in front of you. Look deeply . . . concentrate. . . ."

As they did, Rita, who had no glass, watched something else. She watched Johnny's hands, very busy hands. Poetic hands, she thought.

"Go fire up the truck, sweetheart."

"You don't need any other supplies?" she said.

"Have all I need," he said, dropping one, two, three bullets on the table.

Sheriff looked up from the wonders of the void. "What are you doing?"

"Ammunition is part of that mystique of yours, Sheriff."

"But the cylinder holds eight rounds. Not three."

"Go on, Rita." Johnny Holes nudged her.

As she walked out she flinched with explosion number one. Her dog flew past, howling, but the image of what occurred behind her was immediately replaced by a picture of turning to butter in Johnny's arms. The next four reports fell like raindrops on the desert; gift of a drifter, missionary and—she swooned to think of it—poet.

Creator of private eye Moe Prager in novels including Redemption Street *and* The James Deans, *Mr. Coleman (as Gischler calls him) is a drinking buddy at every convention, always ready with a great story delivered in his rough as sandpaper voice, and a guy who can turn a phrase. He lives and breathes the language of the streets, and it shows in everything he writes, including this story our readers couldn't get enough of. And it's packed pretty tightly, too.*

Kaddish
Reed Farrel Coleman

It was to laugh.

What a stupid fucking expression, but my old man said it all the time. It rolled off his tongue like careless spit. So I say it. My old man, so low on the totem pole he was halfway to Australia. So much an afterthought, he gave forgotten a bad reputation. When they drilled Manny Feingold's boys in the Chink's up on Empire Boulevard, Starker Mench's gang pissed their pants at the sight of my old man crawling out of the crapper, toilet paper trailing out the back of his trousers. He wasn't even worth the price of a bullet. One of Mench's boys threw a broom and a dust pan at my pops.

"Start cleanin' up or say Kaddish. It's your choice."

My old man did both. He would have done a tap dance. All they had to do was ask.

It was to laugh.

Even when I don't say it, I think it. It's like one of them songs that gets stuck in your head sometimes. There are days I almost forget his stupid expressions, the sound of his voice, and the weight of my pop's subterranean legacy stops tugging at me, but then somewheres between my skull and scalp it settles back down into my brain.

109

I'm thinking it now, the blood pumping outta my *kishkas* in a sweet rhythm like the words outta that Olivier guy's yap. I don't understand half the shit that limey prick says, but I bet he could scream "fuck you" and make it land on your ears like a kiss. He's probably half a fag. Even still, I could die happy with that voice in my head. Instead, I got my old man's for company. I never heard my mother's voice, not so's I remember, anyways. She lit out on us before I could crawl. Smart move. What I don't get is what she saw in the loser in the first place. I bet she don't hear the old man clanging around her head no more. It would serve her right if she heard it on her deathbed. I'd like to be there for that.

"Remember me?" I'd whisper in her ear. "It's to laugh, no?"

Now I won't get that chance, but I'll save her a seat in hell like the old man's saving for me.

• • •

"I'm fuckin' bleedin'."

"Me, too. Didn't you hear, that's what happens when you get stabbed or shot? You wanna compare entrance wounds?"

"You stabbed me! What the fuck did you stab me for?"

"I didn't wanna waste bullets."

"I don't even know you. Do I know you?"

"My old man. You knew my old man."

"Call a fuckin' doctor. I'm dyin' here."

"That's the general idea."

"Who's your old man?"

"One of Manny Feingold boys."

"What happened at the Chink's, that was business. Your old man knew the price of admission when he got into. . . Ah fuck, this hurts."

"And what, you think this hole you put in my belly feels like a dip in the pool after a *schvitz?*"

110

"Listen, I'm sorry about your old man, whoever the fuck he was. Now call an ambulance, for chrissakes!"

"Bite your tongue or the rabbi's gonna box your ears."

"You're a sick bastard, you know that?"

"Very sick. Sicker by the minute."

"Call a fuckin' ambulance!"

"No."

"Fuck you and your old man. I hope my boys took their time with him."

"Easy, that's blood dripping down your chin. You can't afford to let your heart pump any faster. You like Olivier?"

"What?"

"Olivier, the actor. You like him? I seen him in some of those Shakespeare movies. When he talks, it's like the rhythm of your heart."

"Anything! I'll do anything, just call somebody. I'm sorry I had your old man killed. It wasn't personal. Just call somebody, please!"

"Your boys didn't kill my old man. They should have, but they didn't."

"You stabbed me cause my boys *didn't* kill your old man? Is that what you're sayin'?"

"Something like that, yeah."

"You're Hymie's kid."

"Yeah."

"Holy fuck! It's to laugh."

"What'd'you say?"

"Hymie's wife was the best piece a skirt I ever had."

"What? What are you laughing at? Stop it!"

"Hey kid, forget the call. Just save me a seat."

• • •

It was to laugh.

111

What else can I say about my buddy, writing partner, fellow grad school alumnus, and co-editor?

How about this: you won't believe the sci-fi novel he's writing. This guy's a multiple threat—a poet, a Crimedog, a sci-fi fan, and, like me, a worshipper of Will Farrell.

Often accused of writing cartoonish noir, Victor's story this time actually contains a cartoon! It's a nice slice of Twilight Zone style noir from a writer who never fails to surprise with his highly original eye for detail and depth of ideas. And he's really goddamned funny. Check out Gun Monkeys, Pistol Poets, *and* Suicide Squeeze.

X's for Eyes
Victor Gischler

We started fighting again because I said I was going down to Walmart to buy bullets for Dad's gun.

Sharon looked up from her drawing board, a pencil behind each pink ear, another in her mouth, the burgundy lips trying to flap words at me while the square white teeth kept a harsh grip on a third pencil. "God damn, Billy. I didn't want a gun in the house, and I sure as hell don't want a *loaded* gun in the house."

She started erasing something hard, shaking the drawing table. That made her body shake too, her heavy breasts swinging in rhythm under her loose tank top. She was mad all over. Pale cheeks flush. Teeth digging into the pencil.

The fight wasn't about the gun. It was about me and Dad and her. She'd bought the tiny one-bedroom house six months ago, and we'd crowded it with stacks of books and half-painted canvases and wicker furniture. It was fall, just turning cool, and we waited for the temperature to dip just enough to justify using the small fireplace.

It was her house, her wicker, her fireplace.

"What's the point of having the gun without bullets?" I asked.

"Fuck you, Billy."

"What's Pinky doing this week?" This was my feeble swipe at changing the subject. *Pinky & Pals* was Sharon's comic strip. Sort of *Mary Worth* with a gen-x edge. We'd met as grad students. I was trying to push some poems together and make a master's thesis out of them. She was wrestling with cubism,

113

trying to get a showing in Soho or the Village or Flatbush or Gary, Indiana—anywhere but here in Ocala, Florida, where they didn't give a rat's ass about anything but horses and Gator football. Certainly not cubism anyway.

Pinky & Pals was pretty popular in our college newspaper. Soon it was picked up by other college papers. Soon it was all over the damn place. Then the *Boston Globe* picked it up and it got the hell syndicated out of it and now it was paying the bills and the rent and buying me new shirts and new shoes and the whole time my dad wanted me to come on down to the furniture store where he said he could put me to work selling couches and bedroom sets at three hundred a week plus commission.

Sharon said, "Shit on that."

I said I couldn't just sit around while she earned all the money. I said she pushed me around because she thought she was the boss because she brought home the bacon. I'd take the job with Dad. She said that was selling out and she made enough to support us fine. I said she should go to hell and was getting fat sitting at the drawing board all day.

We had this fight about twice a week. More lately.

I put on my coat.

Sharon froze at the drawing table, cocked a sideways look at me. "Where are you going?"

"I told you. Walmart."

"No."

"What's your problem? We need toilet paper anyway."

"No bullets."

"I'll just see how much they are."

"I don't care if they're free. You're not getting any."

My face got hot. "Look, I'm going to see Dad tomorrow. I'm going to work for him. I'll buy any fucking thing I want out of my paycheck."

"Billy, I swear to God in Heaven, if you walk out that door to go to the store for fucking bullets for that fucking gun, you'll find all your shit on the lawn when you get back."

"I'll be back in an hour."

"I mean it, Billy"

I left.

When I got back with the bullets and the toilet paper, there was a sloppy pile of my stuff on the grass near the mailbox. On top was the Smith &Wesson .38 police special my father had given me.

• • •

It only took about a week for me to slip into the routine at the furniture store. I learned to tie a tie. I bought dress shoes. I sold couches. I sold bedroom sets.

I was staying at Dad's for a while. Sharon called me there.

"You can't be happy selling furniture, Billy."

"I'm good at it, actually."

"Come home. I'm sorry."

"Too late." I hung up on her.

That Sunday, I turned to the comics. I was curious about *Pinky & Pals*. In the strip, Pinky's boyfriend had taken a job selling furniture. The joke was that he'd sold a whole house full of furniture to some redneck who lived in a one-room trailer. The last panel showed the redneck crowded in with all the furniture saying, "I'm gonna get that furniture guy."

Hilarious.

• • •

Sharon tried calling again. I hung up again.

I sold more furniture that week. Started stashing away money. Once in a while when I was sitting around Dad's house alone, drinking a beer, I'd take out the police special and twirl it around. I kept it loaded the first night, then started getting nervous like maybe I'd drop the thing and it would go off, put a bullet through my brain. I could just see Sharon at my funeral, shaking her head at my corpse and telling my friends and family that she'd warned me about the gun. So I kept it unloaded when I played with it.

That Sunday. The comics.

Pinky's boyfriend was getting the shaft again. A German Shepherd chased him around the yard. The boyfriend ended up hanging from the low branch of a tree, a big bite bitten out of his trousers by the dog.

Three Stooges humor. I would have expected better from Sharon.

I poured a six-pack of Schlitz into my face, stumbled to bed in a fog.

The next morning I woke with a slight hangover. I drifted in and out of the shower, dressed, and went out to my car. I was late for work.

In the driveway between me and the car was a pretty big dog. He looked like he was unhappy. He looked at me like I was the reason why. It was a Husky or maybe a Malamute, the kind with the all-white face. He growled.

I made shooing motions, stomped my foot.

No dice.

I'd always heard that saying about dogs being able to smell fear. If it were true, then Rover was getting a snoot full. He growled. Barked. Then he launched himself, claws making that *clickety* noise on the cement. He moved fast, thick saliva streaming from his mouth like a cartoon beast.

I back-peddled so fast, I think I went back in time. My stomach clenched in a wad of real-life-no-shit-I'm-gonna-die terror. I spit out a little girl yelp.

Somehow I was back in the house, door slammed, dog doing a number on the door's paint job on the other side. I was breathing fast and hard. Sweat formed under my arms, on my forehead. I looked out the window. The dog circled, grum-

116

bling little barks and growls like he was muttering to himself. Was he on crack or something?

I called the police. They sent somebody with a big net.

The police had a few questions for me.

No, I didn't know how the mad dog had gotten as far as my neighborhood without being spotted by anyone else. No, I didn't know who owned the dog. No, I didn't know why the dog had chosen me to vent his embittered doggy wrath on.

The cop who wrote down my information seemed very disapproving. He shook his head while he scratched his pencil in his little book and told me that animal control had taken the dog away to be destroyed. It turned out to be a Malamute.

Of course, I'd remembered Sharon's cartoon, but I hadn't mentioned it to the officer. What could he have thought? What did I think? A coincidence. I tried to imagine her coercing a rabid dog into my yard, training it with one of my old dirty socks to attack me on sight. Sure. Right.

Ridiculous.

But I picked up the phone to call her, dialed five numbers before hanging up again.

Ridiculous.

• • •

The week crawled by. Dad asked about the dark circles under my eyes. I told him girl trouble. He nodded and peppered me with dad advice: Chin up. Buckle down. Nose to the grindstone. Don't take any wooden Injuns.

Sure, Dad. Thanks.

I sold a couch, a love seat, a bedroom set, and a mahogany wall unit. *Cha-ching.*

Sunday sneaked up on me. I shrugged into sweats and sandals and headed for the Quick-Mart. I bought a large coffee and a newspaper. I turned to the comics before I even walked back to the car. Pinky's boyfriend was getting the hell beat out of him by a couple of toughs. Two big guys with big, meaty fists doing a number on the boyfriend.

Splendid.

• • •

I tip-toed my way through Monday morning looking over my shoulder and jumping at loud noises. I spent half my time worried and the other half feeling like a dumbass. By the end of the day, I was laughing at myself pretty good. The dog thing was a coincidence. I was a moron.

I dropped by the Ale House for a quick draft or three after work. The afternoon stretched into evening. Friends trickled in. We bought each other drinks. By the time I left, it was just a little before midnight.

On the way to the car, two great big sons of bitches fell in behind me.

Shit.

"Buddy," said one. "Hold up a sec, eh?"

Shit and fuck.

I walked faster. They kept pace.

"Buddy."

I wasn't quite running, but it was obvious I was on the move. I made it to my car, fished my keys out of my pocket and got them into the lock.

A hand on my shoulder. It spun me around.

The two big guys were right up on me. They looked like they were put together on the same assembly line. Big square granite jaws. Shoulders you could land a plane on. Knuckles like walnuts.

"Didn't you hear us, buddy?" His words floated to me on a cloud of bourbon.

"Sorry." I tried to take the quiver out of my voice. "Just in a hurry to get home, you know?"

"We figured. My pal and me are looking for a ride."

"Sorry."

"Don't be sorry. Just give us a ride."

"Look, I just want to–"

"Fuck that noise," said the other one. "Get his keys."

He put his hands on me, pawed at my pockets. I pushed him away.

The fist came around on me so fast I didn't even see which one of them had thrown it. I felt important things in my jaw go *crunch*, and darkness fell, punctuated by little star-shaped explosions.

I shook my head, slipped to the side. I didn't want to be caught up against the car.

One had a hold on my shirt. The other had his fists up. I tried to remember back five years to the four months of jiu-jitsu I'd taken. I put a knuckle into one's solarplexis. He *whooshed* air and let go of my shirt.

The other one swung at me. I ducked and tried to kick him in the gut. I wasn't limber enough and the kick landed low, my heel connecting with his balls. He grunted and went to his knees.

The other one took a running start at me. I punched, missed. He lowered his head and tackled me. We both went to the ground, and he ended up on top. I tried to punch up at him, but I couldn't get an angle. He started in on my face, knuckles biting into my cheeks and eyes until my lips were bloody mashed meat against my teeth, until my nose was flat. I felt a molar jar loose. Before I could spit, I was hit again, and I swallowed the tooth. The other one came over, and they both started kicking.

As I blacked out, I heard. "Fucking stupid bastard. That's what you get."

• • •

119

I got out of the hospital on Friday, but I still looked like hell. Dad picked me up and drove me home. My face was full of Frankenstein stitches, and I had two busted ribs. I ate painkillers all weekend and slept. Sunday morning, I asked Dad to bring me a newspaper.

Sharon was laying off me this week, I guess. Pinky and pals were on to other adventures—a day trip to Daytona. In the hospital, another dour cop took my statement. I gave him the whole play by play, but once again didn't mention Sharon.

Now, it seemed certain she was out to get me. Artistic types like her can't let things go. Everything has to be all dramatic. I knew all about it. As a poet, I'd dated almost exclusively women with screws loose. That's the kind of gal you meet in dark coffee shops, I guess.

Dad told me to take the next week off and rest. But I couldn't rest. The ribs still hurt, and I was ugly as all hell, but I could get around okay. I grabbed the police special and drove to Sharon's house.

I wasn't looking for trouble and sighed relief when I saw she wasn't home. I only carried the pistol as a precaution. If she'd sent a couple of bruisers to put a hurt on me, she was capable of anything, and I was pretty goddamn tired of getting shoved around.

I went in the house. I still had a key, and Sharon hadn't changed the locks.

I wasn't anything like a detective, but I had to find something to show Sharon was gunning for me. I couldn't go to the police and tell them my ex-girlfriend was slowly killing me with her comic strip. They'd chuck me in the loony bin.

I went through her desk, her bedroom. Nothing. The drawing board had a half-drawn strip, but it didn't tell me anything. The trip had been a bust. Oh, she was a clever one, little

Sharon. She wouldn't leave anything damning just lying around. I should have known that.

The knob on the front door turned, and I froze. It swung open. Sharon saw me. We stared at each other a long, quiet second.

"Billy?"

My mouth opened and closed. Nothing came out.

She took a step toward me and she smiled, and I got mad because I knew what she was thinking. She was thinking I'd come back to be with her, that I was there waiting for her to come home so I could tell her how wrong I was and how right she was and all that. Bullshit.

I pulled the gun, pointed the thing right at her.

Sharon stopped. Her smile fell away a little piece at a time, and we were just looking at each other again, except this time I was holding a revolver on her. That'll stop anybody. Put a gun in someone's face and they come to a screeching halt every time.

"Oh, Billy." She said it like I was pointing the thing at myself. Dumb bitch.

"I've been keeping up with *Pinky & Pals*," I said.

"You're upset."

"I'm fucking beat-up is what I am."

She didn't seem to hear me. "I know it was wrong, but I was really hurt. It was just my way to blow off a little steam."

"Don't play stupid," I said. "I know what you've been up to. You don't think I can do anything, but I'm doing it, aren't I? I'm on to you, missy."

"What the fuck are you talking about, Billy?"

"The dog and the guys beating me up."

"I told you I was sorry. I shouldn't take out my aggressions in *Pinky & Pals.*"

"Fuck *Pinky & Pals!*" I shook the gun at her. "I nearly got

121

my ass chewed by a rabid mutt, and your pals beat the fuck out of me. I was in the hospital for Christ's sake."

"What?"

"The guys you sent to beat the shit out of me."

Her jaw fell open. A hell of an acting job. "That's insane. I would never do that." She spoke each word slowly like I was some little retarded kid or something.

"I was insane to ever get involved with you," I said.

"That's a laugh," she said. "You're nothing. I supported your ass for three years while you were scribbling your precious little poems."

I got hot all up through my face, and my fist tightened on the gun. I jerked the trigger at her three times hard.

Click. Click. Click.

The bullets. I'd unloaded the gun at Dad's house, so I could twirl the damn thing.

The blood had drained from Sharon's face. Each time I'd pulled the trigger, Sharon had flinched, sucked in a horrified breath.

"God damn you, Billy," she whispered. Seething, final hatred seeped into her voice. "God damn you to hell."

I pushed past her. My hands shook. I shoved them into my jacket pockets with my empty revolver. I climbed into the car. Cranked it. Drove home.

• • •

Two Sundays later, Pinky's boyfriend met his comic but untimely end in the funny pages. Pinky had crawled through his bedroom window and presented him with an exploding box of valentine candy. Didn't somebody edit these things? How could they show this to kids?

What struck me about the dead boyfriend in the comic strip were his eyes. You ever see a dead guy in a comic strip?

They put Xs in for the eyes to signal that the guy's a corpse. Pretty damn freaky when you're looking at yourself.

So I don't sleep anymore. Not for a week. I'm jittery and nauseous from so much coffee. I sit up in the chair in the corner of my room. I wait. Sometimes, I start to doze, and a night noise sends the panic up my spine. I clutch the revolver. It's loaded now.

She thinks she has me. But I'm ready. I'm waiting. Waiting for candy covered death to slip in through my window.

Cocked and loaded.

When I found out Robert Skinner lived in New Orleans, my favorite city, I wrote him a note and asked if Gischler and I could buy him a beer and talk about crime writing. He said yes, and these few years later, we'll still stop by when we hit the Big Easy and talk about the city, Westerns, the book business, and . . . the Atkins diet?

If you get a chance, ask Bob Skinner to tell you what he knows about mid-century New Orleans, and you'll be glad you did. We get to soak in that world in his critically acclaimed Wesley Farrell novels, full of shocking language, stunning violence, and tasty surprises mixed in like a spicy gumbo. The story below gives you a taste of that, an exception to our "contemporary setting" rule. But when it's done this well, who gives a shit about the rules?

Spanish Luck
Robert Skinner

I remember asking Mr. Aristide once if he knew why Sal Cortes always referred to bad luck as "Spanish luck," and like usual, the man give me an answer I couldn't quite get my hands around. "Sal's an ironist, Jeff. And maybe a bit of a fatalist, too." I went home and looked those words up in my dictionary, but neither definition got me any closer to understanding what Sal meant.

Don't get me wrong now. Sal was my best friend, and in the late '50s, not many Negroes could call a white man a best friend. The thing about Sal was, he was his own guy, from his pearl gray Stetson to the bone-handled .38 Super he carried just behind his right hipbone. He trusted me and I tried to never let him down.

I got a call from Sal one afternoon in May of '58, askin' me to meet him at Mr. Aristide's office on Gravier. It was already hot and sticky, and I felt sweat runnin' down my back under the sport coat I had on. Mr. Aristide always insisted his men wear a coat and tie, no matter how hot it was. Sal was waiting for me out front, smokin' one of those Mexican *cigarillos* he favors. He dropped it on the sidewalk, ground it out with his silver-toed cowboy boot, and jerked his chin at the door. I followed him inside, pulling my sweaty shirt away from my skin.

"What's Mr. Aristide want us for?" I asked.

Sal shrugged his thick shoulders. "We'll know when we ask him." We took the elevator up to the fourth floor, where Mr. Aristide kept his offices. When the elevator door opened, I saw the gold letters on the wall that spelled out FARRELL & ARISTIDE. Underneath them sat Maxine Smith, giving her typewriter a fearsome workout. She looked up at our approach.

"Morning, Mr. Cortes. Mr. Aristide says to go right in." She shifted her gaze to me, wide brown eyes set in a pale brown face. Her mouth parted in a grin. "Hi, Jeffy."

"Uh, h-hi, Maxine." All I had to do was look at that girl and I turned into a fool. I followed Sal across the reception room, glad that a man my color can't blush.

"Howdy, Sal," Mr. Aristide said. "Jeff, how's your mama and daddy doing?"

"Fine, sir." My daddy was commander of the police Negro Squad before the war, and sometimes told me stories about all the dangerous things Mr. Aristide did when he was a young man. Every time I looked at the neatly dressed, light brown man with his cultured voice and polished manners, I tried to see it, but couldn't. But I could tell he knew things, though, by the glitter in his slate gray eyes, and the way his mouth would sometimes get hard around the edges. Like today, once the greetings was over.

125

"Vic Lacey didn't appear at court this morning. You know what that means?"

Sal nodded. "You're out ten grand unless we find him." He shook his head. "I told you not to go his bail. You can't depend on a guy who beats up women."

Mr. Aristide's eyes got a flat, far-away look in them whenever Sal talked back to him. His mouth crinkled as though he'd tasted a bad oyster. "Okay, Sal. You said 'I told you so.' Now go out and find Lacy and bring him in. I'm damned if I'll write off ten thousand without a fight."

Sal nodded. "Yes, sir. Come on, Jeff."

Sal left the building as though he knew exactly where he was going. When I first started working with him, I thought he was a psychic or something, but I learned by and by that Sal just didn't worry about details, only the outcome. When we got to the street, he pitched me the keys to his Buick Roadmaster and told me to drive.

"Where we goin'?"

Sal settled his narrow hips into the seat beside me and put his elbow on the open window ledge. "Head out to the lake. We gotta see a man." He smoothed his black mustache with a thumb and forefinger, then rested his chin on his fist. I knew better than to bother him, because I could already see he was workin'.

I cut through the Quarter and picked up Elysian Fields, following that all the way to Pontchartrain Beach. By then I'd figured out who we were gonna see. After I parked the Roadmaster in the amusement park lot, we went to the manager's office. The manager was Vic Lacey's brother.

"Got a minute, Phil?" Sal asked from the office door.

Phil Lacey was about fifty, a big, gruff-looking man who still retained the physique he'd had when he was a professional wrestler. He took a cigarette from his mouth and held it

126

between his thumb and forefinger. "I don't know where he is, Sal."

Sal's mouth approximated a smile beneath the neat black mustache that decorated his upper lip. "You're a lousy liar, Phil. You're a good brother, but a lousy liar. You think Vic would lie to keep you out of jail?"

Phil Lacey put the cigarette back into his thin, brutal mouth with a stony look in his eye. "I still don't know where he is."

"Does he know you and Mary Alice got together while he was up at Parchman this last time?" Sal watched Phil's silent face for a minute before shaking his head. "I guess that's why you're staying clammed. He finds out, he'll kill both of you, sure as God made little green apples."

Lacey took one last drag on his cigarette, then crushed it out in the ashtray. "He's got to leave town, Sal. Let him go. He won't come back this time—he can't, for Christ's sakes." I wondered if this were true or not. Vic Lacey had been arrested for robbing a liquor store on North Broad. He'd only just got out of the Mississippi pen, so it was a sure thing he'd be lookin' at hard time. 'Course, Vic's head was mighty hard. I wondered if there were any brains inside it, or just a muddy pool of meanness that kept him in a constant state of hate and discontent.

Sal just shook his head. "Uh-uh, Phil. He leaves town and Mr. Aristide loses a bundle, and you know Mr. Aristide better than that." He stared down at the big man from beneath the brim of his Stetson. "I got a brother, too, Phil. He's an asshole sometimes, but he's my brother. Because of that I overlook things, but some things you can't overlook. Vic's a lit stick of dynamite, and he's probably found himself another gun by now. If I don't find him, he's gonna kill somebody, and I'd hate for it to be you or Mary Alice, so tell me where he is."

Phil Lacey was one of the biggest, scariest white men I knew, but I could see fear bouncin' around inside his eyes like ping-pong balls when he looked back at Sal. For a minute I thought he'd break down and use some common sense, but finally he just shook his head and looked away.

Sal's mouth was a hard, tight line and his face was pale. "You goddamn dummy. Let's go, Jeff, before I do something I'll be sorry for later."

"He's scared outa his mind," I said on the way to the car. "He don't know what he wants to do."

"That happens when you fall in love with your brother's wife," Sal said with a peculiar note in his voice. "You can almost see heaven but hell is where you live. Let's go back to town."

It was a funny kind of a job we had with Farrell & Aristide. I never knew from one day to the next if we were bodyguards, private dicks, or skip tracers. All I knew for certain was that Mr. Aristide had a lot of different concerns, and we were his trouble men. After we went to see Phil Lacey, though, I wasn't sure we were still working just for Mr. Aristide. I could tell there was something personal in this for Sal, because we worked a lot harder that day than we did on other jobs.

We made the rounds of a hundred poolrooms, bars, and whores' cribs where Vic Lacey was known and more-or-less welcome, but ended the day with a big fat goose egg in the leads department. I was kind of wrung out from the heat, but Sal looked as neat as he had when I'd met him that morning. We stopped at a *taqueria* on Magazine for chow, and it was there we got our first break.

Sal ordered barbecued pork, *frijoles refritos,* and Mexican rice, and I asked the girl for the same. We were in the middle of a couple of Carta Blancas, talkin' over the day, when a gambler named Boley Wright slid into the booth beside me. Even for New Orleans, Boley was a flamboyant dresser. He had on a red shirt, purple tie, and a gold-plated tie bar shaped like a flamingo under his hound's-tooth-check sport jacket.

128

Like usual, his narrow-brimmed Panama hat sat square and straight on his narrow skull. He said, "You still lookin' for Vic Lacey, Sal?"

Sal let the smoke of his *cigarillo* escape the corners of his mouth as he studied Boley. "You know where he is?"

"No, but I know somebody who does. It was Babe Shellhouse helped him with that liquor store heist."

"You know that for a fact?"

"Uh, huh. See, Shellhouse is livin' wit' Marcy Blue."

I tried to keep my thoughts out of my expression, but it was hard. Babe Shellhouse had spent his whole life tryin' to play the Bad Nigger. He was stickin' up sweetshops at an age everybody else was out playin' stick ball. Marcy Blue was like him, only worse. She was the kind who'd egg a man on to commit violence for a kick. Blood was an aphrodisiac to Marcy.

"How do you know?" Sal asked.

Boley licked his lips as he tried to look Sal in the eye. "What's in it for me if I help you?"

Sal's eyes flickered in my direction. "Give him a fin, Jeff." I dug out my expense roll and peeled off a five. I put it in front of Boley. I could see him wantin' to touch it, but he knew it wasn't his yet.

"Marcy's in the Fat Man Lounge over on Clio," he said. "She's drunk, shootin' her mouth off about what her man and Lacey gonna do."

"Which is what?"

Boley licked his lips again. "They fixin' to blow town once they build a stake."

"Uh huh."

Boley took off his Panama and mopped his forehead with a silk handkerchief. "She say Lacey know about his brother and Lacey's wife. She say he gonna fix the two of 'em."

Sal blew a stream of acrid smoke through his nostrils. "Take the five and blow, Boley. And keep your trap shut."

"Yessuh," Boley said as he snatched the five and slid to the end of the booth.

When Boley was gone, I said, "You wanna go over to Marcy's or go warn Phil?"

Sal crushed out his smoke and took a long drink of beer. "Let's eat first." He pushed his ashtray to the end of the table as the waitress put the beans, rice, pork, and a stack of tortillas in front of us. "Bring us two more Carta Blancas, willya, doll?" The dark-haired Mexican girl rewarded him with a grin as she went to get the beers.

"Sal, I hope you don't mind me sayin' that I think you're taking this a little too calm. S'pose Vic takes it into his head to go kill his brother and Mary Alice while we're here chowin' down?"

"Eat your dinner, kid. It might be a long evening."

Sal makes me mad sometimes. He knows I hate it when he knows something and I don't. He always tells me, but sometimes I don't get the word until I see the headlight of a railroad engine staring me right in my face.

The sun was well down in the sky when we drove out St. Claude Avenue. Sal made several calls before we left the restaurant and learned Marcy Blue's place was on the top floor of a brick apartment building on St. Roch Avenue. I'd been listening to Sugar Boy Crawford sing "OOh Wee Sugar," trying not to think about what we were gonna do, but I knew it was hopeless. No amount of rock'n roll could make me forget the combined hazard of Babe Shellhouse and Vic Lacey. I snapped the radio off as I coasted to a stop across the street from the apartment building.

"Stay out of sight," Sal said as he opened his door. "I'll scout the neighborhood and meet you back here in about fifteen minutes. You got your piece?"

130

I opened my coat and showed him the .38 Smith in my belt. I preferred to use my head first, then my hands, before I started showing a gun, but I carried it to keep Sal happy. He winked at me and then disappeared.

I watched the street, turnin' things over in my mind to keep from thinking about what we were about to do. I knew that Sal felt bad for Phil Lacey and I knew why, too. Sal's brother, Val, was married to a pretty red-haired woman that he never seemed to have time for. Sal had tried to be a friend to Gloria and her little boy, Nick, but after a while the friendship got to be something else. As cool as Sal seemed, I knew that part of him was in knots all the time. I picked at the edges of my friend's problem until he appeared at my window and told me to follow him.

The entry to the building was dark and the staircase had the usual smells of poverty: sweat, burnt cooking oil, dog and cat urine, fried hair, and failure. We took the stairs to the fourth floor and walked down the hall to the last door on the left. Sal looked at me and I nodded. We'd already talked it out. He stepped back and kicked the door hard, but not hard enough to break it in. He paused, then kicked it a couple more times. From inside I heard the gruff sound of a big, angry man as he approached the door from his side. When he jerked it open, I stepped in and hit him on the hinge of his jaw with all my 180 pounds behind it. Babe Shellhouse staggered from the blow and I hit him twice more before he fell.

By now Sal was inside the apartment and Marcy Blue was screaming like a banshee. I was still workin' on Babe when Vic Lacey came into the room with a .45 in his hand.

"Drop it, Vic! Drop it or I'll blow the guts out of you." Sal had the .38 Super cocked and pointed at Vic Lacey's head. A bigger, nastier version of his brother, Phil, Vic's pale blue

131

eyes were full of crazed fury, but he saw no give in Sal and dropped the big gun to the floor.

I moved away from Babe's prostrate form and shoved Marcy into a chair where I could watch her. I noticed in the corner of my eye that the door wasn't closed, but figured it didn't matter. We wouldn't be there long.

Vic was under control, but just barely. "How did you find me, Cortes? Who told you where I was, so I can kill him after I'm through with you."

"I'll tell you on the way to jail, Vic. Put your hands behind your neck."

Vic grinned savagely. "You think that gun's big enough to let you put cuffs on me, Cortes?" He shook his head slowly. "You get that close and I'll tear your arm out and beat you to death with it."

"He won't cuff you, Vic." I turned my head and saw Phil Lacey standing in the doorway. A .38 Police Positive was almost lost in his huge fist.

Sal didn't seem worried or even surprised. He didn't take his eyes off Vic. "You wanted to know who turned you up, Vic. Tell him hello." He jerked his chin at Phil.

Vic's mouth hung open but his eyes were like something from a bad dream. "What the fuck—? Naw, don't gimme that. Make him drop his piece, Phil. Show the bastard."

Phil's face wore a pained expression. "I thought I had this set up just right, but I guessed wrong."

"Plenty went wrong, Phil. Like you sending Boley Wright to give Vic's hideout away. I've played poker with Boley, and he can't bluff for shit. The whole time he was shoving that crap about Marcy shooting her mouth off about Vic's plans, he had all he could do to look me in the eye. It's too bad you gave him such a lousy story to spread."

Vic was still angry, but Sal had him interested enough to stay put until he knew what was going on. "What's he talkin'

132

about, Phil?" When Phil licked his lips and said nothing, Sal continued.

"He had Boley Wright feed me a line about little Marcy shooting her mouth off in the Fat Man Lounge about what you and Babe were up to. I knew that was a lie, because nobody who knows Marcy is ever gonna say anything that matters in front of her. Even Babe's not dumb enough for that." He shifted his position so he could keep Vic covered and see Phil at the same time. "I called the Fat Man Lounge, too. Big Tony said Marcy hasn't been in there in a week."

Vic's heavy hands had bunched into fists the size of hams. "Marcy? What shit would Marcy spread? That dumb twist stays too stoned to know anything."

Phil took a deep breath, and there was the barest tremor in the hand that held the gun. "About Mary Alice and me. We wanta get married, Vic, but we both knew you'd never let her go. I set this up so Sal would have to take you down. Now I guess I got to do it."

Vic's face had turned the color of bone and his pale eyes went hot and mad. *"You and Mary Alice,"* he shouted. *"You and Mary Alice."* He started for his brother with his fingers hooked into claws.

Phil's gun exploded and a piece of Vic's jaw flew away from his face in a spray of blood. I was clawing for my gun when Sal fired twice from the hip. The high-powered .38 slugs hit Phil in the body and spun him around. He crashed into the door and fell heavily. Marcy Blue was screaming again, but I could barely hear for the ringing in my ears. I ran to Phil and saw blood oozing from two wounds in his side. He was already turning blue from the loss of pressure in his chest cavity so I got out my cigarettes, tore off the cellophane in two pieces, and slapped them down to seal off the wounds. Behind me I heard Sal calling for an ambulance and cops on the telephone. Phil looked up at me, his eyes fluttering like the wings of a small, fragile bird, his mouth moving but making no sounds.

Sal knelt beside us and put a hand on Phil's forehead. "Hang on, brother. I got an ambulance coming." I looked over at Sal and saw him trying to smile in a reassuring way, but his eyes were sick and tired.

"You figure on things workin' out this way, Sal?" I didn't mean to say it like that, but I was still scared and a little sore about the risk we took.

Sal shook his head. "I took a chance and hoped for the best. It's bad luck, I guess, bad luck all around."

I heard sirens in the distance and kept the pressure on Phil's wounds. I couldn't think of anything to say that wouldn't make it seem worse.

Maviano's stories began showing up in our emailboxes, and we were pretty damn glad they did. It took us a couple of hits before we settled on one that blew us away, and that's "Blood Money." After we ran it, we kept in touch. This guy knew his noir and could beat the English language into submission. He was a New Yorker living in . . . Utah? This gave him a unique voice and perspective.

He'd had a run at some movie biz experience with a couple of screenplays, and then he turned to crime fiction. He so impressed us that we signed him up to help us steer the PwG ship for our final two years. He brought his attitude full bore to nonfiction in his column "An Earful from Maviano," a fan favorite that pulled no punches, long after those knuckles were bloody and raw.

Blood Money
Trevor Maviano

The sacrilegious chords of Hendrix's national anthem assaulted my ears, and the dashboard clock glowed 4:15 in the A.M. Seated in the rear of Mikey's van, I tested the weight of a silenced machine gun through thin leather gloves. All misgivings focused on the weapon in my lap. I'd used a pistol before and fired a shotgun a couple times, but an Uzi was out of my weight class. To counter the panic, I reminded myself why I was holding the gun in the first place. Since my release I'd spent twelve months trying to do the right thing–working shit jobs, controlling my temper, doing what I was told. All of which was enough to convince me that *the right thing* wasn't right for me.

"That's it," Mikey's voice broke over the music.

Checking the rearview mirror, I caught Mikey's teal eyes glaring back at me. I responded in kind. It might have been his score, but that didn't mean I had to like the guy. Averting my gaze, I glanced out the side window as we passed by Horowitz Brothers Custom Jewelers. Mikey had gotten the idea for the heist from a guy named "Ducky." He was one of the turd-headed, perma-stoned, Jamaican Yardie boys that Mikey bought blow from. Apparently Ducky used to run with a Jamaican posse who laundered their drug profits through the Horowitz Brothers jewelry store. But after a dispute over some missing cola, Ducky was on the outs and itching to get back at his old pals.

According to Ducky there'd be at least a hundred and fifty large going through the Horowitz Brothers' hands tonight. Ducky had hooked Mikey up with two keys. One fit the outer security door, and the other fit the glass door leading into the shop. According to Ducky there was a video camera inside the front door that could be monitored from the basement. He claimed the monitoring got pretty lax as the Jews hurried to return home to their Long Island mansions and the Rastas zoned out on their sacred herb. It all sounded simple enough– open the doors, take the money and get the hell out. Then again, everything *According to Ducky* might have been bullshit. Nobody would know for sure until we were inside.

What I did know was that machine guns and cash practically guaranteed homicides. Murders didn't bother me. In the three years I spent at Green Haven I'd racked up half a dozen, killing for survival and respect. The first time was tough. I stuck a foot long, razor sharp shank into a big mooley's chest and felt his final heartbeat vibrate into my fist. The whole thing reminded me of my first whiskey shot. It burned a little and clenched my stomach, but it didn't take long before I wanted more.

A hand slapped my knee, jerking me back into the moment. I glanced up at my old cellmate, Joey O. He was riding shotgun and smiling his Hollywood smile.

"Lighten up, Scarselli."

"Fuck yourself," I tried not to grin.

"Oh, that's the thanks I get, huh? Ungrateful son of a bitch."

Thanks to Joey O I'd become the final member of the threesome. Joey and Mikey had grown up together in Hell's Kitchen. I'd come up across the river in Brooklyn. That combined with an Italian surname was enough for Mikey not to like me. If it hadn't been for my Irish mother, Joey O never could've convinced the guy to bring me along. Still Mikey didn't like me, and the feeling ran both ways. In the two weeks I'd known the guy, we'd nearly come to blows a dozen times. I held back out of respect for Joey, but we all knew it was a matter of fuckin' time.

Mikey flipped a U-turn and pulled to a stop in front of the jewelers, "Lock and load, cowboys!"

Joey O pumped his shotgun as I chambered a round. *Cowboys*–Mikey was right about that. A high stakes rip-off of drug money was definitely a no-brains, all-balls kinda move. Up front Joey O used the blade of a tiny pocketknife to shovel white powder up his nose, then passed the vial and the knife to Mikey. I lurched over the back seat, snatching large duffle bags and distributing them around the van.

Hopping out of the sliding side door, I felt October chill kissing the air. Holding my Uzi and crouching low, I followed Joey O to the jewelers. The storefront was glass behind cast iron security bars. Joey O slipped one key into the security door's lock. The lock clicked and Joey O swung the door open. I shouldered past Mikey to stand up front. It was time to show some guts, time to earn some respect.

"Jesus! Look at the tough guy."

Ignoring Mikey's comment, I stared through the glass and into the dark store as heartbeats pummeled my ribs.

"It won't open," Joey O struggled with the key to the second door.

"Hurry the fuck up!" Mikey ordered.

Joey O twisted around with his black eyes menacing, "Would you like to fuckin' try? It ain't the right key!"

Mikey leaned over my shoulder for a better view, "The thing fits, don't it?"

"It fuckin' fits," Joey O confirmed. "But the lock don't turn."

"Goddamn Ducky!" Mikey cursed.

I was still staring into the store when a set of snarling ivory teeth flashed through the blackness. Time slowed. I bulled Joey O aside, leveled my gun and jerked the trigger. The Uzi danced. Gunshots cracked like thunderbolts amidst splintering glass. Instinctively dropping to one knee, I sensed the others scattering behind me. When the bedlam subsided I could hear the gurgling groans of the Jamaican, writhing a few feet inside the shattered door. Joey O crawled up beside me and we ducked inside.

As we passed over the dying Jamaican, Joey exploded the guy's skull with a shotgun blast. Fragments splattered my legs. Wandering past cases of shattered glass and precious stones, we approached the top of the stairwell that led to the basement. Footsteps ascended toward us. Gripped in a rage of stoned confusion, another Rasta raced up from the store's basement. We embraced him with hot slugs and buckshot. Screaming, he disappeared back down the steps.

At the top of the stairs, I gazed down at the broken body lying twisted at the bottom. Mikey crowded in behind us. Our time was short. Automatic gunfire and shattering glass wouldn't go unnoticed. At most we had a seven-minute window to deal with the remaining victims and load up our loot. Looking down, I saw cement walls enclosing the stairwell down to the basement floor.

We descended the steps, trying not to slip in the blood the body had left behind. Reaching the bottom, we hovered behind the concrete that protected us from what waited on the other side. Sweat stung my eyes. Joey O looked pissed. Mikey seemed bored. I took the initiative. Easing my barrel around the edge of the concrete wall, I prayed it offered better cover than the basement's occupants had. The others followed my lead. Together we unleashed a blind hell storm into the room. The occupants responded. Slugs slammed into the concrete at my back. Ricochets swarmed like bees. Blasts bit my eardrums and echoed through my skull. Pandemonium reigned.

Clips emptied. I pulled away from the wall and released

my empty magazine. Taking a fresh one out of my pocket, I slammed it into the Uzi. Realization came as I racked a bullet into my smoldering barrel. All gunfire had ceased. Putting my back to the wall, I shot a shaking hand out from behind our cover. *Nothing!* I waved a couple of times. *Nothing!* With nerves knotting my throat, I scrambled over the dead Jamaican and a pile of smoldering shells.

Upon entering the basement, I discovered that our victory had turned out to be more than twelve inches of concrete versus the thin metal and cheap veneer of a toppled folding table that now resembled a giant cheese grater. A greasy crimson puddle spread out from under it. I walked over for a better look. Both Horowitz brothers lay twisted and broken, flopping atop a bloody Jamaican.

"Let's get this fuckin' money and get the fuck outta here, now!" Mikey's voice barked through my numb ears.

I was done taking orders. Ignoring Mikey, I continued absorbing the gruesome panorama. Half way across the room, another Jamaican lay face down. He'd abandoned his pals to seek better cover and died two feet away. Walking over, I stared down at the body. Several rounds had blasted through his head, mixing a gory cocktail of dreadlocks and brains.

"Jesus fuckin' Christ!"

Spinning around, I found Mikey sneering at me.

"Could you quit lookin' at the bodies and help out a little. I can't believe you vouched for this half-breed, Joey."

Looking past Mikey, I saw green bricks of cash stacked in mountains and scattered in piles. I grinned. Mikey started toward me with gritted teeth and bulging veins.

"The fuck're you smilin' at?"

He kept coming. Raising the Uzi, I fired. Bullets blasted out his back, spreading guts and ripping into the money stacks. Joey O scrambled and dove to get out of the way. Mikey danced, dropped, and died.

Shock and confusion twisted Joey's face. He glanced over at Mikey, then back at me. I watched him close, wondering which way he'd go. Joey needed to decide in a hurry. Just when I was about to pull the trigger, the Hollywood smile broke across his face. I lowered my gun as we shared a laugh.

"Fuck it. Two ways splits a lot better than three," Joey O climbed to his feet.

"Guess so," I shrugged.

Slinging the duffle bags off our shoulders, we started packing up the dough. Thousands of dollars lay shredded by my poorly guided bullets. But it didn't matter. Much more remained. It was the most beautiful thing I'd ever seen—crisp green bills dripping fresh red blood.

Maviano's responsible for bringing this one to my attention, and I think it's the first story he accepted as an editor. Brackett writes low-down and dirty, giving us the unforgettable "Fat Broad" in a story so noir *it sweats black ink.*

Brackett's also got a novel out there called Sacrificed Lives. *Maybe you should look it up.*

Eternal Vigilance: Black Coffee
Beverley Brackett

I was sitting on a park bench, watching my sister's kid play on the jungle gym, when The Fat Broad first appeared. At first I thought she was just another park mom, letting her kid get a little exercise on a brisk fall afternoon. Then I noticed she was paying no attention to any of the kids. When I realized it was me she was watching, I reached into my coat pocket for the comfort of my gun.

The fuckin' thing's a pea-shooter, really, but after fifteen years of being armed to the hairline, it's the minimum I can carry without feeling naked. I've been retired and selling books for the past five years, but I've never forgotten that I once had a hard man's career. And that I still have enemies.

Once she had my attention, The Fat Broad began her approach, slowly, keeping her hands in plain sight. She wore an olive green trenchcoat. Tucked under her arm was a manila envelope.

I kept my hand on the gun.

When she got about five feet away, she spoke, softly, but the wind was blowing in my direction and carried her words right to me. "My employer wishes to engage your services."

"I sell books," I growled. "I don't have any goddamn services. Fuck off."

"We think you do," she said. "We'll be back in touch."

Before I could think of a witty rejoinder, she turned and walked away. But not before dropping the manila envelope. It landed in the autumn leaves with a sharp crack, spilling some photos onto the ground.

I scooped them up and took a look. There, in glorious black and white, was my last job: a charming little number I'd done on the idiot oldest son of a prominent East Coast crime family. He lay on a king-sized bed in a fancy hotel, a nimbus of brains and blood spread out on the pillow beneath his head.

It was all there in the pictures. The body. The blow on the bedside table. The room service cart. My smiling, readily identifiable face.

When I looked up from the photos, intending to chase after The Fat Broad, she had already vanished. But she'd be in touch.

And I'd be offering my services.

• • •

It was five minutes to closing when The Fat Broad strolled through the door and made a beeline for the lit section. My assistant, Lexie, a French major at the University, rolled her eyes as if to say, "They always come in at the last minute. Ain't it a pain-in-the-ass?"

I gave her a half-smile and said, "It's late and I know your boyfriend is waiting. Why don't you go on home? I'll close up."

She didn't need to be told twice. She was out the door in under a minute as The Fat Broad leaned against a bookshelf, pretending to be fascinated by a copy of *The Count of Monte Cristo.*

As Lexie and her boyfriend peeled out of the driveway, she looked up from the book and gave me the once over. "You know," she drawled, "I'd a never had you pegged for a bookstore owner."

I raised an eyebrow. "No?"

She put Dumas back on the shelf and said, "No, I'da thought you were more the bar-and-grill type. There's lots of things you can use for protection in a bar and grill: knives, broken bottles. . . ." She shrugged. "Hell, you can even keep a gun under the counter. But what can you protect yourself with here?"

"Obviously, you've never been whacked upside the head with a copy of Vasari's *Lives*," I answered. "Besides, how do you know I haven't got a gun under the counter now? How do you know I'm not gonna blow your brains out?"

For a second, I thought a smirk crossed her poker face. "You got a bitty lil' thing in your pocket, but you don't keep a real gun here. Believe me, we know. And besides, even if you did, you wouldn't shoot me. There'd be all that cleaning up to do, and let's face it, I wouldn't be the easiest corpse to move, let alone get rid of. . . ."

In spite of myself, I grinned. I like a woman who's not afraid to call things by their right names.

"Not to mention the fact that you'd be on the run from our employer for the rest of your life. Which would be a very wretched and brief affair," she continued.

"Our employer?" Her word choice had not escaped my notice.

"Oh, yes," she answered with a slight nod of the head. "In the twenty years that Eternal Vigilance has been in business, and the twelve that I have been working for Mr. Gray, we have only twice had vigilantes turn down offers of employment."

I folded my arms. "Well, how do you know I'm not going to be number three?"

She permitted herself a small smile. "Because if you were, you'd have run."

"So, what do you and this Gray guy want from my life?" I busied myself with shutting down the cash register as I spoke, trying to look nonchalant.

From the corner of my eye, I watched as she laid a thin black briefcase on the counter, popping open the clasps with her thumbs. "Mr. Gray," she began, placing a quiet emphasis on the 'mister' and opening the briefcase to reveal a manila envelope, "would like you to handle the matter of this gentleman. The lady as well, if you can manage it without too much fuss. But if not, just the man."

I turned to look at the counter top and saw a photograph of a wasp-faced man, about fifty-five years old. He had his arm around the waist of a blonde with tits like missiles and not much else to recommend her.

I thought of that old joke: when rape is inevitable, relax and enjoy it.

"Okay," I answered. "You got an address for them? Names?"

"Everything you need to do your job is in here," she said, sliding the manila envelope across the counter. "If Mr. Gray is pleased with your work, you will receive the standard remuneration, plus up to two negatives."

"Two negatives?"

"Remember the photos I showed you a few days ago?" she asked sweetly.

"How could I forget?"

"One negative for each problem you successfully handle. There are twelve photos total. Once you have all twelve negatives, you will be free to continue your employment with us, or not. As you see fit." She smiled at me, her head cocked to one side. "Do you understand?"

I nodded. "Twelve jobs and I'm shed of you."

She closed the briefcase, snapping the clasps back into place. "If that's what you wish. But you'd be surprised at the number of vigilantes who choose to continue offering their services. The work offers satisfactions that just aren't available anywhere else."

I watched, mesmerized, as she glided to the door. For a large woman she moved with unusual grace and ease. The bell jingled as she opened the door, letting in a blast of chilly autumn air.

"Enjoy Florida!" she called out. "If you have any questions or problems, tough!"

• • •

The quick and dirty was this: the wasp-faced piece of work was Curtis Sullivan. The tail with the missiles was his girlfriend, Zee Baker. Ten years ago, Sullivan had been an ambitious tax lawyer engaged to a lovely young woman named Halley. His life was all set; the road to happiness lay straight ahead. But the problem was, like most people, Wasp-Face's public persona did not jibe with his private self. Behind closed doors he was a controlling, manipulative bastard who liked to play sexual "games." When Halley resisted and tried to break off the engagement, she disappeared. Naturally, foul play was suspected: church-going, dutiful daughters don't usually do a vanishing act.

Halley's diaries revealed Sullivan's sexual practices. They also revealed that the more she objected, the more he pressured her, growing uglier as his grip on her loosened and she began to withdraw from him.

When she'd finally had enough, she broke it off with him. The night she went to his house to return the ring, she

147

vanished. They never found her body. And, God knows, they looked.

Once they found the diary, Wasp-Face was their only suspect, and they did everything but tie him to the rack in an effort to break him. But he was a damn good lawyer. He knew they had no physical evidence, no body, and no hope of convicting him. He held firm.

So they went after Missile Tits, and she broke open like a bag of garbage. Spilled her guts about what the two of them had done to Halley the night she disappeared. How they'd taught her to loosen up, not be such a tight-ass. How they'd videotaped Halley in her final moments. Tits giggled as she told the story. Even her lawyer was disgusted.

When the cops found out about the video, they went to work hard. They dismantled Wasp-Face's house, tore apart his office, even located a storage locker he kept in a neighboring town. They found nothing. Not even the hidden stash of porn that most men keep squirreled away in some corner of their lives. Wasp-Face had seen this coming, and he'd cleaned up with Clorox.

Wasp-Face also went to work, harder. He worked on Tits, wooing her all over again with letters, phone calls, and promises of his undying love.

By the time the trial came around, Tits was a dicey witness gone right to hell. The defense attorney took her apart on cross-examination. In the end, the jury took five hours to acquit Wasp-Face. He walked, and Tits, whose deal had been time served and two years probation, walked with him.

Two years later, the video turned up.

Wasp-Face's mother, a sweet woman blinded by love for her only child, had put up her house as security for the attorney's fees. When her baby boy was acquitted and walked away from the debt, mama lost her house. She died not long after and the house went to an upwardly mobile young couple who set about rehabbing it. One of their first projects was to turn the garage into a family room.

That's when they found Wasp-Face's twisted little home movie, tucked away behind some loose brickwork. Wasp-Face's own personal remembrance of his fiancé.

After that, there could be no doubt. Tits and Wasp-Face fled to Florida when persons unknown torched his car. For six years, they'd been living lives of increasing squalor.

I was about to change all that.

• • •

I took up residence in a saltbox house across from theirs, planted a few bugs and a couple of microcameras while they were out, and started listening and watching. They were an interesting couple. His misadventures with the law had meant a long slide down the social ladder for him. As for her, she'd always been bottom rung material. This was her natural environment.

They both worked at a titty bar on the outskirts of the tiny Florida town where they lived. The place was the kind of dive that employed played-out girls desperate to suck the last bit of cash out of their waning abilities to make men's dicks hard.

He tended bar and kept an eye on her tips. She danced. Sometimes, if he felt they needed a little extra cash, he'd get her to perform other services for the clientele. It was a sad, sordid life, but she didn't seem to mind. She had her man, a roof over her head, and drugs. What more could a girl ask for?

But he knew better. He'd lived better, and now, at the bottom of the ladder, he seethed with resentment. And he took it out on her, rendering her servile and sniveling. I

149

watched this white trash soap opera for two weeks before deciding on a plan.

She took her coffee black. He took powdered creamer, lots of it.

Only now, it was powdered creamer and arsenic.

Arsenic can be slow to kill, but it makes itself felt pretty quickly. Its victims become violently ill with stomach cramps, nausea—all the symptoms that send people to a doctor double quick. Within a couple of days, Wasp-Face was vomiting, sick as a dog, flat on his back in bed. At first they both chalked it up to stomach flu, but as the days passed and his condition worsened, Tits convinced him to go see a doctor.

He went to see a doc-in-the-box at the local strip mall. The doc made a diagnosis of gastroenteritis, gave him the usual advice and a fistful of pharmaceuticals that would do him no good.

Wasp-Face returned home, and I went back to watching and listening from across the street. He continued to suck down that powdered creamer, and just got sicker and sicker. When he was only getting out of bed to go to the toilet or make another cup of coffee, I decided it was time to put an end to it all. Before he got too weak.

One afternoon, after about eight days of taking the doctor's drugs, Tits took Wasp-Face back to the strip mall and I broke into the house one last time. It took me about five minutes to do what needed doing, then I was back across the street.

Tits brought Wasp-Face home, put him back in his bed all snuggly and warm, and headed off to work. He napped for a couple of hours, then shuffled into the kitchen for a cup of joe.

That's when he discovered the package of arsenic. Behind the jar of creamer.

I listened to him curse "the bitch" and vow to the cheap prints on the wall that he was gonna fix her but good.

When Tits got home at three in the morning after a hard night of exotic dancing and selling watered down drinks, he was waiting for her in the living room. The action started right away.

"What the fuck is this?"

I couldn't see them, but I had a mental image of him holding up the package of arsenic. I could imagine her squinting, trying to make out the words on the box.

"What's what, hon?" she squeaked. Fear edged its way into her voice, the last word ending on a tremolo.

"THIS, bitch!"

I heard the sound of something falling over, maybe a chair, and his heavy footsteps pounding across the floor. I imagine he's closed in on her, pushing the box in her face.

She started to get frantic. "I don't know! I don't know! Lemme look at it!"

I heard a thump, followed by the unmistakable slap of flesh striking flesh.

"Fuck you, you goddamn cunt! You know what it is, 'cause you've been poisoning me with it the whole goddamn time! It's fucking arsenic."

"No, no, hon! I would never do anythin' like that to you! I love you!" She started to wail. Terror had taken over.

I almost felt sorry for her, but then I remembered the video they found after the trial. I remembered the look in Halley's eyes. Not just terror, but hopelessness. The sure and certain knowledge that no one was gonna come along to rescue her; that she was alone. And Missile Tits was in just about every frame of that video, laughing and having a grand old time.

I crushed out any sympathy I might have felt for her like a cigarette and listened as Wasp-Face beat her to death. Took about four minutes. I think he used a baseball bat.

He put her body in a Army surplus duffel bag and dragged her about fifty yards into the woods behind their shack. Weak

151

as he was, it took him a few hours to dig a small hole, but he managed.

By the time he staggered home it was early morning.

. . .

They didn't find Wasp-Face until the Sheriff showed up to evict him for non-payment of rent. By then he'd really started to stink the place up. The landlord ended up having to replace the linoleum in the bathroom before he could rent the place out again.

The coroner's report said that his death was a homicide. He had large quantities of arsenic in his system, but what did him in was the cyanide. The cops found it in a bottle of extra-strength headache capsules.

See, I figure after a man's killed his girlfriend and dumped her body in a grave out in the woods, he's gonna have one helluva headache. Even a man as cold as Wasp-Face.

The cops are still looking for Missile Tits. I saw her profiled the other night on America's Most Wanted.

But she's buried deep now. I know. I took The Fat Broad out to her little patch of heaven.

Gischler and I met Doolittle at our first Bouchercon, back in 2001. He had just published Dirt *with Uglytown. Gischler's* Gun Monkeys *was still in the pike, and I had a few short stories to my name. So something about our mutual "Just Starting to Make a Dent so We Should Drink a Lot" society made perfect sense, and Doolittle became a huge supporter and a great friend. We like to make the trek to Omaha every spring for Mayhem in the Midlands mainly to hang out with him in his hometown, play video golf at local bars, and drink until dawn.*

His writing is smart and funny, a hard combo to achieve, and I think he's a natural heir to Elmore Leonard in that sense. He's more serious than Dutch, and his characters are drawn with more care, plenty of layers to peel off as we follow them through crimes, flirtations, frights, and crazy acts of desperation. He's had a banner year. His novel Burn *is out in paperback,* Rain Dogs *is coming soon, and we're just waiting for the rest of the world to catch on to what we take for granted: this Doolittle guy is* good.

Worth
Sean Doolittle

It was a simple question, but Worth didn't mind asking it twice.

"Um . . . paper," the woman said. "I guess."

Worth gave a wink and said, "Paper it is."

As he swiped open a sack, the woman traded glances with the checker, a hazel-eyed community college student named Gwen. Gwen just went back to skimming the cheat sheet taped to her keypad for produce codes. After a few beats, watching him work, the woman finally leaned across the checkstand toward Worth.

"Forgive me for asking . . . but don't they have employees who do this?"

"I don't mind." He really didn't. "They're short-handed. Besides, I was just standing over there looking official anyway." By the time he finished speaking, he'd already placed a perfectly-packed sack of dry goods in the cart at the end of the stand.

Square. Stable. Not too heavy.

"Hey," said the woman. "Wow."

Worth nodded to the young boy at her hip, a tow-headed kid with big round eyes. "Watch the hands, kiddo. My clinics are free."

Nightstick creaking softly in its loop, handcuffs rattling against their snap, Worth quickly reduced the rubble of

155

scanned groceries to three neat bags. He'd already outpaced Gwen, who seemed to be nursing the sprain she'd sprung playing volleyball in some local bar league. He dialed it back a notch.

The woman was smiling now. "Say . . . do you think you could put the meat and frozen stuff in plastic?"

"No problem." Worth nudged Gwen playfully. "Hey. Lefty. Keep up."

Gwen might or might not have grinned. She kept on scanning with her left hand, running the keypad with her bum wing. Worth grabbed and bagged. Soon the cart was full, the total totaled. The woman scribbled out a check.

"Is that a real gun?"

Worth smiled down at the kid, who gazed up at his gear belt with widened eyes. "It's real, all right. But it's only for emergencies."

"Have you ever shot anybody?"

"Not even once."

"Trevor," said the woman. "Don't bother the officer."

"No bother at all." Worth fished a Jolly Rancher from a vacant tear gas holster and handed it to Trevor. "That's official police candy. Do me a favor and don't tell anybody I gave it to you, okay partner?"

The kid glanced at his mother, who grinned and nodded.

And Worth mused, with equal measures of acceptance and disgrace, that this was the only time he really felt like a cop. When a seven year-old kid looked at his gun with utter awe.

"You know," the woman said, regarding her shopping cart appreciatively, "you're really good at that."

Worth flagged one of the aproned kids who had just returned from a carry-out. "The long arms of the law are here but to serve."

The woman laughed. She tried to tip him; Worth politely declined.

156

When the woman and her boy were gone, Gwen tilted her head at Worth and batted her lashes. "You know, you're really good at that."

"And you're hilarious."

Gwen laughed, even though she had no idea how close the joke really came to the truth.

The truth: he was a rotten cop.

But he was one hell of a grocery bagger.

As Gwen closed her register drawer with a hip, Worth strolled back to his spot near the cigarette case at the front of the store. He hooked his thumbs in his belt, planted his feet, and resumed position with a steely-eyed, roving gaze.

• • •

Almost nothing ever happened between 10 P.M. and 5 A.M. at the CostRite on Charles and Bellingham. This was the primary reason Matthew Worth had been assigned to the location, which was not so much an assignment as a demotion pending performance review.

The specific events leading up to Worth's current station were various, a jacket's worth of embarrassments and foul-ups that had earned him his inevitable nickname around the shop. Worth still didn't know who had etched the suffix "less" in thin spiky grooves after the "Worth" on the nameplate of his locker, but it was the closest he'd come so far to being included in the fraternal horseplay that made a cop one of the gang.

In all fairness, the many dings in Worth's short two-year service record almost always involved a helping or two more than his share of bad luck and mitigating circumstances. At least until that stoplight in midtown two months ago, when he'd accidentally rear-ended a family of four in a Plymouth Grand Caravan with his police cruiser.

157

Bad luck? Without a doubt. Mitigating circumstances? Matthew Worth could have made out a list. But as an employee of the very taxpayers into whom he'd plowed, he'd had nothing to offer but sheepish apologies and an insurance card. He'd been off-duty at the time, driving home from his patrol shift during rush hour. Still, even Worth had to admit that it had looked pretty awful on the ten o'clock news: him still in uniform, standing next to his own crumpled bumper, while a fellow cop wrote up the ticket and report.

The only excuse he could have offered was simply too humiliating to bear. Besides, it was no big secret anyway. Almost everybody in the precinct knew the story.

Worth? Guy's a wreck. Wife left him six months ago for Vargas up in Homicide. Yeah. Poor dumb bastard's been walking around in a daze ever since. And he wasn't all that sharp to begin with. Miracle he hasn't gotten somebody killed.

The Friday before Worth had returned to work after a two-week suspension with pay, a certified copy of the psych department's official recommendation arrived in the mail, along with a provisional reassignment slip signed by his Lieutenant.

And the following Monday, Worth found himself on temporary night detail at the CostRite on Charles and Bellingham. Where nothing ever happened.

"Bitch!"

Most nights, anyway.

"Russell. Please. You're hurting me."

"Lower your fucking voice."

Worth overheard the argument midway through his 2 A.M. spin around the perimeter of the store. He'd been strolling along, enjoying the scent of the night's earlier rain showers still lingering in the air.

Backtracking around the corner of the building, Worth saw a woman standing near a tricked-out GTO in the corner of

158

the empty front lot. The driver clutched the woman's arm through the open window.

"Honey, I'm sorry," the woman said. "Okay? I need to get back to work. Please let me go."

As Worth lengthened his stride, he realized that the woman was Gwen. Whoever sat behind the wheel of the goat saw him coming. The driver released Gwen's wrist a half minute before Worth reached the car's front quarter panel.

"Everything okay over here?"

Gwen quickly folded her thin arms and looked down at the surface of the parking lot. "Hey, Matthew. I'm just finishing my break. Everything's fine."

Worth watched her a moment. Then he put his hand on the Pontiac's roof and leaned down.

"How about in here?" he asked.

In the driver's seat fumed a lean, muscular guy in jeans and a tank top. The guy gripped the wheel and stared straight ahead, face glowing amber in the lights from a custom in-dash stereo.

Russell, Worth presumed.

"It's not polite to ignore people when they ask you a question," he said.

"You heard what she said, asshole." Russell spoke without turning his head. "Everything's peachy."

"I think you meant to say *Officer* Asshole."

Russell only glared through the windshield.

Worth watched him for a few seconds. Then he straightened his back and looked at Gwen again. "Care to walk me back inside?"

Before Gwen could open her mouth to speak, the car roared to life. Russell dropped into gear, scratched the tires, and gunned away, leaving Worth standing alone with Gwen in the dim vapor lighting of the rain-slicked lot.

Worth waited until the GTO's tail lights cornered the nearest intersection before he turned to her and asked, "Are you really okay?"

"I'm fine. You shouldn't have done that."

"That's why I'm. . . ."

"No," Gwen said. And when she looked at him, her great green eyes seemed caught somewhere between appreciation, anger, and fear. "I mean you really shouldn't have done that."

As she turned and walked back toward the entrance to the store alone, Worth noted for the first time that evening that the nasty shiner she'd come in with last week finally seemed to be fading. And she wasn't wearing the sling for her injured arm anymore.

• • •

Sorenson, the night manager, told Worth that Gwen seemed to play volleyball all year-round.

"Rough sport," Worth commented.

Sorenson stood quietly in his tie and shirtsleeves, scribbling something on his clipboard. He met Worth's eyes for a moment, then agreed that it must be.

For some reason, the exchange made Worth feel oddly guilty about how much he'd come to look forward to the shifts he worked with Gwen.

He didn't consider it a crush, really. Or maybe it was exactly that. Worth didn't know. Gwen had a sweetness, and a toughness, and a sadness that tweaked him in primal and conflicting ways.

Some nights, as Worth watched her from the cigarette case, he entertained ridiculous fantasy scenarios in which he protected her from whatever it was in her life that burdened her.

Other nights, he found himself unspooling impossible grocery-related, cop-and-checkout-girl porno clips in his mind.

Either way, he couldn't help but feel like a cretin. Worth knew damned well he was no hero. But he was no lech, either. He was just abysmally lonely. And he really didn't know Gwen at all.

He looked for her when his shift ended at five, intending to offer a safe ride somewhere. But Gwen had already punched the clock and slipped away.

· · ·

Worth didn't see Gwen again for almost a week and a half. The night she finally returned to work, she wore a cast on the same arm she'd sprained in the volleyball league. She limped through the front doors. That fading shiner had somehow darkened again. It also had spread to her other eye.

Worth waited until she took her first break before following her to the back of the store.

In the break room he found the Modell twins, Ricky and Curtis, clowning around with box cutters and a target drawn on cardboard. Worth grinned and nodded and said, "Guys."

"Hey, Top Cop, hop in," Ricky said. Or maybe it was Curtis. Worth could never tell. "Best throw out of three. Loser buys."

"Buys what?"

"Whatever."

Worth laughed.

"Cut me a rain check," he said, tipping his head toward the door, "and I'll school you two momentarily."

Ricky and Curtis looked at Worth. They looked at the table in the corner, where Gwen smoked a cigarette. She sat forward, cast across her lap, narrow shoulders bunched.

The Modell boys looked at one another. Then they gave Worth a nod and ambled out of the break room, trading shoulder punches as they went.

Matthew couldn't help but note the way Gwen flinched at the sound of fists smacking flesh. He closed the break room door behind the twins and turned around.

161

"Gwen," he said softly. "I want you to do me a favor."

"Sure," she said. She didn't look at him. "Let's hear it, first."

"Actually, it's a couple of favors." Worth moved across the room and sat down in the chair across from her. "First, I want you to file a report with me. Then I want you to let me take you somewhere."

Gwen took a drag from her cigarette and gazed at the corner of the room.

"Somewhere," she said.

"Yes."

"You mean a shelter. You can say it."

"I mean a place where you'll be safe."

Now she looked him in the eye. "I guess you know where you can find a place like that?"

Her voice remained clear and calm, but the tip of her cigarette trembled in her fingers. Worth took a chance, leaned forward, and placed his hand gently on her left shoulder. When he touched her, Gwen winced and bit her lip. Her green eyes welled.

"Gwen."

And suddenly it was as if the tremble in her cigarette radiated from the glowing ash into her body, traveling up her wrist, into her arm, all the way to the shoulder beneath his hand. She looked at the corner.

Then she looked at him and said, "Can I show you something?"

• • •

She moved with slow, conservative gestures, one button at a time. When she finally let the blouse slip from her shoulders, Worth's heart sagged.

Gwen's slim back was a mass of color. Blues and purples and blacks. He saw knuckle marks along the yellowed edges near her ribs, a scatter of crusted cigarette burns between her shoulder blades. He saw dime-sized keloid patches where old burns had scabbed and gone to scar.

Without thinking, Worth stood and touched her bare shoulders. When Gwen cried out, he pulled back and let his hands hover.

"Christ," he said. "I'm so sorry."

"It's not your fault," she said. "I'm the one who called you by your first name in front of him. You'd think I'd know better by now."

As Worth stood behind her, miming contact, Gwen seemed to shudder from scalp to soles. The longer she displayed herself, the less guarded she seemed, as if she'd shed some crucial protective layer along with the blouse. Gwen's tremble became a hitching quake. For one idiotic moment, the only thing Worth could think to do was offer her a Jolly Rancher from his gun belt. He lifted her blouse back over her shoulders instead.

That was when she turned, and he saw the dull vacancy in her eyes, and he realized she was not sobbing, but shivering.

He could barely hear her when she asked, "Can I show you something else?"

• • •

ronically, his time in exile at the CostRite reminded Worth of the reason he'd decided he wanted to become a cop in the first place.

As a teen, he'd been the one freak who actually enjoyed his part-time job at the supermarket. He liked the atmosphere. He liked to imagine the stories behind the people pushing the carts. He got a kick out of trying to peg somebody's home life based on their purchases, their coupons, their final bill.

Even after he'd graduated high school and moved on to college, Worth remained the one zero who never really wanted to move up to the cash register, or the stock room, or front-end management.

Because Worth had actually enjoyed sacking people's groceries. He valued the personal contact; he loved the challenge, the strategy involved. There was a kind of art in fitting a mountain of miscellaneous shapes and sizes into a few uniform packages. Heavy stuff on the bottom, fragile stuff on top. Solvents and edibles safely quarantined.

Worth enjoyed helping people out to their cars, took satisfaction in getting them on their way. He felt good when they said thanks and meant it.

The irony?

Only in the realization that he'd felt infinitely more useful wearing an apron and a name tag than he'd ever felt wearing a gun belt and a badge.

Gwen's apartment was cold because she'd cranked the air conditioner. She pointed to the bedroom door but wouldn't go inside.

Nightstick creaking softly in its loop, handcuffs rattling against their snap, Worth entered the room and turned on the light and stood at the foot of the bed for a long time.

Russell lay tangled in the red-soaked sheets where he'd died. On the other side of the bed, Worth found the bedside table lamp Gwen had used to smash Russell's face while he slept. The lamp remained on the carpet where she'd dropped it, its stout base still clotted with tissue and hair.

For one numb moment, Worth didn't know what he found most depressing about the scene: the bludgeoned corpse, the thought of Gwen finally finding herself able to swing that lamp down, or the idea that with his luck, he could conceivably wind up playing first-officer-on-scene to that miserable prick Vargas in Homicide.

When he emerged from the meat-locker bedroom, Worth found Gwen sitting on the floor of the kitchenette, arms wrapped tight around her knees. He grabbed a tattered afghan from the back of the ratty couch and took it over to her.

164

"I guess I owe you that favor now," she said.

Worth straightened and tore his radio handset from its mooring on his sleeve. He lifted the mic to his lips, squeezed the button, opened his mouth, and didn't say a word.

After staring at the floor a long while, Worth picked up the receiver to the phone on the wall and started to dial. Then he looked at Gwen, stopped what he was doing, and returned to the bedroom.

Standing there with Russell–with what would surely be identified as Russell with the aid of a forensic exam–Worth found himself thinking, of all things, about his own wrecked marriage.

You want to know your problem? This had been the last thing Sondra had said before dumping him for Vargas in Homicide. *You don't matter. But for some reason, you don't seem to care.*

Worth thought about that.

He thought about Gwen. He wondered what she was studying in school.

He looked at the faceless body on the bed and thought about the Russells of the world. He wondered what a good cop would be doing right now.

For no real reason, Worth thought about how sad it was that people had gotten so accustomed to watching some apathetic teenager drop the milk jug on top of the eggs that a woman had actually tried tipping him for nothing more than trying to put a little extra "serve" in Protect and Serve.

He wondered about the temperature in the apartment. He wondered how long Russell had been down.

Finally, Worth asked himself the only question he felt qualified to ask. When he felt he had the answer, he closed the bedroom door.

Definitely plastic, Worth thought, as he made his way back to the kitchenette to hunt for supplies.

165

Another Maviano discovery, Conard sent us a couple of stories right about the same time his first novel Dark as Night *was published by Uglytown.* PwG *published two "Ralphie" stories from Conard, both of which are flinchworthy and delicious if you like your hard-boiled served cold. And as you read this, keep in mind that the author's day job is working as a university professor. In philosophy. It's a* noir *world indeed.*

Ralphie, The Goods, and the Construction Worker
Mark T. Conard

Annie walked into the saloon. It was called Johnny's Place and it was where everybody hung out. Coming out of the bright afternoon sun, she had to let her eyes adjust to the darkness. She hated the sunlight. It hurt her eyes, gave her a headache, and made her freckle, and she fucking hated freckles. She was wearing her good denim skirt, a tank top, and a pair of sandals. She was thinking now maybe she should've dressed up a little more, but the only thing she really had that was dressier was her black skirt, the one that she wore to her mother's funeral, and that wouldn't have looked right, not in the middle of the afternoon.

When her eyes adjusted she looked around and spotted Ralphie sitting with his friends at a table. She walked over to them, trying not to hurry, trying not to look like she was in a hurry. They were laughing and joking, and it was obvious they'd been drinking. They didn't even seem to notice that she was standing there. Quentin was telling a story about his little brother. His little brother was a retard, and Quentin was telling a funny story about how the kid stuck a knife in a light socket, how he shocked himself and then yelled out in this funny retard way. Quentin imitated the yell and everyone laughed.

Pete asked if he had smoke coming out of his hair, you know the way they do in the cartoons, when he stuck that knife in the light socket, and Quentin stared at him a moment and told him not to be stupid.

Annie spoke up then, saying, "Ralphie? Ralphie, can I talk to you?" and her voice sounded too eager. She fucking hated her voice when it sounded like that.

The guys went on drinking and joking, and Ralphie seemed to be ignoring her. She walked over to his side of the table and put a hand on his shoulder. "Ralphie? Can I talk to you a minute?"

Ralphie drank down the whiskey that was in his glass, then belched.

Pete nodded at her and said, "Ralphie, Annie wants to talk to you."

Ralphie looked over at him like he'd said something very stupid. "No kidding?" he asked. "How'd you fuckin' figure that one out?" Quentin laughed out loud, and spit flew from his mouth.

Annie bent down close to his ear. "Ralphie, can I talk to you?" she said, this time in a warm voice, making sure that he could feel her breath on his ear and neck. She fucking loved her voice when it sounded like that.

He looked up at her. "What about?"

She looked at Quentin and Pete, then said, "It's kinda private," using that same voice again.

He kept looking up at her, and their eyes met, and she felt his hand touch her leg. His hand slid up the inside of her leg, under the denim skirt, and she didn't move and didn't let her

167

eyes move away from his. When his hand slid all the way up between her legs, he realized she wasn't wearing any underpants and he grinned. "Okay," he said, taking back his hand, and he scooted away from the table.

They walked together across the room, over to a table away from the others. He held onto her arm, leading her as they walked. They sat down across from each other. Annie looked over at Ralphie. He was twenty-eight or twenty-nine, with red hair, redder than hers, buzzed short, and he had pale blue eyes and a full mouth. She thought he was very handsome. The only thing that detracted from his looks was a thick scar over his left eye, and that made him look rugged more than ugly.

"Carol beat up Cathy again," she said. Carol was her husband and Cathy was her oldest daughter. "He beats me up all the time," she said, "and I don't really give a shit anymore, but I just can't stand it when he hits the kids."

"Does he hit Linda, too?" Linda was her other daughter, the younger one.

"Yeah, he beats 'em both." Truth was, he hardly ever hit either one of the kids, but she wanted Ralphie to think he did. Ralphie liked the two girls.

"Whyn't you stop him?" he asked.

"I try, but he's so much bigger than me, Ralphie." She felt herself starting to cry, and she was glad that she was. She hadn't even tried; it just sort of happened.

"Whyn't you leave him?" Ralphie asked her.

"I would," she said, sniffling, "only he said he'd kill me, he'd kill all three of us, if I did."

Ralphie sat back in the chair with his hands behind his neck. "You think he's serious?"

She nodded and wiped away a tear. "I know he is. He told me he knows a guy, and this guy drives a tow truck. What he does is, he follows you around, and when he gets you someplace kinda isolated, he shoots you in your car, then takes your car to the pound and they crush it all up, and you're never found."

"I never heard of that," said Ralphie, sounding like he was impressed. "I wonder who it is."

"I don't know, but I know he's serious—Carol, I mean."

Ralphie nodded, still with his hands behind his neck. "So, what do you want me to do?"

Annie looked around quickly, then in a low voice said, "I want you to kill him for me."

Ralphie stared at her and leaned forward, putting his elbows on the table. "What makes you think I'd do something like that?"

"Oh, Ralphie, everybody knows about you," she said. "I mean, you got a reputation. People know how bad you are."

Ralphie nodded. He seemed pleased with what she'd said. "All right. I'll kill him, but I'm doing it for the girls."

She smiled warmly at him. "Thanks, Ralphie. Thanks a bunch."

"It's gonna cost you, you know?"

She nodded eagerly. "I figured that."

"Can you get out tonight?"

She frowned, thinking about it. "I don't know. Maybe. I might be able to use my neighbor as an excuse."

"Well, see if you can. Get out tonight and come over to my place, and we'll start working on that payment."

She smiled and felt herself getting moist and warm. She would've fucked Ralphie for fun or for no reason at all. Making like it was a payment for services made it seem dirty, and that excited her even more.

"If you can't get a sitter, bring the girls," Ralphie said. "We can find something for them to do."

Annie nodded. She liked the fact that Ralphie liked her

169

kids. She didn't care anything about his reputation. So long as he liked her kids, he was all right with her.

She pushed away from the table, stood up, and walked slowly across the floor. She was hoping he was watching her as she walked, but when she reached the door, she turned back to look at him, and he was already sitting at the other table with his friends again and wasn't paying any attention to her.

Quentin and Pete had ordered more whiskey and had drunk theirs but left Ralphie's sitting by his empty chair. Ralphie sat down at the table and took a drink.

"What'd she want?" asked Quentin.

"Oh, nothing," said Ralphie. "She wants me to kill Carol."

Pete whistled.

Quentin said, "Yeah? You gonna do it?"

Ralphie sighed. "I don't know. I guess. I told her I would. I suppose there isn't really any reason not to."

Pete whistled again, then said, "How you gonna do it?"

Ralphie frowned at him. "Don't ask stupid questions, Pete," he said, and Pete shrugged.

Quentin said, "Hey, while you were over there, look what walked in," and he nudged Ralphie and pointed over to a man a few tables away. The man was small, probably in his fifties, and he had small features. He was balding on top, and he had a little moustache, glasses, and he had little girly hands with several rings on his fingers. He was wearing a denim jacket over a faded red tee-shirt. He sat at the table by himself, sipping a drink and reading a book.

"Yeah, so?" asked Ralphie.

"He's funny looking, ain't he?" said Quentin.

Ralphie nodded. "Hey, you're right, he is." Then Ralphie called over to the bartender. "Hey Charlie, come here a minute, will you?"

170

Charlie the bartender came around the bar. He was wiping his hands with a dish towel as he approached the table. Ralphie nodded to the funny looking man. "Who's that?"

Charlie glanced over at him, then looked back at Ralphie. "Never seen him before."

Ralphie frowned. "Stranger, huh? What's he drinking?"

"Coke with a lime in it," Charlie said.

"Coke with a lime!" said Pete loudly.

Both Quentin and Ralphie looked at him angrily.

"You're really stupid sometimes, Pete," said Ralphie.

"Yeah, but Coke with lime in it?" said Pete in a hushed voice. "There's something wrong with that."

Ralphie nodded, like he was agreeing with Pete now. "Let's just go have a talk with this guy," he said, and he stood up. Pete and Quentin stood up with him, and Charlie went back to what he was doing behind the bar.

The three of them walked over to the other table and stood over the little man. For a moment they just stood there, and he kept looking at his book. Ralphie looked down at his glass to see that, sure enough, he really was drinking Coke with a lime in it. Finally, the man looked up at them and closed his book, marking his place with his finger. "Yes?" he said, and he had a rather squeaky voice.

"What you drinking there, stranger?" said Ralphie.

The little man looked down at his glass, then back at Ralphie. "Coke," he said.

"Yeah, but it's got a lime in it!" said Pete eagerly.

The man looked over at Pete. "That's right. It's got a lime in it," and his voice was definitely squeaky and high-pitched. It made him sound like the cartoon mouse on TV.

Pete laughed. "Why the hell do you drink it like that?"

The man shrugged. "I like it like that," and Pete laughed again, even louder this time.

Ralphie tugged on Quentin's arm. The two of them turned

171

aside and took a step away from the table. "I'll tell you what," said Ralphie in a whisper. "That ain't no man."

Quentin frowned and glanced back at the little man. "What d'you mean?"

"I mean, that's a woman."

Quentin frowned harder. "You're joking?"

"No," said Ralphie, "I ain't. That's a woman."

"He's bald and has a moustache," said Quentin.

"She's one of those transsexuals," said Ralphie.

"Get out!" said Quentin.

Then Pete joined their huddle. "What're you guys talking about?"

"Ralphie says this guy's a transsexual," said Quentin, hooking his thumb back over his shoulder.

"You mean he likes to wear women's clothes?" said Pete.

"No," said Ralphie, "I mean this is a woman who had a sex change operation to become a man."

Pete laughed loudly. "You're crazy," he said. "She's bald and has a moustache."

"They take hormones," said Ralphie. "The women take male hormones and that way they can grow moustaches."

Quentin said, "Hey, that's right, they do."

Pete whistled. "No kidding?"

"Yeah," said Ralphie, "and you know what else? If you're a man, they cut off your dick, but if you're a woman, they make a dick for you and sew it on."

"No shit!" said Pete.

"What do they make it out of?" asked Quentin.

"Hell if I know," said Ralphie. "Rubber maybe."

"Whyn't they take the dicks from the guys and sew 'em onto the girls?" asked Pete.

"Don't be stupid," said Ralphie, but then he thought maybe that wasn't such a bad idea after all.

"Why don't we check it out and see?" said Quentin.

Pete nodded. "Yeah, I'd like to see what her dick looks like, if they made it look real, or what."

Ralphie said, "Then it's agreed—we need to get a look at her dick." Then the three of them turned back to the little "man" sitting there. He'd gone back to reading his book, but he had a nervous look about him now, like maybe he knew what they were going to do, or had even overheard what they'd been saying.

Ralphie said, "Excuse me, *Sir*—" and all three of them chuckled, "but we'd sure like to have a look at your goods."

The little man frowned heavily, and his mouth dropped open. "What?"

"Yeah," said Pete, "We'd like to get a look at that homemade dick of yours!"

The man dropped his book and made a scared move like he was going to try to run, and the three of them caught him and dragged him out from behind the table, upsetting the Coke with lime in it. He was yelling to the bartender in his high-pitched voice, and the three of them were laughing the whole time. They started dragging him kicking across the bar, and finally they just lifted him off the floor and carried him towards the men's room. His glasses fell of his face and broke against the floor, and he kept crying out in his cartoon voice for the bartender to do something. When they got to the men's room, Pete said in a loud voice, "Hey, maybe she ain't allowed in here!" and they laughed harder.

They pushed open the door to the men's room and carried him inside. Pete kicked the door closed, and they laid him down on the dirty urine-stained floor. He was yelling and kicking the whole time, and finally he got his arm loose and punched Quentin in the side of the face. Quentin stopped laughing then and drew back and smashed the little man in the mouth, and his head snapped back and hit the tiled floor

173

hard, and he went limp. He wasn't out, but he was dazed and wasn't fighting any more.

Pete and Quentin unzipped his fly then and pulled down his pants. He was wearing white jockey shorts and they were little like a boy's, like they were boy's sized. "Okay," Ralphie said, standing over them. "Pull his shorts down and let's get a look."

Pete giggled and grabbed the elastic and pulled down his shorts, and they all three got a look at the goods. He had a little scrotum and a perfectly formed little penis that was circumcised, and both were nearly hairless. "Wow," said Pete, "that looks real!"

Ralphie straightened up then. "You dimwit," he said. "It *is* real."

"What? So they did like I said and cut this off some guy and sewed it on her?"

"No, stupid," said Quentin. "This ain't no transsexual."

"Huh?" said Pete, standing up too. "I don't get it. How'd she get this dick to look so real?"

Ralphie smacked him playfully on the head. "It *is* a real dick–don't you get it? It's a man!"

"Oh, shit!" said Pete, laughing. "I guess he's allowed in here after all!"

Quentin and Ralphie started laughing with him, and they left the little man laying there on the dirty floor as they walked back out of the bathroom. On the way out Ralphie said, "You know I think I'll try one of those Cokes with a lime in it."

And Pete said, "Oh, man, that's fucking gross," and the three of them laughed even harder.

II

Annie was getting the kids their supper, when there was a knock at the door. She warned them to eat their weenies and baked beans, then walked out of the kitchen, across the living room and opened the front door. Ralphie was standing there on the porch. He grinned at her through the screen door, standing there in the yellow porch light. "Ralphie, Jesus, I didn't expect to see you!"

"Well," Ralphie said, "you gonna invite me in, or what?"

Annie turned her head, like there might've been someone behind her listening. She lowered her voice. "Carol's gonna be home pretty soon."

Ralphie shrugged. "I don't care."

"Well, okay," she said, "just for a few minutes, I guess," and she pushed at the screen door.

He opened it the rest of the way and walked in. He'd been to their house a few times before, but always in the afternoon when Carol was working. He looked around at the mismatched furniture, at the sofa with the holes in it, and at Carol's stupid picture of John Wayne hanging on the wall.

Annie was wearing a faded pair of jeans and a pink Tee-shirt that had a picture of a teddy bear on it. She wished she looked better for Ralphie. She wanted him to want her. "Can I get you something to drink?" she asked him.

He shrugged again. "What're the girls doing?"

"They're eating, having their dinner." She paused, then said, "You wanna say hi to them?"

"Sure," Ralphie said. He'd always liked Annie's girls. They were cute, and both of them were smart as whips.

The two of them walked into the kitchen. The kids were fighting over a spoon. Annie said, "Hey, girls, look who's here!"

175

They both looked up and grinned at Ralphie standing in the doorway to the kitchen. "Hi Ralphie!" they said in unison.

Ralphie walked over to the table. "How are you girls?" He put a hand on each of their shoulders and gave them a little squeeze.

"Fine," said Cathy, the older girl. She had shoulder-length straight blond hair that was almost white and bright blue eyes. She was eight now and very smart. She said things that you wouldn't expect an eight year old to say. "How are you, Ralphie?"

"Oh, I'm fine," he said to her. "What you having for dinner?"

"We're having beans and weenies," said Linda. She was six, and just as cute as a little girl could be, with dirty blond hair that was naturally curly.

"Sounds good," said Ralphie. "Say, me and your mom want to have a little talk."

"Okay," said Cathy, going back to her supper.

"So you'll be all right in here by yourselves for a few minutes?" Ralphie asked her.

"Of course we will," said Cathy. "We're not babies!"

"No, you sure aren't," said Ralphie, and he tousled her hair.

Ralphie looked over at Annie, and she gave him an uncertain, worried glance. He nodded to her, and they walked out of the kitchen. Out in the living room, he grabbed her by the arm and directed her into the master bedroom. He closed the door behind them. "Ralphie!" said Annie. "I'm telling you—Carol's going to be home any minute!"

Ralphie pushed her up against the door roughly and grabbed the front of her shirt. "Do I look like I'm worried?" and he tore at her shirt until it ripped in half, right through the teddy bear. He pulled it the rest of the way off and tossed it to the floor, exposing her chest and the black brassiere she was wearing.

"Oh, fuck," she said, getting very excited. "Oh, fuck."

176

Ralphie grabbed her by the waistline of her jeans and pulled her into him. Their bodies met, and he stuck his tongue in her mouth. Annie shot her hands down his hips, then across his groin, feeling his cock, his very large cock through his trousers. Ralphie pulled away from her and pushed her over to the bed, face down. He reached around and unzipped her jeans, and pulled them down around her ankles. She wasn't wearing any underwear. Annie arched her hips then, and Ralphie unzipped his fly and took out his cock and mounted her from behind. He began to pump her very hard, and she moaned. She was very wet, very excited, and Ralphie came quickly, and Annie yelped when she felt him coming.

Ralphie pulled out of her and stood up. He grabbed her Tee-shirt from the floor and wiped his dick with it, then put it away and zipped up. Annie rolled over onto her back on the bed. "Mmmm…" she said, her eyes closed. She was running her fingers across her breasts. "God, Ralphie, I love the way you fuck me."

Then from the other room they heard the front door open. "Oh, shit!" Annie whispered. "It's Carol—he's home! Shit, what're we gonna do?"

"Relax," Ralphie said.

"You gotta hide!" she said quickly, sitting up on the bed.

"No fucking way," Ralphie said, smirking.

"Ralphie!"

"Hey—you want me to take care of things, right?"

Annie looked up at him. "Tonight? You're gonna do it tonight? Now? Right here?"

Ralphie shrugged. "Sure, why not?"

"Ralphie! The kids are here!"

"That's okay," Ralphie said. "I brought my silencer." He drew his pistol from its holster, then reached into the pocket of his jacket and pulled out the silencer. He fitted it onto the end of the barrel and screwed it into place. "The kids won't hear a thing."

"Fuck, Ralphie! Fuck," said Annie, as she went to the dresser and pulled out a new tee-shirt. This one was yellow and had a picture of a baby duck on it.

The doorknob turned just as Annie was pulling the Tee-shirt over her head, and the door swung open. Carol stood in the doorway. He was thin and muscular, with dark brown hair, and he was unshaven. He was wearing a sleeveless white Tee-shirt, jeans and work boots. Carol did construction work, he was strong, and he had a nasty temper.

Ralphie stood against the bedroom closet with the pistol behind his back. Annie was trying to get herself straightened up, smoothing her hair and zipping her jeans.

"What the fuck's going on here?" Carol said.

"Hey, Carol," said Ralphie casually.

"What the fuck're you doing in my house?" Carol asked. "What the fuck're you doing in my bedroom?"

"Nice to see you, Carol," said Ralphie. "Me and Annie were just having a little chat."

"Get the fucking hell outta my house!" Carol yelled.

"Shhhh," Ralphie said, putting a finger to his lips, the pistol still behind his back. "You're gonna scare the girls."

"I don't give a fuck—!"

"Hey!" Ralphie said, whipping the pistol around and pointing it at Carol now. "I told you not to fucking yell!" Carol's eyes bulged at the sight of the gun. "Now close the fucking door," Ralphie told him. Carol did; he closed the bedroom door and turned back to face the two of them. "Good," said Ralphie, and he quickly aimed and shot Carol through the bridge of the nose. Annie screamed, and Carol tumbled to the floor in a heap.

There was a smear of blood and maybe brains on the white bedroom door about the height where Carol's head had been.

"Shit," said Ralphie, "I was aiming for his eye, but I got him right through the nose."

There was a fast knock at the door. "Mommy?" said Cathy's voice. "Mommy, what happened? What's going on?"

"Nothing," Ralphie said through the door. "Nothing at all. Go back to your dinner, sweetheart."

"Is Mommy okay?"

"I'm fine, honey," Annie said. "Go on back in the kitchen."

They heard her little feet padding across the living room floor and into the kitchen. Ralphie unscrewed the silencer from his pistol and put them both away. He walked over and nudged Carol's body with the toe of his shoe. "He's dead," Ralphie reported.

"Oh, Ralphie," said Annie, stepping up beside him, her hand to her mouth.

"Yeah? It's what you wanted, isn't it?"

"Sure . . . sure it is. I'm just, you know, a little freaked out now, looking at him laying there like that."

Ralphie reached over and grabbed her hand then, and placed it on his cock. "I don't know why," he said, "but killing somebody always makes me horny."

Annie rubbed his swelling cock through his trousers, while she stared at the body on the floor. Ralphie got her attention then, and put a hand on her shoulder and eased her down onto the floor, on her knees. She was kneeling now beside Carol's dead body, and she unzipped Ralphie's pants and took his penis out. She stroked it with her hand, as she stole another look at the body. "Oooo... Ralphie, there's blood on the floor," she said, pointing with her free hand.

"That's okay," he said, "you can clean that up later," and he grabbed the back of her head with his hand and turned it to face him. She opened her mouth then and took his penis and started sucking it.

Annie knew how to give a good blow job, and Ralphie was

179

getting very excited. He didn't like to come standing up, though, so he pulled his dick out of her mouth and turned her around, and knelt down behind her. She was facing the dead body now, Carol's dead body, laying inches in front of her on the floor in a pool of blood. Ralphie reached around and unzipped her jeans again and pulled them down around her knees. He climbed down on the floor on top of her, and mounted her once more. Her pussy was even hotter and wetter than it was the first time, like killing her husband had excited her, too. Ralphie started thrusting into her, pounding her, the both of them looking at that dead body, and in a moment they both started to come. Ralphie could feel her coming, feel the contractions, and it made him come, and they both made little noises and came together.

Ralphie gave her a few more strokes and finally pulled out of her. His knees were weak now, and he laid down on the floor beside her. They both had their heads resting against Carol's dead body. "God, Ralphie," she said. "That was *so* good. I haven't been fucked like that in a long time."

"Carol wasn't giving it to you, huh?" he asked her.

"No. You know that little slut, Lisa Miller? I think he was fucking her."

"Lisa Miller?" said Ralphie like he couldn't believe it. "Jesus, you're way better looking than she is."

"You're so sweet, Ralphie. Carol would never say nice things like that to me. At least he hasn't for a long time."

"Well, I'm not saying it to be nice," he said. "I mean it. You're hands down better looking than she is. I mean, you've got a great little body, and she's fat if you ask me."

"She's a goddamned hippo," said Annie.

Ralphie laughed. "A hippo—that's a good one. I'll have to tell Quentin and Pete you said that. A hippo. Shoot."

Annie reached over and kissed him lightly on the cheek. "Anyway," she said. "I think you're sweet."

Tribe. Mysterious, prolific, innovative. He sent these mind-blowing stories in our early days, at one point even teaming up with artist Haze McEllhenny for a bizarre but fascinating illustrated story. Haze went on to design an issue later and publish a piece of her own.

But back to Tribe. He and Darren Subarton and Kevin Jones Miller and so many others were the reasons we started this thing called Plots with Guns. *They had a tough time getting their work out to the public because no one really knew what to do with a well-written, literary-styled hard-boiled tale that pushed convention, hot buttons, and sometimes moral boundaries. We did. These writers found the audiences they deserved.*

As for Tribe, odd thing. He stopped writing. After several great pieces in a row, he just…quit. We still talk to the guy every now and then, wishing him well, but we're also hoping he'll get back in the game where he belongs—writing gloriously filthy noir.

Twenty-five Variations on "Folsom Prison Blues"
Tribe

We pull off I-75 onto an exit ramp and into Toledo with Johnny Cash singing "Folsom Prison Blues" for the seven-teenth time since we left Detroit.

I've been keeping track.

Ya know, it's like we're wrapped in a cocoon in this Mercedes. Us with Johnny Cash.

These new cars. They seal up their occupants from the rest of the world. All you can hear in them are the sounds you make.

You actually pay extra for this.

Pay up, seal yourself in, and get off on the ride.

In the passenger seat Emma sits with her feet curled under her, looking out the windows, her bare foot keeping time to the song. She never puts her feet on the floor. Her shagged blonde hair flutters in the blast air-conditioning. Her skinny legs are light blue from the chill.

Emma's dirty footprints are all over the black leather. Earlier she'd been sitting with her feet pointing toward me. Two perfectly centered and defined footprints are now imprinted on the side of the driver's seat. It looks like a ghost covered in brown talcum has taken a stroll over the inside of the SLK.

There isn't too much blood. Not as much as you'd expect. Emma shot him outside of the car. He spurted most of it out on the corner of Jefferson and Mt. Elliot a little over an hour ago back in Detroit.

183

Seems like it was weeks ago now. Gun. Flash. Noise. Burn. It's what God must sound like. On one of his better days.

I crammed his body behind the front seats of the roadster. You'd think it can't be done. You'd be surprised.

Emma blotted his blood from the seats with pages from an *Utne Reader* she'd found in the pocket of the passenger door. Heading south, Emma gets bored with the bloody *Utne Reader* not two minutes onto the Fisher Freeway and then starts thumbing through the car's owner's manual. She does something to the leather binding of the manual because its pages are now scattered all over the car.

This all starts seventeen "Folsom Prison Blues" ago. Who would've thought the prep squashed in the back would have Johnny Cash on the CD player of a Mercedes? I would have expected Music from the Rain Forest or Whale Songs or something precious like that. Yet sure as shit, the silver needle twang of "Folsom Prison Blues" comes on as I spin the car south onto Jefferson.

I dare say that "Folsom Prison Blues" sums up my whole worldview on the drive down I-75. It's an unexpected discovery.

There's this one French guy, a writer I think, whose whole life suddenly takes on some new clarity because he smells something that reminds him of his youth. Just one smell and he writes this book that runs several volumes.

I'm not French, much less a writer. Hell, even reading can be a task sometimes.

But "Folsom Prison Blues" takes me back.

I'm sitting in front of our trailer in Hazel Park on a summer evening listening to Ernie Harwell call the Tigers' game. In the background, my mom sings along to country songs. I watch the pus-colored smog over Detroit (or Dee-troit, as we would call it) slowly turn purple, then black, and the game drifts into late innings. Mom sings Patsy Cline. She sings Hank Williams.

It's a Saturday night. I'm coming home from Tiger Stadium. I walk up the gravel road in the trailer court. I see my fuck of an old man's rig parked where it usually is when he's home weekends. Home from some over-the-road run to East Jesus, Arkansas.

The inside of the trailer looks like downtown Detroit after the riots. The 8-track's on full-blast with "Folsom Prison Blues."

My old man's sitting on the couch. Only he doesn't have a face. My momma's on the sofa next to him. She's looking through a shoe box of wedding pictures. The shotgun's propped up between her and what's left of him.

My mom's black-and-blue face breaks into a smile when she looks up at me. She's missing teeth where she had some this afternoon. Right then she breaks into "I shot a man in Reno, just to watch him die."

She sings Johnny Cash. She laughs. She cries.

And I haven't been back.

As "Folsom Prison Blues" winds down, I hit the replay button on the CD player. We head south on Detroit Avenue through the grime that's Toledo. I drive over potholes that ricochet right up through the car's tight suspension.

The dead guy's arm slips out from behind the seats and his hand falls on the stick shift. Emma kicks it toward me with her filthy foot. I shove it back behind the seat.

"Light me a smoke," I ask Emma. She slips hers between my lips and lifts the little fanny pack onto her lap with her big toe. She takes out the gun and her sunglasses.

She lights a Marlboro and says that we're gonna need to stop and get more. "Is there any money left?" I ask. She shakes her head and goes back to looking out the window.

"He's gotta have a wallet," I say. "Check and see." Emma pulls the seatback forward as far as she can. She struggles with the body back there. She hits her head on the roof of the SLK when I plow through another pothole.

I'm not surprised when Emma shoots the guy. She just has this way of dealing with things, I guess. I'm not surprised when I stuff his carcass behind the two seats in a Mercedes Benz SLK.

I don't know. It's what needs to be done. No sense in trying to figure it all out like I'm prone to do.

I didn't exactly expect Emma to blow this guy away, mind you. She has a reputation. From what I've heard anyway.

But, you know, all that being said, I don't have any inkling that shooting people for their Mercedes is a surprise she has in store for me. And then again, it may be a leap to assume that the surprise is for my benefit.

It's when I start to answer my questions with more questions that my head starts to hurt.

So I keep it simple. The fucked stunt that Emma pulls is just not behavior that I typically engage in. I'm not saying that I'm an Angel of God or anything like that.

Far from it. This ain't the only hell my momma's son ever raised.

I guess all I'm saying is I understand.

Things like this happen.

I betcha they happen all the time.

I just want to take the car. Take us for a long drive, dump it somewhere, and come back on the bus. Or not come back. Ya know, however it turns out. The plan's that loose.

And some of that plan, if you want to call it that, is still in place.

If you want my opinion, we're committed.

To a long drive, anyway.

I laugh out loud. It's more of a release than anything. Two sharp barks.

"Emma, this is so fucked up." Johnny Cash growls ". . .that train keeps a-rollin, all down to San Antone." I hit the replay button.

We continue down Detroit Avenue. Gangbangers turn to watch the Mercedes bumping along the pocked street.

The car's tinted windows muddy everything up. It's just sounds from the outside world that are banned from the interior of the SLK. It also makes us invisible.

The sounds and sights inside the car stay here. In this SLK world we're creating. Everyone else in the out there is blind to who the occupants of this car are. No one is wise to white trash from De-troit driving a car anyone with the intelligence of a three-year-old knows is stolen.

People see what they want to see.

We're not entirely moronic. We know people like us ain't supposed to be driving a Mercedes.

Especially one with the dead owner in it.

I stop at a red light. Three homeboys start to cross the street. They check out the Mercedes. They check out Emma's skinny ass as she digs behind the seat.

I lock stares with the skinny one. I reach for the button that will lower my window. I turn Johnny Cash all the way up. The bass distorts the tune like when gangstas turn up their hip-hop. I don't break my stare.

The three homeboys are standing calmly in front of the SLK. The skinny one challenges me first. "Whatchoo lookin' at, beeyatch?" Emma doesn't hear him, what with "Folsom Prison Blues" and rummaging through a dead man's pockets in a cramped car.

I put the gun on the dash and smile. A wide shit-eatin' hillbilly grin. They're close enough to see the gun through the tinted windows. The niggers cross the street. Quickly.

187

The three of them stand at the curb glaring at me. They call me pussy. They call me white trash. The tallest of the three picks up a chunk of concrete and lobs it at the car. It bounces with an ugly thud on the roof. I have no doubt it leaves a dent.

But I could give two fucks about that.

The light turns green. I get out of the SLK. I point the gun at the niggers. I hold up traffic.

All I want to do is scare them away. I don't need no more contingencies. I'm not trying to add more craziness to this thing.

Really. I'm not.

I know the degree of craziness Emma can rise up to. She leaves no fucking doubt about that back at Jefferson and Mt. Elliott.

It's my own level of craziness that I'm not certain of.

But put all that aside. I'm out of the car. I'm holding the gun. I'm pointing it.

I hear a cell phone ringing. I know I don't have one. It would be one hell of a surprise if Emma had one.

Emma kneels on the seat facing the back of the car, her forehead against the headrest, a cell phone at her ear. She turns and touches the replay button.

My face slams against the upper doorjamb. The gun flies out of my hand into the car. I grab at the homeboy. I know there are more where he came from.

He pulls at my ponytail. His knee gouges the middle of my back. My nose bleeds onto the seat.

The shot fills the car. It goes off next to my left ear. My head swells with its echo. The nigger howls. "The bitch shot me. She fuckin' shot me!" I hear him plop onto the street.

Now I move in slo mo. Johnny Cash booms. Emma is on her haunches on the seat. The gun's in one hand, the cell's in the other.

188

She postures herself like some animal. Like something inhuman. Like some skinny, pale, pock-marked virus ready to spread its contagion.

The car door is still open. I see the skinny piece of shit kneeling on the street in a puddle of blood. He moans. He doesn't have a hand no more. The others run down a side street. I want to crack his head open. I want to finish it.

But my poorly defined sense of self-preservation gets the better of me.

The Mercedes squeals through the red light. I don't remember to shut the door. Emma picks a mangled finger off the dash. She drops it into the storage console between the front seats. the door slams shut from the acceleration. There's gore along the windshield. I can't hear Johnny Cash through my left ear.

Emma grunts something into the cell phone. She hands it to me.

She turns in the seat. She curls up with an expensive-looking wallet. She pulls out twenties, credit cards.

"Lookit what I found!" She hits the replay. She holds up an expensive-looking silver one-hitter case. She twirls it in her fingers in an act of delicateness I think her nail-bitten fingers are incapable of. She slides the top to the side. She pulls out the one-hitter. Green-gray weed spills onto her lap as she taps the one-hitter into the case. "He was from Grosse Pointe," she says. The car fills with metal blue smoke.

I cradle the phone between my head and shoulder.

"Yeah?" I can't hear. "Turn it down," I say. Emma doesn't move. "Emma?"

She stares out the window again. "Will you turn that motherfucker down!" I yell.

Emma plucks at the volume control. In the same motion she slugs me on the chin. Her punch jerks my head. The cell phone flies behind the seat. I swerve into opposite traffic,

189

then back into my lane. Emma's finger is in my face. "Don't scream at me, fuck!"

The cell phone rings again.

I take a deep breath. "Emma, who is that?"

"You'd be surprised," she says to her window.

"I have to stop somewhere, Emma."

She exhales a cloud of pot smoke. She leans towards and around me behind my seat. She's exasperated. I know.

She places the ringing cell phone on her lap, takes another toke from the one-hitter. "Take the next left. There's an abandoned hospital there. Pull in behind it."

Emma rubs a sweaty palm across my face, she wipes blood off. She hits the replay button.

I park. These SLKs let the stereo keep on going until a door is opened. Johnny Cash goes on about how the train reminds him of everything he doesn't have while he sits there in Folsom.

I flip the cell phone open. "Yeah?"

"Say that again," says the voice.

"Yeah?"

"Wow . . . priceless . . . another hillbilly. . . ." the voice chuckles.

"Who the fuck is this?"

"Dang, a literate hillbilly. Compared to the slit anyways. Nah, Jethro, regardless of who I am, who we are, you and Daisy Mae there are gonna end up somewhere in Lake Erie. I wanna put that before you right from the get go. It's a done fuckin' deal. Now, how long and how painful it's gonna be for youse . . . well, ya know, we can be reasonable. We can negotiate. Me, I could give a fuck whether you want to negotiate or not. We will find you. We will kill you. We will get our property back."

"I don't want your car," I say.

Emma grabs the phone. "But I do," she says into it. "I want the fuckin' car."

Emma hands the phone back to me, takes another toke from the one-hitter, her feet against the windshield.

"Yeah," I say.

The voice chuckles again. "She just wants the car, huh? I can't fuckin' believe this . . . she wants the car. Carlo, one of 'em wants to keep the car." It chuckles again.

"Do you have any idea the world of shit you're in?"

"Not particularly."

"Tsk, tsk, tsk. White trash. Always cracks me up. You're like children. You want the shiny car. . . ."

"I don't want the car. She does. I just wanted to go for a ride."

". . .you have no clue what you're doing, just wanted to ride the shiny new car, impress Miss Bedbug there."

"Maybe you should talk to her. . . ."

"No, no, no, no. I want to talk to you, Jethro. You listening?"

"Yeah."

"Good. Now, don't try to think too hard, don't want you to hurt yourself. I think when we started this conversation, you wanted to know who the fuck I was?"

"Yeah."

"Dang, boy, you have some power of recall. It's not I. It's we. We are people who don't take kindly to having our shit stolen. Now, we can arrange to have our property returned, and we just . . . well, we just kill you. We can do something orderly like that. Or, we can eventually find you, and trust me when I say this, that your last moments on this earth are indescribably painful and degrading."

"Who are you?' I ask. That they're mobsters is beginning to dawn on me.

"Think of us as the minions of Satan. Think of us as the fucking winged monkeys from the Wizard of Oz, for all I

191

care. I just want to impress on you that you and the cunt have fucked with the wrong people. Where's the guy? You know. The one who was in the car before youse?"

"He's here."

"Well, put him on, Jethro"

"He's here, like I said . . . but he's sort of no longer with us."

"I didn't know there was any mob left in Grosse Pointe," Emma says. "That must explain the *Utne Reader.*"

The voice hears her. "That's cause he was a lawyer, Jethro. Our lawyer. And he was on our time. He was on our clock."

"He says he was a lawyer, Emma."

Emma nods, "Yeah, I knew that." I turn to her. "He has a card in his wallet. I could hardly tell you, what with shootin' the hands off of niggers and keepin' your scrawny ass out of trouble," she says to the window.

"He says he's their lawyer, Emma."

"That I didn't know," she says exhaling the pot smoke. "He didn't say that when I was on the phone with him."

"Damn," I say.

"Damn is right, motherfucker. I just wanted to find out which pieces of shit had pulled this little stunt. Now I know. I'll be in touch. Y'all just sit tight now, ya hear?" The voice chuckles again. It's like gargling bones. The phone is quiet.

I sit and don't speak. I feel alive in the creepiest way. Maybe the knowledge that death is right around the corner makes one that much more in tune with life.

Probably another one of those French fucks wrote that somewhere.

Like Johnny Cash, sitting in his cell at Folsom, listening to that train, thinking about what a grand time those folks on the train are having, how they're going far away. Away from Folsom Prison.

It all makes him that much more aware of where he is.

192

I hit the replay button and turn the SLK on. "Well," I say, "this is one red fuckin' banner day, isn't it?"

"You didn't have to come with me," Emma exhales again. "You coulda stayed behind." She shrugs.

I don't answer. It's an effort to control the overdue panic that's engulfing me.

"Light me one," I say. I light a Marlboro while I wait for Emma to load the one-hitter. I take a left back onto Detroit. "Take the next left," Emma says.

"Why don't I just go straight? Does it make any difference which direction I go?" I say. I take a toke from the one-hitter. Emma stares at a family picking up a moving van at a U-Haul. She points at them. "Everybody's on the run. Get out while you can, motherfuckers!"

I hold the cigarette and suck on the one-hitter. SLKs aren't designed for smoking. "I used to come here when I was a kid," she says. "There's a park and a river and a zoo down here." Emma's feet are on the dash.

We drive through a nice neighborhood. It's the first I've seen since we entered Toledo. We glide around the front of a park across from the Toledo Zoo. We curve down to the river's edge and park near something called the Maumee Bay Yacht Club, or something like that.

If this car belongs anywhere, it's here. The guy with the hole in his head is more likely than not one of them. If they find him, they can keep him. Bury your own, fuckers.

I hit the replay again. In the middle of "Folsom Prison."

It's just a matter of time now. This chain of events that unraveled back in Detroit. It's so . . . it's so unholy. I'm in it. I belong to it now. I allowed myself to participate in it, to be drawn into what I know is this black hole of humanity sitting next to me named Emma.

I'm dead already. Just a matter of when the heart stops beating. There's no question about that.

193

Emma passes the loaded one-hitter back to me. I draw the musky smoke deep into my lungs.

The reefer starts to make my head feel better. I don't know. There's nothing says we can't keep playing this thing by ear. With the inevitable grinning at you, it's easy to be optimistic.

The voice on the cell phone doesn't seem upset about the dead counselor at law. Even our appropriation of the Mercedes seems to be low on its list of priorities. The voice's complaint is with the theft of its property. Their property.

I ask Emma what else she found on the stiff when she was emptying its pockets. "Just the wallet and the weed," she says.

I pop the trunk and walk to the back of the Mercedes.

Everything that has taken place inside the SLK has somehow muted the death stench of the dearly departed lawyer in the interior of the car. Back here it's in full bloom. It's not rot. It's too soon for that. A stench has seeped back here. This smell that shouldn't be in a Mercedes Benz SLK creeps up into the dried blood in my nostrils. The foulness of it that much more threatening, because it mingles with the new car smell back here. It makes the comfort of the factory-installed odor seem evil.

For the first time all-day I'm actually frightened.

Johnny Cash is muffled. Yet, I instinctively hear: "well if they free me from this prison, if that old railroad train was mine, I bet I'd move it on a little farther down the line. . . ."

When I reach into the plastic garbage bag and see the money, the cell phone rings again.

"Guess what?" It's the voice. "Ya know that commotion I heard earlier over the phone when I was chatting with your Daisy Mae? The shots and stuff? We seem to have a pretty good idea where all that shit was happening."

"I could give a shit."

"Well now, that's good, Jethro. It's good you're so accepting of where things stand. It's. . . ."

194

"I think I found that property you were talking about earlier."

"Jethro, in our business we've learned to accept that there are always contingencies. Seeing how contingencies have a tendency to take on a life of their own, well, we get philosophical about it and all. See, we can cut our losses and go on to the next thing. What we don't do is forgive. And believe you me, you two will never be forgiven."

The breeze carries a dank smell rustling through the leaves from the rust-colored river. Cicadas in the trees are screeching at us. The sound reminds me of the music that plays when the girl in *Psycho* is stabbed in the shower. It's like a billion brain-damaged crickets playing a billion fiddles–constant, threatening as all hell.

The veil of sound edges out everything else.

It cuts me off. From me. From the world.

Johnny Cash starts "Folsom Prison Blues" again. I hear Emma get out of the car. Her bare feet scratch against the graveled road. She looks into the garbage bag. She leafs through the currency.

"Remember that movie *Night of the Living Dead,* Jethro? Remember what the brother says to the blonde in the cemetery at the beginning?

"'They're coming to get you.'"

The voice hangs up with a sandpaper chuckle.

I sit on the bumper of the car and close the trunk. Emma sits next to me.

"I like that," she says; she rubs the big black X tattoo on my upper arm.

"I want out of this, Emma."

"You don't have much of a choice now, do you," she says. She traces my tattoo with a finger.

"Shit Emma, all's I wanted was to go for a ride in a Mercedes."

195

Emma laughs through her nose, "I'd say you got one hell of a ride."

I throw a half-smoked cigarette onto the asphalt. Gray lines of smoke spiral out. A couple walks out of the Yacht Club. They look all tanned and healthy and monied. "Nice car," the man says. It's a taunt.

I walk to the passenger side of the SLK. I take the gun. I turn, walk right up to the couple. The woman makes a sound, a plastic squeak doll sort of sound when it's squeezed. I shoot her in the face. The man falls to his knees, he spreads his arms. He looks at me as I shoot him through his ear.

He looked surprised.

About time somebody was.

I turn to Emma. She smiles for the first time today, "Dang, sweetie. Think maybe I've made an impression on ya?" I shoot her in the mouth. She falls back into the trunk, onto the bag. Some of the money flies out in a splash of green. The soles of her filthy feet stick out of the trunk, black as her motherfucking soul.

I walk to the car, get behind the wheel. I keep it in neutral. I hit the speed dial button on the phone. The voice answers.

"Guess what?" I tell the voice. "You lose."

I do the chuckling this time. "Folsom Prison Blues" fades out. I don't hit replay.

"Check this out," I tell the voice.

I put the muzzle of the gun against my foot and shoot it. The shot vibrates through my leg up into my throbbing head, drowning out the beginning of a different song.

I have the wherewithal to hold onto the cell phone. "You hear that, motherfucker?" I scream at the voice.

I hold the the gun against my cheek. I shoot again.

I miss.

Jason Starr keeps noir *real, revitalizing the tradition of James M. Cain-style "Average Guy in Over His Head" storytelling. His protagonists are men in New York working hard to make something of their lives in the business world and in relationships, yet for all their good intentions, everything goes to hell. You can't turn away as events roll downhill quickly—you can flinch and try to put the book down, but you're hooked and can't rest until it's over, much like in this story he's written for us: "One Way Out."*

Try Starr's novels Hard Feelings, Tough Luck, *and* Twisted City *for a glimpse at the darker side of big city life.*

One Way Out
Jason Starr

It was almost twilight in October Mountain State Park in the Berkshires, and Susan and I were walking along the dark rocky path in silence. We hadn't been getting along all day, and there was no sign things would get any better. Later on, back in our room at the B&B, I was going to tell her it was time to start seeing other people. "We both know this isn't working out," I'd say. "Isn't it better that we end it now?" Naturally, she'd be very upset. I'd probably be upset too— after all, two and a half years is a long time for two people in their mid-thirties to be together—but so far this let's-find-out-where-the-relationship-is-going weekend had been a major disaster. We had been arguing almost non-stop, proving that we weren't meant for each other. After we cried all night and drove back to New York where we'd have a tearful goodbye, it might take a few weeks, or even months, to get over her, but eventually I would, and I'd probably thank God for it, too.

After about fifteen more minutes of walking in silence, wishing I was alone, I realized how it was suddenly noticeably cooler and darker, and I said, "Do you remember how to get out of here?"

"You're the one who's supposed to have the brilliant sense of direction."

"I'll take that as a no."

We continued to walk along an unfamiliar-looking path. Occasionally Susan grunted in frustration or disgust, as if it was *my* fault that we had gotten lost. This only annoyed me even more. I started walking faster, keeping a few paces ahead of her.

"What's wrong with you?" she said. "Why are you acting this way?"

I didn't answer her, knowing it would only lead to more arguing. I wished I'd broken up with her before we'd taken this trip. I wished I was back home at my apartment in Manhattan, alone, drinking a beer and relaxing on my couch watching a Yankee's game.

"Great," she said. "So now you're ignoring me. That's really intelligent, Robert. Will you please stop walking and wait for me?"

I walked a few more steps and then stopped, waiting for her to catch up with me.

She said, "So did you figure out where we're going yet?"

"What do you think?"

"You don't have to snap at me."

"Will you stop trying to start an argument every two seconds?"

"You're the one who's arguing."

"When we find our way out of here, that's it."

"What's that supposed to mean?"

I didn't answer her, figuring, at this point, it was best to be ambiguous.

We veered right along another rocky, root-covered path, walking for about a minute longer without speaking; then Susan said, "It's getting dark. What happens if we can't find our way out of here?"

"We will."

"But what if we don't? I'm not gonna spend a night in the woods."

"Can you just stop it?"

We walked for about another minute without talking. I was getting bitten up by mosquitoes, and gnats were swarming around my head.

Susan took out her cell phone and said, "Shit, I still can't get service up here. I told you this was a stupid idea."

"*You* wanted to come."

"You didn't tell me what it was like. You didn't say it would just be a forest."

"It's a State Park. What did you expect it to be like?"

"You know there are bears in these woods."

"Who told you that?"

"The woman who runs the B&B. She told me a story—how one time a bear came into the town or something and they had to call in somebody from the gaming commission."

"We won't see any bears."

"How do you know?"

"I think I see a road."

We walked faster toward an opening in the woods.

"Thank God," Susan said. "This is the last time I ever go hiking with you."

It sure will be, I thought, hearing myself later saying, "I want to break up with you." It was going to be so liberating to finally say that simple sentence, to suddenly be released from the burden of a bad relationship.

"I want to be engaged by Christmas."

199

It was the second anniversary of the night we'd met. We had gone out to dinner at a nice Portuguese restaurant on Restaurant Row, and then we had theater tickets to see The Lion King. *But in the cab ride back to my place she had to put a downer on the whole night by trying to get me to make a commitment to her.*

"Come on," I said. "Let's not talk about that tonight."

"Why not?" she said. "It's been two years you know."

As if I was such a louse I didn't know what anniversary we were celebrating.

"Why do you have to put this kind of pressure on me?"

"I want to know where this is going–if you're serious about me or not."

Staring out the cab window I didn't answer her right away. Then, still looking out the window, I said, "I really don't think this is the time to discuss this."

After that night, I started noticing all of Susan's flaws, which I had overlooked until then. She was too controlling, too demanding, too uptight, too stuffy. I began to forget why I'd started dating her in the first place. True, she was very attractive. She was thin with small toned muscles and long stylish brown hair, and she always dressed well and took good care of herself–dieting constantly, doing Pilates and yoga, and going to the gym fanatically, five or six times a week. But there was nothing very unusual about her appearance either. There were thousands of women in New York, a lot of them better looking than Susan, who didn't come with nearly as much baggage as she did.

I decided that the only reason she was interested in me at all was because I was a successful lawyer. She often talked about how she had broken up with her previous boyfriend, Dave the actor, because he wasn't on "a career track." Outside of having similar backgrounds–we grew up in adjacent towns on Long Island–Susan and I had almost nothing in common. She worked in advertising and always seemed bored when I talked about something that was going on at my job, and I was the same way about her career.

I knew that our relationship was Susan's main topic of conversation with her friends. "Did Robert get you a ring yet?" "Do you think he'll pop the question soon?" "How much more time are you going to give him? "Getting a ring" from me seemed to be becoming her true M.O. It had nothing to do with me anymore or getting married. I felt like it was all a game to her and that I was the prize. Once she got a ring from me, the game would be over, and then it would be on to a new game–having children. I felt like I was being manipulated, used.

"Where do you think this road leads?" Susan asked.

I realized that Susan had asked me the same question a few seconds ago.

"I have no idea," I said, "but it's going downhill. It probably leads to the parking lot where we left the car."

"It's going to be pitch dark in like two minutes."

"Let's just keep walking."

Just then I heard the sound of an engine, probably a truck, and then headlights appeared on the road. The driver had the vehicle's brights on, and Susan and I both squinted, shielding our eyes. The vehicle stopped above the road, about fifty yards ahead of us.

"Let's ask for a lift," Susan said.

Usually, as a paranoid New Yorker, I never would have even considered such an idea. At home, I didn't even know the names of the people who lived in the apartments next door to me and, like my mother taught me, I never spoke to strangers. But now getting a lift down the mountain didn't seem like such a bad idea. It was going to be dark soon and I was tired and I was sick of fighting with Susan. The idea of

201

getting back to the room at the B&B sooner, rather than later, was appealing.

"All right," I said.

We started walking faster, toward the back of what I could now tell was a truck, when the headlights went off. It was still bright enough to see a silhouette taking something off the back of the truck and carrying it into the woods.

I squeezed Susan's hand and stopped walking.

"What's wrong?"

"Sshh," I said.

I pulled her off the road, toward the woods. We were still at least twenty yards away, and I didn't think whoever was in the truck had seen us.

"What are—"

I put my hand over Susan's mouth and whispered, "Be quiet. I think I saw that guy carrying a body off that truck."

I moved my hand away and Susan said in a quieter voice, but not whispering, "Are you crazy?"

"I'm telling you it looked like a body," I said. "And keep your voice down."

I heard a door slam—the guy getting back in the truck—and then the engine and headlights went on and the truck started moving slowly in our direction. I pulled Susan back into the woods and we knelt down as the truck—it was red, probably a flat-bed Ford—sped by.

"You idiot," Susan said. "Thanks to you we're going to have to walk in the dark."

"And I suppose you'd rather get a lift from a killer."

"What killer? You're always so paranoid, it drives me crazy. He was probably dumping something else out—a bag of garbage or something."

"I'm telling you it was body."

"You wanna go look at it?"

The sound of the truck had almost faded completely.

"Fine," I said.

Susan let out on annoyed breath, making that face I hated, the one where her jaw dropped, exposing her lower teeth, and then followed me down the road toward where the truck had been parked. I hoped she was right—I could have lived with her saying "I told you so" and being angry at me for blowing our chance for getting a lift down the mountain—but I'd had my eyes checked recently and my vision was 20-15 and I knew what I'd seen. Still, as we approached the spot, I was praying that somehow I'd made a mistake.

"See? There's nothing here," Susan said.

"Farther," I said. "Toward the woods."

As we walked through the tall grass, Susan whined, "Great, now I'm gonna catch lyme disease"; then she started screaming so loud I had to put my hand over her mouth to shut her up because I was terrified that the man in the truck would hear her and come back. I was pretty shaken up myself, and if I hadn't witnessed a traffic accident in New York a few years ago and seen two mangled bodies removed from the back of a taxi cab, the sight of the young blond girl with half her head blown off probably would've disturbed me even more.

"Relax," I said, pulling Susan away, back through the grass. "Just relax, all right?"

On the road, I could barely see Susan's face.

"Oh my God," she said. "What are we going to do?"

"Come on," I said. "We have to get out of here."

Walking along the road, I was holding Susan's hand. Then, realizing what I was doing, I let go.

• • •

While Susan was showering, I lay in bed staring at the muted television. The walk back to our car along the dark road had

203

taken almost an hour. The plan was to get back to our room as quickly as possible and then call the police, but the most important thing on my mind was still how I was going to break up with Susan.

She came out of the bathroom, her bony body wrapped in a towel.

"Did you call the police yet?" Susan asked.

I stared at her for a moment, confused, then I said, "No."

"What do you mean?" she said. "Why not?"

"I was thinking—it might not be such a good idea."

"What are you talking about? Call them—right this instant."

She reached for the phone, but I already had my hand on the receiver.

"Think about it," I said. "This is a very delicate situation. We don't want to do anything rash."

"Rash? It's been at least an hour since we saw that guy—"

"Exactly. Don't you think that's the first thing a detective is going to want to know—why did we wait so long to report it?"

"We had to get down the mountain, didn't we? And we couldn't get service on our cells."

"But we could've gone right to the nearest phone booth, but we didn't—we came back here."

"That's because we were going to call them from here."

"I know that and you know that, but a detective might see it differently. Then what if they find our footprints in the grass or one of our hairs on the body."

"But we discovered the body."

"That's the truth, but to them it'll be just a story. We'll wind up being suspects or witnesses, and we'll be stuck up here for weeks together."

"Together? Is that what you're afraid of?"

"No, I . . . I just don't think it's a good idea to get involved; that's all. This guy's nuts obviously—what if he comes after us, to try to shut us up? You want some crazy red neck killer coming after you?"

"I knew you were paranoid," she said, "but this is unbelievable. Will you please give me that phone?"

I still had my hand over the receiver.

"Trust me," I said. "I'm an attorney."

"You're a *tax* attorney."

I decided to ignore the dig. Sometimes Susan just annoyed me—other times she was a flat-out bitch.

"I know what I'm talking about," I said. "Can you afford to miss the next two or three weeks of work while the police are investigating? Do you want to have to schlep back up here for the grand jury hearing, then for a trial?"

"A woman is dead in the woods, Robert."

"I'm aware of that, but nothing we do is going to bring her back to life. It's better not to get involved."

"But there's a killer loose out there. What if somebody else gets killed?"

"That's not our problem—that's the police's problem."

"But we saw him—"

"We saw nothing. Can you describe him?"

"I can describe the truck."

"I'm telling you, we have to just forget about it. Believe me, calling the police won't do anything except create a big hassle for both of us."

Susan was quiet for a moment; then she said, "What if the time is important? What if they need to know when the body was dumped?"

"We'll just forget about it," I said. "The body wasn't far from the road—it'll be discovered eventually. We were never there and we never saw anything. It's better that way."

"I don't know," she said drowsily. "My head hurts so much I can't think anymore."

"Did you take any Tylenols?"

"Four," she said rubbing the back of her neck.

Susan tossed her towel onto the chair and took her nightgown out of her suitcase.

"I wanted to ask you something," she said, putting on her nightgown. "Not about the body—about what you said before in the woods."

"What did I say?"

"About how, if we find our way out of there, that's it. What exactly did you mean by that?"

Get it over with, I thought. *Here's your entree.*

"I don't know," I said. "Nothing probably."

"Probably?"

"Definitely."

"Then why did you say it?"

"We were fighting."

"You sounded serious."

"Oh, stop getting so melodramatic," I said. "You know how much I hate that."

She lay down on the bed next to me. There was space between us.

We had planned to go to Tanglewood tonight to hear the Boston Symphony, but now that was out of the question. After a while, I turned out the light on the night table, but I left the muted television on. Blue flickering TV light shone across the bed.

I still wanted to break up with Susan, but I was tired I and decided to wait until morning.

"I know I won't be able to sleep," Susan said.

"Try."

"I keep seeing that poor woman."

"Forget about it."

"I can't."

"You will."

"How?"

206

"Just don't worry so much."

I have no idea how long it took Susan to fall asleep or if she slept at all. Within a few minutes I was out cold.

• • •

In the morning, when I opened my eyes, Susan was dressed. She was wearing khaki shorts, a black tank top, and dark sunglasses.

"What time is it?" I asked groggily.

"Early," she said

"Where are you going?"

This time she didn't say anything.

Starting to feel more awake, I said, "You didn't call the police, did you?"

"No. . . . But I'm gonna go to the police station or wherever right now."

I sat up. "What're you talking about?"

"I'm gonna go there and explain to them what happened. I can't believe I let you talk me into that last night. A woman was killed, murdered, and we did nothing about it."

"You're making a mistake."

"And then," she went on, "you just fall asleep, snoring, like you don't have a worry in the world. What kind of person are you?"

"I'm telling you," I said, "don't do it. Last night was one thing, but now it's way too late."

"If you think I'm letting you talk me out of it *again*–"

"Listen to me. I know what I'm talking about. If you go to the cops now, you'll never get out of here. They'll ask all kinds of questions–Why did you wait so long to report it? Where were you when the girl was shot–?"

"I don't care what you say; I'm going."

"Don't go; let's call. It'll be better that way–less messy anyway. We'll phone in an anonymous tip. We were walking along the road, we saw the body, and now we're reporting it anonymously. People do that all the time. That's why they have those hotline numbers."

Susan thought about it, then said, "I guess that makes sense."

"Of course it makes sense," I said. "It makes a lot more sense than getting tied up in something, maybe for days, having to miss work and everything."

"So let's call right now." Susan started toward the phone on the night table.

"No," I said. "We don't want them to know who called–that defeats the whole purpose. We'll call from the road, from a phone booth, on the way back to city. That way we phone it in, tell them where they can find the body and describe what we saw, and then we're on our way."

"In that case," Susan said, "I guess you can make the call yourself."

Susan picked up her suitcase.

"What's going on? Where're you going?"

"Look, I think we both know this isn't working," she said.

"What isn't working?"

"*This* . . . us . . . everything. This whole weekend has been pretty much a disaster, and it's obvious you're never gonna change. . . . What's so funny?"

"Nothing," I said.

"Then why were you smiling?"

"I wasn't."

"I'm glad you're so amused by this. You know, you should really grow up. You're thirty-four years old, and you go around acting like you're twenty. I think we should have a clean break–no phone calls, no lunches, no nothing–let's just end it right now."

I asked her if she wanted to wait and drive back to the city together, but she insisted on taking a bus from town.

She looked at me for a couple of seconds, her hands on her hips; then she said, "Goodbye, Robert," and let the door slam behind her.

I listened to the silence for a while, letting it soak in. I couldn't believe I was alone again, that she was really out of my life for good.

I checked out of the hotel around ten o'clock and headed back to the city. In Great Barrington, I stopped for gas and noticed the pay phone outside the station. I was about to call in the tip, but then I realized it could be too risky. What if the police traced the call and someone remembered seeing me? It could lead to a lot of questioning and I could even wind up being a suspect in the case. I knew I was just being paranoid, but I decided to at least think it through a little longer first.

I continued driving along the winding Berkshire roads. It was great being single again–driving the rental car with the windows open and blasting 'seventies rock.

During a newsbreak, an anchorman reported that the body of a young woman had been discovered this morning by a park ranger on a road in October Mountain State Park. The woman had been killed by a single gunshot wound to the head. Anyone with any information about the case was urged to contact the police immediately.

Driving through a small Connecticut town, I spotted a telephone booth on a corner outside a coffee shop. I was thinking about the woman's grieving family, how there was a killer on the loose, and how my description of the red truck could be the break in the case that the police needed.

I stopped at a crosswalk, letting a man cross the street, and then I sped away.

One day in the far future, people will reach back in time through popular literature, reveling in the Los Angeles that Michael Connelly draws for us. It's such a huge palette, and he paints it blood-red with crime, deep blue for the victims and their families, and black as night for his character Harry Bosch, a man walking through an absurd hell of his own in novels such as The Black Echo, The Concrete Blonde, Trunk Music, City of Bones, *and his most recent,* The Closers.

This guy has been a monster writer for our times, an alumnus of the class of novelists that inspired me to take this crime fiction thing seriously—Connelly, Pelecanos, Ellroy, Crumley. I stumbled across them all in the mid-nineties and never looked back. I thank him for that inspiration, and I also thank him for contributing to this anthology. Think you've read all the Bosch there is? Guess what? Here's one more. . . .

Angle of Investigation
Michael Connelly

THEN

"This is all because of Manson," Eckersly said.

Bosch looked across the seat at his training partner, unsure of what he meant.

"Charles Manson?"

"You know, Helter Skelter and all of that shit," Eckersly explained. "They're still scared."

Bosch nodded, though he still didn't get it. He looked out the windshield. They were heading south on Vermont through territory unfamiliar to him. It was only his second day with Eckersly and his second on the job. Almost all of the neighborhoods in Wilshire were unfamiliar to him, but that was okay. Eckersly had been working patrol in the division for four years. He knew the neighborhoods.

"Somebody doesn't answer the phone and back east they think Squeaky and the rest of Charlie's girls have broken in and chopped them up or something," Eckersly continued. "We get a lot of these 'check the lady' calls. Four years now and people still think L.A.'s been turned over to the nuts."

Bosch had been away from the world when Manson and his people had done their thing. So he didn't have a proper read on what the murders had done to the city. When he had come back from Vietnam, he had felt an edginess in L.A. that had not been there before he left. But he didn't know whether that was because of the changes he had been through or the city had been through.

South of Santa Monica they took a left on Fourth Street, and Bosch started reading numbers off of mailboxes. In a few seconds Eckersly pulled the squad car to a stop in front of a small bungalow with driveway down the side to a single garage in the back. They both got out, Bosch taking his nightstick out of the plastic pipe on the door and sliding it into the ring on his equipment belt.

"Oh, you won't need that," Eckersly said. "Unless you want to use it to knock on the door."

Bosch turned back to the car to put the club back.

"Come on; come on," Eckersly said. "I didn't tell you to put it back. I just said you wouldn't need it."

Bosch hustled to catch up to him on the flagstone walkway leading to the front door. He walked with both hands on his belt. He was still getting used to the weight and the awkward bulk of it. When he had been in Vietnam, his job was to go into the tunnels. He'd kept his body profile as trim as possible. No equipment belt. He carried all of his equipment—a flashlight and a forty-five—in his hands.

Eckersly had sat out the war in a patrol car. He was eight years older than Bosch and had that many years on the job. He was taller and heavier than Bosch and carried the weight and bulk of his equipment belt with a practiced ease. He signaled to Bosch to knock on the front door, as if that took training. Bosch knocked three times with his fist.

"Like this," Eckersly corrected.

He rapped sharply on the door.

"Police, Mrs. Wilkins, can you come to the door, please?"

His fist and voice had a certain authority. A tone. That was what he was trying to teach his rookie partner.

212

Bosch nodded. He understood the lesson. He looked around and saw that the windows were all closed, but it was a nice cool morning. Nobody answered the door.

"You smell that?" he asked Eckersly.

"Smell what?"

The one area where Bosch didn't need any training from Eckersly was in the smell of death. He had spent two tours in the dead zone. In the tunnels the enemy put their dead into the walls. Death was always in the air.

"Somebody's dead," Bosch said. "I'll check around back."

He stepped off the front porch and took the driveway to the rear of the property. The odor was stronger back here. To Bosch, at least. The dispatcher on the radio had said June Wilkins lived alone and hadn't answered phone calls from her daughter in Philadelphia for seven days.

There was a small enclosed yard with a clothesline stretching from the corner of the garage to the corner of the house. There were a few things hanging on the line, two silk slips and other women's undergarments. There were more clothing items on the ground, having fallen or been blown off the line. The winds came up at night. People didn't leave their clothes on the line overnight.

Bosch went to the garage first and stood on his toes to look through one of two windows set high in the wooden door. He saw the distinctive curving roofline of a Volkswagen Beatle inside. The car and the clothing left out on the line seemed to confirm what the odor already told him. June Wilkins had not left on a trip, simply forgetting to tell her daughter back east. She was inside the house waiting for them.

He turned to the house and went up the three concrete steps to the back door stoop. There was a glass panel in the door that allowed him to see into the kitchen and part way down a hallway that led to the front rooms of the house.

213

Nothing seemed amiss. No rotting food on the table. No blood on the floor.

He then saw on the floor next to a trash can a dog food bowl with flies buzzing around the rotting mound inside it.

Bosch felt a quickening of his pulse. He took his stick out and used it to rap on the glass. He waited but there was no response. He heard his partner knock on the front door again and announce once more that it was the police.

Bosch tried the knob on the back door and found it unlocked. He slowly opened the door and the odor came out with an intensity that made him drop back off the stoop.

"Ron!" he called out. "Open door in the back."

After a moment he could hear his partner's equipment belt jangling as he hustled to the back, his footfalls heavy. He came around the corner to the stoop.

"Did you—oh, shit! That is rank! I mean, that is *bad!* We've got a DB in there."

Bosch nodded. He assumed DB meant dead body.

"Should we go in?" he asked.

"Yeah, we better check it out," Eckersly said. "But wait a second."

He went over to the clothesline and yanked the two slips off the line. He threw one to Bosch.

"Use that," he said.

Eckersly bunched the silken slip up against his mouth and nose and went first through the door. Bosch did the same and followed him in.

"Let's do this quick," Eckersly said in a muffled voice.

They moved with speed through the house and found the DB in the bathroom off the hallway. There was a claw foot bathtub filled to the brim with still dark water. Breaking the surface were two rounded shapes at either end with hair splayed out on the water. Flies had collected on each as if they were lifeboats on the sea.

214

"Let me see your stick," Eckersly said.

Not comprehending, Bosch pulled it out of his belt ring and handed it to his partner. Eckersly dipped one end of the stick into the tub's dark water and prodded the round shape near the foot of the tub. The flies dispersed and Bosch waved them away from his face. The object in the water shifted its delicate balance and turned over. Bosch saw the jagged teeth and snout of a dog break the surface. He involuntarily took a step back.

Eckersly moved to the next shape. He probed it with the stick and the flies angrily took flight, but the object in the water did not move so readily. It was not free floating like the dog. It went down deep like an iceberg. He dipped the stick down further and then raised it. The misshapen and decaying face of a human being came up out of the water. The small features and long hair suggested a woman but that could not be determined for sure by what Bosch saw.

The stick had found leverage below the dead person's chin. But it quickly slipped off and the face submerged again. Dark water lapped over the side of the tub and both of the police officers stepped back again.

"Let's get out of here," Eckersly said. "Or we'll never get it out of our noses."

He handed the nightstick back to Bosch and pushed past him to the door.

"Wait a second," Bosch said.

But Eckersly didn't wait. Bosch turned his attention back to the body and dipped the stick into the dark water again. He pulled it through the water until it hooked something and he raised it up. The dead person's hands came out of the water. They were bound at the wrists with a dog collar. He slowly let them back down into the water again.

On his way out of the house, Bosch carried the stick at arm's length from his body. In the back yard he found Eckersly standing by the garage door, gulping down fresh air. Bosch threw the slip he had used to breathe through over the clothesline and came over.

"Congratulations, boot," Eckersly said, using the department slang for rookie. "You got your first DB. Stick with the job and it will be one of many."

Bosch didn't say anything. He tossed his nightstick onto the grass—he planned to get a new one now—and took out his cigarettes.

"What do you think?" Eckersly asked. "Suicide? She took the pooch with her?"

"Her hands were tied with the dog's collar," Bosch said.

Eckersly's mouth opened a little, but then he recovered and became the training officer again.

"You shouldn't have gone fishing in there," he said sternly. "Suicide or homicide, it's not our concern anymore. Let the detectives handle it from here."

Bosch nodded his contrition and agreement.

"What I don't get," his partner said, "is how the hell did you smell that at the front door?"

Bosch shrugged.

"Used to it, I guess."

He nodded toward the west, as if the war had been just down the street.

"I guess that also explains why you're not puking your guts out," Eckersly said. "Like most rookies would be doing right now."

"I guess so."

"You know what, Bosch? Maybe you've got a nose for this stuff."

"Maybe I do."

216

NOW

Harry Bosch and his partner, Kiz Rider, shared an alcove in the back corner of the Open-Unsolved Unit in Parker Center. Their desks were pushed together so they could face each other and discuss case matters without having to talk loudly and bother the six other detectives in the squad. Rider was writing on her laptop, entering the completion and summary reports on the Verloren case. Bosch was reading through the dusty pages of a blue binder known as a murder book.

"Anything?" Rider asked without looking up from her screen.

Bosch was reviewing the murder book in consideration of it being the next case they would work together. He hadn't chosen it at random. It involved the 1972 slaying of June Wilkins. Bosch had been a patrolman then and had been on the job only two days when he and his partner at the time had discovered the body of the murdered woman in her bathtub. Along with the body of her dog. Both had been held under water and drowned.

There were thousands of unsolved murders in the files of the Los Angeles Police Department. To justify the time and cost of mounting a new investigation, there had to be a hook. Something that could be sent through the forensic databases in search of a match: fingerprints, ballistics, DNA. That was what Rider was asking. Had he found a hook?

217

"Not yet," he answered.

"Then why don't you quit fooling with it and skip to the back?"

She wanted him to skip to the evidence report in the back of the binder and see if there was anything that could fit the bill. But Bosch wanted to take his time. He wanted to know all the details of the case. It had been his first DB. One of many that would come to him in the department. But he'd had no part in the investigation. He had been a rookie patrolman at the time. He had to watch the detectives work it. It would be years in the department before it was his turn to speak for the dead.

"I just want to see what they did," he tried to explain. "See how they worked it. Most of these cases, they coulda-shoulda been cleared back in the day."

"Well, you have till I'm finished with this summary," Rider cautioned. "After that we better get flying on something, Harry."

Bosch blew out his breath in mock indignation and flipped a large section of summaries and other reports over in the binder until he got to the back. He then flipped the tab marked forensics and looked at an evidence inventory report.

"Okay, we've got latents, you happy?"

Rider looked up from her computer for the first time.

"That could work," she said. "Tied to the suspect?"

Bosch flipped back into the evidence report to look for the summary ascribed to the specific evidence logged in the inventory. He found a one-paragraph explanation that said a right palm print had been located on the wall of the bathroom where the body had been found. Its location was 66 inches from the floor and seven inches right of center above the toilet.

"Well. . . ."

"Well, what?"

218

"It's a palm."

She groaned.

It was not a good hook. Databases containing palm prints were relatively new in law enforcement. Only in the last decade had palm prints been seriously collected by the FBI and the California Department of Justice. In California there were approximately 10,000 palms on file compared to the millions of fingerprints. The Wilkins murder was 33 years old. What were the chances that the person who had left a palm print on the wall of the victim's bathroom would be printed two decades or more later? Rider had answered that one with her groan.

"It's still worth a shot," Bosch said optimistically. "I'll put in the SID request."

"You do that. Meantime, as soon as I'm done here, I'll see if I can find a case with a real hook we can run with."

"Hold your horses, Kiz. I still haven't run any of the names out of the book. Give me today with this and then we'll see."

"Not good to get emotionally involved, Harry," she responded. "The Laura syndrome, you know."

"It's not like that. I'm just curious. It was sort of my first case."

"No, it wasn't."

"You know what I mean. I remember thinking she was an old lady when the detectives gave me the rundown on it. But she was only forty-six. I was half her age so I thought anybody forty-six was old and had a good run of it. I didn't feel too bad about it."

"Now you do."

"Forty-six was too young, Kiz."

"Well, you're not going to bring her back."

Bosch nodded.

"I know that."

"You ever seen that movie?"

"*Laura?* Yeah, I've seen it. Detective falls in love with the murder victim. You?"

"Yeah, but it doesn't hold up too well. Sort of a parlor room murder case. I liked the Burt Reynolds take on it in the eighties. *Sharky's Machine.* With Rachel Ward. You seen it?"

"I don't think so."

"Had Bernie Casey in it. When I was a youngster, I always thought he was a fine-looking man."

Bosch looked at her with a raised eyebrow.

"Before I switched teams," she said. "Then I rented it a couple years ago and Bernie didn't do it for me. I liked Rachel Ward."

Her bringing up her sexuality seemed to put an uneasiness between them. She turned back to her computer. Bosch looked down at the evidence report.

"Well, we know one thing," he said after a while. "We're looking for a left-handed man."

She turned back to looking at him.

"How do you know that?"

"He put his right hand on the wall over the toilet."

"And?"

"It's just like a gun, Kiz. He aimed with his left hand because he's left-handed."

She shook her head dismissively.

"Men. . . ."

She went back to work on her computer and Bosch went back to the murder book. He wrote down the information he would need to give to the latent prints section of the Scientific Investigation Division in order for a tech to look up the palm print in their files. He then asked if Rider wanted him to pick her up a coffee or a soda from the cafeteria while he was floating around the building. She said no and he was off. He took the murder book with him.

• • •

Bosch filled out the comparison request forms and gave them to a print tech named Larkin. He was one of the older more experienced techs. Bosch had gone to him before and knew that he would move quickly with the request.

"Let's hope we hit the jackpot, Harry," Larkin said as he took the forms.

It was true that there was always a sense of excitement when you put an old print into a computer and let it ride. It was like pulling the lever on a slot machine. The jackpot payoff was a match, a cold hit in police parlance.

After leaving SID Bosch went to the cafeteria for a cup of coffee and to finish reading through the murder book. He decided he could handle the constant background noise of the cafeteria better than he could handle the intrusive questions from Kiz Rider.

He understood where his partner was coming from. She wanted to choose their cases dispassionately from the thousands that were open. Her concern was that if they went down a path in which Bosch was exorcizing ghosts or choosing cases with personal attachments, then they would burn out sooner rather than later.

But Bosch was not as concerned. He knew that passion was a key element in any investigation. Passion was the fuel that kept his fire burning. So he purposely sought the personal connection or, short of that, the personal outrage, in every case. It kept him locked in and focused. But it wasn't the Laura Syndrome. It wasn't the same as falling in love with a dead woman. By no means was Bosch in love with June Wilkins. He was in love with the idea of reaching back across time and catching the man who had killed her.

221

• • •

The killing of June Wilkins was as horrible as it was cunning. The woman was bound hands and feet with a dog collar and a leash and then drowned in the tub. Her dog was treated to the same death. The autopsy showed no bruising or injuries on Wilkins suggestive of a struggle. But analysis of blood and tissue samples taken during autopsy indicated that she had been drugged with a substance called ketamine hydrochloride, a veterinary sedative that acts as a paralyzing agent. It meant that it was likely that Wilkins was conscious but unable to move her muscles to fight or defend herself when she was submerged in the water in the bathtub. Analysis of the dog's blood found that the animal had been drugged with the same substance.

A textbook investigation followed the murder, but it ultimately led to no arrests or the identification of a suspect. June Wilkins had lived alone. She had been divorced and had one child, a college student who went to school in Philadelphia. June worked as an assistant to a casting director in an office in a building at Hollywood and Vine, but had been on a two-week vacation at the time of her death.

No evidence was found that she'd had an ongoing romantic relationship or that there were any hard feelings from a former relationship. It appeared to neighbors, acquaintances, co-workers, and family members that the love of her life was her dog, a miniature poodle named Frenchy.

The dog was also the focus of her life. He was of pure breed, and the only travel Wilkins did in the year most recent to her death had been to attend dog shows in San Diego and Las Vegas where Frenchy competed. The second bedroom of her bungalow had been converted into a grooming salon where ribbons from previous dog shows lined the mirrors.

The original investigation was conducted by partners Joel Speigelman and Dan Finster of Wilshire Division. They began with a wide focus on Wilkins' life and then narrowed in on the dog. The use of the veterinary drug by the killer and the killing of the dog suggested some connection to that aspect of the victim's life. But that avenue soon hit a dead end when the detectives found no indication of a dispute or difficulty involving Wilkins in the competitive world of dog shows. They learned that Wilkins was considered a harmless novice in that world and was neither taken seriously by her competitors nor competitive in nature herself. The detectives also learned that Frenchy, though a pure bred animal, was not a champion caliber dog, and the ribbons he took home were more often than not awarded for simply competing, not winning.

The detectives changed their theory and began to consider the possibility that the killer had purposely misdirected the investigation toward the dog show angle. But what the correct angle of investigation should have been was never determined. The investigation stalled. The detectives never linked the palm print on the bathroom wall to anyone, and lacking any other solid leads the case was pushed into the wait-and-see pile. That meant it was still on the desk, but the investigators were waiting for something to break—an anonymous tip, a confession, or even another murder of similar method. But nothing came up and after a year it was moved off the table and into the archives to gather dust.

While reading through the binder Bosch had written down a list of names of people who had come up in the investigation. These included family members, neighbors, and co-workers of the victim as well as acquaintances she encountered through veterinary services and the dog shows she attended.

In most cases Speigelman and Finster had asked for birth

dates, addresses and even social security numbers while conducting their interviews. It was standard operating procedure. Their thoroughness back then would now help Bosch when he ran every name from the list through the crime computer.

When finished reading Bosch closed the murder book and looked at his list. He had collected 36 names to run through the computer. He knew he had the names and the palm print and that was about it. He could also run ketamine hydrochloride through the computer to see if it had come up in any other investigations since 1972.

He decided that if nothing came out of the three angles of investigation, he would drop the case, admit defeat to his partner, and press on to the next case that had a valid hook.

As he finished his coffee, he thought about the palm print. There had been no analysis of it other than to measure its location on the wall and have it ready for comparison to suspects that might come up in the investigation. But Bosch knew that there was more to it than that. If the print was 66 inches up the wall, that meant it was likely that the man who had left it was over six feet tall. He came to this conclusion because he knew that if the suspect leaned forward to brace himself while urinating, he would probably put his hand on the wall at shoulder level or slightly above. Add a foot in height for his neck and head and you have a man ranging from six-two to six-six in total height. A tall, left-handed man.

"That narrows it down," Bosch said to himself, noting his own sarcasm.

He got up, dumped his coffee cup, and headed out of the cafeteria. On the elevator up to five he thought about the times he had leaned his hand on the wall over a toilet. He was either drunk, middle-of-the-night sleepy, or burdened by something besides a heavy bladder. He wondered which of these conditions had fit the tall, left-handed man.

224

Most of the police department's civilian offices were on the fifth floor along with the Open-Unsolved Unit. He passed the unit's door and went down to the Personnel Department. He picked up contact information on Speigelman, Finster, and his old partner, Eckersly. In years past such information would be jealously guarded. But under order from the office of the Chief of Police, detectives with the Open-Unsolved Unit were given cart blanche because it was part of investigatory protocol to contact and interview the original investigators of a case that had been re-opened.

Eckersly, of course, was not one of the original investigators. He was there only on the morning they had found the lady in the tub. But Bosch thought it might be worth a call to see if he remembered that day and had any thoughts on the re-investigation of the case. Bosch had lost contact with Eckersly after he completed his street training and was transferred out of Wilshire Division. He assumed he was no longer on the job and was not mistaken. Eckersly had pulled the plug at 20 years, and his pension was sent to the town of Ten Thousand Palms where he was the police chief.

Nice move, Bosch thought. Running a small-town police force in the desert and collecting an LAPD pension on the side. Every cop's dream.

Bosch also noted the coincidence of Eckersly now living in a town called Ten Thousand Palms and the fact that Bosch was currently running an angle through a database of 10,000 palm prints.

• • •

Rider was not at her desk when Bosch got back to the unit. There was no note of explanation left on his desk, and he figured she had simply taken a break. He sat at her desk and looked at her laptop. She had left it on but had cleared the screen before leaving the office. He pulled the list of names

225

out of the murder book and connected to the National Crime Index Computer. He didn't have his own computer and was not highly skilled in the use of the Internet and most law enforcement databases. But the NCIC had been around for years, and he knew how to run names on it.

All 36 names on his list would have been run through existing databases in 1972 and cleared. What he was looking for now was whether any of the 36 people had been arrested for any kind of significant or similar crime in the years after the June Wilkins murder.

The first name he entered came back with multiple hits for drunk driving arrests. This didn't particularly get Bosch excited, but he circled the name on the list anyway and moved on. No hits came up on the next seven, and he crossed them out. The next name after that scored a hit with an arrest for disturbing the peace. Bosch circled it but again was not feeling the tug of a hook yet.

The process continued with most of the names coming up clean. It wasn't until he entered the 29th name that Bosch looked at the screen and felt a tightness grip in his chest.

The 29th name was Jonathon Gillespie. He had been described in the murder book as a dog breeder who sold miniature poodles in 1972. He had sold the dog Frenchy to June Wilkins two years before her death and was interviewed by Speigelman and Finster when they were trying to run down the dog show angle on the case. According to the NCIC records, Gillespie went to prison on a rape charge in 1981 and served six years in prison. He was now a registered sexual offender living in Huntington Beach. There had been no other arrests since 1981. He was now sixty-eight years old.

Bosch underlined the name on the list and wrote down the case number. It had an LAPD prefix. Though he immediately wanted to go to work on Gillespie, he finished running the rest of the names through the NCIC database first. He got two more hits, one for a DUI and one for a hit-and-run accident with injuries. He circled the names to keep with his procedure but was not excited about them.

Before signing out of the NCIC system he switched over to the crime-tracking database and entered ketamine hydro-chloride into the search window. He got several hits back, all within the last fifteen years, and learned that the substance was being used increasingly as a date rape drug. He scrolled through the cases listed and didn't see anything that linked them to June Wilkins. He logged off the database to begin his pursuit of Jonathon Gillespie.

Closed cases from 1981 had gone to microfiche archives, and the department was slowly moving backwards and entering case information into the department's computerized database. But 1981 was too far back. The only way Bosch would be able to look at the sexual assault case that had sent Gillespie to prison would be to go to the records archives, which were housed over at Piper Tech, the storage facility and air squadron base at the edge of downtown.

Bosch went to his side of the desk and wrote a note to Rider telling her he had come up with a hot angle and was chasing it through Piper Tech. The phone on his desk started to ring. He finished the note and grabbed the phone while standing up to reach the note over to Rider's desk.

"Open-Unsolved, this is Bosch."

"Harry, it's Larkin."

"I was just going to call you."

"Really? Why?"

"I have a name for you."

"Funny, I have a name for you. I matched your palm and you're not going to like it."

"Jonathon Gillespie."

"What?"

"Jonathon Gillespie."

227

"Who is that?"

"That's not your match?"

"Not quite."

Bosch sat back down at his desk. He pulled a pad over in front of him and got ready to write.

"Who did you come up with?"

"The palm print belonged to one of ours. Guy must have left it while at the crime scene. Sorry about that."

"Who is it?"

"The name is Ronald Eckersly. He worked for us sixty-five to eighty five; then he pulled the pin."

Bosch almost didn't hear anything else Larkin said.

" . . . shows that he was a patrol lieutenant upon retirement. You could go to personnel and get a current location if you need to talk to him. But it looks like he might have just screwed up and put his hand on the wall while he was at the scene. Back then they didn't know anything about crime scene protocol and some of these guys would—hell, about twenty years ago I was dusting a homicide scene and one of the detectives who had been there all night started frying an egg in the dead guy's kitchen. He said, 'He ain't gonna miss it and I'm goddamn starved.' You believe that? So no matter how hard you drill into them not to touch—"

"Thanks, Larkin," Bosch said. "I've got to go."

Bosch hung up, grabbed the note off of Rider's desk and crumpled it in his hand. He took his cell phone off his belt and called Rider's cell number. She answered right away.

"Where are you?" Bosch asked.

"Having a coffee."

"You want to take a ride?"

"I've got the case summary to finish. A ride where?"

"Ten-Thousand Palms."

"Harry, that's not a ride. That's a journey. That's at least ninety minutes each way."

228

"Get me a coffee for the road. I'll be right down."

He hung up before she could protest.

• • •

On the drive out Bosch told Rider about the moves he had made with the case and how the print had come back to his old partner. He then recounted the morning he and Eckersly had found the lady in the tub. Rider listened without interrupting; then she had only one question at the end.

"This is important, Harry," she said. "You are dealing with your own memory and you know from case experience how faulty memories can be. We're talking thirty-three years ago. Are you sure there wasn't a moment that Eckersly couldn't have put his hand on the wall?"

"Yeah, like he might've leaned against the wall and taken a leak while I didn't notice."

"I'm not talking about taking a leak. Could he have leaned against the wall when you found the body, like he got grossed out or sick and leaned against the wall for support?"

"No, Kiz. I was in that room the whole time he was. He said, 'Let's get out of here,' and *he* was the first one out. He did not go back in. We called in the detectives and then stood outside keeping the neighbors away when everybody showed up."

"Thirty-three years is a long time, Harry."

Bosch waited a moment before responding.

"I know this sounds sad and sick but your first DB is like your first love. You remember the details. Plus. . . ."

He didn't finish.

"Plus what?"

"Plus my mother was murdered when I was a kid. I think it's why I became a cop. So finding that woman–my second day on the job–was sort of like finding my mother. I can't

229

explain it. But what I can tell you is that I remember being in that house like it was yesterday. And Eckersly never touched a thing in there, let alone put his hand on the wall over the toilet."

Now she was silent for a long moment before responding. "Okay, Harry."

· · ·

Ten Thousand Palms was on the outskirts of Joshua Tree. They made good time and pulled into the visitor parking space in front of the tiny police station shortly before one. They had worked out how they would handle Eckersly in the last half hour of the drive.

They went in and asked a woman who was sitting behind a front counter if they could speak with Eckersly. They flashed the gold and told her they were from the Open-Unsolved Unit. The woman picked up a phone and communicated the information to someone on the other end. Before she hung up, a door behind her opened and there stood Ron Eckersly. He was thicker and his skin a dark and worn brown from the desert. He still had a full head of hair that was cut short and silver. Bosch had no trouble recognizing him. But it didn't appear that he recognized Bosch.

"Detectives, come on back," he said.

He held the door and they walked into his office. He was wearing a blue blazer with a maroon tie over a white shirt. It did not appear to Bosch that he had a gun on his belt. Maybe in a little desert town a gun wasn't needed.

The office was a small space with LAPD memorabilia and photographs on the wall behind the desk. Rider introduced herself and shook Eckersly's hand, and then Bosch did the same. There was a hesitation in Eckersly's shake and then Bosch knew. Instinctively, he knew. He was holding the hand of Ruth Wilkins' killer.

230

"Harry Bosch," Eckersly said. "You were one of my boots, right?"

"That's right. I came on the job in seventy-two. We rode Wilshire patrol for nine months."

"Imagine that, one of my boots coming back to see me."

"Actually, we want to talk to you about a case from seventy-two," Rider said.

As planned, she took the lead. They took seats and Bosch once again tried to determine if Eckersly was armed. There was no telltale bulge beneath the blazer.

Rider explained the case to Eckersly and reminded him that he and Bosch had been the patrol officers who discovered the body. She asked if he remembered the case at all.

Eckersly leaned back in his desk chair, his jacket falling to his sides and revealing no holster or weapon on his belt. He looked for an answer on the ceiling. Finding nothing, he leaned forward and shook his head.

"I'm drawing a blank, Detectives," he said. "And I'm not sure why you would come all the way out here to ask an old patrol dog about a DB. My guess is we were in and out, and we cleared the way for the dicks. Isn't that right, partner?"

He looked at Bosch, his last word a reminder that they had once protected each other's back.

"Yes, we were in and out."

"But we have information—newly developed information—that you apparently had a relationship with the victim," Rider said matter of factly. "And that this relationship was not brought to light during the initial investigation."

Eckersly looked closely at her, wondering how to read the situation. Bosch knew this was the pivotal moment. If Eckersly was to make a mistake, it would be now.

"What information?" Eckersly asked.

"We're not at liberty to discuss it, Chief," Rider responded. "But if you have something to tell us, tell us now. It would be

231

best for you to clear this up before we go down the road with it."

Eckersly's face cracked into a smile and he looked at Bosch.

"This is a joke, right? Bosch, you're putting her up to this, right?"

Bosch shook his head.

"No joke," Bosch said. "You're in a spot here, Chief."

Eckersly shook his head as if uncomprehending the situation.

"You said Open-Unsolved, right? That's cold case stuff. DNA. This a DNA case?"

Bosch felt things tumbling into place. Eckersly had made the mistake. He had taken the bait and was fishing for information. It wasn't what an innocent man would do. Rider felt it too. She leaned toward his desk.

"Chief, do you mind if I give you a rights warning before we go further with this?"

"Oh, come on," Eckersly protested. "You can't be serious. What relationship?"

Rider read Eckersly the standard Miranda rights warning from a card she's pulled out of a pocket in her blazer.

"Chief Eckersly, do you understand your rights as I have read them?"

"Of course, I understand them. I've only been a cop for forty years. What the hell is going on here?"

"What's going on is that we are giving you the opportunity to explain the relationship you had with this woman. If you choose not to cooperate, then it's not going to work out well for you."

"I told you. There was *NO* relationship and you can't prove there was. That body had been in that tub for a week. From what I heard, it practically came apart when they were taking it out of there. You got no DNA. Nobody even knew about DNA back then."

Rider made a quick glance toward Bosch, and this was her signal that he could step in if he wanted. He did.

"You worked Wilshire for four years before that morning," Bosch said. "Did you meet her on patrol? When she was out walking the dog? Where did you meet her, Chief? You told me you were working solo for four months before I was put in the car with you. Is that when you met her? When you were out working alone?"

Eckersly angrily grabbed the phone out of its cradle on his desk.

"I still know some people at Parker Center. I'm going to see if they are aware of what you two people are doing. Coming to *MY* office to accuse me of this crap!"

"If you call anyone, you better call your lawyer," Bosch said.

Eckersly slammed the phone back down into its cradle.

"What do you want from me? I did not know that woman. Just like you, I saw her for the first time floating with her dog in the bathtub. First *and* last time. And I got out of there as fast as I goddamn could."

"And you never went back in."

"That's right, boot. I never went back in."

There, they had him.

"Then how come your palm print was on the wall over the toilet?"

Eckersly froze. Bosch read his eyes. He remembered the moment he had put his hand on the wall. He knew they had him.

Eckersly glanced out the office's only window. It was to his left, and it offered a view of a fire department equipment yard. He then looked back at Bosch and spoke in a quiet voice.

"You know how often I wondered when somebody like you would show up here . . . how many years I've been waiting?"

Bosch nodded.

"It must have been a burden," he said without sympathy.

"She wanted more, she wanted something permanent," Eckersly said. "Christ, she was fifteen years older than me. She was just a patrol pal, that's what we called them. But then she got the wrong idea about things, and when I had to set her straight, she said she was going to make a complaint about me. She was going to go to the captain. I was married back then. I couldn't. . . ."

He said nothing else. His eyes were downcast. He was looking at the memory.

Bosch could put the rest of it together. Eckersly hatched a plan that would throw the investigation off, send it in the wrong direction. His only mistake being the moment he put his hand on the wall over the toilet.

"You have to come with us now, Chief," Rider said.

She stood up. Eckersly looked up at her.

"With you?" he said. "No, I don't."

With his right hand he pulled open the desk drawer in front of him and quickly reached in with his left. He withdrew a black, steel pistol and brought it up to his neck.

"No!" Rider yelled.

Eckersly pressed the muzzle deep into the left side of his neck. He angled the weapon upward and pulled the trigger. The weapon's contact against his skin muffled the blast. His head snapped back and blood splattered across the wall of police memorabilia behind him.

Bosch never moved in his seat. He just watched it happen. Pretty soon the woman from the front counter came running in, and she screamed and held her hands up to her mouth.

Bosch turned and looked at Rider.

"That was a long time coming," he said.

• • •

Laura was already rented at Eddie's Saturday Matinee so Bosch rented *Sharkey's Machine* instead. He watched it at home that night while drinking beer and eating peanut butter sandwiches, and trying to keep his mind away from what had happened in Eckersly's office. It wasn't a bad movie, though he could see almost everything coming. Burt Reynolds and Bernie Casey made pretty good cops, and Rachel Ward was the call girl with a heart of gold. Bosch saw what Burt saw in her. He thought he could easily fall in love with her, too. Call girl or not, dead or alive.

Near the end of the movie there was a shoot out and Bernie Casey got wounded. Bleeding and out of bullets, he used a Zen mantra to make himself invisible to the approaching shooter.

It worked. The shooter walked right by him and Bernie lived to tell about it. Bosch liked that. At the end of the movie he remembered that moment the best. He wished there was a Zen chant he could use now so Ronald Eckersly could just walk on by him, too. But he knew there was no such thing. Eckersly would take his place with the others that came to him at night. The ones he remembered.

Bosch thought about calling Kiz and telling her what he thought of the movie. But he knew it was too late and she would get upset with him. He killed the TV instead and turned off the lights.

Gary Phillips is the quintessential pulp writer, keeping alive the tradition of fast, dirty, crime fiction that feels like a firecracker blowing up in your hand. The man is everywhere—writing the Ivan Monk books (Violent Spring, Monkology, *and several others*), *the Vegas books (including* Shooter's Point, *my personal fave*), *thrillers like* The Perpetrators, The Jook, *and* Bangers. *And now . . . comic books! The man is writing kick-ass comics like* Shot Callerz *and* Angel Town. *When I met him for the first time, I remember he heard my name, laughed, and said in that booming voice of his, "Oh, man, Plots and Guns, baby!" Then went on to scratch into my copy of* Shooter's Point, *"Plots with Guns,* cars, whiskey, *and* women." *Yes, indeed.*

Chatter
Gary Phillips

I'm just walking out now. I parked on the street because I spotted an open meter, and since I was running late, it was faster to do that than go into the parking structure. Yeah, uh-huh. It went as good as it could I guess. You know whatsher-name from the mayor's office? Je-zus, what the fuck crawled up her ass? I've yet to be in a meeting with her on this and see the hint of a smile cross her face. Every fuckin' thing with this woman is like it's down to her and another broad on Survivor Island, and she's gonna bite a chunk out of the other's throat to be the last ball-cruncher standing.

"Huh? You're shitting me. Her and Morrell from the planning department? He's like what, 58, 60? And she's no more than 38, right? What the hell does she get out of doing him? I mean, God bless Cialis, but Morrell is a functionary at best. Yeah? That so? Huh.

"Hey. Shit. No, I'm all right. I was crossing the street and this asshole in an Escalade swooshed right in front of me. Naturally he had tinted windows and blasting some rap number. Probably juiced on his chronic. Ha. Come on, you know me, live and fuckin' let live, but goddamn, whatever happened to simple civility? And this is what I'm talking about in this matter, right? Wait, hold on. No, I just got to my car and fumbled my cell phone getting my keys out and working the latch.

"Anyway, we've got these do-right, moaning and groaning idealistic and unrealistic lefty organizations going on about oh what about the poor, the less fortunate, where are they going to live if the only concern is the bottom line? If you developers just build these upscale complexes without setting aside so many units for the low income . . . yeah, so their poor unfortunates can hog two spaces parking their Escalades after a hard day of selling dope.

"No, I'm not being racist. But it's true. We could have broken ground on this part of the project by now. We've complied with the Mello Act. We've built in the proper amount of set-asides for low-income units, but no, that's not enough. It's never enough with these people. Christ."

• • •

"Look, I know what the fuck I'm doing. The mark ain't on to me. I just wanted to scope him out, make sure I had the right gee, you know how I do. Plus it don't hurt to get the blood up, shit. Get the smell in the air, ya feel me? Hold up, hold up. I'm coming to this light and there's some po-pos. I gotta be cool. Don't want to fuck this up now. Yeah, I'm turning my sounds down. No, I'm straight. Ain't even got a throat lozenge on me let alone any weed. Yeah, I'm at the

237

light. Yeah, naw, uh-huh. They're giving me their cop looks. I know these fools be running my plate.

"Hell naw, it's all good. We been over that, man. I'm going to use stolen plates for the job. Just like we're using these throw away cellys too so it can't be traced to us. And I'm gonna be creepin' anyway. Ain't no way I'm getting' made. Told you, this is the shit, baby. Watching that black and white that night, with you know, the old dude, Colombo, playing Albert Anesthesia. What? Wait, light's changed. Cops be hanging back, letting me go first so they can try and gank me. Stupid motherfuckahs. Like I don't know what they're up to. Come on, you can't play a playah. Ha.

"Okay, they followed me for a couple of blocks, then turned off. Come on, home, don't be paranoid. We got this tight. We taking that Murder Incorporated thing into the 21st century, dog. Them fools be trippin' using it for the name of a record label to show how hard they are. Shit. When this goes down, we gonna be set. Ain't nobody going to find out who we are. Everything handled by text messaging on throwaways. Man, we geniuses. I know, I know, you're right, don't get all hyped. I got that. Yeah, Huh? What? I lost you for a second going under this overpass. Uh-huh, I can hear you now. Right. Right. Homeboy gets taken out of this world tonight on the dot, and we make our bank and our rep. Man this is the shit."

• • •

"You can not believe how bored I am. No, really. And the munchables, weak. Sautéed Portobellos, ahi with dill, that's so last year. And oh my God, Wood's speech. Snore time, I'm not shitting you. How the hell did this man make the money he's made, own a basketball team, and none of that sophistication rub off on him? Mister one note. Here we are among the movers and shakers, where he has the chance to

238

lay out his vision of downtown redevelopment – what? Yes,
I know it's the choir, but that doesn't mean you half-ass the
work. He has to inspire, not just reiterate the obvious. A
goddamn chimp can do that. You've got to lead, inspire.
Especially now when there's this scrutiny.

"Yes, of course I know that. I'm being hyper-critical because
this is about real consequences. Not only are there multi-
millions on the line overall, but there can be a domino effect
should any part of it derail. This means so much more than
mere physical structures and the anchor businesses we attract
for the mixed-use portion. This is about setting the standard
for decades to follow. Yes, that's true. Why do you think I'm
being so careful?

"Oh, hello, what's this? No, I'd stepped out to the patio
and just spotted this bootylicious honey. I think she's cream
and coffee if you catch my meaning. Ha, yeah, see, I'm down.
Look, I'm going in. Let's synchronize watches 'cause it's poon
tang time, brah. Okay, I'll call you later."

• • •

"Yeah, he was handsome, but he was way too full of himself.
Going on about how he was the man, how he was at the
center of this deal to end all deals that was going to revitalize
downtown and what have you. Make us the rival of Manhattan
we're destined to be. Girl, he went on about all this with
straight-up seriousness. Can you imagine that? Like this
project of his was the greatest thing like whenever. Really it's
just fancy cracker boxes with a Target and a super market
thrown in. One more big, ugly thing gobbling up more land
till there's no green space whatsoever.

"No, I didn't give him my number, I lied telling him that I
didn't currently have a working cell phone—which, yes, I'm
on right now. Ha. But I did give him my e-mail and he of

course gave me his card, writing his personal e-address on it. He's a VP with Wood's company. Then he gets a call on his cell phone and naturally he just had to take it being so important. You know, being all hushed and whispering into it like it was really important.

"Huh? No, I didn't see a ring, but it could have been his wife or girlfriend. Then he said he had to run off to an important meeting. Girl, don't I know that. What kind of meeting would he be going to at this time of night? Uh-huh, that could be.

"I don't know, maybe. It would at least be entertaining in a sociological way to go out with him I suppose. But then I'd have to sit through a lot of him talking about himself, and me trying not to yawn or looked bored. I tell you, though, it's a good thing–oh, sorry, excuse, me. Huh? Yeah, I just bumped into one of the servers from the party while I was stepping outside. He was like rushing off, struggling out of his jacket. Funny, the others are still here, starting to clean up.

"Wow, it's warm tonight. I just stepped back outside. The air smells good after that rain we had this past weekend. So, what I was going to say was it's a good thing he didn't learn I'm temping for Dizaksun. No, I don't think this was some ploy. Girl, please, I surely don't think I'm all that. I'm not getting the swelled head. But yeah, it seemed genuine him coming over to talk to me, and not about him getting some kind of inside dope. And if it was, why me? I'm going to be gone when the regular secretary returns once her ankle heals.

"Oh, so now I'm desperate for talking to him. Too late, dammit, you can't take it back. Of course I know Dizaksun is angling for a pretty big stake in this downtown stuff. But I think this guy, ah, Martin, Martin Conrad, was his name, wasn't that smooth or what have you. He wasn't trying to get anything from me other than what any man wants from a woman.

240

"Uh-huh, Uh huh–ah, goodnight Mr. Browne–yeah, he's the one that invited me. Please. Girl, your imagination is working overtime. Can I help it you couldn't get a babysitter tonight and couldn't come? I am not working anything. Browne and some of the other senior staff invited several of us.

"Okay, now you're just getting silly. You acting like I'm some kind of Sydney. What? You know, Jennifer whatsher-name on that TV show, Alias. Yeah, like I'm some kind of spy or something. Listen, Mr. Browne is orthodox, under-stand? Very upright. Been married for eons to the same woman. He's short and he make it a point to always look up into my face and not at my chest. The three weeks I've been at the firm he's never tried to put a hand on me, unlike a couple of others there I could mention. Exactly, Jack Crane is out of control, isn't he? I'm surprised he hasn't been slapped with a sexual harassment suit.

"I'm sure glad he wasn't here. Worry about him, not this guy Martin. He's okay. Yeah, the more we talk about him, the more I might just–ah, here. The valet just went to get my car. Huh, that's something. That server I told you about? He just drove past me going down the hill behind the wheel of one of those nasty SUVs. Nope, not sure what kind it was except it was shiny black and big. How could he be blinging like that on his salary?

"I don't know. That doesn't sound right. Yeah, I guess this could be a second or third job, but what does that say about his priorities if he's working just to keep up with payments and gas in that thing? No, that's true. I'm going home and crawl under the covers. Might try to watch Tavis but those blankets are calling my name. You need to stop. I am hardly not going to a motel to meet Mr. Browne for a quickie. You the one that needs it more than me. You realize that, don't you?

"Well, well, you can dish the dish but . . . oh, shit. I'm so busy yakking with you I damn near put a ding in this Porsche coming up while I drive down the hill from Wood's house. Look, I better let you go and use both hands to get off this narrow pass, because I can't afford to have my insurance jump up after paying that kind of bill hitting a fancy car. Okay, right, see you in the morning. Let's try that new place for lunch. 'Night."

• • •

"Mom, how can you say that? Yes, I've got you on the head set, cognac on my nightstand and finishing up tweaking the report on my laptop. But I hear every word you're telling me. Really. Cute, very cute. Well, let me tell you, when this deal goes down, they will have my picture next to multi-tasking in the dictionary. Yeah, uh-huh. Hold on. Just need to do this last calculationnnn . . . hell, yes. Sorry. Just keyed up. This is the shit. Sorry. Sorry, just getting carried away. But it's my passion for this project that's kept it online despite, ah, never mind. What?

"Yes, I know you understand business, mom. You ran the shop when dad passed. And who was there each summer and winter break? Look, I'm not trying to be condescending. It's just I shouldn't be talking out of school, understand? No, it's fine, really. Wall Street Journal article? When was this? About a week ago? Hmmmm. No, you know that's just those also rans at Dizaksun trying to muddy the waters. That's an old trick competitors do to sully the winner. A unnamed source alleges there're accusations of double-dealing and kickbacks.

"Mom, think about it. I'm the VP of community relations. I'm the one that's smoothed this project through with all the pols hungry for headlines, the tree huggers, and the bomb throwers. That's just a term, mom. That just means the so-

called community leaders who stand around, not producing
dick, sorry, and then howl and moan supposedly in the name
of their people when something positive comes along from
the Man. But really it's just a way for them to get theirs, too.

"No, I don't mean anything illegal. But a consultant fee
here, a rec center there that employs some of their cronies.
It's just how business is done. So there's nothing to worry
about. Everything is fine. There's no investigation. Huh? What
about next Tuesday for dinner. Sure, that Italian place. I love
you too, mom."

• • •

"Fifteen-Adam-eighty-three, fifteen-Adam-eighty-three,
report shots fired, one-four-nine Ocean Shore Drive, one-
four-nine Ocean Shore Drive, Brentwood. Residence of
Martin H. Conrad. Thirty-four, male, Cauc, brown hair,
brown eyes. Five-eleven. Repeating information."

• • •

"What the fuck, dog? Naw, I got there. The side gate was
unlocked and the alarm was off like we'd been told. I'm
creeping up, Glock ready and shit. I go through the sliding
glass door off the pool also like we wuz told and the mark,
Conrad, has already been capped. One to the chest and one
dead ass center in his forehead. He's still sitting in his bed,
spilled glass of something in his limp hand. Motherfuckah
never saw it coming. I could tell he had a laptop in there
'cause I saw the connection, but no computer.

"Hell, yeah, that's why I'm out of breath. Think I just waitin'
around there for Entertainment Tonight to fuckin' show up?
I bounced out of there like my baby's mama was after me for
money. No, I didn't leave no prints. Like we planned, I wore
rubber gloves.

243

"But straight up, man, they trying to punk us. This is some shit, that's for sure. Hey, you hear that? Ain't that a ghetto bird? Man, that's a chopper, only I'm straining and I don't see nothin' over me."

"Aw fuck, it's you, dog, they at your crib, you hard-of-hearing motherfuckah. Run, goddamit, run."

• • •

"I don't know how else to tell you this, man. I had car trouble, I don't know why the fuck it stopped running, but it did. I went to that dude, that Wells' house because that's where my car stopped. And the reason, like I've told you several times before, I was in that area was because I was coming back from this bar called the Shanty up there on Sunset. I know you checked that shit, Sergeant, 'cause I know you. And I can't tell you why nobody remembers me. That place was crowded. So if some nosy desperate housewife spotted my south of La Brea ass in her precious Brentwood neighborhood, that's why.

"And I ran because how crazy was it gonna sound that me, who's done time, for a beef you busted me for I might add, and here it was I just happened to stumble on a croaked bastard. Wait, I know what you're about to say. But I can't explain that gun in my apartment no more than I can explain geometry. That ain't my gun, ain't no prints on it. I know what your lab said, that was the gun that smoked homeboy. But look here, sarge, you been knowin' me since Eazy E cut his first record. The fuck would I be doin' sneaking around Brentwood. I got some kind of OJ fixation going on? I'm not crazy."

• • •

"Hi, honey. Yeah, I'm still at the station. I was just replaying the videoed interrogation of the suspect. Huh, I'm laughing because I first encountered this character, Choo-Choo, when I was in uniform and he was this snot-nosed look out for the slangers. Yeah . . . uh-huh. His real name is Antonio Stevens, and I got him for receiving once. Right, and now it looks like I've got him for the Conrad murder, but I don't like the fit.

"Choo-Choo would never be mistaken for a mastermind, but even he's not stupid enough to leave the murder weapon in his crib. From what one of my CIs tell me, it seems Choo-Choo and his running buddy, Twin–huh? No, he's an only child. They call him Twin because he has a habit of always repeating himself. Anyway, it seems they were setting themselves up as hired killers.

"I know, pursuit of the American Dream. So these two numb chunks set out on this new venture, right? But you just can't advertise something like that on the radio. And they want high-end customers who can pay some real money. No rooty-poot shit for them, no sir. So, how do they get the word out. Guess. You'll never guess.

"They go to pilates and yoga classes, trendy bars and what have you in Beverly Hills and the Westside and leave cards on people's windshields. I'm serious. I've got a few as evidence. Check this out. It says, 'Got a serious problem? One that the normal methods can't fix? Need a permanent solution? Call and leave a text message at,' and they leave a number which leads to a disposable cell phone.

"Actually, yes, that was kind of clever. Something like that old show, the Equalizer, right? Only it's reverse. Sweetheart, I'm not making this up. Twin's saving grace is his computer skills, so he's like Mister Nerve Center in all this. And you've got to ask yourself, what moron would actually get in touch with someone who left this kind of notice?

"You know the more we talk about this, the more it might be that Choo-Choo would leave the incriminating weapon in his place. The Beretta was wiped clean, and except for

245

that and what I got from the streets, that's all I have on him. A uniform found a bowtie and jacket like a waiter would wear in a trashcan a couple of blocks from Conrad's house. And the jacket is Choo-Choo's size, but what does that mean? A disguise of some kind?

"Conrad's alarm had been shorted and the lock on his gate had been jimmied. I guess, could be that Twin helped his boy do all that, but it just don't fit, honey. There's none of that kind of equipment at Twin's apartment or Choo-Choo's.

"Now you've got me believing what that chump said was true. He was set up. Oh, I agree. He needs to be locked up. But more and more I'm feeling there's someone else behind all this. I mean, it's not that hard putting two clowns who would leave post cards advertising that they are killer-for-hire into a frame.

"All right, I'm taking one more run at Mr. Twin, who's so terrified he's given up Choo-Choo, Michael Jackson, and Robert Blake. Want me to bring anything home? Sure. Okay, see you in about an hour, baby doll. Don't worry about that. I'm not that tired. Don't you know doing this gets the blood up. Yeah. . . ."

• • •

"Oh yes, it's me. I know what hour it is and I know it's your home. I dialed it, didn't I? Before you continue ranting, know that your clutch player, shall we say, has been checked. I find it insulting you didn't think I wouldn't make him. Driving that Porsche, shadowing me from the party. Like I'm going to get played like those two delusional homeboys I set up. When I came down the hill, he tried to be clever, turning around and going the opposite way to make it seem he was just some Westsider returning home.

"Don't cut me off when I'm talking, Mr. Wood; that's impolite. And you already have a price to pay for challenging

246

me. Don't pretend to protest. You're not good at playing naïve, Mr. Wood. You now owe me double what we agreed to since you tried to break your contract with me, sir.

"What? I'm chuckling because you still insist on this bluster as if I'm one of thousands of ubiquitous real estate brokers or developers or what have you seeking your largess. We both know that you will gladly and promptly arrange to have the proper amount of cash, in non-sequential bills, ready to be delivered to me. In fact, you will deliver my funds. If you don't, that daughter of yours at that college on Long Island might trip down the steps and crack her skull open one sunny day on her way to biology.

"I make it a priority to thoroughly know about my clients. Just as you have so arrogantly and clichéd *ad nauseam* proclaimed over and over to the public in such media venues as Forbes and CNN about your position is testament to your due diligence. Hmm, yes, well, now we're achieving some understanding. Very good, I knew you were a fast learner. Oh no, it will not be the place or time we previously discussed. Sad to say, I simply don't trust you. Get the cash together and you will hear from me specifically to make the drop, precise time, and what have you."

• • •

"Our top story on Action News is that police are looking into the violent death of Douglas Wood, a key figure in the multi-million dollar downtown redevelopment boom. Inexplicably, he was out walking underneath the Santa Monica pier after midnight. Why he was there, and at that hour, is part of the ongoing investigation. Action News is following a lead that there may be a witness. A Marine just returned from Iraq had been out celebrating with his friends and reportedly was sleeping if off beneath the pier when he may have witnessed some sort of altercation with Wood and an as-yet-unidentified woman.

"And in what may be a related incident, the murder of Martin Conrad two days ago, a man who worked in Douglas Wood's company, is also under investigation. Action News is following up a report that the Securities and Exchange Commission had approached Conrad about possible irregularities in some of Wood's dealings. Particularly as it relates to monies involved in the massive downtown redevelopment.

"But this is unconfirmed as of this broadcast, and we will of course keep our viewers informed as we learn more."

Jim Nisbet is one of those maverick authors who write whatever the hell they feel like all the time. Poetry, essays, seriously whacked-out crime novels. All on his resumé. His The Price of the Ticket *and* The Syracuse Codex *are both available from Dennis McMillan Publications, and are also plentiful in France. It seems that Jim turns the French on quite a bit.*

Since I was born and raised in the Deep South, I definitely feel the atmosphere and the vivid characters at work in "Brian's Story," and I understand that impluse to tell stories to strangers, embellishing with precise and quirky details that make you give your full attention, the whole time wondering if this is truth or lies—and not caring much which as long as you're satisfied!

Brian's Story
Jim Nisbet

Brian rented a tidy white clapboard bungalow, with a porch and swing, tucked under a walnut tree on the far side of a pasture across the road from the store. His car was a British racing green MGB convertible, a two-seater and unusual for Chatham County, or anywhere else in North Carolina in 1971, where most people drove American stock cars or pickup trucks, and at least two of the store's regular customers piloted tractors when they came up out of the woods. One of the latter, a rear-engined Alis-Chalmers, whose original orange had become indistinguishable from the colors of advanced oxidation and red dust, always towed a two-tired flatbed wagon which bore the three-hundred-pound matriarch of the family, enthroned upon its oak planks, in full lotus position with a tiny velvet change purse clutched to her lap.

Brian often bought gasoline on Friday evening, which was my shift, and he never purchased anything else. He never stepped inside the store either, waiting in the yard by his car if I had to make change out of the register. Perhaps he savored the moment alone there. That yard would get so quiet you could hear the powder post beetles, minute as they are, as they chewed their way through a wooden church pew that stood to the left of the screen door. An elderly neighbor often whiled away his morning on the pew, after seeing his grandchildren onto the school bus, and he enjoyed telling the youngsters that an experienced ear could distinguish a species of wood according to how loudly the powder post beetles had to chew to get through it. Others among the pew's regular idlers propagated another story, equally unverifiable, concerning Brian.

The store faced the paved road, to the west. Fifty yards south a dirt track, little more than a pair of graveled ruts blanketed in pine straw, teed off the paved road across a culvert and meandered through white oaks and jack pines to a turkey farm, almost two miles behind the store. When rain came on an easterly wind, people sitting on the pew could smell the turkeys; which, as the old man always pointed out, beat the aroma of even a single hog.

Judging by the number of mailboxes at its intersection— clustered like a line of birds along a sagging two-by-four be- tween a pair of posts in front of the ditch—twelve or fifteen trailers and four-room houses were sprinkled through the woods along that dirt road. All of these tenants rented from the turkey farmer, at least two of them were pot dealers, and one of these had declared that the guy with the MGB was an undercover narcotics agent.

Of all these people, only I had troubled to learn the name of the MGB driver. I also knew that he drove to town in the morning, returned in the afternoon, and, later in the evening drove back to town, five and sometimes six days a week. I'd noticed stacks of medical textbooks on the MGB's passenger seat, too, and eventually came to know that Brian was in the second semester of his first year of medical school at Chapel Hill, twenty miles up the road. And right away I'd spotted the cute Browning automatic pistol affixed by a spring clip to the driver's side of the MGB's transmission tunnel.

Since I wasn't dealing pot, however, I didn't think that much about it. As I am often at pains to point out to people from elsewhere, guns are extremely common to the rural South. I'd been raised 125 miles south of this country store and gas station, about five miles above South Carolina. Less than a mile north of the border and along one of only two paved roads that ran between the pair of counties abutting it, the father of a schoolmate had kept his own modest store. This individual distinguished himself as the only man I ever knew to readily admit to me his membership in the Ku Klux Klan. He called it the "Ku-Klux," as in, "I'm a Ku-Klux." He said other things, too, that, on the theory that once I die they'll stand a chance of being forgotten, I won't repeat. Beneath his own cash register counter a cardboard box overflowed with little revolvers and automatics of calibers .22, .25, .32, rarely a .38, and never a metric bore. Some lacked a handgrip or a screw or a serial number, some shone in the gloom under the counter, nickel-plated, and a few were properly blued. But most of them were tarnished and all of them were Saturday-night specials, which my friend's father bought, sold and traded, singly and by the handful, for any one example of which I never saw more than twenty dollars change hands.

Brian's Browning cost fifteen times that. I once apprenticed for a carpenter who owned one, too, and we had passed a pleasant evening with it after work one summer, drinking corn liquor from a jug and throwing lead at a poplar stump. This target stuck a foot or two up out of the shallows of a pond, and we sat on the dam some sixty or seventy yards away, yet each of us hit the stump often. The smack of a hit reverberated over the water, and the misses whined through the healthy poplars beyond the cattails at the water's edge. And so, one Friday evening, as the MGB's tank filled, I observed aloud, "That's an accurate, short-barreled pistol."

Brian glanced at the gun. The convertible top was back, and there it was, not thirty inches below the rearview mirror, about as obvious as a leech on a courtesan's flank.

253

"It's a good pistol," Brian agreed.

"Take practice with it much?"

Now Brian looked me in the eye. His eyes were brown and these, along with his straight, jet-black hair, contrasted strongly with his pallor. It was a very good example of what musicians call a studio tan, exactly the color of skin you'd expect on a man who spent all day at medical school and half the night in the library. "Not really," he shrugged. "If I ever need it, accuracy probably won't be an issue." His eyes remained frank—and unamused, it seemed to me.

The tank filled. I told off the metal digits in the face of the pump. Brian handed me a ten-dollar bill.

The following Friday, he arrived at dusk.

Although not so slow as the kerosene pump, which was cranked by hand, those old gas pumps were pretty deliberate. It was almost as if, having done their part to outpace the life around them, they were now content to rest on their laurels. This particular evening was particularly quiet. Excepting Brian and myself, nobody was around. He stood out of the driver's seat without a word. I set about fueling the car. Gas in those days was fifty or sixty cents a gallon, but that evening the tin numerals revolving in their die-cut windows seemed to take a greater time than usual to account for the exchange of pennies for tenths of gallons. It wasn't unpleasant. The evening was warm but not hot. The humidity was damp but not claustrophobic.

A flock of crows flew overhead, chuckling contentedly and calling raucously. We watched them circle the tops of a stand of tall pines on the south side of the pasture across the road, both of them, crows and trees, silhouetted against the darkening sky like their own, eponymous, ideograms.

"Settling in for the night," I observed, "and you're just

heading out." I nodded toward the pistol. "Do you leave that thing in the car when you park?"

No way, of course, and the implication was that where Brian went, he went armed. As to why I was being so pointedly inquisitive, I figured if the guy were straight up, he'd talk to me; if not, he might take his gun and his business elsewhere. Brian glanced at the pistol, then looked across the road again, and for a while longer we listened to the crows. The gas pump hummed in pulsing rattles. The gnats bit only occasionally.

"My brother," Brian said suddenly, without turning around, "was two years older than me."

In the slightest of breezes the leaves of a willow behind the store would sound like waves receding from a beach, as its drooping limbs swept the pea gravel on the flat roof. But on this night the willow's boughs hung suspended in almost perfect stillness. Among them a tree frog spoke twice, as if tentative about the solitude, and ceased.

"Randall was a lot of the things I wasn't," Brian continued. "As an athlete, he simply dominated. He was popular with the girls and his classmates. Even though he rarely studied, he was a passable student, and his teachers liked him anyway."

I politely cleared my throat. "Where was this?"

"Other side of Durham." Brian moved his chin toward the northeast, the correct direction.

There was as yet no such thing as a pollution sleeve attached to the hose on a gas pump, let alone an automatic shutoff. In order to avoid washing down the fender of a customer's car or filling one of your shoes, you had to listen for the sound of gasoline backing up the filler neck. This sound was the reverse, more or less, of a drain emptying a basin.

"Randall was wild, though. All that success occasionally went to his head. It came easily and early and he wasn't stupid enough to not let it bother him, so he was somewhat conflicted. But he was a good guy. A really good guy."

255

About half a mile north along the paved road and two hundred yards west up a dirt one, in a shack-filled hollow along Three Mile Creek, a coon dog barked.

"Did he watch out for his little brother?"

"Oh yes. Randall took good care of his little brother." Brian nodded toward the darkness accumulating trees to itself. "He even took me along with his crowd, up to a point."

"That's a big deal in high school."

"It can be. But we were close. Randall carried authority among his friends, his friends weren't insecure people, and they accepted me quite naturally. Of course, when Randall began dating the homecoming queen, he didn't invite me along so much any more."

"Well, hey," I laughed.

"Sure, sure, and it was just as well. She was an olive-skinned brunette with black eyes and a brilliant smile, Cherokee and French and smart as a whip. I was completely tongue-tied in her presence." Brian almost smiled. "Many nights in his senior year he'd come home late, and the next morning he'd sleep in. He'd make it to school in time for lunch, study hall, and football practice. But by then he was the captain of the football team, and nobody seemed to mind him cutting classes."

"Let's see," I mused, "would study hall have taken place in the coach's office?"

"That's true." Again, Brian didn't quite smile. "After practice he'd come home, shower, grab a bite, and head out again."

The tank's filler neck began to back up, and I released the handle. "Aren't girls wonderful?"

"Randall used to say that, lacking girls, we'd have to call this planet Mars."

"The god of full-time war." I hung the spout on the lever, and the pump fell silent.

I hadn't turned on the yard light yet. There weren't even any lights on inside the store. Save for the western-most tail-

256

end of dusk, light came only from a pair of fluorescent tubes behind a translucent panel in the soft drink machine, which was chained to the outside wall of the store to the right of the screen door, opposite the pew. About this pearlescent rectangle, moths had begun to flutter. Brian and I stood silently in this modestly augmented twilight, and I wondered if we weren't mutually aware in that moment of a small country, on the other side of the world, where our setting sun was about to rise over last night's carnage. It occurred to me then that Vietnam might be where his brother's story was headed.

"Came the big game," Brian said. "With a three-point lead and thirty seconds to go in the fourth quarter on our own ten-yard line, Randall fumbled a handoff."

"Oops, oh dear, and you shouldn't be handing off under those circumstances."

"Tell me about it. The biggest and slowest doofus on the other side's defensive line picked up the ball and fell face first into the end zone to score the winning touchdown."

"If it happened tonight, we'd hear the screams all the way out here."

Brian nodded. "For just a moment, until the other side started yelling, because even they were shocked, all I heard was the shutter open and close on somebody's camera. Then the place went nuts."

"How big was big?"

"The doofus?"

"The game."

"As a matter of fact," Brian sighed, "it was the regional championship."

I have always felt uncomfortable with the presumed gravity of such situations, but in this case, as a polite or at least sub-sociopathic gesture of sympathy, I refrained from quoting

Jacques Elull's opinion that organized sports pave the road to fascism.

"That photo or one just like it wound up above the fold on page one of the sports section in next day's *Durham Morning Herald.* The caption read, 'A Senior Moment.'"

Again I checked my reflexive response, *And soon forgotten.*

"Among other results," Brian continued, "the homecoming queen couldn't handle the embarrassment."

"She dropped your brother because he dropped a football?"

"So it seemed."

"It's not like *she* dropped it."

"Not a bad point," Brian ruefully agreed. "Nevertheless...."

"Not that it's any of my business," I interrupted, "but Randall should have counted himself lucky to discover this detail about her sooner rather than later."

Brain didn't look at me. "That's what I told him."

"Did he listen?"

"No."

This was a slight wrinkle on the Vietnam vector, but I still thought that Vietnam was where Randall was headed. "So what did he do?" I retrieved the MGB's gas cap from the top of the pump housing. "Quit school and join the Marines?"

"Worse." Brian made an odd sound, more grunt than laugh, which conveyed a hapless, brief amusement. "For the simple reason that she knew what was going on, and I didn't, it turned out that the homecoming queen had done the right thing. It was months before I figured it out, and by then it was too late for Randall."

"Maybe so," I said stubbornly, "but you didn't quit him."

Brian looked at me and blinked. For a moment it seemed as if he no longer trusted whatever instinct had tempted him into telling me his story.

Then it was my turn to blink. "Found out what?"

We endured another short silence, in which I thought that

I could just about hear him thinking, *I don't even know you, man.* True enough; but, as I realized right away, maybe Brian didn't know anybody.

"Heroin," he said abruptly.

I fumbled the gas cap and it rolled under the car. "What?" I knelt to retrieve it and stood up again. "What?"

By now it had gotten pretty dark, but even by the faint light of the drink machine, I could see that Brain was considering that he may have misjudged his man at the gas station. Either that, or his man at the gas station was coming on mighty ingenuous. He gave it another try. "It's a drug," he said patiently, "made from poppies."

Close by a cricket breedled, just once, and now I was thinking that I was the one doing the misjudging. "Opium poppies," I said testily. "The CIA smuggles their distillate to us direct from Laos. Something about supporting indigenous Hmong culture with more than mere automatic weapons and twisted logic."

"Opium poppies," Brian repeated softly.

"Is that what the homecoming queen knew?"

"Yes."

"So I misjudged her."

"As had I. She wouldn't explain it, either. Except for me, when we discussed it much later, she told nobody, and only then did I discover that she had tried to help Randall. In the beginning, like myself, she had no idea. When she figured it out, she confronted him. Randall brazenly admitted to it, as if daring her to do something about it, and she saw that as a cry for help. She learned quickly. Randall was addicted and he'd been adrift, out of control, for nearly a year. He'd lost his scholastic touch, he'd diluted his athletic talent, he sacrificed his . . . his. . . ."

". . .His intimacy with her?"

"She tried. She even sniffed a little of his powder to see

259

what it was like, to share the high with him. She told me she put it down immediately because she didn't care for it, but she didn't quit Randall until she finally admitted to herself that he no longer cared for anything else. He didn't care about dropping the football or losing the big game. He didn't care that he'd been too out of it to play at all, or that only his natural talent had allowed him to help the team get as far as it had. She realized that he was high whenever she saw him, which was less and less frequently. It turned out that, much of the time, when she thought he was with us at home and we thought he was out with her, he wasn't in either place. Instead he was alone in his car, parked on some dead-end road in the woods next to the river, nodded out. Then her parents started taking her on weekend trips to look at colleges and, well. . . ."

"But, Jesus," I blurted, "what an awful thing for your family to go through. Did you tell your father? Your mother?"

Brian dismissed this. "We barely knew our father. Momma worked all the time to support us. Randall and I had been on our own—and doing good on our own—since we were little boys."

"So Randall's coming and going wasn't so unusual."

"Not at all. By the time he—" Brian stopped and stared straight up. After a moment I looked up, too. Despite a haze of humidity, Venus and a few stars were visible, and the sight reminded me that the pew attracted star gazers and pot-smokers after hours. Three of them claimed to have seen a UFO out there.

Whole days passed when not ten cars drove by that store. At night, traffic was even scarcer. Walking the road after midnight you were more likely to encounter a deer or a possum than an automobile. It was one of the reasons I liked it there. It probably had something to do with people seeing flying saucers there, too. And it certainly had something to do with people telling each other stories there, in the dark.

Brian said to the sky, "One night he was supposed to come home in time to drive Momma to work. She was working nights, then, in one of the cigarette factories. When he didn't show, I put down my lessons and took her to work. Then I went looking for Randall.

"By then he'd quit school, too, even though it was close to the end of his senior year, and even though it made him liable for the military draft. He probably would have flunked out anyway. His last football season being over, the athletic department wasn't so inclined to help him get by as they used to be. That was an eye-opener. For that matter he was in such bad shape he might have flunked the draft physical. At any rate, days passed with no sight of Randall around the house. I never found out where he was getting the money, but I did know where he was buying his dope. So, after I dropped momma at work, I drove her car down there.

"It was a place called Keaton's Chicken Shack, and, I don't mind telling you, I'd never been anywhere near it. It was way down in Lee County, about sixty miles from home, so far out in the country it made this place look like Atlanta."

"You all been to Atlanta?"

He ignored this. "Nobody else I knew frequented Keaton's, even though segregation had been over for years, and even though one is always surprised by the number of drug addicts in the world. As you no doubt know."

"As I no doubt know," I repeated amiably.

"I hope you don't mind. . . ."

"I've never been there either," I told him.

Brian blinked. "No," he said, after some thought. "Why would you go?"

"I never went chasing after my brother," I said evenly, watching him.

"No," he replied carefully.

"In fact," I added, "I've never even heard of the place."

"Of course not," Brian responded, after a pause. "Anyway ... his car wasn't there. I was glad it wasn't there, too, because I didn't want to go inside and I didn't want to confront Randall, either. I was confused."

"What sort of place was it?"

"A low cinderblock building, no more than ten or twelve feet high. No windows. Painted white a long time ago. A badly delineated chicken with a flamboyant red comb, topped by a chef's hat, wearing an apron, and pointing a barbecue fork, had been painted onto a piece of plywood which leaned against a tree next to the road. It was a county road—dirt—and the parking area was dirt with cars and trucks parked every which way. A thick layer of road dust coated everything. Stripped-out cars, doorless refrigerators, upside-down stoves and all kinds of other junk lay scattered through the woods around it." He moved an arm. "It's way worse than this place."

I cast a critical eye at the darkened storefront. "Maybe if we sold chicken and heroin, we'd be too busy to keep things tidy, too."

"Maybe that's the difference," Brian said dryly. "Keaton also sold whiskey. Bootlegging whiskey was his idea as a cover for selling dope. The sheriff got his cut from the bootlegging and stayed away."

Then, as now, hard alcohol was the state's own concession, jealously guarded, and many counties, Lee among them, were dry. "That's brilliant," I grudgingly allowed. "It's examples like Keaton's that bring me face to face with the possibility that when it comes to enterprise I exhibit very few symptoms."

"Keaton made a lot of money."

"I'll bet he did." I was still holding the gas cap. I looked at it and said, "How did a white high school boy so much as get his foot in the door of such a place?"

262

"It seems to me," Brian said measuredly, "that a junkie always finds a way."

I thoughtfully screwed on the gas cap before I allowed, "It's one of the verities."

After we'd savored this point for a moment, I said, "So you found him elsewhere?"

"I didn't know where else to look. I drove straight home. Only to find. . . . His car was in the yard. . . . He. . . ." Brian took a breath. "He was in bed. Dead."

I must have inhaled sharply, for Brian held up his hands, as if in apology, as if to indicate that he didn't know how else to tell it. I shook my head and waited for the rest.

"He was already . . . blue. And cool. His belt was looped around his biceps. The spike was still in his arm. If he'd come home right after momma and I had left, he could have been dead for two hours at least. Maybe three."

"Son of a bitch," I said softly.

"It was curious," Brian continued in a dull voice. "He was sitting against the headboard. His head drooped forward. His right hand was curled in his lap, very life-like, but a thin line of blood ran diagonally across the back of it, from thumb to wrist, directly beneath his nose. It was maybe an eighth of an inch wide and three inches long. Even in the dim light the line glistened, as bright as a streak of scarlet nail polish."

"Ahm," I hesitated, "hemorrhage?"

Brian shrugged.

"Do you think he. . . ?"

Brian finished the thought for me. "Maybe screwing up momma's ride to work put him over the top, maybe his death was an accident. Maybe not. It's hard to say. It's not possible to say." He stopped a moment. "It doesn't make any difference." He paused. In the silence the tree frog tried again and gave up again.

"Momma had moved us into the garage when we got old

263

enough to play the radio loud. We had it fixed up with a wood stove, a box fan in the back window, and a big army-surplus mosquito net over the garage door, which we left open all summer. The two beds stood against opposite walls with bookshelves, stacks of records, a couple of rugs. . . ."

"He came home to die," I inferred lamely.

"All the signs were there. We just didn't understand."

"It's hard for the rest of the world to understand if he didn't," I suggested, somewhat coldly.

"I checked for a pulse. I even pinched his nose and held a mirror to his mouth. Nothing. By the time I had proved to myself that he was dead, I had made my decision."

"Decision?" Had it been Brian, then, who enlisted?

"I took Randall's car and headed back to Keaton's."

"You what?"

"Randall had five dollars on him. I had a twenty. It's a solid one-hour drive, and this time I walked straight in. Keaton was sitting in a booth by the jukebox staring at nothing. He was a man who had been a heroin addict and a heroin dealer for thirty years, a guy who had seen everything. You've never met him."

"We practice divergent yogas."

"He's black as the eight ball and his teeth are all gold. He weighs 250 pounds and shaves his head. He often wears a brown suit jacket with thin mustard pinstripes over a pair of denim overalls with no shirt, no matter what the weather, and brown tasseled loafers with no socks. He sports little, black round shades which are sometimes parked up on his dome, and he carries a gold-handled walking stick, intricately carved, that somebody brought back from Africa and traded to him for dope. He spent most of his time stoned in that booth, collecting money."

"But why did you go there? To kill him?"

Brian shook his head. Negative. He was looking my way

now, but it wasn't because it was dark that he wasn't seeing me.

"Keaton's shades covered his eyes. I introduced myself. He tilted his head. The shades made it look as if he were looking over my shoulder at the wall behind me, or like he was blind. But he wasn't blind. He said, 'What you want, white boy?'

"'Sir,' I said, real nervous-like, 'I'm Randall Cook's little brother.'

"Keaton just sat there.

"'Brian Cook,' I added. "'Randall sent me.'

"A section of his upper lip rippled and showed a little gold. It looked like a snake crawling over a rock. I held out the twenty and the five.

"'Randall's sick, sir—I mean, Mr. Keaton. Randall's real sick.'

"Now Keaton allowed himself a little smile, and I knew I hated him. I hated all that gold in his mouth, I hated the formica table, I hated the jukebox, I hated the flies stuck to the spiral of yellow paper that hung from the ceiling in the corner behind him, and I hated that his dope had brought my brother back time and again until it killed him.

"'What's Randall took sick of?' Keaton asked, not bothering to conceal his amusement.

"I stood there holding out the damp and wadded money, and I told him, 'He said you'd know what I mean, Mr. Keaton. He said you'd have medicine for him.'

"Keaton touched his breast with the gold knob of his walking stick. 'He said that? About me? How I know what's makin' him sick? Huh, boy? How?'

"No doubt my desperation came across, plain as day. 'That's what he told me, Sir. Randall sent me because he's so sick he can't even drive.' I gestured toward the door. 'He gave me his car.'

"'Well,' Keaton said after a moment, 'I'll be dogged.' He

leaned over the table and had a good look at me. 'You ain't even old enough to drive yourself.'

"Now for a long time I looked younger than my years, but I don't know what came over me, to turn a color like I did and declare, 'Am too, Mr. Keaton. I got my permit last fall.'

"'Permit,' he snorted. 'What's that make you? Fifteen?'

"'Yessir,' I lied.

"'What you gonna do if the polices catches you drivin' at night?'

"'Show them Randall's license, Mr. Keaton," I replied as if slyly, "like I always do.'

Now by this spontaneous fib I managed to scare myself half to death. I was driving Randall's car, sure, but I did not have his driver's license. What possessed me to say such a thing? If Keaton asked to see it, what would I tell him?

"But Keaton enjoyed the story. 'Always? How many polices you been talkin' to lately?'

I looked completely caught out and said, 'Why none, sir,' and added, real sheepish, 'Lately.'

"'Haw!' Keaton banged the ferruled end of his stick on the floor so loud that I jumped. 'Listen at him!'

"'I ain't afraid of the police," I declared, stubborn and earnest.

"Keaton couldn't restrain himself. He reached out and ruffled the hair on my head, and I let him do it. His palm completely covered my skull. 'That's a good boy. You keep it that way. Let's hope you don't ever talk to no polices.'

"'Nor sheriff neither,' I extrapolated brightly.

"This elicited a great guffaw. 'Oh no sir,' Keaton roared, 'Not ever that damned sheriff!' He could hardly speak for laughing. When he'd settled down, he sat back on the naugahyde and mopped his brow and his face and his eyelids, up under the little glasses, with a canary-yellow kerchief imprinted with black polka dots. 'How much you got there, boy? What's your name?'

"'Brian, sir.' I held up the money. 'Twenty-five dollars, sir.'

"He leaned over the laminated table top, had a look at the money, then peered up and over the rims of his glasses at me. His brown eyes were so bloodshot and jaundiced they looked like the heart of a fresh papaya with two dilated pupils for seeds. 'That all the money you got?'

"I have to admit, if I hadn't hated that man so much, I'd have found it in me to be plenty scared. As it was, I stammered and beat around the bush until Keaton finally fished out of the bib of his overalls the biggest wad of cash I'd ever seen. As if it were as heavy as it looked, he rested the wrist of his money hand on the table top, licked the fingers of the other, and peeled through the wad until he found a ten. 'Here. Trade me.' We traded my twenty-five for his ten. "Elroy," Keaton shouted. 'Yo,' came a high, thin voice from kitchen pass-through.

"'Bring this here boy fifteen cents' worth of candy.'

"'Alreet.'

"Keaton had the twenty folded in among forty or fifty others and was working on the five likewise when Elroy came around the end of the cafe counter. Keaton gestured with his stick. 'Him.'

"Elroy was skinny and sick and old beyond his years. He wore a sauce-stained apron over filthy checkered wool trousers and a sleeveless undershirt. He hadn't shaved in weeks, his teeth were brown stumps or gone, his eyes looked worse than Keaton's, his spittle was flecked with snuff, his breath reeked of fortified wine, and his complexion was as runneled as a topographical map of southern Utah. There was a filter cigarette parked over one of his ears. On his head perched a formerly white double-ended paper hat. It looked like capsized dinghy with desperate handprints all over the

267

hull. Despite all these details Elroy manifested no more of a physical presence than a ghost. Without a word he handed me a bright green penny balloon with a knot in its neck and disappeared into the kitchen.

"I stood with the ten dollar bill in one hand and the balloon in the other, speechless, with little idea as to what was supposed to happen next.

"Keaton, idly thumbing the money in his fist without counting it, said, "If the polices pulls you over cause they think the car is driving itself cause you can't see over the steering wheel, you be sure to swallow that there balloon before he ever so much as gets out of his patrol car, and then you be real nice to him. Nothin' but polite. Show him Randall's license and tell him you just dropped you momma off to work at the chicken plant down at Guffries and you going straight home. Everything be fine. If he sees the need, let him search the car. Whenever he turns you loose, you praise the lord for watchin' over you and go straight home. Do you hear? Randall will know what to do then. Won't hurt a bit.' Keaton showed a lot of gold teeth. 'Heh heh heh.'

"I said thank you, sir, and got the hell out of there. A Cadillac had blocked the Fairlane and I never saw who was driving it, but I'd be goddamned if I was going back inside to ask for somebody to move it. I jacked that Ford around eight or nine times until it must have turned ninety degrees standing in place, and that with straight drive and a clutch and no power steering. I got on the road and even though it took an hour to make it back home, I arrived drenched in sweat.

"Momma was still at work. Randall lay right where I'd found him. I'd already covered him with a blanket and turned off all the lights, but I touched him anyway. He'd begun to stiffen. I switched on his reading lamp. His tongue had begun to swell behind his teeth. I turned off the light and went into the kitchen to the phone and figured out how to call the SBI."

268

The State Bureau of Investigation was an organization peculiar to North Carolina, so far as I knew, and it was a surprise
to me that any kid would ever have heard of it. I myself had
never heard of the SBI until two of its agents took away one
of the local pot dealers very early one morning just a few
months previous to my conversation with Brian. Later the
same day they returned to ask questions which betrayed a
startling collage of knowledge concerning daily life in the
vicinity of the store, an account as muddled as it was detailed.
For one example, their information held that the pot dealer
in question ran a tab with the store, and this was not accurate.
His girlfriend, who was nowhere to be found at that point,
did all the shopping, maintained the account, and settled up
promptly on the first of every month in cash. In fact, as I
pointed out to the agents, who didn't seem to be listening, I
so rarely saw the boyfriend I wasn't even sure what he looked
like. But, while these agents surely learned little enough from
me, my impression of them was passing strange. The leader
of the two was a white man less than thirty years old. He
wore a blue blazer, black penny loafers with dark blue socks,
a light blue dress shirt with a red striped tie, carefully pressed
khakis, after-shave, and a college ring. He was closely
barbered and his receding hair was clipped short, not quite
in the military fashion. For a guy who spent his days chasing
small-time pot dealers, his self-confidence, while certainly
informed by sociological contempt, seemed quite baseless.
This impression was only reinforced by his colleague, who
struck me as little more than a clone of his boss. If they packed
guns, I didn't see them, but the highway patrolman driving
them, and a sheriff's deputy accompanying them, were both
armed. The deputy I knew; being the sort of peace officer
who made a point of acquainting himself with everything
that went on in his jurisdiction, he stopped by the store every
month or two, just to say hello.

269

That Brian had heard of the SBI, however, was but one of his surprises.

"Two days later, I returned to Keaton's wearing a wire and bought three bags of dope for forty-five dollars."

"A wire?"

"Everything was recorded."

"The SBI let that go down? Your mother let it go down? Keaton let it go down?"

"Keaton treated me like a long-lost customer. He even offered me a beer."

"Did you accept?"

"I don't drink," Brian replied seriously.

"Hang on a minute. What happened to the corpse in your brother's bed? And, okay, let's suppose you found a way to handle your grief. What about your mother's?"

"The SBI had a morgue adjunct to their crime lab in Raleigh. They—we—convinced momma to put Randall on ice and postpone the funeral. She quit her job at the textile mill, the SBI put her on their own payroll, and they sent her to visit her sister in Memphis. It was the first time she'd ever been on an airplane. Aside from that and Randall's death, it was one of the nicest things that ever happened to her, too. She met my stepdad in church about two weeks later and she's never been back to Durham but once, to bury Randall and sell the house."

"What do you think?"

Brian shrugged. "He's okay. I don't see them that much."

I shook my head. "So then what happened?"

"An agent moved into our house and more or less acted like Randall, except he never went out. I made incrementally larger buys every few days, but not so large that one badly strung-out junkie couldn't run through them. After each trip I handed the dope and a cassette to the agent."

I didn't bother to conceal my incredulity. "This sounds risky for anybody, let alone a kid."

"Actually, Keaton wasn't the dangerous part. The SBI was interested in him, of course, along with his supplier, but what they really wanted was to roll up that sheriff. They'd been after him for years. But he was a cagey old boy."

"They were willing to risk a fifteen-year-old kid on that possibility?"

"Sixteen going on seventeen. They would have put their own people in the mix, but only if it could have been rationalized as helpful."

"I guess nobody saw the necessity."

"On the contrary. I ruled it out."

Could it be, I puzzled, that his brother's death had made a man out of Brian, overnight? "They wanted the sheriff; you wanted Keaton."

"The last night I went to the Chicken Shack, about three months after Randall's death, Keaton was a quieter than usual. He hadn't seen me in a couple of weeks, and this time I carried $300 with me, all grubby small bills, all of their serial numbers recorded."

"He suspected something?"

Brian smiled grimly. "He let on not a word. He was seated at his usual booth, back to the wall, facing the door. I laid the money on the table. He told me to count it and watched. When I got to three hundred, he said, 'I ain't got that much here.'

"This surprised me.

"'Tonight,' Keaton added, 'I ain't got nothing here at all. Not at all,' he added thoughtfully. It almost sounded like 'not ever.'

"I couldn't read him behind his shades, and it made me nervous. I said, 'Well, how about I come back tomorrow? Or maybe the next day?'

271

"Keaton said, 'What's today?'

"'Tuesday.'

"He thought about it. 'Come back Friday night.'

"'Friday night?' I said. 'Randall will be sick as a dog by Friday night, Mr. Keaton.'

"'Can't be helped," Keaton said. "Buy him some cough syrup." When I started to object, he pointed at the pile of money and said, 'You can leave this here and come get your stuff on Friday, or you can come back on Friday and we can do it all over again.'

"'You mean . . . leave a deposit?'

"'That's right.'

"'But we, you and I–'

"He shook his head. 'Elroy don't keep that amount of shit around here, and he ain't gonna front for you nor Randall neither.'

"Laying the onus of the whole operation on Elroy was one thing; but running short of product was something else. I wasn't sure what to do about it, but uncertainty was a luxury I couldn't afford. The money was marked. It seemed important to leave it. So I said I would.

"Keaton smiled, but he didn't seem pleased, exactly. I realized I'd made a mistake.

"'Well,' I ventured, 'this makes for a new level of trust in our relationship, Mr. Keaton." I eyed the pile of cash like it was a lifering and I was drowning.

"'Take your goddamn money,' Keaton said suddenly, without raising his voice, 'and git the fuck out of here.'

"The change of tone was unmistakable. Something had gone wrong. I didn't wait to find out what. I scooped up the money and headed for the door. It seemed a long way. As I passed the kitchen, I glimpsed Elroy, watching from the pass-through.

"I pushed open the screen door, and it felt like a great,

silent wind was resisting it. Like an idiot I turned and said, 'I'll see you on Friday, then?'

"Nobody said a word.

"Despite three or four cars parked out front there was no sign of anybody else, as usual. Except for the light from the screen door, and a metal-shaded clip-on lamp at the far end of an orange drop cord, which illuminated the plywood sign, it was quite dark. I went straight to the Ford, threw the money into the passenger footwell, and started the engine.

"I was tempted to drive off in the direction opposite the way I always went, just to change my luck. But somewhere back along my usual route an SBI agent was sitting in an unmarked car, backed off the county road onto an old sawmill or field access, waiting for me to pass by. I only occasionally spotted him, but I knew he was there somewhere and if I didn't behave according to pattern, things would go even more haywire. So I reversed onto the road and headed for home. Before I got out of first gear, the Ford's rear window exploded.

"I must have heard the shotgun, but I don't remember it. The glass just dissolved. I tromped on the accelerator so hard the engine almost choked. But then the little V8 woke up all of a sudden and gave me all I could handle just to keep the car on the road. When I reached for second gear, the rear end fishtailed like it was trying to get out from under the chassis. I got it straightened out and hauled down that county road like a bat out of Hades. It was all I could manage just to keep that Ford between the ditches. Through every curve the shattered safety glass sloughed over the rear shelf, the Ford wallowed sideways, and the tires threw gravel into the trees while I sawed at the wheel. A plume of dust trailed us hundreds of yards long and dozens high. The dollar bills spun around in the gloom of the passenger footwell like barn swallows over the mouth of a cave.

273

"Two or three miles north a pair of headlights swerved onto the road behind me, but I didn't let up. I couldn't be sure who it was. The headlights had to drop back on account of the obscurity of the dust, which was fine with me, but once back on the paved road they tightened up and followed me all the way home. I ran about 80 the whole way and almost missed the turn into the yard and barely got it stopped before I ploughed through the garage.

"My handler took a statement and made a call. Keaton was arrested that night."

I heard the willow limbs before I felt the breeze moving them. As I turned to face the possibility of cooler air, the compressor in the soft drink machine kicked on. The draft was refreshing but it didn't last. After a while I said, "That's a hell of a story." And I meant it. Then, "Did the court nail Keaton?"

"You could say so."

"What's that mean?"

"Elroy caught the assault charge."

"For the shotgun."

"Correct."

"What was wrong with attempted murder?"

Brian shrugged. "He snitched off the guy who sold them their whiskey and pled out to misdemeanor assault."

"Nice for him."

"Happens all the time."

"What about Keaton?"

"Keaton wouldn't deal and caught one to three in Raleigh Central."

"One to three years for dealing heroin?"

Brian shrugged. "The bastard had been telling the truth. There was heroin on his premises, but not much and he wasn't holding it. Nobody was holding anything. We figured that bad sheriff had got wind of our operation, told Keaton, and

Keaton cleaned up everything except for what he and Elroy needed to keep themselves straight. After about two days of searching a couple of balloons turned up, parked on the top plate between two rafters in the outhouse. Keaton didn't have a single marked bill from the previous buys, and none ever turned up. But the cops had the recordings I'd made, and they had all the dope I bought. What with one thing and another, he pled it down to something called possession with intent to sell. It's a felony, but not much of one."

"What about the sheriff?"

Brian shrugged. "They got him about two years later on something else, some chicken shit thing, taxes or something, and let him resign."

I considered this. "Keaton must be out by now."

"He served about fourteen months."

"He returned to Lee County?"

Brian nodded.

"Back in business?"

He turned his palms up.

"Son of a bitch. What about you?"

"I graduated from high school the next spring, one year early, and joined the Marines a few months after that, one day after my eighteenth birthday."

So somebody in Brian's story had made it into the armed forces after all. "But," I objected, "you were the only surviving son. You should have been exempt from service."

Brian nodded. "I volunteered as a corpsman. But because of my law enforcement experience, modest as it was, I saw no hospitals or combat. I spent my tour with the MPs, investigating drug smuggling at Fort Bragg and various other military facilities."

"Any sign of that CIA heroin?"

Brian smiled thinly.

"I suppose I would have heard about something that

spectacular," I conceded. "But it sounds as if you were destined for a career in law enforcement." Who was fishing now? "Practically from the cradle," I added.

Brian smiled, a little more broadly this time, and shook his head. "It was none of my doing. Once we took down Keaton, I was done. It was a lot more revenge or justice or whatever you want to call it than most people get. No . . . I joined the Marines so I could go to medical school on the GI Bill."

"Which is what you're doing now."

For the first time Brian genuinely smiled, though he looked tired. "What I'm doing now is going to work."

"The GI Bill doesn't cover everything," I concluded.

"The GI Bill doesn't cover everything," he confirmed. He pulled out his billfold and gestured toward the gas pump.

By then it was so dark I had to read the figure off the side of the pump that faced the soft drink machine. Be assured, there are people who might have lit a match.

We straightened out the bill. One last time, my thoughts returned to the pistol clipped to the transmission tunnel. "So the Browning is just in case."

Brian glanced toward it. It was too dark to see the pistol, but that didn't mean it wasn't there.

"Keaton made some threats."

"That was a long time ago."

"Almost seven years."

"I hope you never have to use it."

Brian shrugged. "As far as I know, he's right down that road, about twenty-five miles. Only half way to Sanford." He pointed a finger in that direction, straight south. "I'd like to see that bastard try to put a move on me."

We could see less than a dim quarter of a mile down the road before it curved out of sight.

"So now I'm late," Brian said. But he didn't move.

"Medical school by day and a job by night," I said. "That must be tiring."

He nodded wearily. "Chemistry class is a little somnambular. I catch a little shuteye on the job, too."

"What's the job? Something amenable to napping and studying? Parking lot attendant?"

"Close. That's pretty close." Brian sat into his sports car and started the engine. He snapped on the lights and said, "I'm the night man at the county morgue."

The top was down on the MGB. The night was warm. It would be a pleasant drive to town.

"See you next week," Brian said.

I stood in the dark and listened to the MGB run through its gears until it was no longer audible. In the ensuing silence a cricket started, and the tree frog in the willow, and a whippoorwill.

Inside the store I turned on the lights. I still had an hour till closing, but business was unlikely. I stood behind the counter and stared at nothing, straining the hair on the back of my head through the fingers of one hand, as if studious or absentminded. They look the same. After a minute or two I pulled the hand away to regard, between the tips of the thumb and middle finger, the slowly wavering, inexorable forelegs of a wood tick, now deprived of its chance to dig in.

I turned it loose on the back of my hand and watched it make its way toward the wrist, as unerring in its instinct for mammalian blood as nature could possibly refine it. But I've seen a lot of these creatures, everybody has, and when it got to clambering among the hairs of my forearm I plucked up the tick and dropped it into a fruit jar, half-filled with kerosene, kept under the cash register for just that purpose.

277

While we had published a couple of stellar issues before, it wasn't until the Winter 2000 issue that we really started to define what it was we hoped to do with the magazine. Miller's story appeared in the same issue as Darren Subarton's seminal "Nil Desperandom" (which should have been in this book, but I couldn't find Darren to ask him!) and Victor Gischler's depraved Christmas story "Santa and the Concubines." We couldn't stop laughing at the awfulness of these hyper-violent and wonderfully written pulp tales. Miller's story is over the top, to say the least, and worth the pole vault it takes to get there. This is the first of several Miller published with us through the years.

Stealing Klatzman's Diary
Kevin James Miller

Getting Klatzman's diary meant killing Klatzman and taking it off his dead body, and a whole bunch of people had tried to kill Klatzman.

Sherman and Little Tucker sat at an open-all-night donut shop. They planned jobs here. A neon sign in the window spelled "DONUTS."

"Sherman, my faithful colleague," Little Tucker said, "isn't there a way to get out of this job?"

Sherman always looked sleepy, but he never took his eyes off what interested him. "We did the bank job in Berteau's territory, didn't pay the commission."

Sherman used to be a garbage man and Little Tucker used to teach high school. Crime didn't pay more than sanitation or education, but had more challenges.

Little Tucker looked like his name—a small, thin man with feminine features and clean. He wore a gray tee-shirt, black suit coat, vanilla white sneakers, faded denim, and brown leather. He had encouraged the underworld nickname of "Little Tucker" because "the Elf" sounded way too soft and cute for a professional crook.

Sherman had the casual, rough majesty of an ape. He always sat or stood with an artful slouch. His hair looked like frayed black and gray rope.

They had done the First Millennium Bank.

A few days after that job, a thug appeared in their apartment, a loft near the river that looked over a street of bars and antique shops. The thug had the large chest, gut, and box-like build the two thieves always associated with professional wrestlers. He wore an expensive suit.

The thug introduced himself as Snooker, said whom he worked for, and went on to describe the names and personal lives of all of Sherman and Little Tucker's relatives. No formal threats, except the last moment when Snooker said, "This has been a threat."

"Yeah," Little Tucker said. "We picked up on that."

Little Tucker made some calls (he carried the cell phone, and stayed in touch with Sally, he and his partner's police contact), worked the streets, and found out about their error. Sally had been the lover of Little Tucker, then Sherman, then both of them, and then neither of them. Her brother, a drug dealer, got beaten up by a cop to get a confession to two murders. Sally's brother died, the cop got away with it, and Sally chose some long-term revenge.

Berteau asked for a meeting in a neighborhood gym, a red brick building, after it closed for the day.

Two uglies escorted Sherman and Little Tucker inside the gym, to the pool, one of them their old friend Snooker.

He had a new statement to make, that everyone present also all knew. "You're here to see Mr. Berteau."

"Thank you," Little Tucker said, trying to avoid sarcasm.

The other thug looked eighteen. The left side of his face had a dozen shiny metal studs and pins in it, plus his beige suit was too big.

They walked through a cramped room, filled with free weight equipment.

The chlorine from the pool smelled strong. Berteau never came out of the pool. Berteau, a distinguished-looking man about sixty with a full head of steel-gray hair, had a hard, rough build. He swam and did laps.

"I control this territory. You guys did the bank and didn't give me a cut." He kicked back off the deep end.

"Sorry, sir." Little Tucker wished he had a hat to take off and hold in front of himself.

"We didn't know." Sherman took off his cowboy hat and held it in front of himself.

"Well, you know now." Berteau reached up out of the water and hung off the diving board. "How did you do the bank anyway? The media and police reports are confusing."

"We got some sort of knockout gas from an elderly manufacturer of LSD." Little Tucker felt like he was giving a book report in primary school. "He decided to leave the country and needed some quick cash. So we bought the gas. Sherman and I came in wearing masks, deployed the gas, spray painted the security cameras, emptied the cash drawers, left. We can get you half the haul from the bank job, in any form you want. American money, Euros, bonds. . . ."

"Independents never understand." Berteau swam on. "I let you two pay me my cut now, you're like club members paying late fees. Then, in a month or two, any of a dozen possible guys feeds my own balls to me. This way, I look innovative, and in charge."

"Uh, what way, sir?" Sherman squirmed in his cowboy boots.

"To make it up, you two are going to steal Lou Klatzman's diary and give it to me."

So the two thieves sat in the donut shop and bought more coffee.

Little Tucker said, "We need information!"

They went to see Petrovich. In a converted warehouse that was now a movie theater, Petrovich, a young man, worked as a projectionist. He had a solid reputation as a source of underworld information. (He had gangster uncles.)

The theater's owners had slapped together the projection room from old, cheap wood and then saturated it with a dozen coats of black paint. A fading yellow bulb in the ceiling lit the room. The movie Petrovich showed screamed in French.

Petrovich was skinny, but with lots of sagging, pale, hairy skin. He wore black jeans and a white Tee-shirt, with the faded logo of a band on it.

Sherman sat in a corner eating popcorn.

Little Tucker listened to Petrovich as he made reel changes.

"Lou Klatzman is a fence." The young projectionist chewed on a fingernail.

"Know this already, Petrovich," Little Tucker said, standing, rocking back and forth on his heels.

"You don't know what kind of fence. You steal it, he'll find a buyer." He shook an index finger to emphasize a point, a habit Little Tucker hated in anybody.

"Example."

Petrovich smiled. "A 1987 college biology textbook."

Little Tucker shrugged. "Big deal."

"Every sixth page with a detailed pornographic drawing on it, in black ink?" He looked over his shoulder at the two of them, and adjusted the movie's sound.

This made Sherman look a little less sleepy. "What?"

"Once this buyer in, get this, Finland, looked for just such an item. It had to be every sixth page. Heard Klatzman got a million for it."

Sherman sat up straight. "Where did such an item come from? Who would buy it?"

Little Tucker shook his head. "It doesn't matter. So our man, Klatzman, records his business, numerically, porno illustrated college textbook and all, in his diary." Petrovich nodded. "Description."

Petrovich described what the diary looked like.

Sherman had his pocket sketchbook out. He knew what his partner intended and they hadn't even discussed what the big plan might be.

Sherman held up the new drawing. "Like this?" The drawing showed a small, hardcover book with a Florida postcard taped to the front and KLATZMAN written down the left side, also on the front cover.

Petrovich nodded. "Yeah, that's it."

The boys left. They were almost to the parking lot when a beige van appeared and stopped. Doors flew open, arms pulled them inside, and off they went down the streets of the city.

The interior of the van was a glossy sky blue. That's all the two thieves could make out, because people pressed tight around them.

These people looked young, clean, athletic and sharp. Betty Sue Janger, new head of the local FBI office, sat on a little stool. A lady of about forty-five, with a thin face, she wore her long, gray-streaked hair up. She wore, just like Petrovich, sneakers and black jeans, but these looked shiny and new. She wore a dark blue windbreaker, too, every snap fastened, with the stylized image of an eagle.

Ms. Janger looked at her watch. "Good evening, boys."

"We know who you are." Sherman paused, because the woman's expression seemed a battleground for two moods: anger and patience. "Ma'am." Sherman took off his cowboy hat.

Some of the feds smirked, and some growled at Sherman's remark.

"Well, you're a bright young man," Ms. Betty Sue Janger said. It must have been sarcastic but sounded sincere.

Little Tucker decided he didn't care if forty lay behind him.

People who called you "young man" but looked like they didn't have ten years' lead on you were just damned annoying.

"I know who you are." She rattled off their full legal names, and then added one word. "Thieves."

Little Tucker faked concern. "There's been some sort of mistake. My colleague and I find promising pieces of art by struggling artists and sell it for them to collectors and galleries, and take a small commission."

They needed a cover to please cops and IRS agents. Art worked.

"Listen to her," said a young fed with blond crewcut. He looked at his boss. "Oh, uh, sorry for interrupting."

"You aren't, Agent Norbert," Ms. Janger said.

Little Tucker wanted to be polite. A crook who tried to be tough with cops, especially federal cops, fell out of the game. "You look like a decent, reasonable woman."

She shifted her attention to him and him alone. "I am."

"A good wife and mother." Little Tucker had no idea why he babbled like this.

"Sure." She shrugged.

"Which is what you always wanted, even when you were a little girl." Little Tucker paused. "Right?"

"Not always." She looked far away, then brought her attention back. "You two are crooks. I'm FBI. I can arrest you, hand you off to the next musical chair, or you two and I can play friends. Would you like to know how?"

Little Tucker indulged in a pause. "Okay."

She touched Little Tucker on the shoulder. "You can help me put Frankie Berteau away."

Sherman said, "Well, if we were criminals, how would we go about helping you with this mission of yours?"

"You're a bright young man, and I'm in the book." The smile dropped off her face. "Let them out."

She dropped them off back at their car. They watched as the beige van drove off.

Sherman looked at the departing van, then his partner, then the van, and back at his partner. "What do you think?"

"I think she has some information on us." Little Tucker looked at his colleague. "Just some."

"Wwwwweeeellll, Frankie Berteau must have pissed off the wrong people to be drawing this much federal heat this soon. He's controlled this territory for, what? Three months?"

Little Tucker took out his cell phone and tapped it with an index finger. "Got a call from Sally. Berteau cut a deal with terrorists. He got them heavy firepower off the black market."

"Arabs?"

Little Tucker looked at the ground. "Americans. American terrorists, Sherman."

"The Army of the Lost?" Sherman closed his eyes and pulled news stories out of his memory.

Little Tucker looked at him. "No. Those other guys. The Flaming White Sword."

In the next few weeks, Sherman and Little Tucker tracked Lou Klatzman and mulled over his movements and schedule.

Part of Little Tucker felt sorry he had to do this job, because Lou Klatzman had lots of height, weight, and baldness. Little Tucker had affection for the general idea of big fat bald men. All of his male relatives, including his father, had been (or were) big fat bald men.

Klatzman spent lots of his time around booze. Klatzman had "liquor distributor" for IRS cover. It made honest criminals wonder why he needed to work the crooked path. The liquor distributorship dodge allowed much legal cash to flow one's way.

Klatzman went all places with his two bodyguards, identical twins. The two men were close to seven feet. They bleached their hair and wore long orange coats.

285

Were Little Tucker and Sherman going to rob Klatzman at the roller rink? Bowling alley? The planetarium? None of Klatzman's haunts seemed the right place to make a grab, and switch, for the diary.

Sherman, his cowboy-boot-shod feet up on a cheap coffee table, drew his and Little Tucker's ideas for the robbery and taped them up on the walls. "Do you want to sell out Frankie Berteau to Ms. Janger?"

"I think that she doesn't care, exactly, about following her rules. She didn't quite make a deal with us. She floated a possibility."

The week they were finishing planning the robbery, they got another phone call from Sally. Berteau didn't get those terrorists, the Flaming White Sword, guns. Then, what? Sally told them Betty Sue Janger didn't know either but wanted to. (Janger now wore a silver locket on a gold chain and acted weird about it.)

The solid bones of a plan appeared. Tuesday afternoons, Klatzman, barreling alongside his twin bodyguards with bleached hair and orange leather coats, went to a high stakes poker game in the back room of a hardware store. Klatzman and his men took the alley to the back door. Now about halfway up the alley there hung an old brown door with a crack in it, leading to an empty storefront.

Sherman had checked the foot and traffic patterns around the entrance to the alley, moving his cowboy hat, which had been covering one of his drawings. He gave Little Tucker a verbal summary of the hand-drawn map.

Little Tucker picked up his scribbled notes. "Cops have a foot patrol man who comes by that time." He tapped his red pen against his notebook, lost in his thoughts.

They looked at each other and smiled. "The Cop And The Robber," they said together.

Next Tuesday afternoon, Little Tucker got the foot patrol

cop from behind. Nothing permanent. Knocked him on the head and dragged him away. Tied him up and gagged him.

Klatzman, the hot afternoon sunlight gleaming off his bald head and his twin bodyguards (almost running to keep up with their boss, pulling their orange leather coats tighter) came out of the hardware store and started up the concrete alley.

A pistol in each hand, Sherman appeared at the end of the alley. Sherman had replaced his usual cowboy gear with black shoes, black pants, shirt, long coat and big hat, black scarf covering his face. He shot down the two bodyguards as they reached into their long orange leather coats, and then started shooting at Klatzman, missing by inches. Sherman had lots of spare ammo. Klatzman took cover behind a garbage dumpster and had his piece out and engaged in a firefight with Sherman.

Klatzman cracked off more than a dozen shots toward Sherman, popped the spent ammo clip out, bouncing it off the alley wall as he slammed a new clip in. Then he rationed out his shots.

Little Tucker rushed to Klatzman's "help." Little Tucker's disguise, besides the cop uniform (from the back of his closet, for jobs like this one), made him look like a tall blond guy with a mustache and 1970s sideburns. The two of them took cover behind the dumpster.

"Are you okay?"

"That bastard down there is trying to kill me!"

"He's killed your two friends!"

Klatzman shrugged. "That, too!"

Little Tucker had the radio in his hand as Sherman and Klatzman continued to blast away at each other. "Request immediate backup at 2159 East Lang Street!" He described the whole situation, the working radio tuned to a real police dispatcher.

The dispatcher acknowledged over the radio speaker and

Little Tucker, fake cop, turned off the walkie-talkie as the dispatcher started to ask for more information.

Little Tucker had his pistol out. He threw a few shots down the alley to make it all look good.

"This man might be a lot more than just a mugger, sir."

Klatzman took out his diary. "The bastard probably wants this."

Little Tucker took the book with the Florida postcard and KLATZMAN on the cover. He looked at it, front and back cover, and spine, but didn't open the book. Little Tucker scratched his head. "All this just for this book?"

Klatzman got distracted long enough by Sherman's shooting not to be looking at Little Tucker for a moment. Then he looked back over his shoulder and demanded his book back. "Those are my business records," he added.

"Sorry, sir." Little Tucker gave the copy back, having switched it for the original.

Sirens in the distance, and Sherman disappeared.

"You wait here, sir."

Sherman disappeared by the time the police patrol unit, red lights spinning on top, slammed to a halt at the end of the alley. Little Tucker ran toward the street.

He ducked into the door to the empty storefront and made his way to the rendezvous point, leaving the cops, the real cops, to sort things out.

Little Tucker made phone calls to Ms. Betty Sue Janger and Frankie Berteau.

Sherman set up the actual logistics for phase two, making sure he wiped the book clean of their fingerprints.

He came back to the apartment. Little Tucker got off the cell phone again with Sally. Police detectives who had worked kidnapping cases had been sniffing around Klatzman's and Berteau's lives.

Kidnapping? Who did Klatzman and Berteau snatch?

288

Klatzman's diary rested in a safety deposit box at First Millennium Bank.

"Why didn't you two just bring the diary?" Berteau demanded when Little Tucker and Sherman went to see him again, again doing laps in that pool. In his red swimsuit, the crime boss looked like a comic book superhero who'd lost his cape.

Sherman said, "Because with special items like this, Mr. Berteau, sir, the receiving party often likes to take the merchandise and then wrap up loose ends. None of us are going to try to hurt each other in a bank."

"Shit. I got to go into a stupid bank." He dogpaddled over to them and scowled. "That breaks my rule about my accountant doing all the details involving money. In business, you have to have rules. Okay. Fine. All this gets you guys is clear with me for doing that robbery and not getting me a cut."

Near the safety deposit vault, beyond a door, ran a corridor and small rooms where safety deposit box owners could, in privacy, go through their safety deposit boxes, putting in and taking out what they needed. In one of these little rooms, Berteau and his bodyguards (Snooker and the kid with all the metal on half his face) and Sherman and Little Tucker stood around a table.

Five people and a table were a tight fit in that room. Light shone down from the ceiling. Air conditioning hummed. Snooker looked like he needed drinks. The kid with metal in half his face smelled like he had objections to deodorant.

Sherman put the box on the table.

Snooker said, "The boss will now look at the object in question." Why didn't this guy just pass out programs?

Berteau wore a black and gray ensemble, a blue silk tie with large, faint blue polka dots on it, and glasses with thin metal frames, shiny and yellow like gold.

Berteau opened the box and took out Klatzman's diary.

Little Tucker got a cell phone call. After the conversation, he told everyone that his and Sherman's police department contact said the cops had a warrant for their apartment. They had incriminating items to remove!

Sherman and Little Tucker walked through the bank lobby, toward the street exit. Betty Sue Janger put her tiny black and green cell phone away. Around her neck, she wore the locket that Sally had mentioned. It went well with the white blouse she wore with the lace collar and sleeves, and the large navy blue suit coat. She combed her gray streaked hair straight back, plastered down with hair spray, making her face look thinner than the last time.

"Now why did I just call you, as you asked me?"

Sherman said, "So we're not in the way when you arrest Frankie Berteau for possessing an object from an armed robbery a few days ago–Lou Klatzman's diary."

"Deposit box Privacy Room Three," Little Tucker added.

Ms. Janger smiled and went to the BOX OWNER PRIVACY ROOMS door, taking out her FBI identification and pistol.

The two thieves stepped outside. Petrovich appeared, gun in hand with overcoat over gun, an eighth of an inch of barrel showing. The projectionist wore a gray suit coat and pink silk tie. The loose, pale flesh on his young face didn't help the look of knowing sophistication that he tried to pull off.

Sherman said, "That's a new look for you isn't it, Petrovich?"

"Let me guess," Little Tucker said. "You were Berteau's backup, just in case."

Petrovich said, "Go back into the bank."

Under the persuasive power of Petrovich's gun, they walked back into the bank, wearing wide smiles of stiff insincerity.

Back in deposit box Privacy Room Three, Berteau played

generous host. Betty Sue Janger still had her pistol out and held it level.

"These are the two gentlemen I told you about. I am a legitimate independent consultant to securities and investment firms. I wanted to invest in gallery art. These two represented themselves to me as legitimate art dealers. They said the book contains sketches by an artist I want to invest in. However, it seems a record of activity by some criminal named Lou Klatzman."

Janger turned to the two thieves. "What do you two have to say?"

Little Tucker said, "You won't find our fingerprints on it."

Ms. Janger's cell phone rang. She took it out and answered it. "Janger. Go ahead . . . are you sure? Okay. Stay there. I might need the team in a moment." She put the phone away.

"The Army of the Lost assassinated Lou Klatzman three hours ago." The criminals in the room looked at each other. "I'm sure you're all wondering why a left-wing terrorist group would kill a fence. Oh wait. You're all law-abiding citizens and you don't know Lou Klatzman was a fence. Right?"

Berteau said, "My lawyers and I will be happy to explain."

Agent Norbert came in.

"Uh, I'm not interrupting anything, am I?"

Ms. Janger said, "What is it?"

"I finally got a straight answer from the Anti-Terrorism Unit," Agent Norbert said.

"So?"

Agent Norbert looked at Berteau and his bodyguards. "Our colleagues allege that, per the request of the Flaming White Sword, Mr. Berteau and his men kidnapped an African-American, an Hispanic, a lesbian, a Muslim and a Jew, sold them to Lou Klatzman, and Klatzman in turn sold them to the Flaming White Sword, who tortured them to death."

It got quiet.

291

Ms. Janger took off the necklace and opened the locket. Inside were two photographs of a pretty, redheaded woman. She showed it to Agent Norbert. "Is this one of the people they killed?" She held her breath.

Agent Norbert looked right into her eyes and hesitated. "Yes."

She breathed again and gave the locket to Agent Norbert. "Keep that for me for now."

"'Not always,'" Sherman said, echoing the conversation in the van, pushing back his cowboy hat.

"Not what you always wanted, Ms. Janger," Little Tucker added, starting to rock back and forth on his heels in tiny movements.

Agent Norbert pocketed the locket.

Berteau flicked a speck of dirt off his golden-framed glasses. "If everyone is finished framing me and making outrageous accusations, my associates and I would like to leave."

Ms. Janger's grey-streaked hair gleamed. "You aren't going anywhere."

Berteau made a tight little grin. His small teeth were very white. "You have nothing to hold me on."

The lace at the FBI station chief's collar and sleeves bristled. "This is isn't about the law anymore."

Agent Norbert's blond crewcut looked sweaty. "Uh, Ms. Janger. . . ?"

"Be quiet, Agent Norbert," she replied.

Not in a bank, Little Tucker thought. *My list of places where I don't have to worry about my safety is too small already.*

Sherman thought, *Little Tucker and I must get out of the city. Berteau will want our skins. Might be a good idea to see about leaving the country.*

Ms. Janger said, "I'm going to ignore that little pipsqueak covering the two thieves with the little girl's gun."

Petrovich said, "Hey!"

292

"Then I'm going to kill your two thugs, and then you, Mr. Berteau."

Berteau laughed.

Which Ms. Janger took in stride. "Why are you laughing, little boy?"

Berteau, surprised by the "little boy" crack, stayed with the matter at hand. "Because you're a federal cop."

"You're something worse than a criminal," Ms. Janger replied. "You service the needs of monsters."

Berteau smirked. "Isn't that just a little too politically correct?"

Janger, who had been holding her gun level all this time, let it dangle at her side. "You want to spend your last moments of life ridiculing me? I'm your executioner. Interesting tactic."

Berteau's bodyguards began to reach into their coats. "No, you morons! You draw first she can fake self-defense!"

Ms. Janger said, "You're a lousy conversationalist. Better a corpse."

Janger snapped her Glock 17 up and Agent Norbert yanked out his, and Snooker and the kid with all the metal in half his face started to take out Beretta 92s, and Snooker's enormous gut and chest seemed to roll right off his body, and Berteau pulled out his Beretta 92 one second faster than his men, and the two thieves dived toward the floor together, and while they were doing that the shooting started, and by the time the thieves got to the floor to cower, the eliminated Snooker and the kid with all the metal in half his face, now corpses, part of their skulls gone, hit the floor with Sherman and Little Tucker, along with Petrovich, who never fired, just collapsed into a ball and pissed his pants, and two seconds into the shooting, cowering on the floor, pressed up against two dead men, and a fellow coward, who at least had a gun, the two got glimpses of running and scrambling, intense but not going very far in the cramped room, and the flashing of gunshots, and the stench of gunpowder, and the stupid animal banging and booming of the weapons, and the two thieves half understood that Berteau must have avoided the first couple of rounds from Ms. Janger and Agent Norbert, and so the crime boss must have got off two or three or maybe five shots, and then he got shot eight or nine or ten times and how many rounds does a Glock 17 hold again oh isn't this bastard dead yet, and finally Berteau took a hint and died.

When they heard five seconds of silence, the two thieves let out breaths they didn't know they were holding.

On the floor, they took their hands away from their eyes. The three slaughtered gangsters, and the gore that dripped away from them, piled up in one corner of the room. Together, Little Tucker and Sherman rolled the whimpering Petrovich, who still hadn't fired and still had his coat over his gun, off themselves, and stood up into a lingering cloud of gun smoke.

Uniformed bank security appeared at the door, large men in black uniforms. Ms. Janger flashed her ID. "FBI station chief! No one in this room until I say so!" The bank guys disappeared.

Ms. Janger looked at the thieves. "As far as you two are concerned, this never happened. You were never here."

Little Tucker said, "Are you sure you wouldn't want to shoot us also and cover that up as well?"

"You two just got thrown a bone. Take it and leave town. I want what happened in this room always to be a little fuzzy."

Later, as they packed to leave town, Sherman said, "I thought we could plan for everything."

Little Tucker finished packing a suitcase. He sat on it. "I guess that's just about it. Oh yeah, I almost forgot." He took out a piece of bluish white paper and tossed it over to Sherman. Sherman looked at it. "Another goodie from Sally. Copy of the autopsy report on one of Berteau's thugs."

"Snooker?"

"No. The kid with all the metal in half his face. He had partly digested paper in his stomach."

"So Berteau had him eat the part of the diary with the kidnappings recorded on it after we left the room and before Ms. Janger walked in," Sherman said.

Little Tucker shrugged. "I'm trying to decide how much she suspected, about what Berteau and Klatzman did."

"Bet she still doesn't think she's a criminal. Even after what she did in that room."

"No," Little Tucker disagreed. "She knows she's one of us now. Even if she never does anything illegal again. Guys like Berteau and Klatzman know that jokers like you and me will do anything to win. People like Ms. Janger are supposed to be by the book and steady as a rock. Anybody can be pushed too far, even people who are supposed to hold everything together."

"God help the Flaming White Sword, or whoever tracks them down."

"Partner, they are totally, completely worthless shits."

"I know. God help them anyway."

295

I remember Gischler telling me, "The Ice Harvest, man. You've got to read this!" So I gave it a shot, not sure what to expect. I tell you what, though—the title is spot-on. That book is cold, unflinching, and funny as hell. A man after our own hearts. Scott dares to think that violence and vulgarity are the best places to dig up humor. And I do mean "dig," because it's dirty and black—try his gonzo-Western, Cottonwood, *to see what I mean.*

We met Scott in Austin at Bouchercon, chased him down and bought him liquor, and then told everyone at nearby tables that this guy was the one to beat. His writing pretty much sums up the Crimedog philosophy.

Crow Killers
Scott Phillips

T he cold Monday before Thanksgiving, we skipped out
on school after lunch, bought a case of Falstaff at a
blind pig, and headed out of Wichita on a joyride. By
late afternoon, the sky was grey and drizzling and we'd ended
up way the hell out west in Stafford County, shooting roosting
crows out the windows of a brand new '38 LaSalle doing fifty
or sixty, blasting the bastards with a twelve gauge just to
watch them disintegrate. By five o'clock or so, when the sun
started getting really low, you could find crows all over hell
and gone in that part of Kansas, sitting on fenceposts and
cawing at one another. Grady Cherkas was at the wheel with
a Falstaff in his left hand, scared shitless of driving that fast,
his eyes popping out of his bucktoothed skull. I had the
shotgun pointed out the passenger side window; I'd nailed
ten of them in less than half an hour.

"Come on, Wayne, let me shoot some of 'em." The girlish
whine came from Sylvester Halliburton, pouting in the
backseat because I hadn't let him take the wheel or the
shotgun yet even though it was his old man's car. He was
unhappy we were still out this late and this far west, still
more so that we'd had to put the spare tire on after a blowout.
Eager as he was to get back into our good graces, he'd readily
agreed when I'd suggested we borrow the LaSalle. I'd been
on poor terms with him since I'd stolen his girlfriend, but he

297

seemed ready to forgive that offense and be friendly again. He even claimed I'd done him a favor because he was now going steady with the lovely Bobbi Brickman. He was putting a brave face on it, though; swell tits notwithstanding, Bobbi was a lousy lay and a notorious semen-spitter, certainly no peer of my ravenous Sally's. I had other reasons to be uncomfortable in his presence, though; there are transgressions sufficient to inspire the docile to mayhem and murder, and I preferred to keep Sylvester in the dark about certain recent ones of mine.

"Lookit, a hawk," Grady yelled, beer slopping out the sides of his mouth in his breathless excitement. "In the tree."

"Too big for a hawk," I said, taking aim.

It sat motionless in an old cottonwood, hard to make out in the cold haze of the coming evening and much farther than any crow I'd shot that day. When my first shot missed, it took off flying across the road, and I saw for the first time how big the son of a bitch truly was. I fired with the other barrel as it crossed the road overhead, and this time he went down tumbling at a forty-five degree angle, hitting the dead grass on the other side of the gravel road.

"Turn around," I yelled at Grady, and he spun the LaSalle right onto the shoulder and stopped, stalled. He looked at the wheel for a moment, confused as to why we hadn't ended up on the road where he'd been aiming.

Grady leaned over to grab another Falstaff from the case at my feet, his belly hanging down like a pregnant sow's. He opened the bottle and took a long, happy swig. "This goddamn LaSalle don't steer for shit," he said. "Let's go have a looksee at that carcass."

The bird lay sprawled a dozen yards ahead of us. Its head and neck were white, its massive wings and body dark brown except for the white at the end of its tail.

"Holy shit," Sylvester yelled. "That's a goddamn eagle."

"Bald eagle," I said, unable to resist the temptation to correct Sylvester.

"Shit," Grady said. "Isn't that against the law?"

"Against the law my ass," I said. "Farmers shoot hawks every damn day and nobody gives a hot shit."

"For your information," Sylvester said, "the bald eagle happens to be our national bird, and it's illegal to shoot them." His fists on his hips, he looked just like the shitbird little hall monitor he was at heart.

I grabbed him by the lapels of his corduroy jacket. "You little prick, how was I supposed to know it was a goddamned bald eagle? You're just as guilty as me."

"How do you reckon that? I was sitting in the back seat." He looked a little scared, as though I might be planning to pin the whole criminal enterprise on his frail shoulders.

Grady knelt for a closer look. "I never saw one of these in Kansas, that's for sure. Aren't they supposed to live up in Alaska or someplace?"

"Hell if I know. We'd better make ourselves scarce before someone happens along and we end up in the poke."

The eagle had his revenge: he had drained the joy out of our carefree teenage sport. After fifteen minutes and five assassinated crows, I was so dispirited I let Sylvester ride in front and gave him the twelve gauge. He missed three of the four crows he fired at, but to give him his due the night had pretty much fallen by then.

In the back seat I was deep in reflection, and when it was finally too dark to shoot, and Sylvester rolled up the window, I spoke up. "I bet you could get a couple hundred dollars or more for a bald eagle, stuffed and mounted. Museum or a high-class speak, maybe."

"I bet you could," Grady said.

"It's our national bird, fellows. We can't sell it. We'll get in a world of trouble."

299

"Open your mouth about that one more time, Halliburton, and I'll tell the cops you fucked it first."

Sylvester didn't say anything more until we got pretty close to where we thought the thing lay.

"It was close to those Burma Shave signs," he said, and as it happened, Grady and I both remembered the signs, too. We got out of the LaSalle with the headlights still burning and started off in search of our trophy. It was colder now, and the drizzle was getting to be more like sleet. I had an electric flashlight in my hand that barely illuminated the patchy yellow grass in front of us.

"You sure it wasn't the other Burma Shave signs?"

Right then the eagle, alive as you or me, half-flew, half hopped into the flashlight beam and made a horrible kind of squawking complaint at us, his enormous golden beak wide open and threatening to bite our collective nutsacks clean off.

Sylvester and Grady both yelped and retreated a few paces. I was too surprised and scared to do anything for a second, and by the time I could move, I'd realized that the thing couldn't fly; he was too badly hurt to do us any damage except at extremely close quarters.

"Sylvester, you hold this light on it so it doesn't get away." I handed him the flashlight and, with some reluctance, he shone it at the bird while I humped it back to the car. The tire iron was in the trunk with the busted tire, and when I got back, the two of them were discussing in low tones whether this was such a good idea or not.

Sylvester spoke up first. "Say, Wayne, maybe we ought to just leave the thing alone. We were worried about how killing an American eagle's against the law, and here it turns out we haven't killed it after all."

In the faint, diffused beam of the LaSalle's headlamps Sylvester found it impossible to return my basilisk gaze. "That

300

bird'll be dead in twelve hours one way or another, and I mean to have that trophy eagle. So you just hold that flashlight on it."

"You gonna shoot it again?" Grady asked.

"With a twelve gauge at this range? Wouldn't be anything left to stuff." I turned to Grady. "Now you distract the cocksucker while I sneak up behind."

He nodded and entered into the periphery of the flashlight's beam. The bird's attention was focused completely on him as I sidled around its flank until I stood three or four feet behind the tailfeathers. Grady was doing a good job of holding its attention, bobbing his shoulders up and down and making gobbling noises, and the eagle advanced toward him hissing and listing to the right, its one good wing flapping. I lunged forward and brought the tire iron down on its head; it went down but kept moving so I struck again, and this time it stopped moving. Sylvester brought the flashlight close to the head and shone it into the black, half-closed left eye. I turned the head to one side and was pleased to note no damage to the beak, upper or lower.

I grabbed onto one of its legs, which had curled underneath it as it collapsed, and then the other. It was all I could do to get both legs with one hand.

Sylvester trained the light on the talons, sharp as needles. "Jesus, will you look at those feet? Big as a hand, just about." And so they were, a kid's hands anyway, clenched into scaly, terrifying fists of a slightly paler yellow than its beak.

Grady helped me fold the wings so I could carry it like a baby instead of a dead pheasant, and I laid our prize gently down onto a blanket in the trunk, on top of the busted tire.

• • •

Sylvester took the wheel on the way back while Grady tried to get some sleep in the backseat. When we got to a paved

301

road it was slicker than gooseshit, and for a while we didn't talk much, listening to KFH radio as we got closer to Wichita. The announcer giving the farm report sounded like he wanted to get off the air fast so he could take a squirt.

"Notice how this model's got the radio controls mounted right into the dash?" Sylvester said.

"It's a swell car, all right."

"Cost well over a thousand dollars."

"I'm impressed. Your old man must be making a lot of dough."

"He does all right. My Ma's driving our old Plymouth these days, so I guess you'd say we're a two-car family."

"Guess you would say that." While an Ipana commercial played on KFH, I opened a bottle of Falstaff and tossed the cap at Grady, snoring on the backseat. When he didn't react to that, I tossed the churchkey, too, and hit him in the face.

"Jesus," Sylvester said. "Don't do that. If my old man finds out we've been drinking in the car, I'll catch all kinds of hell."

"Sorry," I said. There were three bottles left in the cooler at my feet, and we'd started with twenty that afternoon. My friend Norman, who operated a blind pig around the corner from Sylvester's house, had warned us that we'd be needing more than that when we bought them. He must have seen a thirsty look on Grady's face; this was only my fourth or fifth, and Sylvester had only drunk two before quitting; it was no goddamn wonder Grady was passed out back there.

"Where do you think we ought to take the bird?"

"Grady's brother-in-law does some stuffing. Hey, Grady," I yelled. When he didn't respond, I took the tire iron and whacked the soles of his feet.

"Ow, shit. Cut it out." He sat up and took his glasses out of his shirt pocket. "How far are we?"

302

"Another twenty, twenty-five minutes. Your brother-in-law, what's his name?"

"Who, Vernon?"

"Is he the man we should see about stuffing that carcass?"

"I don't know. I never seen him do anything bigger than a mallard."

"If he can't, maybe he knows someone who can."

Grady thought about it for a minute. "I guess we can give it a try. One thing, though, is Vern's pretty patriotic. He might not like us killing an eagle."

"We'll tell him we found him."

"We're going to have to just leave the bird with him and get this car right back to my Dad," Sylvester said. "Won't be able to stay."

"Bullshit. How are Grady and me supposed to get back to my car?" I asked. My old Hudson was parked downtown next to the Miller theatre, where we'd run into Sylvester. The sleet had stopped, but it was still cold.

"I'll take you there after you guys help me explain to my old man why we were gone so long with the car."

"That's not our problem." I had no intention of going to Sylvester's house ever again under any circumstances. My girlfriend's house was around the corner; in a pinch I could get her pop to give us a ride downtown.

He pleaded with us for a while, and by the time we got to Vernon's house, it was still up in the air. Vernon lived with Grady's sister Polly and their kids on Jeannette, not too far from the Halliburton's house in Riverside. When we backed into the driveway and honked the horn, a light came on next to the side door. A second later Grady's sister Polly showed up in it, a dishrag in her hand and her panties in a wad because it was past nine and the little ones were asleep.

"Go wake 'em up, Polly, and go get Vern. Wait 'til you see what we got in the trunk."

"You've got some brass, bringing your hooligan friends over here at all hours and drunk, too."

That hooligan business hurt, because I'd been sweet on Polly since I was about ten. Her hair was done up in a platinum wave, and she'd put on a few pounds since I'd last seen her, mostly aft; her mascara was smudged and there was a spot of bright red lipstick on her upper left incisor. She swung around and stuck her finger at me like a mind reader.

"And what the hell are you staring at? You get on my nerves, creep. I'm a married woman and a mother."

Vern stepped behind her in the doorframe. He squinted at us and hooked his wire-framed glasses behind his jug ears. I knew him from a couple of times Grady and I had drunk beer with him in his basement when Polly wasn't home. He was all right for a drip. "What's the matter, Sweetie? Hey there, Grady. Wayne."

"I was just telling these boys to clear out."

"Vern, go get the kids. We got something to show 'em. Something for you to stuff."

Vern shrugged and turned around, and Polly followed him, yelling. "Oh, no you don't, Vern. Goddamnit, don't you wake those children up." She slammed the door behind her.

"Look at that fat ass on her," Grady said about his only sister. "He's knocked her up again."

"Is that so?" I said. You'd think that would have doused my enthusiasm for Polly, instead of giving me a boner I had to fight to suppress. Pregnancy certainly did something for her tits.

"Maybe we ought to go, Grady. Your sister doesn't seem too happy to see us." Sylvester was already heading back to the car.

Grady beckoned him back. "Forget it. She doesn't run this house. Vern does."

The side door opened again to the sound of Polly yelling at

Vern. He was in a coat pushing a bleary-eyed, confused-looking boy and girl, aged about four and six. They were dressed in their Doctor Dentons with sweaters on over them, and still they shivered in the evening cold. Only Polly braved the night air dressed for the indoors; it seemed to bother her not at all.

"All right. Let's see what you've got to show these kids."

"It's in the trunk of the car. Come on in close, kids; Uncle Grady's gonna show you something swell."

Sylvester unlatched the trunk and hauled it open. Out shot an angry flurry of brown and white feathers, accompanied by a girlish scream from Sylvester, who went down to the driveway beneath the eagle, one set of talons digging into his forearm and the other into his bicep. The claws had already perforated the sleeve of his corduroy jacket, soaking it with blood. The babes were fully alert now and clinging to their mother's legs, their eyes wide—had their Daddy really awakened them to witness a boy being killed by a vicious bird?

"Jesus! Sweet Jesus, get him off me!" Sylvester's howl swung upwards into a register I wouldn't have thought him capable of reaching, one sure to attract the attention of the neighbors. He had to be shut up, one way or the other.

I ran for the tire iron. The children were shrieking now, as was Polly, the three of them coming close to drowning out Sylvester's cries. Vern had hold of the bird's lower legs, trying to pry those talons loose, and Grady's hand around its throat was all that prevented that beak from slicing into Sylvester's trachea. The iron was under the driver's seat, and I sprinted back towards the fray swinging it. Grady caught my intention and let go of the eagle's neck a fraction of a second before impact; it was remarkably like one of those moments when a fast pitch seems to slow to nothing as it nears the strike zone, and in mid-swing you know it's perfect, unstoppable. I damn

305

near took that big head clean off with a solid blow to the side of it; its talons relaxed, allowing us to pull it off Sylvester, who was crying as plaintively as the children were.

"Holy cow, is that an eagle?" Vern said, delighted as a boy on Christmas morning.

"Are you out of your goddamned minds, bringing that here? He could've mauled the children," Polly said, the kids whimpering behind her.

"Sorry, Pol. We thought it was dead. It's okay, kids; take a look. He can't hurt you now." The older child, the girl, crept gingerly towards the supine bird, but the boy remained at a safe distance.

"Can I touch it?'

"Sure," Grady said, and the child touched the beak, pressing the tip of her index finger cautiously against the tip of it.

"Jesus, Jesus," Sylvester whimpered. "I'm bleeding."

"You stop using the Lord's name in vain. Come on inside, I'll get you bandaged up." She led him in, the blood copiously flowing from the deep multiple punctures in his arm, the little boy following and sobbing along with Sylvester.

"Hot diggedy. You gonna let me stuff this?"

"Sure," I said. "We thought you might know someplace we could unload it, afterward."

"Yeah, maybe so. Oh, boy. A bald eagle. Where'd you boys find him?"

"Out in Stafford County."

"Huh. Must have been migrating south, hunting ducks out there. I haven't ever seen one in Kansas."

Very carefully we lifted it, trying to avoid any further damage to the feathers. As I was passing through the door, an elderly man, tiny and hunchbacked and wearing a faded, raggedy G.A.R. cap, stepped into the light of the driveway. A corncob pipe jutted from the side of his toothless mouth, and cradled in his arms was a rifle. I damn near laughed out loud.

"What was all that caterwauling about, Mr. Griese?"

"Nothing, Mr. Packer."

"Is that an eagle that boy's got in his arms, there?"

"No, sir, Mr. Packer, it's a big old tom turkey for Thanksgiving."

"Looks like an eagle to me. Good night, Mr. Griese."

"Good night, Mr. Packer."

In the kitchen Vern told me not to worry about the old man. "He won't turn us in. Remember Packer's Hardware on Broadway? That was him. Since his wife died, he's been window peeping. Been arrested four, five times in the last year. Scared to death of the cops."

Before we got the cellar door open, the eagle roused in my arms, startling me so that I dropped it. Scrambling, dazed, it made its way back to its feet, scratching at the new linoleum.

"Oh, shit," Vern said.

Behind me was the icebox; I opened the ice compartment and yanked out the pick. There was something wrong with the bird, all right, but in the close quarters of the kitchen it looked even bigger than before, and the look in its eye was one of demented loathing, of the unquenchable desire for bloody vengeance. Its reflexes had slowed enough that I was able to get behind it and drive the icepick through the back of its head, like pithing a frog for dissection. It made an awful choking hiss and went down so that its chest was resting against the floor, but that Rasputin of a bird was still conscious and snapping at the air.

Behind me Grady was inexplicably filling the sink up with water. There was blood all over the kitchen floor, the eagle's and Sylvester's, and I wondered if I'd have to go out to the car for the shotgun and blow the bird to his eternal reward strictly out of humanitarian kindness. Damn it, though, I didn't want to damage the hide or the feathers any more than I already had; for all I knew I might have already rendered it unstuffable with that damned icepick.

By now the sink was full, and Grady was yelling for me to pick the bird back up, something I was reluctant to try.

"What the hell for?"

"Drown it," Grady yelled. "Drown the son of a bitch!"

It was a big sink, but not big enough for the whole eagle. Vern stood watching with his hands in his pants pockets while I screwed up the courage to swoop down on the wounded bird and pick it up by the sides. It tried to extend its wings but only succeeded in ruffling them, and its great yellow feet grasped ineffectually at the air beneath it. It didn't struggle much harder than that when I plunged its head into the tepid water, apart from several vigorous attempts to flap. It may have taken less than a minute to finish it off or it may have been ten; I don't know; I do know that around the time it finally stopped moving altogether, Polly came in, followed by a sheepish, bandaged Sylvester Halliburton, and started yelling at me for what had happened to her kitchen.

"And just what in the hell do you think you're doing with that foul bird in my kitchen sink? And what's the idea getting all this blood all over my new linoleum?"

As she yelled, I hauled the bird from the water. She continued to berate me despite my lack of response.

"Vern, here's what you have to do with him." I raised the dripping, blood-spattered corpse high above my head with one hand under the torso and one gently cradling his head, his neck stretched gallantly outward. Polly stopped hollering, curious as to my intentions and still nervously protective of her kitchen floor.

"Grady, Sylvester, each of you take a wing and make like he's flying." His wings extended into a reasonable semblance of flight, feet dangling beneath him, talons open as if preparing to seize at some lesser creature, he now looked for all the world like a live American eagle, soaring magisterially over the land he ruled.

No one spoke. Vern stepped back and appraised the bird like Michelangelo taking stock of a block of marble; tears came to Grady's eyes, only partially the result of the dozen and a half beers he'd drunk. A look I interpreted as a variety of shame or self-loathing crossed Sylvester's bland mug as he stared at the eagle's unmistakeably dead eyes; I was focused, though, on swollen, fecund Polly, on the wonderful fact that I had finally done something sufficient to impress her into an awed and slightly horrified silence.

Kent Anderson wrote one of my all-time favorite cop novels, Night Dogs; *a psycho-romp through the streets of Portland, Oregon, in the 1970s. That might have been the first time I heard about Dennis McMillan, too, when I looked up Kent online to see what else he'd written and discovered the story of* Night Dogs' *trek from hip indie crime novel to heavyweight Bantam hardcover. Anyway, I devoured the book and then said, "Can't wait for his next one." And I waited. and waited. . . .*

and. . . .

In the meantime, I couldn't resist his collection of shorts called Liquor, Guns, & Ammo, *and was happy to see his contribution to Dennis'* Measures of Poison *collection. I'm still waiting for that new novel, but I'm honored that Mr. Anderson has contributed this shotgun blast of a story to our project.*

Elvis Hitler
Kent Anderson

Febuary in East Oakland, windshield wipers hot-wired and out of synch. Warped, brittle, thudding like speed-bags—working *hard*—scoring the glass and tossing rain back&forth, useless.

A Saturday night, radio traffic heavy in spite of the weather, other cops barking radio codes out of the dark from districts three and four, the dispatcher on channel two rapping like an auctioneer:

Three –L forty two nine oh nine, now the other unit...Three L ten code four...anyone else? The car with the traffic stop go ahead...

Three L five three at seventy third and east fourteenth on a red, uh, red Pontiac adam mary king, seven three seven...

Three L forty four, nine oh nine...

Three L forty four is nine, and, three L forty four, a four fifteen F at sixteen forty four eighty first, the wife says her husband is beating on her, no weapons indicated, we could hear him shouting in the background. . .

Three L forty two's got the cover...

I have three L forty two covering...Unit with the car stop go ahead

...at seventy third and Olive on a black LTD John Frank Mary one oh two...

Unit with the car stop, repeat your number only...

Three L five one...

Three L five one, copy...

Hanson drove past the address and pulled to the curb half a block down, putting the car in PARK, his eyes on the house in the rearview mirror. *Domestic Dispute. A four-fifteen...F.* People who needed a cop with clubs and a gun to make their decisions for them.

The overheated engine dieseled out, the pounding wipers *stopped,* and the urgent radio voices went silent.

Rain hissed on the hood of the filthy patrol car.

Closed up in his wall locker, his wool shirt and trousers didn't have time to dry out between shifts. They'd been damp for three days now, heavy and hot, smelling like a stray dog. He was hung over, with a headache and diarrhea, pissed off at himself for not calling in sick.

He flexed his right hand, *making* it hurt, on purpose, to put a little more edge into his attitude. It seemed to help, so he made a fist, squeezing the festering blue puncture wound in his palm that he'd gotten Thursday night, going over a chain-link fence. "Fuck you," he thought, glaring at the fist, "how about *this,*" and squeezed the pain harder.

Keeping his eyes on the dark street and rearview mirrors, he reached into the black leather case on the seat beside him and pulled out a 16 oz. bottle of Pepto Bismol. For a moment, he saw his ghostly reflection in the windshield as a brooding magician producing a pink rabbit.

He slugged down the chalky antacid, tilted the bottle and squinted at it–already half empty–screwed the cap back on, and put it away. He licked his lips, checking his mouth and teeth in the rearview mirror for pink residue, when his stomach cramped up again. He reached back into the case, felt around for the bottle, and took one more swallow. Maybe, he thought, he should design a holster for the pink bottle, like the one he carried Mace in.

At least he'd finally gotten assigned to a late Tac "Wild Car," a ten-and-a-half hour shift, 6 P.M. till 4:30 A.M., four days a week. Only one sergeant for all five districts, so he didn't have to watch his ass *all* the time. And it was Sergeant Hicks, who was as crazy as Hanson. In a different way, but crazy understands crazy. That's why all those 5150s, *scared* of the other cops, always spotted Hanson right away, fuckin' *jay-walking* to tell him about Department of Defense transmitters the VA had installed in their heads.

Radio had assigned a cover-car–standard procedure–to Hanson's call, but, as usual, Hanson declined, telling them, "I'll advise," and hung up the mike. He'd let them know if he needed one of the cops who worked adjacent beats, young hot-dogs looking to pump up their arrest statistics, who pissed people off–"raised them up"–sometimes on purpose and sometimes because they didn't know any better, hard-ass and in-your-face from the get-go, the way they'd been taught in the academy. He'd rather take his chances working alone.

He pulled on his left sap glove, eight ounces of powdered lead stitched into five pouches, one behind each finger, and a single bigger one across the back of the hand. He kept the other glove tucked under his belt buckle–freeing his gun hand–the glove's cuff hanging out so he could snatch it out if he had to. He got out of the car, pulling his nightstick from its door-clip, dropped it through the ring on his belt, quietly closed the driver's door, and walked up the street in his steel-toed, ankle-high combat boots. His socks were wet, and one of them—he could feel it—had worked its way down past his heel.

At the door he listened for a moment, called out "Police Officer," hit it three times with the ten-inch Billy, the lead-filled "short wood" they all carried in addition to the longer nightstick—for close work—then dropped it back into the little pocket along his leg when he heard the clatter of locks opening.

She opened the door a crack, then wider, barefoot, wearing cut-offs, no bra, a black tee-shirt with white letters across the front, EAT SHIT AND DIE, a cigarette going between her swollen lips, one of them split, but scabbed over now. She wasn't *bad* looking, Hanson thought, her tits stood right up against the tee-shirt, but she was out of shape, her skin pale. She looked . . . *tired*.

Her black eye was a couple days old, the bruises blue-green and yellow. *Traumatic eye-shadow,* Hanson thought, even as his guts seized up again. *Violence, sex, and pain,* he thought, *all beating as* one *in each of God's human hearts,* pleased with the phrase, fighting a smile, looking away so she wouldn't see it in his eyes.

"What?" she said.

He shook his head and followed her inside, checking behind the half-open front door.

"I want him outta here," she mumbled, cigarette bobbing between the swollen lips. "I want the fucker outta here. Now! Right now!"

But of course, Hanson thought. *Right away! Forgive me for taking so long to arrive.*

"And what *is* the problem this evening?"

She took the cigarette out of her mouth and shouted over

her shoulder, *"He's* the problem. He's an *ass*-hole! And I want him *out."*

"And fuck *you,"* a man yelled, his voice coming up through the floor.

Yeah, yeah, Hanson thought, *how many times had he been in this movie before?* Then his stomach cramps were back. He tried to *breathe,* a "stress-reduction technique" some homosexual psychologist–real nervous–had taken an hour to explain one day in the academy, and sucked in menthol cigarette smoke, mildew, and cat piss from the sofa and carpet.

It was hard to find a bathroom in East Oakland, the way they moved you from beat to beat, and radio too busy to give him time for a 980-B anyway. 980-B. OPD had a number for everything.

Maybe he could take care of this quick, whip it out on an assignment card–915-F. Problem resolved upon departure. Date and time, the complainant's name and DOB– then ask this woman to use her bathroom before radio sent him to another call.

His stomach calmed for a moment, and it was only then that he realized the house was filled with Elvis memorabilia, like a fucking roadside attraction in North Dakota. Black velvet paintings–probably from Tijuana–darker skin and eyes, pompadour and sideburns curlier, with subtle blond highlights, even one with a skinny little mustache– "Mexicanized" Elvis–"Greaser Elvis." Porcelain busts, hand-painted by machines, the red not *quite* aligned with his pouting lips, the blue of his eyes slightly off-center, unfocused . . . his whole damn face that way, like he was disassembling into another dimension.

Molded rubber figurines, Barbie Doll Elvises–mostly from his last Las Vegas period–the final triumphant tour before he got fat and OD'd on a toilet in Graceland–that she'd dressed in the spangled white jumpsuit, boots and sunglasses . . . but there was Hillbilly Elvis, too, a GI Elvis, Elvis in a Hawaiian shirt and lei from the movie *Blue Hawaii*. Karate Elvis in a blackbelted gi, whose cocked, deadly-weapon arms rotated at the shoulders. Foot-long Elvis suspended from a wire, ascending to Rock&Roll Heaven in a flowing, almost robe-like leisure suit, legs spread, bell-bottoms wide as wings, that lock of black hair over one eye, his final sneering "goodbye" smile, holding a glitter-lighting guitar at arm's length, just below his crotch, rising to Glory like he was rocket-powered.

Movie posters, Elvis liquor decanters filled now with colored water, behind a sad little red&white Naugahyde bar, the kind of thing you'd see in a strip-mall LOST OUR LEASE–EVERYTHING MUST GO store-front, with a sign that said *Buy me for only $14.95 a month.*

Hanson saw himself in the Elvis-profile-etched mirror behind the bar. He looked awful, sick and beat-up, worse than the woman.

The *clang* and boom of free weights shook the floor like a minor quake, colliding tectonic plates, little ones, shrunk down like Elvis.

"Could I please have your name, ma'am? And date of birth."

She stubbed out her Kool in an ashtray stolen from the Reno *Circus-Circus* Hotel and took another from a musical cigarette box that plucked a few hesitant notes of . . . *Love Me Tender?* before the spring wound out.

"Mine? What you need *mine* for? *I'm* the one who called the cops," she said, twitching the unlit cigarette between her fingers, her chipped red nails chewed to the quick. "I need some *help*, not a census taker."

"I need the 'complainant's' *information*. The rules, you know? Statistics for the, uh, data base," starting to get twitchy *himself*. Already. *Elvis*. Everywhere, watching him. *Be cool*, he told himself, *be cool, man.*

"Can't *you* just *tell him* to leave? That's all I fuckin' want."

She stuck the cigarette in her mouth and rewound the music box. It *was* "Love Me Tender," but now, spring-tight, it played at double-speed, like music in a Chinese nightmare.

Her name was "Racine," and she was twenty-five years old. The guy downstairs was Paul.

"He do that to you?" Hanson said, leaning closer, tilting his head, squinting at her bruised face. "How'd that happen?"

"He . . . lost his job. Got, uh, laid off. . . ." she said, looking into Hanson's eyes now, drifting, ". . .laid off at the door factory."

Hanson imagined himself spending eight hours every day making doors, the whine of power saws and planers in his head.

". . .he *changed*. Started getting *mean*."

The *bang* of iron on iron shook the floor. Then again. *Adding weight to each end of the bar,* Hanson thought, *A* lot *of weight.*

"Using steroids?"

"No."

"I don't care if he uses steroids. I'm not a *narc*," he said, spitting out the word. Half the people in Oakland were heroin addicts, winos, crack heads, paint huffers. And why not, if it took them out of this shit-hole they'd been born into. Jesus, *he* got drunk every chance he got.

"It'd help if I knew what to expect."

She nodded.

"Thank you, Racine," Hanson said, his guts burning.

The stairway, built with warped, knotty, unpainted 2X4s and 2X8s and about forty pounds of nails, shuddered as they started down. Hanson wondered if the materials had come from the door factory. *Of course they had,* he thought. *Jesus.*

The windowless, concrete basement was as bleak as a torture chamber, blinding at first, ten thousand watts of warehouse guard-lights hanging from the ceiling. *They* probably came from the door factory, too, one at a time, every Friday after

317

work, in the trunk of the car. *Half the shit in Oakland is stolen,* he thought, ducking his head to clear the overhang, *A trickle-down, drug trade economy.*

The walls on either side of the weight bench were paneled with K-mart door mirrors, four feet high and not much more than a foot wide, mounted knee-high, edge-to-edge with black-tar adhesive, half a dozen of them on each wall. A four-foot Nazi flag hung on the far wall, behind the weight bench. *Weight,* Hanson thought. Every house west of 24th Street came with a set of weights for staying in shape till the PO violated them back to the joint with the random, 4 A.M. urine sample.

Paul was being cool, like he didn't even notice them, half-way through a set of bench presses, maybe 300 pounds on the bar. He raised it, slowly, held it at arms' length without a quiver, then, again, *slowly* lowered it. Impressing them. It *was* a lot of weight. He sat up, six-pack abs shiny with sweat, and *studied* them, blue veins wriggling along his arms.

Dark blue spandex shorts to the knee and a white tank top with a pair of Nazi SS lightning bolts bracketing the word *BLITZKRIEG!* 90-IQ blue eyes. Blond—the crew-cut, and, of course, a Fu Manchu mustache. 6'1", 220 pounds at least. Tattooed arms as big as Hanson's legs, the bat-hooded no-neck.

"Hi," Hanson said, his mouth dry, head throbbing, doing his best to ignore the stomach cramps.

"'Hi?' Fuckin' 'Hi?'" Paul said, a little out of breath but trying not to show it. "'Hi' doesn't cut it. How about, *you got a warrant? Dude?*"

"Don't need a warrant. *Sir,*" Hanson said, "It's not a tee-vee show. Your wife called the police and *let* me in."

"*Wife?* That what she told you? I'm not married to the cunt."

Hanson opened his eyes wide, slightly unfocused, inno-cent . . . psycho innocent. He called them "Shirley Temple

318

eyes." He used them when he wasn't sure what to do yet, and needed a little time. The eyes confused people, and they hesitated. Most people had never seen eyes like that, up close.

"What's your name again, man?" he said.

"Paul, okay? My name's Paul."

"Right. Paul. *Paul.* Your uh . . . *Racine,* here, called the police. *Asked* me inside. So I don't need a warrant . . . Paul.

"She wants you to leave," he said, stepping off the stairs onto the concrete, his weight on his toes, balanced, *set,* but easy, subtle, the eyes covering it. When his stomach seized up again, he clenched his fist, *beating* the cramps. *The worst pain wins.*

"I pay rent, Dude. So fuck that," Paul said, laying back again, looking up, into the lights, doing three, quick, angry presses.

"He hasn't paid rent in four months," Racine said from the stairs. "He sleeps mornings, hangs out with his 'buddies' at the gym all afternoon, gets drunk, then, hey, it's time to come home and give me shit.

"I'm fuckin *through.* Payin' the rent, fixing his special *HI-PRO* meals, walking on egg shells. Watching tv. Every night. Alone. While he's down here grunting, *looking* at himself in those cheap-ass mirrors like some faggot."

Paul sat up like he was spring-loaded.

"Fuck you, you stupid . . . cow. *You're* the faggot. Queer for Elvis. I been thinking you must use him for a dildo. 'Cause that's the only way *you're* gonna *get* any. *Look* at yourself!

"I'm a queer?" he said, hitting himself on the chest. *Like a bow-legged chimpanzee,* Hanson thought. *What was it called . . . aggressive display? If they were outside, he'd probably start throwing dirt and leaves.*

"I'm *hard.* I'm *bad. Nobody* gives me shit. . . ."

"Fuck you. . . ." was all she could manage before her voice broke.

319

"And what did I tell you about the next time you called the fuckin' cops? Huh!" the sound coming from deep in his chest, pumping up the anger. "Huh?" he said, pressing both hands, palms down, on the bench, between his legs, lifting his body off the bench like a gymnast.

Hanson watched it like a movie, in the mirrors. His uniform looked like shit, creases steamed out by the rain, the shirt *hanging* on him, pants too big, like hand-me-downs from a big brother. With all the weight *he* carried—the pistol, night-stick, packset, mace, handcuffs, speed-loaders, the short wood in its own little pocket—his pants kept slipping over his hips and he had to hitch them up, hooking his thumbs in the belt loops. *Must be down to one-forty-five, maybe less,* he thought. Radio sending him from call to call, the whole ten and a half hours too busy for supper, burning adrenalin instead. Most of his calories came from Mickey's Big Mouth Malt Liquor and the little half-pint bottles of oily Popov vodka he sucked down after work, watching dawn come up over the Oakland Hills before passing out in his bed.

"Huh?" Paul said again, "*Huh!*" *Working it, lifting and lowering his body—like the Alpha Chimp,* Hanson thought. Finally, he pushed up and *off* the bench onto his feet.

The stairs shuddered as Racine ran up and slammed the door. Paul sneered, spit on the floor.

Very classy.

"You call a cover car, Dude?" he said, *looking* at Hanson, the Fu Manchu & bunched jaw muscles tough guy again, *His Gold's Gym badass look,* Hanson thought.

"Say, you must be of German heritage," Hanson said, big eyes, nodding at the Nazi flag, the black swastika on a red background.

Paul hesitated, looked at the flag, back at Hanson.

"*Deutschland. Now* I can see it. In your physiology. Naw, your physiognomy! That's the word."

320

Paul held back, his eyes wary for just a moment, then he flexed his arms, shuffled like a boxer, to the left, the right, then toward Hanson

"That's a fuckin' Roge, Dude. Both sides of the family. . . . I *asked* you if you called a cover car. 'Cause after I kick your punk ass, I'll kick the shit outta *him,*" he said.

"No."

"Call one then. Call *two,* dude. I'll take 'em as they come, one at a time. Like an assembly line, motherfucker, like hammerin' fuckin' door frames."

"No, Paul."

"NO? No *what?*"

"No, you're not gonna kick anybody's ass."

Paul laughed, "Why is *that. . . ?*"

"Because you're gonna be dead," Hanson said, as he pulled the sap glove from behind his belt buckle and backhanded Paul across the throat with it.

Paul froze, his eyes empty, huge, then full of fear as he realized he couldn't breathe. With an easy, casual, almost contemptuous wrist motion, Hanson flicked the leaded glove into Paul's face, dropping him to one knee, gagging, sobbing, *whooping* for air.

Hanson tucked the glove back behind his belt, wrapped his hand around the grip of the stainless steel .357, and popped the clam-shell holster open.

Coughing, Paul looked up.

"I want to explain something," Hanson said.

A bubble of blood swelled from Paul's nostril, then *popped.*

"And it's *very* important that you believe me, because I'm not gonna 'verbally negotiate' any more. If you see it in my *eyes,* you'll *know.*"

"Right *here,*" Hanson snapped. *"Look,* goddammit," he said, pointing at his own face. Then, when Paul looked up, Hanson turned on his eyes, locking into Paul's.

"Turning them on." That's what he called it, but what he did was release *them, let them go, where they wanted to go, always—the way a compass needle sweeps north and* holds*—back to the eyes they'd become during the war, when Hanson was free to do* anything, *already dead, with nothing to lose. Nothing had changed. They were still, and always would be those eyes, but he had to control them now, conceal them, but sometimes . . . those times when the world, when* everything *seemed hopeless, and Hanson picked up his off-duty Hi-power 9mm—just to feel its cool weight in his hand—thinking it over—just once in a while, he'd let his eyes go free. Let them go to a place not many people ever visit, but once you do, it's always there, waiting for you. He'd look up from the pistol and the eyes would take him back there, to the walking-dead killer he would always be. Two, maybe three, seconds was all he could risk, before they could, he knew, take him over—where the eyes go, the body follows—holding . . . then coming back. He'd always made it back, so far. And afterwards he'd feel good, sane, for a few hours, like he was still home for a little while. It was then, if he was alone, he might weep with relief.*

But he was in the basement now, with Paul, when he turned them off this time, having held them there a split second more than he should have. Okay, though. He'd gotten back okay.

Paul was looking up at him.

"I'm hung over, man. I got *diarrhea.* If I had to arrest you— I'd grab you, you'd grab me, bla-bla. . . ." Hanson sighed, *it was always the same old dance.* ". . .and I'd shit my pants, my Oh Pee Dee uniform pants, and I'd never live it down. That's the only thing anybody would remember about me. Fifty years from now rookies would still hear the story. 'Hanson was so scared that he shit his pants.'

"So you gotta leave now, and not come back till tomorrow morning, or I'm gonna shoot you. Six times. *Kill* you. Because you can't testify in court if you're dead. That's how it works. It's that simple.

"I'll say you came at me with a weight plate and I had to shoot you in self-defense. There'll be powder burns all over you. This thing," he said, glancing at the pistol, "might even set your shirt on fire. 'He was *on me,* man.' That's what I'll tell 'em. 'Didn't have any choice.' Shit, you weigh twice as much as me, all those big muscles you worked so hard for, steroids in your blood. 'Roid Rage.' And you're *white.*

"Do I have to shoot you?"

Paul shook his head.

"You got somewhere you can spend the night?"

"I *live* here. . . ."

"Paul."

"I can sleep down at the gym."

"Good. And I think I can trust you to keep your word," Hanson said. "I think you're an honorable man," he said, looking at the Nazi flag. *"Mein wort es mein ehre."*

Paul looked at him, still trying to clear his throat. Respectfully.

"'My word is my honor.' Waffen SS. The *soldiers,* not those fuckin' SS camp guards. That was the *creed* they lived by. Some of the best soldiers in the world, and that stupid *fuck* Hitler," Hanson said, nodding toward the flag, "used 'em for cannon fodder there at the end. They were *soldiers,* man. So I'm gonna trust you not come back till tomorrow. Not before noon. Can I do that, Paul?"

Paul nodded. "Sure," he croaked. "Absolutely."

Hanson sat on the toilet, pants down below his knees, the pistol resting in the crotch of his trousers, just in case Paul was stupid enough to come back early. Unloaded, it weighed 38 ounces, say . . . two and a half pounds with six rounds in it. He smiled at the nightlight, a translucent bust wearing a red&black check bandanna around his neck. Elvis looked happy.

And Hanson sure felt better.

He was pleased with that Waffen SS stuff. He'd made it up, but it *could* be true. And he was pretty sure Paul would wait till morning before he came back, pounded on the door, told Racine to let him in, then beat the shit out of her again.

"Okay," he said, his hand on the doorknob. Racine *looked* at him, biting her lip, waiting, till Hanson asked her, "What was the *real* problem?" regretting it instantly.

"He doesn't want me anymore," she said, her eyes tearing up. "Pushes me away. Then he gets angry, even if I don't *say* anything. I think it's those steroids," she said, putting her hand over Hanson's.

"Of course it is. You're a very attractive woman, Racine." And she wasn't bad, really. He could smell her now, standing this close. A little skanky, but skanky was okay. It was all, pretty much, okay, he thought. Looking again at her breasts beneath the "Eat Shit And Die" tee-shirt, the straining buttons on her Levi's.

He put his thumb against the split in her lip, softly, barely touching it, feeling the heat, blood close to the surface, healing it. A tiny pulse in there. Then, slowly, but with increasing force, she pushed her lip against his thumb . . . until it split again, warm blood seeping out, forming red drops that fell, one by one, onto the top of her shirt, while she kept eye contact with him, never flinching, only her eyes–the pupils growing–as they fell.

He took his thumb away. "Look," he said, talking fast, "gotta go. Clear from the call. Here's my card. Call me if you have to," handing her his card, his bloody thumbprint on it.

"Gotta go. Lock the door behind me, don't let *anyone* in."

She was giving him that *look,* and he almost added, *especially me.*

"Get some sleep," he said, letting himself out, walking to the car, knowing she was watching from the window.

He'd be crazy to go back after he got off his shift. Although, Paul *wouldn't* be back till morning.

"Well, *shit,*" he asked himself, "You gonna *worry* about it?"

What happens, happens. *No changing that. It's all Zen, 'Dude.' God's big ferris wheel of suffering and rebirth. Might as well get laid while you can.* Gott Mit Uns.

Paul was just a stupid asshole. He was glad he didn't have to kill him. The more time he spent out here, the harder it was to get really pissed off at people.

But then, he shouldn't have hit him the second time. It was that mean streak coming out again, getting worse. A *lot* worse, lately. Maybe something he'd been born with, like a talent, a *gift,* because the more he used it, the better he got. He was almost starting to. . . . *Starting to, my ass.* He *did* like it. He was *good* at it. *Meanness.* About all he had left any more.

He drove a few blocks to an empty parking lot in front of a boarded-up furniture store, where he could see in all directions, while he filled out an assignment card on the call– 915-F. Problem resolved upon departure. The date and time, Racine's DOB, and that was it. If one of those hot dogs had come by to cover him, he'd have turned it into a big deal, a felony to boost his monthly arrest quota. Paul would have gone to jail, and the paperwork would have been at least an hour's worth–most of it Hanson's as "primary officer" on the call.

He dropped the 3 by 6 inch card into his aluminum report notebook and cleared from radio, "Nine-oh-nine," and immediately the dispatcher gave him a 647-F. "Public Intoxication." A "man down" by the dumpster behind Carl's Country Market. Drunk and passed out, probably. They were passed out everywhere you looked—sidewalks, gas station bathrooms, city parks and front yards—sometimes in the middle of the street where they got run over by drunk *drivers*. A fatal 901-D. *There's* a night's worth of paperwork.

"Make that a 415–C," the dispatcher said. *"We're getting reports of possible shots fired. We've dispatched a 945, inbound from Highland Park."*

Hanson jerked the mike loose. "904."

"Car to cover. . . ."

"I'll advise. I'm almost there," he said, looking at his watch, "but I'm on overtime in fifteen minutes."

If the guy was DOA, maybe a 187, they'd try to send a beat car to take it, and he'd only have to fill out a Supplemental Report. The City wasn't handing out overtime if they could help it. They couldn't afford time-and-a-half for a murder in East Oakland, not when they had 200 a year. But if they couldn't free up another car, he might as well forget about Racine tonight. Too bad—

No. He'd rather go home tonight, get drunk watching the sun rise, pass out in his own bed. At home.

Driving the dark streets to the location, he thought about changing his name to Elvis Hitler. *Officer* Elvis Hitler. People would remember you with a name like that.